TOP HARD

Stephen Booth

Published by Westlea Books

ISBN 978-0-9569027-7-1

Westlea Books
PO Box 10125, Tuxford, Newark,
Notts. NG22 0WT. United Kingdom

www.westleabooks.com

TOP HARD

September 1998

Nottinghamshire, England

1

This lorry I'd been watching was a brand new Iveco with French registration plates. All tarted up with flags and air horns and rows of headlights, it was like a space shuttle had just landed in a layby on the A1.

I'd got myself a position no more than thirty yards away, slumped in the driver's seat of a clapped-out six-year-old Escort that had last been driven by a clapped-out brewery rep. Or that was the way it looked, anyway. It was one o'clock on an ordinary Friday afternoon. And all I had to do was wait.

The trouble was, this lorry hadn't been doing very much. I had nothing to look at except a red and white sticker on the Escort's dashboard thanking me for not smoking, and a little dangling plastic ball that told me what direction I was heading in. I might have been facing the soft south, but at least I was nicotine free.

I already knew a few things about this truck by now, of course. I'd counted its sixteen wheels and admired the size of its tail pipes. I'd seen the sleeping compartment behind the cab, with its ten-inch colour telly, a fridge, and even a microwave oven for warming up the driver's morning croissant. I knew that its forty-foot trailer was packed full of leather jackets, jeans and denim shirts - all good stuff that's really easy to shift. I also knew that somebody was going to be really pissed off about that trailer very soon.

Well, it definitely looked like a solid job so far - good information, and a plan that might actually come together for once. That's saying something in this part of the world. So all I needed to do was sit tight and wait for the action. But it's funny how things can start out really good and solid in the morning, and then turn totally brown and runny by tea time. It's one of my own little theories, this. I call it the Stones McClure Vindaloo Lunch Rule. It's as if the bloke up there with the beard likes a bit of a joke now and then. And today was going to be one of his joke days. Well, I

1

might just die laughing.

Meanwhile, sitting in a tatty motor was in danger of ruining my image. The Escort just wasn't worth looking at. Well, that's the point, I suppose. But you can take low-profile a bit too far. There were an incredible eighty-five thousand miles on the clock of this thing, which proved it hadn't been handled by a used car dealer recently. The floor was covered in empty sweet wrappers, the mouldy debris of a cheese sandwich, and dozens of screwed-up bits of pink tissue. The inside panels looked as though they'd been trampled by a gang of miners in pit boots. The cover had fallen off the fuse box, and a tangle of wires and coloured plastic hung out of it, for all the world as if I'd just botched a hot-wire job. The car smelled of stale beer, too. Maybe a pack of free samples had split open some time. Or maybe a brewery rep just goes around smelling like that.

In a word, it just wasn't the sort of motor that folk round here are used to seeing Stones McClure in. My style is more poke than parcel shelf, if you know what I mean. More turbo charge than towbar. Not to mention a spot of F and F across the fake fur covers. That would be me, definitely.

So for the last few minutes, I'd been dozing a bit, clutching my plastic bottle of Highland Spring in one hand and a half-eaten Snickers bar in the other. Don't believe that means I had no idea what was going on. I've got this trick of keeping one eye half open at all times, like an old tom cat. It's saved me a lot of grief on jobs like this.

One-fifteen. I sat up to take a quick look round. Along the road was a roundabout where traffic was heading into the service area or grinding its way west on the A57 into Lincolnshire. Apart from a roadside cafe, there was nothing around me in the layby - just empty fields on one side, and a bit of Sherwood Forest on the other. I mean there was nothing apart from four lanes of traffic thundering by on the A1, obviously. But the drivers weren't taking notice of much. They were busy fiddling with their carphones, or counting the miles ticking off as they hurtled towards their next meeting or their latest delivery of widgets. This is what vehicle thieves rely on. Nobody sees anything happening around them when they're on the road.

2

Well, people never learn, do they? That's my second rule. And thank God for it, because this is what keeps blokes like me in beer and Meatloaf CDs for life.

I glanced at the clock again. Shouldn't be long now. Half an hour ago, I'd watched the driver who brought the lorry disappear into the cafe, shrugging his shoulders at the smell of hot fat drifting from the window of Sally's Snap Box. He was a short, thickset bloke wearing blue overalls and a five o'clock shadow. You could practically hear him singing the *Marseillaise*. This bloke's load might be headed for Leeds or Glasgow, or anywhere. But it wouldn't make it to its destination. Not today.

It's the load that's important, see. Thieves don't target brand new trucks for their own sake. If you're planning to cut a vehicle up for spares, you go for an ancient Bedford or something. There's a big export market for old lorry spares. But if you're nicking the load, it's a different matter. That's where the real business is - at least £1.6 billion worth a year, they say. And people will do anything to tap into dosh like that.

For the sake of authenticity, I was tuned in to a local radio station on the Escort's battered old Motorola. The presenter had just stumbled off into one of those endless phone-in segments they seem to like so much. Grannies from all over the county were passing on tips for getting cocoa stains out of acrylic armchair covers, or offering to swap back copies of *People's Friend* for a second-hand budgie cage. It was dire enough to kill my remaining brain cells – I mean, the few that last night's booze had left intact.

And then – bingo! An unmarked white Transit van left the inside lane of the A1 and pulled slowly into the layby in front of the French truck. Action at last.

I have a really good memory for registration numbers, but the plate on the Transit was a new one to me. That was no surprise, though. It would have been nicked from a car park in Worksop or Mansfield during the past hour, and that was someone else's worry.

From my position, I could just see a bloke jump down from the passenger side of the van. He had the collar of a red ski jacket turned right up and a woollen hat pulled low over his face, making it impossible to get an ID on him. As soon as he'd slammed the door shut, the Transit pulled out into the traffic again and

3

disappeared south.

I stayed low in my seat and ate a bit of my Snickers. The chocolate was starting to melt and my fingers were sticky. I rubbed them on a windscreen wipe from a little packet I found in the door well. I would have stuffed the used wipe into the ashtray, but it was already jammed with crumpled tissues, all yellow and crusty. Anonymity is fine, but I draw the line at catching some disgusting disease for the sake of camouflage.

The bloke in the cap was fiddling with something I couldn't see, right up close to the near side of the Iveco's cab. No one took any notice of him, except me. Then he looked round once, took a step upwards, and was gone from sight.

I speed dialled a number on my mobile, then waited a minute or two more until I heard the rumble of a diesel engine and the release of air brakes. As I started the Escort's motor, I glanced in my rearview mirror and saw a large figure emerge from the cafe. It was a bloke so big that he had to duck and walk out of the door sideways to avoid bringing the side of the portakabin with him. He lumbered up to the side of the car, hefting something like a lump of breeze block in his left hand. And suddenly it was as if the sun had gone in. Oh yeah, meet my sidekick, Doncaster Dave. He's my personal back-up, my one-man riot squad. A good bloke to have watching your arse.

Dave had been stuffing himself with sandwiches and cakes in Sally's at my expense. Well, it's better than having him sit in the car with me. He gets twitchy when there's food nearby, and he'd probably enjoy the phone-in programme and laugh at the DJ's jokes. And then I'd have to kill him.

"Come on, Donc. Come on."

Dave was starting to go into the monkey squat necessary for him to manoeuvre his way into the passenger seat, when the door of the cafe flew open and a second figure came out. This one was dressed in blue overalls, and he was gesticulating and shouting. The sight of the lorry pulling onto the A1 seemed to infuriate him, and he ran a few yards down the layby, yelling. Then he turned and ran back again, still yelling. This was far too much noise for my liking. And definitely too much arm waving. Even on the A1, he might attract attention.

I put my foot on the brake. The bloke came eagerly towards me, and I sighed as I wound down the window.

"*Mon camion*," he said. "My truck. It is being stolen."

"Let him in, Donc, why not?" I said.

So Dave opened the back door of the Escort without a word. The Frenchman climbed in, and Dave squeezed into the front. The breeze block in his hand turned out to be the biggest sausage and egg butty you've ever seen, dripping with tomato sauce. The car filled with a greasy aroma that would linger for days. It didn't go too well with the stale beer either.

The Iveco was already a few hundred yards away by now, and the Frenchman began bouncing angrily.

"What's up, monsieur?" I said, as I indicated carefully before pulling out. I was waiting until I spotted some slow-moving caravans to sneak in front of. Getting onto the A1 from a layby is a bit dicey sometimes - you can end up with a snap-on tools salesman right up your backside, doing ninety miles an hour in his company Cavalier.

"We must follow the thieves. They steal my truck."

"Dear, oh dear. It happens all the time, you know. You can't leave anything unattended round here."

"Hurry, hurry! You are too slow."

I shook my head sadly. Well, there you go. You give somebody a lift, do them a favour, and the first thing out of their mouths is criticism of your driving ability. The world is so unfair.

"It's always been like this," I said helpfully. "This bit of the A1 was the Great North Road. You know, where Dick Turpin used to hang out? You've heard of Dick Turpin, have you, monsieur?"

"*Comment?* What?"

"Highwayman, you know. Thief."

This is straight up, too. Well, the original Great North Road is a bit to the east, but it's well and truly bypassed now. Some of it has deteriorated to a track, fit only for horses and trail bikes. But make no mistake. This whole area is still bandit country.

"Then there was Robin Hood," I said. "Robbing from the rich to give to the poor. Oh, and we had Mrs Thatcher, of course, who got it the wrong way round."

The Frenchman wasn't listening to my tour guide spiel. He was gesturing towards the bottom of the fascia, where my mobile phone sat under a pile of music cassettes and the world's worst in-car stereo system.

"Yeah, you're right, it's crap, this local radio. *Le crap*, eh? I don't know why I listen to it. What do you fancy then, mate? Some Sacha Distel maybe?"

I poked among the cassettes as if I was actually looking for *Raindrops Keep Falling On My Head*. It wasn't likely to be there. Not unless there was a cover version by Enya or UB40. Whoever normally drove this Escort had different tastes from mine. No doubt about it.

"How about this? This is French." I held up a Chris Rea tape. "*Auberge*. That's French, right?"

I slipped the cassette into the deck, and Rea began to sing about there being only one place to go. It's funny how you can always find Chris Rea tapes in sales reps' cars. I reckon they have them so they can play *The Road to Hell* and feel all ironic.

"No, no. You must call for help," the trucker shouted in my ear over the music. "Police. Stop the truck."

And then he reached forward, trying to make a grab for the phone. Dave barely moved. He gave the Frenchman a little flip and the bloke hit the back of his seat like he'd bounced off a brick wall.

"Sorry, mate, but the signal's terrible round here," I said. "It's all the trees. Sherwood Forest, this is."

The lorry driver called me a *cochon*. I failed French 'O' level, but even I know that isn't polite.

"Look, I'm really sorry it's not Sacha Distel, but I'm doing my best, right?"

As we approached the big roundabout at Markham Moor, the Iveco was already halfway up the long hill heading south, growling past the McDonald's drive-thru and the Shell petrol station. I could catch up with the lorry easily. No need for lights and sirens - which was lucky, because we didn't have any.

But the sight of those yellow arches by the carriageway put me in mind of something.

"Hey, it's a bit like a scene in that film, what's it called? You know, with John Travolta and the black bloke in a frizzy wig? What do they call a Big Mac with cheese in France?"

6

Dave's ears pricked up at the Big Mac, but he didn't know the answer. He has no culture, see.

The Escort's steering juddered and the suspension groaned as I twisted the wheel to the right and we swerved into the roundabout, across the A1 and towards a little B road that leads past the Markham Moor truck stop. As we passed, I couldn't resist a glance for professional reasons. On the tarmac stood two orange and white Tesco lorries, a flatbed from Hanson Bricks, and a Euromax Mercedes diesel, all backed up against a couple of Cho Yang container trucks. There was a load of NorCor corrugated boarding, and even a Scania full of Weetabix. To be honest, though, I couldn't see anyone shifting fifty tons of breakfast cereal too easily. Not in these parts.

The Frenchman started gibbering again and pointing to the main road, where the back of his lorry had just vanished over the hill.

"*Non, non.* Turn round. That way. The thieves go that way."

"It's a short cut, mate. What do they call a Big Mac with cheese in France?"

"*Merde!*"

Then he began to poke his finger at Dave's shoulder. Well, that was a mistake. Dave stared at him, amazed, like a Rottweiler that finds a cat pulling its whiskers. His immense jaws opened and his teeth came down on the round, stubby thing in front of his face. It disappeared into his mouth with a little spurt of red, and he began to chew. The Frenchman pulled back his finger fast, in case it went the same way as that sausage.

We passed through a couple of villages before I turned onto a road that was more mud than tarmac. A track led us over the River Maun, past a few derelict buildings, through some woods, over another river and into more woods. The trees closed all around us now, dark conifers that wiped out any hope of a view.

But in the middle of the trees a space suddenly opened up. It was a vast expanse of wasteland - acres and acres of black slurry and weed-covered concrete. There were old wheel tracks in that slurry, and some of them were two feet deep. This was one of our dead coal mines, whose rotting bodies lie all over Nottinghamshire these days - a memory of the time when thousands of blokes and their families lived for the seam of coal they called Top Hard.

Finally we ran out of road and pulled up by a series of lagoons. These lagoons are pretty deep too, and I wouldn't like to say what the stuff is that swirls about down there.

"Okay, Monsieur Merde. Out."

The Frenchman looked from me to Dave, who helpfully leaned back to unfasten his seat belt. The trucker flinched a bit, but looked relieved when the belt clicked open. He got out and looked at the devastation around him, baffled.

Well, this bit of Nottinghamshire is no picnic site, that's for sure. We were on the remains of an old pit road, where British Coal lorries once trundled backwards and forwards all day long. In some places, wagons have been dragged off the underground trains, filled with concrete and upended to stop gypsies setting up camp in the woods. But there are always ways in, if you know how. Up ahead was a bridge where you could look down on the railway line that carried the coal trains. The lines are rusted now, but the coal is still there, way below ground. Top Hard, the best coking and steam coal in the country. It made a lot of the old mine owners very rich.

Yes, this was once the site of the area's proudest superpit. A few years back, when it was still open, a report came up with the idea of making it a Coal Theme Park, preserving the glory days of the 1960s. There would have been visits to the coal face, a ride underground on a paddy train, and maybe a trip to the canteen for a mug of sweet tea. They had a dry ski slope planned for the spoil heap. I kid you not.

But you'd need a heck of an imagination to picture this theme park now. The buildings have been demolished, and the fences are a futile gesture. There's just the black slag everywhere and a few churned up roadways where they came to cart away the debris.

The Frenchman stared at the lagoons, then turned and looked across the black wasteland behind him. It would be suicide to try walking through that lot. He shrugged his shoulders and waited, his eyebrows lifted like a supercilious customs man at Calais. Suddenly, his complacency was starting to annoy me.

"Take a look at this then, mate. What do you think? Pretty, isn't it? This is what's left of our mining industry. Coal mining, yeah? It may not mean much to you. You grow grapes and make cheese in France, right? But coal was our livelihood here in Nottinghamshire, once. Blokes went down into a bloody great black hole every day and got their lungs full of coal dust just so that we could buy food after the war. You remember the war, do you? When we kicked the krauts out of your country?"

Of course he didn't remember the war. He wasn't old enough. Nor am I, but I've read a history book or two. I know we bankrupted ourselves fighting the Germans, and it was the miners like my granddad who worked their bollocks off to get this country out of the mess afterwards. Their sons and grandsons carried on going down those holes day after day to dig out the coal. Decades and decades of it, with blokes getting crushed in roof falls and burnt to death in fires, and coughing their guts out with lung disease for the rest of their lives.

And this is the thanks they got, places like this and a score of other derelict sites around Nottinghamshire, Derbyshire, Yorkshire. Maggie Thatcher betrayed us, the whole country let us down. Workmates stabbed each other in the back. That was 1984. Write it on my gravestone.

Somewhere north of Newark, the French truck would be picking up speed on the flat right now. In a few minutes it should it hit the bypass and turn off on the A46. Within the hour it would be in a warehouse on an industrial estate outside town, and that would be nothing to do with me at all. All thanks to Slow Kid Thompson.

Oh, I forget to mention Slow Kid, didn't I? He's one of my best boys. He has a lot of talents, but his number one skill is driving. If Slow can't drive it, it hasn't got wheels. Today, he'd just delivered our first big load, a job worth quite a few grand to me and my mates. After years of doing small-scale business, shifting dodgy goods and re-plating nicked motors, we were finally moving into the big time. That Iveco represented the start of a new life of a crime, and goodbye to a past I wanted to forget.

"You're lucky, monsieur. I'm feeling in a good mood today."

By now the Frenchman had gone as quiet as Doncaster Dave. I guess it had finally dawned on him that we weren't going to help him catch his stolen lorry after all. Maybe he'd realised there would be no nice British bobbies rushing up to arrest the villains who'd ruined his day. No high-speed pursuit, no rolling road blocks, no one to pull him out of the brown stuff.

Oh yeah, that's the main thing I forgot to mention - you can't trust anyone these days. I call it the Stones McClure Top Hard Rule.

2

It would take the trucker a while to find his way out through these woods. There was a farm half a mile away, but I happened to know that the bloke there was a sheep farmer who exported lamb. He was more likely to welcome a French lorry driver with a shotgun than with an invitation to step in and use his phone.

I spun the Escort round and headed away again. But after a few yards I jammed on the brakes and reversed back to the Frenchman. I wound down the window and handed him out a Mega Mac Meal. Then we drove off. In my mirror, I saw the trucker stare at the bag for a second before dropping it on the floor and jumping on it. What a waste. I know it was probably a statement of his national culinary superiority, but that Mega Mac Meal cost me £3.89.

Heading south now on the A1, I put my foot down for a few miles. Just before Newark we caught up with the French truck. It was going well and picking up speed on the flat. We tailed it as it hit the Newark bypass and turned off westwards on the A46. After a few minutes it disappeared into a lorry park at the back of the cattle market.

Dave and I sat in the car by the junction for a bit, checking out the traffic. Then we turned round, eased our way back onto the bypass and pulled straight into the forecourt of one of the fast food places, where we sat and ate our Mega Macs. Dave was ready for another snack after all that effort.

I checked my boots and scraped off a bit of mud from the pit site. It wouldn't make much difference to the floor of the Escort. I'm not exactly a snappy dresser, as anyone will tell you who's ever seen me coming. A pair of old Levis and a leather jacket suit me fine. But I've got a soft spot for these boots. They're Dan Post tan Gamblers, with snip toes and cowboy heels, and a nice bit of fancy stitching in the leather on the sides. I reckon they must have cost a few hundred dollars, these things. I got them as a present years ago from some American bird with too much money. You don't see many of those round these parts, so she's worth remembering, if only for the boots.

A few minutes later, a young bloke walked out of the bushes near the back of the cattle market and dodged and jinked his way across the road to the cafe. He was medium height, with hair cropped so short he looked bald from a distance. He was wearing a grubby t-shirt and carrying a red ski jacket, and a woollen hat was shoved into the pocket of his jeans. I eyed him in the mirror as he slipped into the back seat of the Escort.

"All right, Slow?"

He pulled out a fag before he answered, adding to the stink in the Escort. Then his eyes met mine in the mirror, bright with excitement, and he grinned suddenly, looking like a little kid who's just come down from a ride on the Corkscrew Rollercoaster at Alton Towers. He gestured at me with a sharp jab of his index finger.

"All right, Stones. All right."

I left Dave to finish off the extra large fries while I went outside with Slow Kid. There was another bit of business to see to that Slow had set up, but we had a few minutes to wait. The roar of engines and the screech of air brakes from the heavy traffic approaching the roundabout didn't help conversation, but you don't expect the car park of a microwave mecca to be scenic.

"Good job that, Stones, don't you reckon?"

"Sure, Slow. Let's hope there'll be lots more of them. What are you going to spend your share on?"

"Dunno really. My mum's talking about moving. Maybe it'll help. She wants to get out of Beech Street. Move into one of the Crescents maybe."

"A Crescent? Going upmarket?"

"Well, Mum's not happy. She's says they're all drug addicts in our street now."

"Yeah, probably."

The Thompsons are a big family - there are several households of them on our estate alone. Slow Kid has lots of brothers and sisters and cousins, and they're so close they form a separate clan.

Although they argue all the time, they also protect each other. Very few of them have jobs.

Slow Kid nudged me as a blue Renault Master high-roof van nosed into the car park. It picked out the quietest corner and backed into a spot where its rear doors were facing towards the shrubbery.

"That's the bloke, Stones."

"Right. Let's see what he's got. Rawlings, is it?"

"Yeah."

The owner of the Renault was a heavily built bloke in a check shirt with receding hair pulled back in greasy strands over his ears. He was sweating, though the weather wasn't all that warm, and his manner was a bit too slimy for my liking.

"Hey up," I said.

"Hey up. McClure, is it? I'm Rawlings."

"Nobody ever calls me anything but Stones."

"Right, right."

His hand felt clammy when we shook, even though he wiped his palm on his jeans first. He had the back doors of the van open, glancing slyly around him like some Russian spy from a Cold War thriller. I was already getting a bad feeling about him. I only stay free and in good health by keeping clear of blokes like this. But I decided to take a look at his stuff since we were here, and Slow Kid had set it up himself.

The back of the van was half full of cardboard boxes.

"Trainers, that right?"

"Right. Reeboks." He winked at me, and I had to fight a shudder. This jerk was putting me right off crime.

"And there's some sweatshirts and tracksuits too. Umbro. All top-notch gear, you know, Stones. Reeboks, now, they go like mad with the youngsters these days, eh?"

"Let's have a look then."

"Sure thing." Rawlings leaned round the side of the van and bellowed towards the driver's seat. "Josh! Open a couple of these boxes."

A lad with a streaked flat-top slid out of the cab and slouched towards us, pulling a nasty-looking combat knife from his pocket. Slow Kid, who was standing behind me, took a couple of steps backwards as if to give himself room for action. Without looking round, I could feel him stiffen.

But Flat Top took no notice of us. He hoisted himself into the van and hacked away at the tape sealing one of the nearest cases. I could see it was packed with plain white shoe boxes stuffed with tissue paper. The lad watched me as I lifted a couple out and unwrapped the tissue.

The trainers were real top-class stuff. They were well made, with solid stitching and thick soles that flexed like something alive in my fingers. They smelled new and expensive, and the gold and black labels on the heels looked genuine. They looked really good. Too good.

Flat Top had another box open by now, and was dragging out a tracksuit top. But I didn't want to see any more. I shoved the trainers back in under the tissue paper and turned to Rawlings.

"No thanks. I'm not interested."

"What?" His eyebrows shot up towards his freckly bald head. "You must be joking. Look at them! That's good stuff, that is. You won't see any better."

"Maybe. But I'm not interested. Sorry."

"Stones, look. You don't know what you're saying. I'm offering you the best here."

"Sure. But offer it somewhere else, okay?"

Rawlings was sweating even more now. He took a revolting rag from his pocket to wipe his head. "If it's the price that's worrying you, I'll drop it, okay? Just make me an offer. I need to unload the stuff. It'll make you a bomb."

"No."

I turned to go and caught sight of Slow Kid's expression. He looked as though he'd come face to face with a rattlesnake on the living room carpet and was just waiting for it to blink before he stamped on its head. He bared his teeth as I felt a sweaty hand grab my arm and pull me back towards the van. It was Rawlings, and his mood had suddenly changed.

"McClure, I don't appreciate being messed around. I came here because I heard you'd be interested. I was told you were straight up, a bloke who knew a good deal when he saw when. So don't muck me about. Take this deal or tell me why not."

I don't like being grabbed very much, especially by jerks like Rawlings. But Flat Top was poised by the back doors of the van, the knife held in his hand almost casually, as if he was waiting for someone to ask him to slit open another cardboard box or something. His eyes were fixed on me, and I hadn't noticed them until now. They were blue, but dead, like the eyes of a stuffed cat.

The knife was too near me for comfort, and Rawlings had a good grip on my best arm. I knew Slow Kid was probably carrying his own blade, but he was behind me. An accident can happen at a time like this - and the thought that I might be the one it happens to makes me unhappy.

I don't reckon to be a coward, but self-preservation is my middle name. In fact, I'm thinking of changing it by deed poll to 'alive'. Stones Alive McClure. It doesn't sound too bad, does it? It'll give someone a good laugh when they chisel it on my memorial. But it's sussing out situations like this that has kept me on two feet all this time. Well, that and the good money I pay Doncaster Dave to be my minder, anyway.

I don't know whether Rawlings and his mate could see me weighing up the odds with my lightning-fast brain, or whether it was the sight of Dave himself leaning on the side of the van and crumpling the door that made Rawlings let go of my arm. The odds had shifted, and retreat had become a sensible option for him. That's the way I like it.

Rawlings gave a jerk of his head to Flat Top, who followed him back to the cab, looking frustrated. Rawlings put his boot down and the van shot off across the car park, leaving us with just a few lungfuls of exhaust fumes to remember them by. When they turned to go past us to the exit, I thought Rawlings looked worried. Scared even. Maybe I ought to give Dave a pay rise.

The three of us walked back in silence to the Little Chef, and Dave happily went back to his place at a table by the window.

"Something go wrong then, Stones?"

That's Dave all right. Nothing much gets past him.

"Well, you were watching, weren't you, Donc? That's what I pay you for, ain't it? To watch me? You must have seen what went off, right?"

"Course, Stones."

I was irritated with him because it had nearly gone very badly wrong, and I didn't like the fact he'd turned up at the last minute, even though it was probably my fault. I hadn't been cautious enough for once. Just then I didn't realise quite how badly everything had nearly gone wrong.

Dave was looking shifty at my tone of voice, and his eyes slid sideways. I followed his glance and saw a muscly waitress with a dyed blonde crop. She grinned back at him, and I sighed. Why does my minder have this effect on some women? I can't understand it. He frightens the life out of me.

Then the mobile phone rang. When I say 'rang', the Motorola can be set to vibrate instead of ring if you don't want it going off noisily somewhere where it might not be very discreet. This vibration can be an interesting experience if it's in your pocket. Luckily, on this occasion it was on the table, and began to rattle quietly on the plastic surface until I picked it up.

"Yeah?"

"Delivery on the way," said an unidentified voice.

"Okay."

And that was all I needed to know.

*　　*　　*　　*

Half an hour later we were back on the road. But a mile or two down the A614, traffic slowed and gradually came to a crawl.

"Oh shit, what's this? More roadworks?"

Slow Kid is always impatient with delays. But me, I look for the positive side, watch for the opportunities.

"If there's some new roadworks, keep your eyes peeled. Some of these contractors are very careless with their equipment."

"Right."

But as we got nearer to the hold-up, we could see there was no chance of any mobile generators or JCBs going spare. Instead, there were flashing lights, police cars slewed across one carriageway, an ambulance, a fire engine and a cloud of steam and black smoke.

We crawled by the scene as traffic was filtered into one lane

16

past the accident. Like all the other drivers, we craned our necks to see what had happened. The blackened and smouldering remains of a van stood at the side of the road, and fire had scorched a patch of grass and tarmac around it. The van was a Renault Master high roof. It might once have been blue.

"Hey, isn't that - ?" began Slow, his eyes popping as he stared out of the window. He began to brake for a closer look.

"Don't make us noticeable - drive on," I said.

"But Stones - "

"Yeah, I know," I said. "Rawlings and his mate."

This wasn't good. The smile had frozen on my face. It was as if a blast of icy air had suddenly blown in through the window, straight from the smoking wreck of that van.

3

The village I live in is Medensworth. It's in an area called the Dukeries, on account of all the dukes. Medensworth is in the Domesday Book, according to our county's tourist office, which seems to think it's a mark of historical importance. Back then, some bloke by the name of Roger de Busli held eight bovates of land here, and a fishing yielding one hundred eels. It seems de Busli was one of William the Conqueror's minions. His reward for backing up his gaffer in 1066 was getting his hands on about half a million acres of Nottinghamshire and Yorkshire that had belonged up till then to some poor bloody Saxons. The Saxons happened to have been on the wrong side in the Battle of Hastings. So it goes.

Whenever I happen to read that bit about the bovates and eels, I can just picture some fat Norman landowners living it up in their manor houses on venison and French wine while Saxon carls slaved away in the fields and ate mouldy turnips in their dingy hovels, knowing that they weren't worth mentioning, not even in the bloody Domesday Book.

A few centuries later on, a load of dukes divided Nottinghamshire up between them, like greedy kids with a big cake. They built these vast monstrosities of houses for themselves, surrounded by acres and acres of parkland, outdoing each other to spend their cash. Worksop Manor once had five hundred rooms. How could anyone actually live in a place like that? It can't have been a home, just a huge stone box to contain someone's ego. And this was Worksop, for God's sake - it ain't exactly Florence.

Meanwhile, these peasants were still pissing about in the fields, eating the same rotten turnips - at least, those of them that weren't already being sent into the pits and factories, or shipped off to die in a war somewhere. *They* weren't worth mentioning either. The area's called the Dukeries, not the Peasanteries.

The rich gits may change a bit over the centuries, but it's

18

always the same bloody peasants. These days we don't slave in the fields so much. In fact, we don't slave anywhere much since the pits closed. Instead, we stand in a dole queue for our pittance. And instead of rotten vegetables we eat packets of Fry Dry frozen chips, which I don't think are even made from anything as exciting as turnips. Have things changed since Monsieur de Busli? I think not.

Well, we all know it's going to be like that for ever and ever, unless someone breaks a few rules here and there. That's where I come in. I help to share out a bit of wealth. That means breaking more than the odd rule. But they're other people's rules, not mine. If a load of stuck-up magistrates don't like the way I do it, then tough shit. Maybe now and then I re-distribute more of it than strictly necessary towards the Stones McClure Benevolent Fund. So? Double tough shit.

We dumped the Escort where it would probably rust away quietly forever and switched to my Subaru Impreza Turbo 2000. I dropped Slow Kid and Dave off and watched them disappear into the darkness towards their houses. They belonged in Medensworth, and they blended into the background the moment they walked out of the light of the nearest working street lamp. Being on my own felt strange after the excitement of the afternoon, and somehow the elation was starting to turn bitter in my stomach as I drove onto the monster of a housing development they call the Forest Estate. This is my home.

You'll find Medensworth north of the Major Oak and left a bit. Tourists looking for Robin Hood in Sherwood Forest Country Park don't know it exists, and they wouldn't want to. It's one of those big pit villages that were thrown up for miners' families when the mines were first sunk, villages that are wondering what to do with themselves now the pits have gone.

They're not pretty, these places. But there's some sort of symbolism in the fact that the most visited bit of Nottinghamshire, where visitors gape at a decrepit oak tree and walk along leafy woodland paths thinking they're in the heart of rural England, is completely surrounded by pit villages and the remains of their pits. I mean places like Ollerton, Edwinstowe, Welbeck, Shirebrook. Their slag heaps are cleverly screened, but they're still there. They look like hills thrown up by some delayed spasm of the earth. It's like nature, or God, or whoever, spent a hard week sweating to build all those really nice mountains and rolling hills and lakes and stuff, then decided to get rat-arsed on the seventh day and spewed up all these slag heaps. They may have come from the same place as the rolling hills, but the quality isn't the same. It's the shitty end of creation. Medensworth is one of those places, mostly.

It was all quiet as I drove into Sherwood Crescent and round the corner into the back alley to park up. Houses in my street don't have garages. They weren't made for folk with cars - after all, men only had to walk up the road to reach the pit gates or the Miners Welfare. Where else would they want to go?

Now we do have cars, though details like tax and insurance and MoT certificates tend to get a bit neglected. Well, we're not used to it. Can't read the small print on the log book (it fades when you photocopy anything). But the number of cars parked at the kerb and blocking up the street meant we had to have garages. So there are rows of them, ramshackle corrugated iron things in the back alleys and on bits of wasteland round the estate. My motor's in one of those - except there's nothing ramshackle about my garage and nothing cheap about the locks either. You can't be too careful, because you never who might decide to take a look inside. Maybe even some nosey copper. And we wouldn't want that.

The Impreza is red and it's new, but not too flash. Lisa wanted me to get a BMW. I could have afforded it, I suppose. But driving one of those things round here might make people think you were a criminal, right?

Oh, Lisa? Lisa reckons she's my girlfriend. At least she comes round to my house a lot, even talks me into taking her out occasionally. And we have sex in my bedroom quite often - sometimes not even in the bedroom. So I suppose it might seem there's some truth in what she thinks.

I let myself into 36 Sherwood Crescent, turning off the alarm and listening carefully to the sounds of the house. You get into the habit of being careful - you want to be sure that the house is empty. There wasn't much to check out in the little hallway. Just one of the local free papers on the mat, shouting the attractions of a new fitness centre in a garish clash of coloured inks. I left the door into the sitting room open while I switched on the lights, skirting the settee and a couple of armchairs on the way to the kitchen. Apart from the telly and a good stereo, the room was pretty much empty. There are a few books on the shelf. Some local history, loaned to me by Lisa for my education. Some law books, a few crime novels -Inspector Morse and P.D. James. The certificates and the other stuff are buried in a drawer with balls of string and spare fuses and the rest of the dross.

No end of women have told me the place looks like a hermit's cell. But so what? I've never been on any holidays where I'd feel tempted to buy a straw donkey or a glass paperweight to bring back for the mantelpiece. I don't have any reason to collect things that remind me of the past. And a certain sparseness means there's less to dust. This is important when you're a bloke living on your own, but birds don't seem to see it. And another thing - why make the sitting room too comfortable? You don't want a bird getting warm and cosy in front of the fire, do you? You want her keen to get out of there to the warmth of the bedroom. So the sitting room needs to be bare, and a bit cool. It's stick and carrot, if you know what I mean.

In the kitchen, I switched the kettle on and pulled a pizza out of the freezer compartment to stick in the microwave. I didn't look too closely at the interior of the fridge while I had the door open. There were a few cans of beer in there that looked all right, but everything else was likely to cause a major European health scare if it ever escaped. There was a milk carton that had taken up a new career as a penicillin factory, and a bit of Cheddar cheese that would have cracked the floor if I dropped it. There were other things, too, that didn't bear looking at, and the smell was getting bad. I'd have to buy a new fridge soon.

With the kettle hissing and the microwave humming, I switched on the telly and caught the climax of an American film, all guns and screams and cars getting blown up. But the house still sounded empty, and this is what made me think of Lisa, I suppose. It never feels empty when Lisa's there.

It's funny, really. You see, me and women don't usually last longer than a few weeks together. I get bored easily, and just when they're talking about a steady relationship, I'm off eyeballing something different and it comes to a nasty end, one way or another.

Obviously, I expected this to happen with Lisa once she'd been coming round for a month or so. It's a natural cycle, like Autumn coming after Summer. You don't even think about it - you just start sorting the woollies out of the drawer when the drain gets blocked up with leaves and the kids start chucking sticks at the chestnut trees for conkers.

But it hasn't happened this time, and I don't understand why. It's as if nature has decided not to bother with Autumn this year because it's too messy, what with the dead leaves and all that, and she's quite happy with Summer, thank you very much. Surely Lisa must have clocked the way I am? She's not stupid - far from it. Sure, she gives me some hammer now and then. She has a fair old temper, so I don't answer back much. And there she still is. She's been around so long the lads have learned her name and even ask after her health. Every time that happens, I get this nasty feeling in my guts, like I've just eaten curried chips from the Bombay Duck takeaway. It's going to cause a real problem one day soon. You see, I was so sure that Lisa would drift away like all the others, that I've already gone and found the next one. And, like I said, Lisa's got a real temper.

When I first met Lisa, I'd been going around with some bird whose name I can't quite remember now. One day she decided she wanted to visit Newstead Abbey, where Lord Byron used to live. She'd been gawping at the oak-panelled Great Hall and its minstrels' gallery and twittering on about how grand the Byrons must have been, and how wonderful the place must have looked when they lived there.

My attention was already wandering a bit, and I was wondering whether what's-her-name would be interested in a bit of sex down by the lake. I had also, of course, noticed the blonde bird standing nearby. She was slim and smartly dressed, with short, well-cut hair, and she had that rare quality in a woman - style. Looking sexy and dying your hair blonde is okay, but if a woman knows how to wear clothes and how to hold herself when she moves, that's what really catches my eye. You don't see it too often, but Lisa has it. From her expression, she was several shades brighter than the bird I was with, too. Her eyes looked amused as she listened to the twitter. I like a woman with a sense of humour.

"Actually, the fifth Lord Byron let the Abbey go to rack and ruin," she said suddenly. She seemed to be talking to me rather than Miss Twitter. "He died in the scullery, which was the only room left in the house where the roof didn't leak."

"Yeah? Was he the poet?" I asked.

"No. The poet was his great-nephew, Alfred, who inherited the Abbey from him. This Great Hall was so derelict by then that he only used it for pistol practice."

"No kidding."

The blonde woman began to talk about the monks who lived in the original abbey from 1150 until they were kicked out by Henry VIII. Then she told us about the follies built by the fifth Lord Byron - the two mock forts by the lake, where he used to stage miniature sea battles - and his sheer bloody-mindedness in neglecting the building and deliberately laying waste to the estate. She talked about his great nephew's riotous lifestyle and dubious friends, and his permanent money problems. She moved on to point out the cloister court, laid out as what she called a Mary Garden, with a carved sixteenth century water conduit, and then she led us into the kitchen next to the Sussex Tower, which she said had been modelled on the Abbot's Kitchen in Glastonbury Abbey.

And something really funny happened as I listened to her talk. Suddenly I could see it. I could actually see and hear and smell everything that she was talking about. I could picture the holes in the roof, and the damp running down the walls, soaking into rugs that smelled of mould. I could see a journeyman carpenter painstakingly carving out the patterns by hand on yards of water conduit, his hands and clothes smelling of fresh wood shavings. I could hear the kitchen servants chattering to each other as they prepared yet another ten-course banquet for the eccentric poet and his disreputable friends. I could smell the sweat of those servants as much as the sides of venison roasting in the ovens and the hot, steamy aroma as the maids scrubbed stone-flagged floors on their hands and knees.

This had never happened to me before. Until then, these places had just been tourist traps, somewhere for the Americans and Japanese and a few local folk like Miss Twitter to be parted from their money in exchange for postcards and Newstead Abbey key rings. But Lisa made it real. I think it was then I knew she was going to be part of my life.

After the pizza was finished, I made a few calls. Though I was feeling good about the lorry load of gear we'd just got away, the big stuff was new to me just then. I still had my main business to run, the small scale stuff that's done so well for me and quite a few other people, since I fell out with a system that won't let you help out people worse off than yourself.

But let's get this straight. Some folk think I'm a criminal. A thief even. Me, I call what I do redistribution of wealth. Wealth is the stuff that the rich gits have, and the folk who live round here don't have. It's always been like that, you know - right back to the time when some Stone Age bloke called Ug grabbed the best cave for himself and collected every flint arrowhead that was going and made all the other Ugs do the hunting and mammoth gutting. I'm just sharing out a few bits of flint that some modern day King of the Ugs has carelessly left lying around.

So the first call was to Fat John, my best supplier. This is a two-way business, you see. I supply blokes in other areas with goods they want. In return, I buy in stuff I can sell on my own patch from their areas. You don't mess on your own doorstep, right?

Once or twice the Trading Standards blokes have tried to make out some of the gear was counterfeit. But honest to God, I bought it in good faith, your honour. Well, what I say is - if people can have faith in the British justice system, I can have faith in Fat John when he tells me I'm buying top grade stuff. John says you you're getting Reeboks or Levis, and just like the constitution tells you, you're innocent until proved guilty. Well you either buy that shit or you don't. As far as I can see, the only difference is that Fat John gives it to you in black and white, and it's right there on the labels. But the constitution? The constitution only ever exists in the head of some decrepit judge, and depends on whether his piles are playing him up or the cheese he had for lunch is giving him indigestion. British justice? Don't make me laugh. I've seen more

24

attractive concepts on the pavement after the pubs have shut.

A fat voice answered the phone with a string of numbers, giving nothing away.

"John? Stones. All right?"

"Ah. Hello there, my friend. How goes it?"

"Fine, fine. You trading, John?"

"As ever, my friend. More watches for you. Rolex and Seiko. They shift well for you, yes? Also lots of videos and perfumes. Good names, good stuff."

"I can take a load at the end of the week."

"You have it, Stones. Usual arrangement?"

"I'll see to it."

"It's a pleasure, my friend."

"See you, mate."

The next call was to one of the boys. He goes by the name of Metal Jacket, because his shoulders are never out of a car engine. He took a long while to answer the phone.

"Yes?"

"Metal? Stones."

"All right, Stones?"

As usual, he was somewhere noisy. There was the banging of metal and a radio turned up too loud in the background, and a terrible echo. I could picture him pulling the phone out from under a pile of junk in a blacksmith's shop or something.

"What's this message about a motor?"

"Yeah, yeah. You ought to take a look at it, Stones. Nice wheels."

Metal Jacket is one of the best when it comes to motors, but scores of them go through his hands. I couldn't understand what he was on about here.

"Why should I take a look? I've already got a motor."

"Yeah, I know. But this one's a real nice motor. Special. You know what I mean?"

"No." I sighed. Communication isn't all that it's cracked up to be sometimes. "Where is it, Metal?"

"Oh, down the workshop."

"I'll be along tomorrow."

"Right, man. See you."

"See you."

The third call was to a legit contact. I do still have some of these, and they're really useful. It's like a packet of condoms - they're no fun at the time, but it's always best to keep a few in your pocket, and you're always glad you had them afterwards.

"Hello. Newsdesk. Can I help you?"

"Nah then. Is that the whatsit, the editor?"

"This is the news editor, Mel France. Can I help you, sir?" The voice was cautious, like someone who never knows quite what to expect when he answers the phone.

"Well, I've got this bit of news, like, that I thought you might be interested in."

"Oh yes?" Encouraging, but non-committal. A professional.

"It's about my dog, you see. My neighbours are taking me to court complaining about the noise he makes."

"Oh. And how do you feel about that?"

"Well, I'm barking mad."

There was a brief silence, then a click, like your car key turning in the central locking.

"That's McClure pissing about, isn't it?"

He still sounded annoyed, but relieved too. It wasn't some irritating member of the general public to deal with, but just me after all.

"Shit, Mel. You're so sharp, you catch me out every time."

"I'm up to my neck in deadlines here, Stones. What the hell do you want?"

"I want to be informed, educated and entertained. Where do you think I can find those things, Mel?"

"Piss off. You're bad news."

Mel France is one of my favourite contacts. I think it's the way he falls over himself to be helpful. I must have done him a real big favour some time in the past. Now that he's news editor on a big evening paper, he's always delighted to get the chance to pay me back.

"You journalists are so full of bullshit. Why don't you just cut the guff and get to the point?"

"I'm pretty close to the point, Stones. To the point of hanging up."

"There was a van fire on the A614 last night. What have you got on it?"

"Why don't you read the bloody paper and find out?"

"You'd have to write it in language I can understand first, Mel."

"There's a limit to how much you can say in words of one syllable."

"Oh yeah? I mean, there was a headline the other day that said 'Bespoke oak folk are tree-mendous' What the hell does that mean? Is it in English?"

"What did you want to know about this van?"

"Anything you've got. What are the police saying?"

"Damn all, as usual." There was a rustling of papers at the other end of the phone. Somehow I'd imagined everything being on computer screens in newspaper offices these days. Maybe Mel was doing the Sun crossword. If so, he wouldn't keep me long. "We're talking about a Renault Master, right? Near the Clumber Hotel? Normanton entrance to Clumber Park?"

"That's it."

"The fire service were called, but the van was totally destroyed, it says here. No other vehicle involved."

"Casualties?"

"Two. Taken to Bassetlaw Hospital and treated for minor burns, but not detained. No serious injuries."

"Pity"

"What?"

"Names?"

"Er, no names given. Withheld at the request of the victims."

"Victims, right."

"That's perfectly normal these days. People can say they don't want their names giving out to the press."

"Yeah, I know. So if there were no other vehicles involved, what was the cause of this fire?"

"Mmm, doesn't say. Some sort of electrical fault, surely."

"Maybe."

"Do you know otherwise, Stones?"

"No, no. I was just passing, and I thought it was someone I knew."

"Oh yeah? Nobody important, then."

"Ta."

"Well, as long as the van was insured, there's no harm done, is there? I mean, it wouldn't have been nicked or anything, by any chance? We're not talking about a crime here, after all, are we? Just an insurance job. So nobody loses."

"That's right, Mel. Dead right. Nobody loses."

I hung up and tapped my fingers. Nobody loses. You've heard people talk about victimless crime. Well, there are some crimes that not only have no victims, but everyone benefits from them. Nearly everyone, anyway.

Did you know those big companies write off huge losses to theft? In fact, they take them into account in working out their budgets for profit and loss. They call it slippage. It's one of those words business types like to use to cover up something they'd rather not talk about. They probably call going to the toilet 'dumpage'. Anyway, the point is that if a few loads of their stuff didn't go missing now and then, it would throw their accounts out completely. So I'm doing the accountants a big favour. Right? They ought to pay me for it. I could be a Freelance Slippage Consultant.

As for insurance companies, they already make more money than is good for them. Fatter profits would only make people take a closer look at their activities. So let them share the money out a bit. The government can't seem to manage it, whatever its colour. But I can.

When I talk like that, I feel good. And when I count the money, I feel even better. There's only one more thing that can make life perfect, and here it comes now.

"Hello. Who's that?"

Lisa has a warm, sexy voice. Hearing her speak is like drinking your first cup of coffee in the morning and finding it spiced with rum. You're already looking forward to it, then you realise it's even better than you thought.

"It's me," I said, original as ever.

"Stones?"

"Yeah. How are you?"

"Fine. Are you busy?"

"Well, you know, so-so..."

"Got much on tomorrow?"

"Always things to do. Business." I was beating about the bush here. Lisa has no idea what I actually do for a living, and I need to keep it that way.

"Oh. I thought you might have time to see me. I'm not working tomorrow afternoon."

"Right. Where? What time?" I didn't want to sound too eager. But, well, the sound of her voice was doing strange things to my hormones that kind of over-ruled anything my brain might be telling me.

"Can you pick me up at the hall? I should be out at twelve-thirty."

"No problem. I've got something to do in the morning, then I'm free."

I signed off feeling pleased with myself. Lisa had made the first move. That always makes a guy feel good.

When I think back, it was her who made the first move that day we met at Newstead Abbey. She may have been listening in to what the other bird was saying, but it was me she was talking to. That's the way it felt, anyway. And that's the way she hooked me. After I'd listened to her talking for a while, with my mouth hanging open like one of those roast pigs without the apple, it hadn't seemed at all difficult to find out her name and where she worked.

When I'd finally walked out of Newstead Abbey that afternoon, the other bird had to run after me and remind me that she was there. I never saw her again after that.

4

Next morning, when I arrived with Slow Kid at the workshop on an old industrial estate outside Medensworth, there was another bit of solidity waiting to trip me up. Half a ton of fancy motor, in fact.

Metal Jacket had picked up an old Citroen BX. That's one of those French jobs that crouches at the kerb like a whippet with the squitters. It always looks as though its suspension's gone, until you turn on the ignition and the hydraulics kick in to lift its skirts off the road. Trust the French to be different. I've never got over sitting in a Citroen Dyane once and finding both the gear lever and the handbrake sticking out of the dashboard at me like a couple of bread sticks. The BX wasn't quite as eccentric as that, but it was trying. They don't make them any more - not since the EC decided that all cars had to look the same.

"What did you nick this for, Metal?"

He ran the back of a greasy hand across his nose, leaving a dark smear among several other dark smears on his face. Metal was well camouflaged for work in a garage, being mainly covered in engine oil and rust. He wore a baggy old grey sweater that matched the bags under his eyes, and the holes in his jeans were more likely to have been caused by spilt battery acid than any attempt at fashion. He was chewing gum, and he hadn't shaved for a while. When he shouted at me above the racket from the radio, I could tell that he hadn't used much breath freshener recently either.

Metal Jacket is a real hard worker. He has several kids at home, and a Mrs Jacket who thinks she has a licence to stack up store credit cards now her husband has a proper job for once. This gives him a sharp eye for any chance of turning a few extra quid.

"Slow told me to nick it. He says there's a bloke wants one nicking, so I nicked it."

"What bloke's that, Slow? Local?"

"Nah. Whatsisname, Sharma, in Leicester. He's got a customer for one. But he wants it cheap. So I put the word out for the lads to look out for one."

"All right," I said. Jotindar Sharma was a regular customer, canny and safe. In any case, there'd be no way of tracing the car back to where it had come from by the time it reached him. Metal could render a car unrecognisable in an hour or two.

The Citroen wasn't what he'd called me about, though. He'd brought in an old Morris Traveller, one of those half-timbered little estate cars that make you think of 1950s comedy films and tea on the vicarage lawn. Did they used to call them shooting-brakes, or am I mistaken? Apparently I'd once mentioned them fondly to Metal as being part of our heritage, and the jerk had remembered it.

But this particular Morris had belonged to some old farmer out near Newark. It looked as though it had spent the last couple of decades being used as a hen house. There were white streaks on all the seats, and various bits of the car were fastened on with lengths of baler twine.

"And this one? Don't tell me some rich eccentric German businessman or somebody is itching to get his hands on this, Slow."

"Nowt to do with me, this."

"So. Metal? What's the excuse?"

Metal had to chew his gum a few times before he could translate the grinding of his mental gearbox into English.

"Well..." he said. "It's difficult to explain, like."

"Shit, Metal. How many times have I told you? You nick the rich gits' cars - the Mercs, the BMWs, the Bentleys, that stuff. Or you nick the company motors. That don't matter. But I don't want you nicking stuff like this, from people who can't afford it. You got me, Metal?"

"I know all that, Stones."

"So why did you nick it then?"

"I didn't."

"What do you mean, you didn't? Oh yeah, so you found it, then. Or maybe it took a fancy to you and followed you home?"

"I bought it," said Metal.

"You what?"

Metal Jacket hung his head, looking shamefaced, and fiddled with the ratchet on his spanner. Behind me, I heard Slow Kid gasp in disbelief.

"Metal? What do you mean? Tell me you're joking."

"I paid a bloke for it. I bought it. He gave me the log book, look. I reckon it's a real one too."

"Holy shit."

"Man, that's really weird," said Slow Kid, awed.

"It's even got its MoT certificate and everything," said Metal.

"Yeah? And I suppose the MoT's genuine as well?"

Metal glanced at the nearside headlamp of the Morris, which would have been pointing at the floor if it hadn't been jammed into place against the wing with a bent six-inch nail.

"Well... sort of. I had one lying about in a drawer."

"And you're really telling me that you bought this thing?"

"It needs a bit of work on it," he admitted. "Restoration, that's called. But it'll be worth quite a bit when it's done, I reckon."

"Well, maybe." I was seeing a new side of Metal Jacket. I'd never put him down as a bloke who needed a hobby. But people never cease to surprise me.

Then I looked again at the Citroen. Other than its odd posture, it was fairly anonymous. A bit of flashy French styling, true. But it was plain white with no distinguishing marks, as they say, apart from a small blue and red sticker in the back window with the initials 'PF' on it. I had a sudden nasty suspicion. It was like the feeling you get when you're caught short and there isn't a toilet for miles.

"Was there a radio in this one, Metal?"

He sniffed and shuffled his feet uneasily at the tone of my voice. "We took it out, Stones."

That was normal, but the feeling in my guts didn't shift. "Show it to me."

Reluctantly, Metal disappeared into the cupboard he called an office and came back with a small cardboard box trailing wires. It was a radio all right, but not a cheap Motorola that had been pre-tuned to Radio 4 and Classic FM, as you might expect. It was a short wave two-way set, with a hand mike on a coil of cable and a tuner no doubt locked onto the Nottinghamshire Constabulary waveband. It looked to me like Alpha Bravo Charlie had just gone off the air for good.

"Where did you say you got this motor, Metal?"

"Car park at Trowell Services. Dead easy. No alarms, nothing."

So some plain clothes cop on the M1 had made the mistake of stopping for a piss, or a plate of chips at the Granada restaurant. Served him right for being careless. And I don't just mean for leaving his car where Metal might find it.

You see, some of us aren't totally ignorant round here. We know a thing or two that's useful - like, for example, that the letters 'PF' stand for Police Federation, the coppers' trade union. The PF is one of those rare beasts these days - a union that fights tooth and nail for its members, and it doesn't care who it takes on. Criticise a copper and the PF's solicitors will be after you. Sometimes you might think the police are more likely to sue you than bang you up for a crime.

"Don't you recognise this, Metal?"

"Just a radio, in't it?"

"No, it isn't. Haven't you ever sat in a police car?" Stupid question. I realised it when Metal stared at me as if I was gone out. "Yeah, course you have. But only in the back seat, eh? With the cuffs on."

He shrugged. He had no idea what I was talking about. "Last time they done me was for that bit of bother at the races, Stones. It was a whatsit..."

"...a misunderstanding. Yeah, I know. Your solicitor said so."

"You want the radio, Stones?"

"No, no. Get rid of it, Metal. Chuck it in the river, bury it at the refuse dump. But wherever you ditch it, make it somewhere safe. Unless you want the owners round here turning you over. You've nicked one of the plods' little toys."

"What? You mean the motor's a pig wagon?"

"That's about it. You're hot, boy. You need to cool off quick, before they decide to put you on ice somewhere."

I shoved the radio back into his hands, watching him swallow his gum. Metal's day had turned runny already. I should have taken it as a warning.

*   *   *   *

Twelve o'clock already. I got back in the Impreza with Slow Kid. From Medensworth it was about twenty minutes to the hall.

"Where do you want dropping, Slow?"

"I got to see a few boys down the Welfare, Stones."

"Business, is it?"

"Well, you know... a few games of pool, a bit of chat, a drink or two."

I looked at him, but said nothing. He'd got rid of the ski jacket and the woolly hat and was wearing a Chicago Bulls baseball cap.

"Yeah... and probably a bit of business," he said.

"That's good, Slow. Let's keep it up. That load was only the start. We need to keep our eyes open for some more like that."

"Sure thing. Trust me, Stones."

"We ought to get confirmation on that load soon, shouldn't we?"

"They've got your mobile number, yeah?"

I dropped Slow Kid off at the top of Medensworth, near the old Miners' Welfare, and picked up an onion bhaji and a couple of Danish pastries at the deli on the corner. There'd be crumbs in my car, but it was a small price to pay.

Then I carried on through the village, passing under the railway viaduct that carries the old mineral line to Warsop. From here, the line goes on east past Tuxford to the power stations in the Trent Valley. Those power stations were the biggest customers for local coal for years, and at one time the mineral line was the only way coal could get to them from the pits. Then they started switching loads onto the roads, and the result was thousands of lorries trundling through the villages every day.

But the viaduct is still there. Five hundred feet long, with five stone arches standing over the River Meden like swan's necks, full of power and grace. To me, it's the best sight in Medensworth, not excepting the old church. Funny, though, that it took Lisa to point the viaduct out to me. Until then I hadn't noticed it much. It was just part of the scenery, like the street lights or the back wall of the Welfare. How had I missed that craftsmanship? It was built in 1819, said Lisa, out of the local stone. Wagons originally carried stone from local quarries to a canal wharf, and brought coal back from the pits in the other direction.

The amazing thing is that this was before the invention of steam railways, and the wagons were pulled by bullocks, and later by horses. Yet here the damn thing is, still standing, a monument in its own right, totally ignored by people passing it in their cars day after day. And totally ignored by me, too, until I had my eyes opened.

Some folk sneer at stuff like this. Pit headstocks, Victorian pumping stations, the framework knitters' cottages, canals, windmills, lace mills. Industrial archaeology, they call it. But it's all part of our heritage, isn't it? Just the same as Sherwood is, or Hardwick Hall or Creswell Crags. And so is what's left of the pits. Even the godforsaken housing estates like the Forest, built for long-gone miners. Because this is how people lived, you see.

That's what heritage is all about, right? It's not just about the dukes and mill owners, not just about the rich gits who lived at Welbeck Abbey and Clumber Park. It's about the ordinary folk too. The poor buggers who got chopped to bits fighting for King Edwin of Northumbria against the Mercians and were chucked into a big hole at Cuckney. The poor bloody women who went blind straining their eyes to make lace by candlelight in dingy hovels. All those Victorian mill workers and brewers and bicycle makers. And, of course, the bolshie sods who spent the whole of their working lives underground digging out coal until they got kicked onto the spoilheap like the rest of the unwanted rubbish. They're all part of our heritage, and they've all left their mark on this landscape.

When I stop and think about it in some of the places round here, I can practically see and hear and smell them still. I haven't got the right words for it, but I think what I mean is that they're the people who really make a place. Aren't I right? You see a bridge over the road as you're driving along. Who built that? Was it

35

erected personally by Sir Robert McAlpine? Did Mr Taylor and Mr Woodrow heave those slabs of concrete into place with their own hands and ring up Mr McAdam to come out with his tip-up truck and put the surface on? Or was it really built by a gang of sweaty, beer-bellied labourers with Guinness hangovers, holes in their socks and handkerchiefs on their heads, who had to work as much overtime as possible because they each had six kids at home eating tons of fish fingers a week, peeing on the carpet and kicking the telly in? You know which it was. I rest my case.

When the phone rang again I expected it to be the call telling me that the load had arrived safely at its destination. But the voice at the other end sounded upset, despite the terseness of the message.

"Delivery lost."

"Lost?"

There was the pause of somebody being careful. "It attracted a bit of attention at a truck stop. Driver safe."

"Right."

This was bad news. There was a good load in that trailer. But it sounded like a bit of bad luck. It does happen sometimes. I know that as well as anyone. I didn't know my luck was about to get even worse.

Now I only had a few minutes to get to the hall, and I was already in a bad mood.

The hall? I suppose that sounds bit grand. Now you're thinking that Stones has got off with some rich bird who lives in a bloody great mansion somewhere. What a hypocrite, you think. Well, tough - you're wrong. Lisa is a tourist guide at Hardwick Hall. That's Bess of Hardwick's gaff, right on the border with Derbyshire. You'll no doubt have noticed its graceful Tudor turrets from the M1 on your way south between junctions 29 and 28? Like hell you will. Like everyone else, all you'll have noticed is the bumper of the car in front and the signs telling you how far it is to the next service area.

But take my word for it, it's there. In fact, there are two halls - the Elizabethan mansion built by the Countess of Shrewsbury (that's Bess's Sunday name), and next to it the ruins of an earlier effort.

Lisa has the shitty job of shepherding hordes of ignorant visitors about all day, answering bloody stupid questions. You wouldn't believe some of them. Most of these people don't know Bess of Hardwick from Tess of the d'Urbervilles. They've come because it's next on the list of places to visit on their tourist board kitchen calendars. Or maybe they got lost on the M1 at Heath and ended up somewhere real, not knowing quite how to handle it. When they arrive at Hardwick, they expect Shakespeare to have written Romeo and Juliet there or something. Lisa has to explain two thousand years of English history in thirty seconds, and do it fifty times a day. But then, she's good at it. She's good at a few other things as well, but I'm keeping those to myself for now.

Thoughts like these kept me warm while I drove the Subaru west through Meden Vale, Church Warsop and Warsop Vale to reach Shirebrook, a village that is all back streets, plus a one-way system that directs you away from the shopping centre, which is shut anyway. By the time I got to this gem in Nottinghamshire's crown I'd already passed four pits - Medensworth, Welbeck, Warsop and Shirebrook itself. But then I began to wind my way through some lanes towards Stony Houghton, and the pits might as well have been in a different country. I started to feel quite cheerful. Hardwick and Lisa were ahead, both of them nestling invitingly in a bit of parkland that was as far from the Forest Estate as you can get and still be within ten miles.

Getting to Hardwick Hall is a bit of a neat trick, though. The hall lies east of the M1, on the Nottinghamshire side. But to get there you have to go past it, cross the motorway at junction 29, then sneak back under again on a little side road. If it weren't for the little brown tourist signs at the junctions, you'd never find it, even though you can see the towers up there on the hillside.

Like all the big historic gaffs in this part of the world, Hardwick Hall is well within a miner's spitting distance of slag heaps - in this case, the remains of Teversal Colliery. Of course, this didn't bother Bess of Hardwick when she built the place (the hall I mean, not the pit). She'd lived in the Old Hall until her husband died. This particular husband - number three - was the Earl of Shrewsbury, and of course he was loaded with dosh. So Bess used his money to build a bigger, grander hall. She was already seventy at the time, and it took seven years to finish the place. But what else would you do with so much money at her age?

It's been written that Hardwick is 'a milestone in the history of civilised taste'. Some folk would think it's more of a millstone. Think of all that money, they say, poured into a bloody enormous house for one batty old woman to live in. Paintings and tapestries and carpets and staircases and wood-panelled corridors. Who needs it?

But not me. I think about the blokes who worked on it. It took them seven years - so they weren't your average cowboy builders, were they? We're not talking the old 'sling up a bit of breeze block and slap some paint on it before the plaster's dry' techniques of the late twentieth century. They were craftsmen, these blokes, who put their whole lives into producing places like Hardwick. The Great High Chamber has a coloured plaster frieze a hundred and sixty-six feet long that will knock your eyes out. The Gallery has three bay windows - each of them about the size of a modern council house.

Then you should go and look at the Great Kitchen downstairs. Who do you think slaved away at those sinks and chopping boards? Who lugged crates of wine up from the cellars, and who broke their backs to produce vegetables all the year round from the garden? Not Bess of chuffin' Hardwick anyway. It may have been her money, or her dead hubby's. But it was ordinary folk's sweat that built the hall and kept it running.

*　　*　　*　　*

While I waited in the car park, I eyed up some of the tourist types drifting in and out of the hall and wandering about the grounds. Most of them looked as though they might just as well have been at Alton Towers or Disney World. Today they'd been for a whiteknuckle culture ride. Really scary stuff. There was a carved ceiling in there that could make you forget which way up you are. And then, of course, there's the usual souvenir shop, where they turn you upside down until the coins fall out of your pockets. Who needs the Corkscrew Rollercoaster?

I felt sorry for some of the kids being dragged about. It's supposed to be part of their education. But they just get the impression that in the old days everybody lived in massive houses and had servants. It makes them wonder why their own family lives in a shoebox-sized semi made out of cardboard and have to move their own wheelie bins to keep the binmen happy. Nobody bothers to explain to the poor little sods that if they had lived in Bess's time, they would have been the servants. No Nintendos or telly, no designer jeans or Big Macs. Not even any school. Or wages. Or shoes. And no Sunday afternoon outings to places like Hardwick either. Yes, you can make them learn from history if you take the trouble. But if you don't do it properly they grow up feeling all deprived because they haven't got three maids and a footman.

I was loitering near one of the side entrances, where a sign at the gate says 'Residents only'. But we're not talking Bess herself here, or even her impoverished descendants. The residents now are caretakers, National Trust staff - there to see that the hoi polloi don't get in at night and nick the tapestries. As if we would.

When Lisa came out, she wasn't alone. From a distance, she always looks small and fragile. She's fair, and I suppose a bit plain really, if you forced me to it. But her smile and that style she has make up for it. She'd got this way of holding herself as she talks to you that makes you feel you're the most important person in the world. It's a kind of a tilt of the head, a look in the eyes, an angling of the shoulders. And then when she smiles at you, you feel as though you're already in bed together. What a trick. But just at the moment that smile was turned on someone other than me. I'm not a jealous bloke - emotions like that are dangerous in my business - but I like to know who my bird's being chatted up by, just in case I have to feed him a knuckle sandwich.

This bloke was one I didn't recognise. He looked like a tourist, but not the ordinary sort. For a start, he was wearing a suit instead of M & S casuals and he wasn't carrying a Canon autofocus camera. He was much too smart. In fact, he stood out like a working man in a workingmen's club.

I expected him to go in a moment or two. Probably he was just asking the way to the nearest craft shop. But he kept Lisa talking on the doorstep. She was nodding and chatting back, and she hadn't even noticed I was there. This wasn't on. It looked as though I'd have to take action.

I slipped out of the car and checked my jeans were suitably grubby. Levis never look right unless they're a bit grubby, do they? One of the back pockets was hanging off, and there was a curious stain near my crotch which I couldn't properly explain. I'd left my leather jacket off, because the weather was quite warm, and my check shirt was rolled up to the elbows and just about clinging together, held at the front by a couple of buttons. I had on my favourite belt with the big brass VW buckle ('Very Wicked' - get it?), and my boots were still streaked with mud. Somehow my hands had got covered in black oil at Metal Jacket's workshop. My hair had been cropped to a number two on top only a couple of days before, but I'd left it long at the back, where it was starting to get in need of a wash. I reckoned I looked about right.

My boots crunched satisfyingly on the gravel as I marched across the car park towards the elegant doorway. At times like this I feel as though I ought to be going round to the servants' entrance, but what the hell. The rich gits are long gone from this particular pile. It belongs to us now, via the National Trust.

Lisa clocked me first, and I gave her my best grin. I watched her eyes, and several expressions seemed to pass across her face. This is normal. Well, you know what women are like - they can feel eight things at once and communicate six entirely different ones at the same time. And God help you if you choose the wrong one, mate. I thought I detected pleasure in there, along with wariness, apprehension, and a touch of amusement. But did this mean she wanted to be rescued, or not? It was no use waiting to find out. It isn't the way I operate anyway. And I must say the closer I got to the bloke in the suit, the less I liked the look of him. My antennae were picking up the sort of aura about him that told me I would either have to touch my forelock or drop him with a Mansfield kiss, depending on whether I needed his money. By the time I arrived on the steps, I'd decided to dispense with subtlety entirely.

"Fuck me, I'm sweating like a pig in a sauna. Me kecks are stuck so far up me arse it feels like I'm being buggered by a randy stair carpet. Talk about shagpile, eh, mate?"

I saw the suit stiffen like a sudden case of rigor mortis. And that was even before I nudged him amiably in the ribs. Lisa covered her face with a hand. Whether she was laughing or about to be sick I couldn't tell, but it was too late now, whatever.

"I've got to have a slash soon an' all, or I'll be filling me pants legs. I've had ten pints of bleedin' Mansfield Bitter and I'm not even near pissed. I don't know how the bastards get away with it."

I managed a nice loud, unrestrained belch just as the suit turned reluctantly to face me. His long nose wrinkled and his lip curled. His hands began to move nervously about the pockets of his jacket as if he was searching for a scented handkerchief to hold to his nostrils. I laid a hand on his sleeve, like a bloke who just couldn't help being friendly.

"You met my kid sister then? Bit of all right, in't she? What about them knockers, eh? Bloody hell, talk about selling 'em by the pound. You've got enough there to start a European tit mountain."

The bloke seemed as though he'd been about to say something suitably condescending. Now he stopped and his face coloured. Obviously the tits had been exactly what he'd been thinking about.

His feet were moving on the gravel, and he might have backed away if I hadn't got hold of his sleeve. All right, I'd wanted to get rid of him, but I was enjoying myself now. It's a funny reaction. I suppose it's a bit like a fox who wishes like hell that the idiots in the red coats would go away and take their horses and dogs with them, then when he gets round the next corner he finds a huntsman off his horse and having a slash against a tree. He wouldn't be able to resist the sight of that solitary fat backside, right? The bloke saw this too. Contempt had been replaced by anxiety on his face. He wasn't sure what I was going to do next, and this is the way I like it. Would I to try to borrow money off him, or might I vomit on his polished brogues? Or worse, was I intending to be his friend for life?

Lisa recovered first. Very cool, that one.

"This is Mr Michael Cavendish," she told me. "He's a regular visitor to Hardwick. In fact, he's a descendant of the original family. About the ninth generation from the Countess, would it be, Mr Cavendish?"

"What? Oh yes."

Cavendish sounded a bit croaky. Either he had a touch of laryngitis or he was scared shitless that I'd pollute his Hugo Boss suit with a steaming beer and carrot stew. But his colour was getting back to its normal aristocratic puce, and any minute now he might even think of something to say.

"I must be going," he said. Brilliant. He'd got his line word perfect at the first attempt.

He had another go at tugging his sleeve out of my grasp. I hiccupped and gave him my best lopsided grin.

"Oh, but we were just discussing the fourth Earl, weren't we?" said Lisa.

"No matter, no matter. Another time."

While he was looking at Lisa, I took the opportunity to brush up close to the bloke and feel for his side pocket with my free hand. He looked as though he might have a useful cheque book or two about his person.

Cavendish lost patience then. He took hold of my fingers with his right hand and prised them from his sleeve. I was taken by surprise at the strength of his grip. My fingers felt bruised where he'd held them, as if I'd accidentally trapped them in a door.

"Goodbye then, Miss Prior," he said.

We stared into each other's eyes for one more moment. Then he turned on his heel and marched away towards a gold Range Rover without looking back.

"Stones," said Lisa. I still couldn't tell what she was thinking. Was I in deep shit for upsetting an important visitor? Had I just put the total kibosh on a really crappy day?

"Yes, love?"

"You're such a pillock. Just get in the car."

5

After we'd been in the house for an hour or two, Lisa had pretty much forgiven me for the incident at Hardwick Hall. At least, she'd quietened down a lot. In spite of the fact that I'd washed my hands, I could see there were slightly oily handprints on her bare back when she turned over onto her side. Also, I had to find a clean shirt, because the buttons had gone completely on the old one.

"Why were you so foul to Michael Cavendish?" she'd asked me at one stage, just before we came unglued.

"He asked for it," I said.

"How do you mean?"

"He was a stuck-up rich git."

"But you'd never met him. You'd hardly set eyes on him."

"So? I'm very perceptive like that. I can sense it. Rich gits make my ulcer hurt."

"You haven't got an ulcer."

"I will have, if I meet that Cavendish bloke again."

She seemed to think about it for a bit, clinging on to my arm when I tried to ease myself away.

"It wasn't because you were jealous then, Stones?"

"Jealous? Give over. I could get a suit like that, if I really wanted to."

"Mmm."

I left Lisa dozing in the bedroom and went back downstairs. Despite the onion bhajis and other stuff from the deli earlier, I was feeling a bit peckish after my efforts. I felt my performance had been pretty good, but giving your all to your art fairly takes it out of you. I'm talking about my bit of acting at Hardwick, of course.

When the phone rang, I automatically picked it up. I could have let the answerphone deal with it, but you never know when it might be urgent business.

"Stones? It's Nuala."

"Oh, hi," I said, cautious.

Nuala's the new bird. She's at that stage where she actually thinks I'm a non-stop sex machine, a hilarious stand-up comedian, and some soppy romantic Mills and Boon hero all rolled into one. Women like their delusions, don't they?

"How are you, love?" she said. "I've been missing you something terrible."

"Oh yeah? Right."

Then she started to make conversation. It was the kind of stuff that women expect you to put up with when you've recently started having sex with them. I'm not very good at tolerating this at the best of times, but just now I really had to cut her off. Lisa was upstairs, and I thought I could hear her putting her knickers on. You know that sort of slither and snap that you're usually only half aware of while you're still sleeping it off? That's what I could hear, and it sounded like approaching trouble.

"Yeah, yeah, Nuala. Right. I might be able to see you tomorrow afternoon. Yeah, well, I'm really busy, love. You know what it's like." Well, she soon would if she was around me for any length of time. Nuala is a bit of all right, but my God can she talk. When she opens her mouth, it's like a slagheap shifting - it just never stops coming at you.

Nuala is an Irish name, and it's pronounced Noo-lah. She tells me her long-disappeared dad was from County Wicklow. I don't mind this, because I'm part Celt myself. My old granddad was one of a band of Lowland Scots who trekked down to find jobs in the pits back in the 1930s. We're a Nottinghamshire family now all right, though. My dad never went to Scotland in his life. And me? I wouldn't know a haggis from a sheep's intestines.

I met Nuala when I called in the travel agent's one day. No, I wasn't going on holiday. All those foreign countries leave me cold. Or too hot. You can keep your villas and bistros and your Hotel Paso Doble. It seems to me that most folk travel out there and straightaway run into some family called Cunliffe who live in the next street back home. Am I right? And then they spend a whole fortnight talking about people they know and getting pissed together watching Blind Date on the telly with Spanish sub-titles. Bloody marvellous. Why couldn't they just have nipped round the corner to the Cunliffes' house and saved the money? You can get sloshed on cheap Spanish wine just as easily if you buy it from Tesco's as you can if it came over-priced from Manuel's Los Bravos Bar. Why bother with a seafood paella on the harbourside at Tossa de Mar when you can give yourselves the thundering squitters just as quickly with a few out of date haddock fillets from the fish stall at Medensworth market? The blokes could even shag each others' wives without having to go through all that business of swapping hotel bedrooms and getting lost in the corridors. And they wouldn't have to risk getting skin cancer from falling asleep on the beach on the first day; and they wouldn't have to wear those bloody stupid straw hats for the rest of the fortnight to stop their noses falling off. So why do they bother? Well, at least the Cunliffes save them from having to come into contact with the natives, I suppose. Y viva bloody Espana.

Anyway. I was in this travel agent's. I wanted some travellers' cheques, you see. Yes, there are reasons for wanting travellers' cheques other than going abroad, but now isn't the time to explain it. All I'll say is that it's a neat trick, but you can't do it too often.

Nuala wasn't actually serving me. That job had fallen to some other bird that I hardly noticed. This was because I was distracted by an Irish voice that was going on and on about some tour company rep she'd got off with in a hotel room during some steamy weekend freebie in Rotterdam. Apparently he'd seemed very promising when he was handling her bookings, but he'd failed to check the entire party in at reception, if you know what I mean. Nuala didn't quite put it like that. But the way she did put it, you couldn't quite ignore what she was saying.

It was when she noticed me that the situation changed. She peered over the other bird's shoulder to see what she was doing, and then became an instant expert on Brazil. Yes, Brazil - but don't ask.

"The basic unit of currency is the *real*," she said helpfully. "Portuguese is the official language, but German and Italian are spoken by many Brazilians, especially in the southern cities."

"Thank you very much," I said. "Now about these travellers' cheques - "

"The climate ranges from tropical to subtemperate. The average temperature in the capital, Brasília, is a comfortable seventy degrees Fahrenheit, and rainfall is about sixty-three inches a year. Hundreds of species of beautiful exotic plants abound, including begonias, laurels, myrtles, and mimosas, as well as palms and mangroves."

"I'm not actually going - "

"And did you know that Brazil is the home of the puma, jaguar, ocelot, and the rare bush dog? Anteaters, sloths and armadillos are also common."

There was a lot more of this stuff. Brazil is the fifth largest country in the world, and the Amazon basin occupies one third of its surface. You can vote there at sixteen, and the capital, Brasilia, was only built in the 1960s.

These and other fascinating facts were force-fed to me while I looked at Nuala. Looked, I said, not listened. She's worth looking at far more than she's worth listening to. The trouble is, that was how I ended up taking her for a drink, then later on going back to her flat. By not listening to her, I mean. She tells me she did discuss it with me in great depth at some stage. It must have been somewhere between the population of Sao Paulo and the length of the River Amazon. But, like the Amazon itself, I just seem to have gone with the flow.

"Haven't you ever thought of getting some nice curtains for this room, Stones?"

Lisa had come down the stairs behind me. Thank God I'd already cut off the call. But she was well used to me being on the mobile, setting up meetings, that sort of thing. Poor tart, she thought I was a scrap metal dealer or something.

"I don't need them. I don't have the lights on much."

"Some cushions, at least. I know where you can get some lovely ones, not too expensive. They'd go with the carpet. Sort of."

I said nothing while we both looked at the floor and tried to picture something that would go well with curry stains.

"Perhaps a rug would be a good idea," she said. "Something big and furry that you could cuddle up on in front of the fire."

"There's nothing wrong with this room," I said. "Nothing at all."

But she was drifting about, looking classy and smart in a pale green trouser suit, deliberately trying to make my wallpaper seem shabby and clashing with my off-yellow paintwork.

"You could really make something of it, if you tried," she said. "There's the basis of a nice home under this rough exterior."

She'd somehow sneaked up on me and laid a hand on my chest. The look in her eyes set alarm bells clanging in the back of my head, even as the soft hairs began to stir on my belly.

"It suits me, this house. It matches my personality," I said.

"Of course." She backed down then, smiling as she watched me pick up my jacket from the floor. Somehow I wasn't quite sure whether I'd said what I meant to say.

"Are we going out somewhere, Stones?"

"I've got things to do later," I said. "Business. I'll take you home, but I've got to call at the church first."

"Oh?"

I didn't like the way her eyes lit up then. She was supposed to be disappointed that I was taking her home. Then I realised it was the word 'church'. Women's minds only run on one track after they've known you for a bit. They start thinking about white dresses and wedding rings and revolting nephews in bow ties, all that shit. I really had to get out from under this one very soon. A pity she was so sexy and good in bed. It sort of takes your mind off the risks.

"On second thoughts," I said. "I can call there some other time."

"Where else are you going, then?"

"Me? Up the Cow's Arse."

* * * *

Everyone knows they can find me up the Cow's Arse when I'm not out on business. Officially, it's called the Black Bull, and that's the name over the door. But then, who ever cared about 'officially' round here? The sign outside the pub looks like a cow's arse, so that's its name. Medensworth folk aren't too good at reading, but they can make out pictures. Besides, the landlord there is Baggy

Prentiss, and he has a wife who looks like a... well, I'll let you guess.

I had to make a bit of a detour out of Medensworth to drop Lisa home, and by the time I got to the pub Doncaster Dave was there waiting for me. When I say waiting, I mean he had his face in a plate of steak pie and chips, with plenty of gravy. It was a bit late for lunch, but at the Cow's Arse they tend to serve him whenever he feels hungry, which is all day. The pub was full, except for two spare seats at the table where Dave was sitting. It wasn't that he was saving them for us exactly - just that no one else wanted to sit with him.

"Lo Hones."

I rocked back in admiration. The standard of Dave's conversation is blistering, even when he's concentrating on destroying a steak pie. Oscar Wilde, eat your heart out.

I looked around for Slow Kid and sent him to buy the drinks. It's easier than writing it down for Dave. Besides, I wanted a tequila, and Dave has never seen a word with a 'q' in it before. He'd probably think I'd written a 'g' the wrong way round.

Oh yes, a tequila. So you thought the Cow's Arse would be the sort of place where the bar has a choice between lager and lager, and you don't dare ask for anything in it? Wrong. Didn't I tell you not to be fooled by a name? You maybe pictured a scabby pub with bloodstains on the walls and sawdust on the floor to soak up the spilled beer? Wrong again. Baggy had the bloodstains painted over last week.

"How's Denise then, Donc?"

"Aw-right."

"Yeah? She's got over that flu, has she?"

Dave shrugged. I took this for a 'yes'. Dave and his sister are really close, actually. Denise has been married once, but she left her husband to move in with Dave and look after him when their mum died. That's what it seemed like, anyway. Of course, she knew that Dave would have eaten the furniture in no time if she hadn't. Now they share a council house and Denise has a full time job trying to feed him. She worries like mad that he's not eating properly when he's out of the house.

"She went to the doctor," said Dave.

48

"Oh good. Did he give her something?"

"Useless bastard."

That seemed to be the end of the conversation. I'd distracted him from his food for too long. He went back to the pie. Watching Dave eat isn't much fun at the best of times. The way he constantly has to stoke up his reserves reminds me of a Sperm Whale I once saw on one of those wildlife programmes on BBC2. This huge animal ploughs through the sea with its mouth permanently stuck open, sucking in plankton and seaweed and whatever else drifts about in the water out there, including beer cans chucked over the side of cruise liners probably. Anyway, the point is that it can never stop feeding, because its bulk uses up so much energy keeping it moving. And it has to keep moving to take in the food to give it the energy... What a life.

Come to think of it, a whale is shaped a bit like Dave too. And doesn't it have a very tiny brain, about half the size of a human's brain? That's where they differ then - Dave's is much smaller than that.

I had to get a stiff drink inside me to make sitting with Dave even halfway tolerable. At least Slow Kid was reasonably articulate. And there was something niggling at me that I wanted to ask him.

"Hey, it's like a madhouse in here," he said when he came back with the drinks, winding his way through slot-heads playing fruit machines and video games. *Trivial Pursuit, Cops 'n' Robbers.* Baggy Prentiss's idea of irony, I always thought.

Slow was drinking some expensive American beer straight from the bottle, but Dave was putting up with Baggy's bitter, which is about as interesting as those dregs in the bottom of the milk carton that's still in my fridge from last year.

"Slow, I need to know what went wrong with that load."

"Oh yeah. What a pisser."

"Pisser is right. I'm seriously dischuffed here and I need to hear what went off."

"Well, it seems their bloke stopped at the services on the M1, near Leicester, you know it? And when he came out there were the cops, all over the rig."

"Silly sod."

"Obviously the bloke stayed well clear. He legged it as fast as he could. Got a lift out of there with a trucker. Left ten grands' worth of gear sitting in the service station car park. Mind you, it could have been worse. If the cops had any sense, they'd have laid low and waited for him to come out, wouldn't they? No sense, Stones, eh?"

"The cops were quick off the mark for once, though. You don't think they had a tip-off?"

"What? How could they?"

"I don't know. But I don't like it."

"Hey, Stones, it was just bad luck. The next one'll be okay. Just watch."

"This was the first. It should have gone right."

"Like I said, bad luck."

"That van's bothering me too," I said. "Rawlings and the other bloke."

"Wow, yeah. That was real, that fire. You'd never have guessed Reeboks would go up so well."

"What would make it burn like that?"

"Big fuel tanks on them things, Stones. Smash it sideways into a tree or something and do it hard enough, you'd split the tank. Bit of a spark from the electrics, and wham! Get that smell of burning rubber."

I shook my head. "That van hadn't crashed into anything. There were no trees, no concrete bridges. And there was no third party involved."

Slow Kid looked at me curiously. "Yeah, well. There's other ways of making something go bang, if you really want to."

"Like?"

"Like, well..."

"A bomb?"

"Right. A couple of bags of sugar, some fertiliser, a milk bottle full of petrol. No problem."

"And a timer maybe?"

"A doddle, Stones. There's plenty of blokes round here who know how to do that. There were a couple went off in Worksop a year or two back, remember? One at the cop shop, one at the Miners' Welfare."

50

"They didn't do much damage, though."

"Nah, they weren't planted right. They were shoved up against brick walls or something. They go off, see, but they don't get hold on anything."

"But plant one in the right spot, over a fuel tank for instance..."

"Right on. Barbecued van. You reckon somebody had it in for Rawlings and his mate, then?"

There was something that wasn't right about Slow Kid. He always plays his cards close to his chest. Well, don't we all? But I had the feeling there was something here he wasn't telling me.

"No, not them," I said.

"What do you mean, Stones?"

"I think somebody had it in for us. If I'd gone for that deal with the Reeboks, the stuff would have been in our van."

"Yeah. I got you." Slow Kid stuck the neck of the beer bottle in his mouth and squinted at me over its base. "But who'd do that? Who've we pissed off recently?"

"If you've got a bit of paper, we'll make a list."

"Nah. We always treat folk fair." He sucked a bit of beer out of the stubble on his top lip. "Except the ones we nick stuff from, obviously."

But then, before I could get to the bottom of what Slow Kid knew, before I'd even got halfway down my tequila, before Doncaster Dave could even stuff away six more mouthfuls of pie and chips, my whole afternoon was ruined. A shape appeared in the doorway, lurking in a vaguely familiar manner that could only mean one thing. Wow, what a treat. My favourite visitor, Detective Inspector Frank Moxon. And behind him, the untidy bulk of his sidekick, DS Wally Stubbs.

DI Moxon is one of that new breed of CID coppers who have pissed from a great height on the old Inspector Morse types. He's too serious. His parents managed to find a grammar school to send him to, and he has a degree from Nottingham University in some really handy subject - Anglo Saxon Poetry or Nineteenth Century Russian Trade Union Reform, or I don't know what. Something useful enough, anyway, to get him on the fast track to promotion, leapfrogging the more mundane blokes on the way - the ones, that is, who wouldn't know their Beowulf from their Bolsheviks, but only know about catching crooks, the poor sods.

Moxon wears gold-rimmed glasses. He has a neat little blond moustache and a nasty habit of turning up in snappy suits and bright ties. He doesn't drink, not even off duty, and he doesn't smoke either. He plays squash to keep fit, but hasn't managed to keep his balls in play long enough to give his wife any kids. His manners leave something to be desired, but then I suppose I never see him at his best. His bosses at Sherwood Lodge seem to love him. As for Wally Stubbs, he tries to copy his boss's style, but he hasn't got the build for it - or the will power to keep off the fags and booze.

When Moxon and Stubbs came in, a sort of self-conscious hush fell over the bar of the Cow, as if three quarters of the people in the place knew exactly who these two were. I could see Baggy Prentiss sigh at the damage to his custom.

Moxon and Stubbs paused in the doorway, surveying the room. They wanted everybody to know they were there. But you could hardly miss them in those shiny jackets and ties like smears of technicolor vomit. Their hands were shoved casually into their trouser pockets and their eyes were everywhere, like maggots on a fresh corpse.

We all sat very still, like a roomful of schoolkids willing the teacher to pick on someone else to read the next page of *Jude the Obscure* out loud. The only sound from our table was the continual slow munching of Doncaster Dave's jaws. His mouth doesn't have any gears, it's on automatic. You put food in, engage 'drive', and it won't slip into neutral until the plate is empty.

But it looked as though we were about to get something else on our plate. It was definitely our table that Moxon and Stubbs were wandering towards. Behind them, there were smiles of relief. Three or four customers took the opportunity to slip casually out of the pub, hoping they hadn't been noticed. This was just what Baggy was afraid of. There went the blokes whose bail conditions said they had to stay away from licensed premises, the ones who didn't want to be seen in the wrong company, the ones who simply weren't supposed to be in the area just now.

But the deserters were too late, of course. In those first moments, as he and his sidekick stood in the doorway, Moxon had no doubt logged the identity of every single customer, his evil little eyes sending a stream of messages to his evil little brain.

I've seen him do this before. I reckon he uses one of those 'pegging' techniques they teach you on management courses. You know the sort of thing - every number from one to ten has a peg, and you hang a mental picture on it. So it's 'two - zoo' and you imagine a picture of Stones McClure swinging from a rope next to an orang-utan. Not difficult. Then 'three - key' and there's a picture of Slow Kid Thompson with a bunch of skeleton keys in his hand.

Moxon could remember all of our names that way, plus what we were wearing and exactly what order we were sitting in at the table. He probably downloads the contents of his brain onto a computer when he gets back to his office. Maybe he slips a floppy disc out of his ear and logs onto the mainframe for a quick virus check. Let's have Inspector Morse back, that's what I say. That lad would have been too busy weighing up what beer was on draft behind the bar and whether Joanne the barmaid was the type who fancies older men.

"McClure." Ah, here was Moxon himself practising his pronunciation. They hadn't given him elocution lessons at his grammar school, so he had to keep trying to get it right. "Underwood." He swivelled his head slowly. "And Thompson."

Full marks, three out of three. This bloke was good. Only Donc acknowledged his name. Or maybe he was just belching.

"Nice to find the three of you together. Saves a bit of trouble," said Moxon. "We can kill three birds with one stone, eh, Wally?"

Wally Stubbs laughed. This might suggest he has no sense of humour. But we know he must have, to be wearing a tie like that.

"Are you buying the drinks then, Inspector? Baggy knows our order."

"Hey, get me a packet of those spicy nut things while you're at the bar, man."

Dave chortled, rattling his fork on his plate,

"Yes, you might be able to help me," said Moxon, just as if someone had been stupid enough to make the offer. He pulled over a chair that someone on the next table had suddenly vacated and sat down between me and Slow Kid. Stubbs hovered in the background, blocking out the sunlight - presumably so that it didn't fall on his boss and turn him into dust.

Moxon looked from one to the other of us, amending his mental identikit pictures slightly where he found that Slow's hair had been shaved a bit shorter at the sides, or Donc had put on an extra six pounds since he'd last seen him. I knew Moxon couldn't have anything on us, because I'm very careful, like my mother always told me to be. But his presence made me a bit uncomfortable, like I was sharing a table with Mussolini - after he'd been hanged from the lamp post, that is.

"We were wondering, you see, whether any of you gentlemen could assist us with a little bit of information."

Moxon said 'information' precisely and carefully, pronouncing each syllable distinctly, as if he thought it was a word we might not have heard before. The flickering lights of the *Trivial Pursuit* game were glinting off his glasses, and I couldn't see his eyes.

"We're always glad to help," I said, smiling genially into the glare of his spectacles. Notice that I didn't specify who we were glad to help.

"Delighted to hear it, McClure. So tell me where you were last night at around, say, eight o'clock."

"Oh. That sort of information."

"Yes, please. What else did you think?"

"I thought you might have wanted to have a go at *Trivial Pursuit*. I'm really hot on Countries of the World. Just ask me the currency of Brazil."

"Eight o'clock last night."

"It's the *real*. And did you know the capital was only built in the 1960s? And Dave here - he's our expert in foreign languages, I think. I can't tell what he's on about half the time anyway."

"It's much pleasanter asking you here. But if you want to play Mastermind, I'm sure we could find a chair and some nice spotlights back at the nick."

He waited expectantly while I thought about this. "I believe I was out with a couple of mates. Had a meal, a few drinks, a bit of a chat, you know the sort of thing mates do. Or perhaps you don't."

"What mates?"

"Ah. I thought you wouldn't."

Moxon looked at Slow Kid and Doncaster Dave. They looked at me.

"Was there a point to these questions?" I asked. "Were you getting round to asking me to lend you a quid for the machine?"

"I'd like to know whether you had any dealings with somebody called Les Rawlings."

"Rawlings? Goodness me. Wasn't that the bloke who tried to sell us some trainers out of the back of a van, Slow? We didn't buy anything from him, of course. You never know whether you can trust these people, do you?"

"Quite."

I got the feeling that Moxon had more that he wanted to ask me, but either he wasn't sure how to phrase the question, or he didn't want to ask me in front of the other two. It was a bit unnerving to see him struggling, but I wasn't about to help him. His hesitation made me feel more confident. Superior even.

Stubbs shuffled from one foot to another, and we could hear conversations getting back in full swing around the pub. Dave and Slow were beginning to relax. They thought I had the situation under control as usual. But they were wrong.

"I thought that would be your answer," said Moxon. "But I had to ask. Thank you very much."

I nearly choked on my tequila. Had Frank Moxon just thanked me?

"One more thing," he said.

"Hit me with it."

"We had a very upset French gentleman in the station yesterday. A lorry driver."

"Pulled him in, had you? Some of those foreign lorries are really dangerous. If you blokes are managing to get some of them off the road, you've got my full support, no worries."

"This particular gentleman had his lorry stolen."

"No?"

"Oh yes. And then, he says, he was kidnapped."

"Sounds like a bleedin' crime wave."

"The description he gave us of the two suspects sounded a lot like you and Underwood here."

55

"Ah now. Perhaps I can help you there then," I said. "You remember that bloke, Dave?"

Dave grunted. He didn't remember anything, but he knew he was being spoken to.

"There was this little foreign bloke," I said. "Jumped in our car in a layby on the A1. We reckoned he just wanted a lift, and we thought we'd help him out. As you do."

"Oh yes? Very admirable." Moxon's face was expressionless. "And where did you give him a lift to?"

"Well, that was the funny thing. We couldn't figure out what he was saying to us at all. Come to think of it, he *might* have been French. But me and Dave, you know, we're not educated. So we had a communication problem, like they say. In the end, he started to get stroppy. Shouting and that. So we stopped and made him get out, thought he might be a nutter, you know. You can't be too careful these days, can you? But that's what you get for being a Good Samaritan."

"This place you stopped. Would it have been a derelict pit site?"

"We were passing."

"Passing?"

"I like to go there, to reminisce. My dad was a miner, you know."

"Yes. How poignant."

I waited. Words like 'poignant' seem to dry up the sentences in my mouth. Moxon waited too, but he had less patience.

"So that's your story, is it?"

"Does it help?"

"And you, Underwood? I suppose your version is the same?"

"Yeah," said Dave.

Moxon sighed. "I want you both to come down to the station some time in the next forty-eight hours and make a statement."

"'Course, mate. No problem."

"And I'll be in touch if I think you can help me any further."

"A pleasure."

Moxon stood up to go, his tie clashing with his sergeant's like a couple of garish tropical fish in a tank full of sticklebacks.

"By the way, McClure," he said. "I met a friend of yours the other day."

"Oh yeah?"

"Funny, isn't it? I just popped into that travel agent's on Ollerton Road to make some inquiries for my summer holidays next year. We fancy Turkey. Have you ever been to Turkey, McClure? No, I don't suppose so. Anyway this travel agent's was recommended to me by a friend, you might say. A friend of *mine*, that is - not yours. And the young lady in there was very knowledgeable, and somehow we got chatting. It turns out she knows you very well. Very well indeed. Quite a coincidence, it was."

Moxon smiled at me. When he did that, his little moustache climbed towards his glasses like a furry centipede slithering over damp stones.

"I promised her we'd have a nice long chat some time. Swap a few reminiscences, that sort of thing. I think it should prove very interesting for us both. I'm sure she's the sort of person who's absolutely bursting with useful information."

After Moxon had drifted out, with Stubbs grinning behind him, Slow Kid was the first to recover.

"What's he on about?" he said. "He's got nothing on you, Stones. He must have been joking, wasn't he?"

I lifted my tequila. Suddenly it seemed just as tasteless and depressing as Baggy Prentiss's beer.

"Actually," I said, "I don't think he was."

6

Next morning there was business to do. Sunday business.

Well, Sunday never really was a day of rest. Even all that praying and confessing they used to get up to all day long must have been real hard work. Once I was on holiday on the West coast of Scotland and got dragged along to one of their Free Church of Scotland services. We were damned and abused so thoroughly from the pulpit for a couple of hours that we all went home exhausted. I felt as though I'd just gone five rounds with a spiritual Mike Tyson. So don't tell me Sunday is a day of rest. We peasants have always known different. Before and after they went to church, my ancestors still had to milk the cows, plough the field, scrub the floors, empty the cesspit, and make their masters' breakfast, in that order. There were convenient exceptions in God's rules about the Sabbath to allow your servants to do all those things.

These days, you can do almost anything on a Sunday, including all the things that are specifically forbidden in the Ten Commandments. Most of them have become a commercial necessity, in fact. 'Thou shalt not covet thy neighbours' goods' has become 'Get thee down to B and Q and get some new kitchen units that are better than hers next door'. These are the commandments of the new gods - envy and greed. They're a lot more fun to follow than the old boring ones.

Not that I'm complaining, don't get me wrong. Envy and greed are what make my life worth living. There's money in them sins. And on Sunday the sin business is booming. Me, I stick to the cheaper end of the iniquity scale. You'll find me doing my bit in that growth industry of the 1990s - the car boot sales and Sunday markets.

It's incredible what some folk will do at the prospect of a bargain. The chance of saving a few pence on something they don't really want seems to turn their brains to strawberry jam. It never seems to occur to them that they could save even more money by not buying that old sink in the first place, or by leaving those Val Doonican 78s where they are on the trestle table with the rest of the tat.

No, round these parts folk are up and about before dawn, lurking around the car boot sites waiting for the pitch holders to arrive, shining their torches into the cars like highwaymen, weighing up the contents. Arriving and setting up your pitch at one of these places can be life threatening. The punters descend on you like vultures, haggling with you and sneering at your prices. Some of them are traders themselves, who think they can sell your tatty bits of china for a few pence more than they bought them for. Others just live really sad lives.

But the rush is over in the first couple of hours, and then you're left to stand around in the drizzle smelling the hotdogs and onions and the wet anoraks until it's time to go home.

And all of this stuff they're buying is crap, of course. The grottiest dross that you can dig out of your attic or scrape off the shelf at the back of the garage is meant to be a bargain for someone. You'd be amazed at the stuff some folk collect. Jampot lids, milk bottles, postcards of Skegness from your Auntie Gladys, 1950s knitting patterns, old spark plugs, used hair grips. Don't believe it? You name it, and there's some punter desperate to waste his money on it. Having a load of junk cluttering up your attic or your garage is one thing - they tell me it can happen to anyone once you get domesticated. But at least it's your own junk. Buying up other people's junk to put in your attic is just so sad it almost brings tears to my eyes while I'm paying the money in at the bank.

Sunday markets are a bit different. A bit more up-market, if you like. There's still the same punters out to get something cheap. But the people getting them to part with their dosh aren't the car boot amateurs any more, they're professionals. And where you've got professionals about in this business, you're likely to find Stones McClure. I think of myself as a sort of Premier League football manager. The pros go out there to do the work and score the goals, so they can bring home the trophies. But they couldn't do it without me organising the business end, deciding the tactics, getting the best out of them, sussing the opposition. It's hard work, and a lot of responsibility. Of course, I take my share of the cash bonuses too. That's only fair.

There's a Sunday market near Medensworth that's one of my best money earners. I won't tell you which one it is - there are plenty of them in this part of the world, so you'll have to visit them all to find it. You'll have a good time doing it, though. I never said there was no fun in being fleeced, did I? This is Sunday - so I want you to enjoy yourselves, right?

The police do a good job at these markets. As you drive up the road, they practically force you to turn off into the site, where the market boys charge you for parking in a muddy field. If you try to drive straight past, the fuzz glare at you as if you'd just gone through sixteen red lights. God help you if one of your brake lights isn't working. After all, you must be mad to drive round here at this time of the morning if you're not going to the Sunday market. Through all this traffic? Definitely suspicious.

As far as I'm concerned, it's only at times like these that the cops make themselves useful. They're actually helping the less fortunate to make a living here. Careful - that could be frowned on by the bosses.

When I got to the site that morning, it was already full of punters. The fields were lined with cars, and the sound of money changing hands was deafening. The first stall I checked out was down at the end of one of the main aisles. It was loaded with leather jackets and handbags, belts and purses and wallets. Did I say leather? Well, you know what I mean.

The stall was run by Ernie and Stella. They're into leather in a big way. Selling it, that is. The kids come in droves to buy the stuff, and think they're conning the old pair. It's good to let someone think they're shafting you. It makes them less likely to come back and complain when they find out it was the other way round.

Ernie and Stella are a lovely couple. Ernie is an ex-miner gone to seed - a big, beer-bellied bloke without much hair left and a grin that is more gap than tooth. Stella looks much the same, but with more hair. She was attending to a group of giggly teenage girls when I arrived, but gave me a big wink from among the racks of jackets.

"Now then, Stones. How you doing?" said Ernie. "What can I sell you? Nice leather waistcoat?"

This is Ernie's idea of a hilarious joke. He says it every time. But I never claimed he was a comic genius, did I?

"How's business, Ernie?"

"Brilliant, brilliant."

This was all I wanted to hear. After a bit of small talk and a wave to Stella, I moved on, letting a couple of bikers get to the stall to try out their smirks.

Down the aisle a bit were Carl and Vince, two brothers who once ran a joinery business until the building industry ground to a halt. They were in their late forties and not likely to get a job, but both had families to keep. Now they were selling watches and jewellery.

"It's been quiet in the summer, but it'll build up now for Christmas, I reckon," said Carl, re-arranging the jewellery with a hand more used to handling a saw. "We won't be complaining. And neither will you."

Down the line again was Marlene, with two of her five kids helping her out on the display of shirts and socks, underwear and handkerchiefs. Some of this stuff looked like Marks and Spencers surplus. Maybe it actually was. Maybe that was a pig flying by, wearing a St Michael's vest.

Sometimes people have the nerve to tell me there might be a problem with the Counterfeit Goods Act. What I say is, if there's a problem with the Counterfeit Goods Act they should have worded it properly in the first place, instead of bothering blokes like me about it.

Marlene had been with me a long time, even before her old bloke was killed when a load of pallets fell on him at the warehouse he worked in. She was too busy at the stall to talk, but gave me a big smile and a thumbs up as I paused. The kids waved too. One big happy family. But I was thinking mainly of the punters' cash going into the canvass pockets slung round Marlene's waist.

61

Over the far side of the field was the area set aside for car-booters. This part of the event seems to get bigger all the time. It's mainly for amateurs, of course, but there are definitely a few pros in there. I know, because it's where I made my start. Now look at me - I never use my car boot for anything but keeping the spare wheel in. That's success, that is.

I went to do a check on Marky Benn's set-up - radios, cassette players, telephones, electric alarm clocks and hair driers, stuff like that. Small electrical items. Easy to shift, and pretty easy to get hold of too, usually. This is one of the most profitable stalls. As I arrived, Marky was flogging a radio alarm clock to a woman who looked as though she had more trouble sleeping than waking up. Her face was pasty and lined, and her hair hung in greasy strands either side of her forehead. She looked so tired and worn out that I wanted to offer her a chair. She was all of twenty-one, but she had three kids in tow.

Mind you, Marky wouldn't be one to criticise the looks of his customers. His years working in a gypsum quarry had left their mark on his skin, white dust getting deep into his pores like the black coal dust that taints the skin of miners, making them look as though they're wearing eye liner. In Marky's case, his eyes had suffered worst. An allergy, he said, that he'd taken no notice of for years because he needed the job. Now his eyeballs looked like rotten tomatoes, swollen to unnatural size by the thick lenses of his glasses. He coughed like a miner, too - long, rasping barks that hurt the ears. Marky hadn't been able to hold down his quarry job for a while now, but he still had a family to support and a mortgage to pay. He seemed to be making a good job of the electrical goods stall.

"Everything all right, Marky?"

"Things are going great, Stones," he said, turning his awful eyes towards me. "This stuff sells really well. Can't get enough of some items."

"Yeah? Like what?"

"CD players. That's the thing they're all asking for at the minute. I sold out last week, but folk keep asking for 'em all day long."

"I'll see what we can do about that."

"Ta."

Finally I went to see Jean and her daughter Wendy, selling perfumes and cosmetics in bottles with familiar names. People were trying out the samples, sniffing and nodding approvingly and opening their purses without hesitation. None of them would know the difference between a counterfeit and the real thing if it jumped up and bit them. Just shows that folk only pay for the name. Jean and Wendy were right there on the main drag the same as Marky Benn, two really good pitches. All satisfactory. There were plenty of folk about, so many that in places you could hardly get by in the crush.

As I walked back towards the car park, I passed a small crowd gathered round a sort of covered pulpit, where a bloke in a blue suit and a short haircut was demonstrating a fancy device that could slice carrots, peel apples, chip potatoes and probably boil water for tea as well, all at the same time. His patter was non-stop, and he had the admiring housewives in fits of giggles. Soon he would have their hard-earned cash out of their purses, and maybe later on he would have the knickers off one or two of them as well. God, I really hate crooks.

*   *   *   *

Slow Kid was waiting for me by the car, trying to look cool and inconspicuous at the same time. He doesn't like Sunday markets and car boot sales. He has bigger ideas, does Slow.

"Stones. Are we out of here or what? These places give me the creeps."

"Sure, let's go."

He hopped in the car, pleased to be behind the wheel again. He'd been wasting his life as a boy racer when I found him. Burning up somebody else's rubber on the old pit roads at the back of the Forest. But at least he'd been the best of them, and the fastest. That's why they called him Slow Kid.

He set off across the grass eagerly, but soon had to jam on the brakes and change down to first gear when he got near the exit. You don't get out of a Sunday market that fast - especially when everybody else wants to do the same thing. We got a glower from the special constable on duty as he waved us away. I'm sure some of these boys must be on commission. Get 'em in and don't let 'em leave.

It being Sunday, we didn't head straight for the pub. Instead, we met up with Dave in Medensworth's top caff, the Riviera. Dave was already halfway through the contents of the kitchen, but there was probably a few crumbs left for us.

As soon as we were settled at a table, I lost no time getting straight to the point. This thing had been niggling me ever since Friday night.

"Okay. Spill it, Slow Kid."

"What?"

Slow looked suddenly as if he'd like to leave, but it just so happened that he was sitting between Dave and the window, with me opposite him. He was trapped, and I wanted to know what was eating him. But he didn't always get on with Dave, and maybe he didn't want to talk in front of him.

"Dave, are you awake?"

"Eh? Yeah."

"Fetch me a cup of tea then. And one of those Danish pastry things, you know."

"Right, Stones."

"And plenty of milk in the tea, but no sugar. Got it?"

"Yeah."

Dave struggled painfully for several seconds to extricate himself from the narrow gap between the bolted-down chairs and the table. He seemed to have added several pounds to his already massive bulk while he'd been sitting there. One day he'd get stuck completely and they'd have to send for the fire brigade with cutting gear to get him out.

Dave might not look too bright, and his education definitely owes more to Teddy's Amusement Arcade than King Edward Grammar School. A lot more time spent in greasy friers than the Dreaming Spires. Not the sharpest knife in the drawer, our Dave. But he does have a memory like an ox.

I watched him wander off towards the counter, then swerve with the grace of a drunken elephant to bring him closer to a tattooed waitress. You could see she was a Worksop lass. They look pretty much like Mansfield women, but they have a better class of tattoos.

Then I saw Dave drop her a massive wink. If women like that could blush, she would have been beetroot. Her biceps rippled alluringly, and a heart tattoo glinted. After food, muscle-bound women were Doncaster Dave's major weakness. I'd be lucky to get my tea before the tannin ate its way through the polystyrene cup.

"Go on then, Slow," I said.

"What do you mean, Stones?"

"I mean, what do you know about those people with the load of Reeboks? You recognised that lad with the flat-top, didn't you? Right?"

"Yeah, I did," he admitted. "His name's Josh Lee."

The name Lee made me think of a certain family of travellers who move around Nottinghamshire in small convoys of caravans towed by vans and flat-bed trucks. They park up on grass verges, disused forecourts, even school playing fields - any acre of accessible ground, but preferably belonging to a district or county council, because it takes that much longer for them to get moved on. It drives the local residents wild of course, being as how the travellers never seem to have to pay Council Tax, road tax or income tax. North Notts seems to get more than its fair share of them, and the Lees got a few lessons to teach blokes like me about how to stay the wrong side of the law without getting caught.

"Should I have heard of him, Slow?"

"No." He hesitated again, but I wasn't in the mood for kid gloves after entertaining thoughts about a knife in the guts. I could remember those dead eyes, and they were putting my stomach off thoughts of a Danish pastry.

"Let's have it. Now."

"Our Sean told me about Josh Lee. They came across each other in Lincoln."

"Oh, right." He wasn't talking about a chance encounter while boating on the River Witham or admiring the architecture of the cathedral. Slow's big brother Sean had recently done a spell inside for armed robbery, and Lincoln Prison was one of the local institutions favoured for a short break away from the hurly-burly of crime. Armed robbery is a respectable crime on the inside, the sort that gets you looked up to by all the petty thieves and twockers and Saturday night piss artists who get too handy with their fists and boots. Sean would have made acquaintance with influential types, and would no doubt have been offered a few jobs for when he got out. Did I say it was a break away from crime? More of a chance to make contacts, learn new tricks, and plan the next job. The good citizens who are paying for it all don't know the half of it.

"Sean said Lee is connected with some of the big pushers. He came over real friendly inside, asking all sorts of questions, he was."

"About what?"

"Oh, people Sean knew. Who was involved with what, you know. I guess it's the sort of thing they talk about in prison."

"Yeah, maybe. So did he offer Sean a job?"

"Well, yeah - I reckon he did. But Sean didn't want anything to do with him. He said Lee was big trouble."

"Why exactly?"

"Just the talk, you know. There's stories about him. Tasty bloke, he is. Well, you saw him yourself."

"Yeah. But how come you recognised him, Slow?"

"Sean pointed him out to me one day in Nottingham. It wasn't long after he came out. Sean told me to stay clear of him. Well, you know what our lot's like about drugs, Stones."

The Thompson boys had just been kids when they were forced to watch their dad plumbing the depths. An addict himself, he'd made money selling third-rate stuff to kids the same age as his own and nicking money wherever he could get it, including the pitiful family allowance in his wife's purse. He'd learned the trick of telling his customers that the stuff he was selling was 'brown'. They aren't so streetwise as they like to think round here, and they thought it was just another form of cannabis, until it was too late. By the time they found out 'brown' was heroin, they already needed it too much.

Sean and Slow, and their mum Angie, had lived among the degradation and despair and danger that Des Thompson had brought upon them, until his body finally disintegrated under the abuse and he OD'd. Slow didn't need his mum to warn him about the danger of drugs. He'd seen it all for himself.

My cup of tea and Danish pastry finally arrived. The tea was coffee without milk but loads of sugar, and the Danish was a piece of dried-up Dundee cake. Like I said - Dave's got a memory like an ox.

While I chewed, I thought about this Josh Lee for a bit, then about his mate Rawlings. When I finished thinking, Slow Kid hadn't even touched his coffee, but Dave had several empty plates in front of him and was looking round for more.

"When this Lee was asking questions," I said, "did Sean get the idea that it was for someone operating in this area? Someone Lee was working for?"

Slow shrugged. "Dunno. Could be. One of the big outfits, you mean? But what about Eddie Craig?"

"Just what I was thinking, Slow. What about Eddie Craig?"

Yes, Craig. Anybody trying to survive round here has to remember that name. The likes of Josh Lee might be nasty, but Eddie Craig is poison. He runs the big operations in this area - the protection, the clubs, the illegal gambling, the prostitutes, the pornography. And there are a few exotic substances changing hands at the odd club or amusement arcade too.

There are some small fry who get away with running their own little franchises out of the night clubs and that sort of thing. But God help them if they get ideas above their station and think about branching out. Eddie has his ear firmly to the ground and stamps on anyone who even smells like a rival. And when you've been stamped on by Eddie Craig, you stay stamped on. This bloke is big time.

Officially he's as clean as a whistle, of course. If you checked his criminal record, you'd probably find he's gone straight as a die, your honour, ever since he was nicked for riding his bike without lights in 1954. It was such a shock to his dear old mother that her little Edward could have got himself into trouble with the police that he's been a model citizen ever since, in honour of her memory.

I'm clean, too, obviously. But I do it by being a bit cleverer than the plods. Craig has the sort of organisation where blokes are queuing up to take the rap for him and thank him for the privilege.

He possesses enough dosh to make it worth their while, and the clout and the hard men to make it not worth arguing the toss, inside or out.

If somebody else was operating on Craig's territory, it could get quite interesting. If two of those somebodies were Rawlings and Lee, it could be a real pleasure.

Despite the sweet coffee and the Dundee cake, I felt a smile coming on.

7

When Lisa rang, it was to remind me that I was supposed to be giving her a lift to the station. Which station? Oh yeah. She was going to Sheffield on a course. Away for three days. How could I have forgotten that?

Soon I was on the road, heading for Lisa's place a couple of villages away. She lives in a mid-nineteenth century terraced house right on her village's main street, but with a view from the garden at the back that you could die for, if that's what turns you on. Me, I'm more interested in the things that tell you people have lived here for a long time. Weavers' windows or Yorkshire ranges. Keeping cellars or those stone steps worn into hollows by centuries of feet. Or, in this case, the carved stone set high up in the centre of the row of houses giving the date and the name: Balaclava Terrace, 1895.

It was a strange custom they had in those days to name streets and terraces after famous battles, even ones the British had lost. Oh, we had six hundred men slaughtered at Balaclava, did we? Russians shot our troops to bits with cannon? Thousands of widows, orphans and bereaved parents in some working class areas now, are there? Jolly good, we'll sling up a few new houses to commemorate the glorious event. Eh, what?

Funnily enough, the Dabbling Dukes did much the same on their vast estates, only in their case it wasn't houses, but trees they planted. There are plantations called Ladysmith, Culloden and Corunna. Even Spitfire Bottoms. But then the Dukes also planted woods named after their racehorses when they won a big prize. That many trees must have done the landscape a world of good, but you can't help finding their motives a bit puzzling.

Still, these terraces are solid and well-built, which is a bit more than you can say for some of the rubbish that's been put up since.

Lisa has done her little house up in what I think of as single girl's style - you know, lots of frilly curtains and chair covers, floral patterns and porcelain nicknacks, rugs and dried flower arrangements and pot pourri. Everything smelling very fragrant and always in its right place. There's even a teddy bear on the bed. Awful, the place is. You couldn't really ask for anything more different from my house on Sherwood Crescent. A colour TV, a freezer, and plenty of beer in the fridge. Now, that's a home.

"What did you say this course was that you're going on?"

Lisa gave me that exasperated look that says 'you're an ill-mannered pillock, but you're a bloke, so I don't expect any better.'

"Heritage Management," she said, but from her tone of voice she might as well have been saying "How to turn water into wine". She sounded reverential, almost. I gathered that this was the latest in-thing, like all those American executive gimmicks that came round in the 1980s, when I was in another life. As soon as you'd got your head round one of them, it was totally out of date and the next one had come along. To be in management, it seemed as though you had to follow the old eighty - twenty rule. Eighty per cent of your time reading memos and going on management courses, and the other twenty per cent actually managing.

"Right. Heritage Management. Who else will be there?"

"I don't really know."

"Heritage managers maybe?"

"Oh, the usual crowd, I suppose."

She said this a bit too casually. It made me suspicious, though I couldn't think what she might be hiding from me. Another bloke she'd met somewhere? That could only be a good thing from my angle. It was time I moved on. If Lisa was going to make the break, that would be all the better. God alone knew why I couldn't get round to doing it myself. It had never been a problem in the past. Perhaps I had a touch of social constipation - there was something I had to get rid of, but the system was bunged up. Send for the sexual senna pods and stand clear of the loo.

"Middle-aged biddies from WI groups and Local History evening classes at the Tech then?"

"That's about it, I expect," said Lisa placidly. She gave me no argument, you see. A warning sign in a woman, that is. McClure's

Rule number three. I call it the Adam and Eve Rule - never trust a woman when she agrees with you.

There wasn't much conversation on the way to the station in Mansfield. Lisa had a suitcase with her in the car, and it was only when I happened to glance at this that it dawned on me she was stopping the night somewhere. Presumably a couple of nights. I don't know why this hadn't clicked before, but there it was.

"Where are you staying then?"

"Stones, I've told you all this. Weren't you listening?"

Why do you have to justify yourself to women all the time?

"I've forgotten. I've had a lot on my mind."

"The seminars are in a hotel. We stay there overnight as well. It's all organised as part of the course, and they book the rooms for us."

"I see. You and all the other course members will be there then. In this hotel."

"Yes."

"All the middle aged biddies."

"Yes." She sighed. "I'll be back on Friday."

"Okay." We turned into the station car park and Lisa hopped out. There wasn't much time to spare before her train arrived, so all I got was a quick peck on the cheek before she went off to meet the biddies. I could barely muster the grin as she walked off.

I watched the carriages pull away northwards towards Shirebrook and wondered whether Robin Hood would be waiting to waylay her.

For a long time Mansfield was the largest town in Britain without a railway station - one of the achievements of Dr Beeching. Now it has passenger services again, connecting southwards to Nottingham and north through some of the villages to Worksop and on to Sheffield.

This has helped to put a bit of life back into some of the old pit villages like Creswell, Whitwell and Shirebrook. But naturally tourism was foremost in the minds of the people who named it the Robin Hood Line. Perhaps they think loads of Americans and Japanese will come over and ride the diesel units backwards and forwards looking for signs of outlaws in green outfits with bows and arrows, lurking among the slag heaps and the fields of oilseed rape.

Actually, it wouldn't be all that surprising if some of them did just that. A few years ago they put up signs on the A619 into Worksop warning motorists of speed cameras. You know those signs with a little illustration of a camera on them? Local folklore has it that there were Japanese tourists stopping their cars at each one they reached, thinking they were viewpoint signs telling them the best spots to take photos from. There must be a lot of baffling holiday snaps being shown around in Nagasaki and Kyoto with nothing on them but a few telegraph poles and the odd bored cow.

But I digress.

You might call me a bit of a bastard, but by the time I'd turned the car round at the station and was on my way back towards Medensworth, my thoughts had already left Lisa and were hovering around Nuala. But I've already explained that, haven't I? It's just the way I am.

I was hoping Nuala would be my senna pod. She could certainly talk the shit out of anybody I know.

I drove across Medensworth to the new estate, where they slung up some low-rise flats a few years ago and moved folk in from the grottier bits of Mansfield. These flats have got their own garages, private parking for residents and their own graffiti. It's not a place for a miner to live - all miners want to be outdoors when they're not working. But you can't even do a bit of gardening here. Since the gardens are only ten years old, the grass hasn't managed to force its way through the rubble left by the builders yet. Luckily, the folk who live here spend all day indoors watching soaps on the telly.

Nuala was waiting for me in the bus shelter near the flats. At first glance, she looked to be half naked. When I looked a bit closer, I could see she wasn't wearing as much as that. Apart from the usual pelmet round her bum, she had on a low-cut top that hung away from her breasts at the side and failed to get anywhere near covering her navel. There was a gang of teenagers behind her, ogling her legs, but she pretended not to have noticed them.

"Hi, love. You look great."

I gave Nuala my grin as she climbed in the car and got a quick kiss. I heard shouts and hoots behind me and turned to stare at the youths. One of them gave me the finger. There's no respect in this part of town.

"Where are we going, Stones?"

"Well, I thought you might fancy something hot."

She pouted at me. "You'll never believe the sort of day I've had."

"Yeah? You live such an exciting life, Nuala."

"Too right. We had the accountants in from head office all afternoon. Going through the books, they were. And do you know why?"

"They wanted something to read?"

"Them at head office couldn't believe that we'd made so much money this month. What do you think of that? It's because of our bonus, of course. They think we've fiddled the books to make it look like we've reached our sales targets. But I told one of the blokes - you ought to see me selling holidays, mate. Then you'll know why we're so good. You can't argue with that. They ought to be thanking us, not accusing us of fiddling."

"It's a disgrace."

Nuala went on for a bit longer on the same theme. And then a bit longer again.

"Can we go to that Italian place?" she said after a while.

"What? Rome? Venice?" I thought she was still talking about holidays.

"Stupid. That Italian restaurant in Edwinstowe. Luigi's or something."

"Oh. You want to eat, then?"

She looked at me funny. "I want you to spend some money on me for once."

"Come on, sweetheart."

But the appeal got me nowhere.

"Well then, what's it to be?" said Nuala. "Luigi's, or I go straight back home. On my own."

I looked at her, giving her a careful consideration. The seatbelt across her chest was pulling her top really tight in the middle, and her tits were bursting out at the sides like the corners of a bouncy castle. She uncrossed her legs, pushing her feet against the footwell so that her long thighs tensed and stretched. Tensed and stretched.

"I'll spend the money," I said.

*   *   *   *

And afterwards I took her to Clumber Park, which in the summer is like a sort of open air knocking shop and picnic site combined. Clumber is always a revelation for me. The Dukes of Newcastle lived there for a couple of centuries, until they eventually had to demolish it in the 1930s when even the ducal money bags couldn't keep such a vast pile from developing dry rot in the joists and cracks in the plaster in the downstairs toilet.

Although there's no house there any more, they've left nearly four thousand acres of wooded parkland - not to mention a big lake, a coach house, stables, estate offices, a brew house, vineries, a fig house, a palm house, a huge range of greenhouses, a walled garden, a family chapel, mock Roman and Greek temples, and pleasure grounds. You can't say they didn't know how to live, those dukes.

The best feature of Clumber Park, though, is the Duke's Drive, three miles long and better known as Lime Tree Avenue because of the double row of limes. It's around this area that you find most of the visitors who flock to the park to eat their picnics, run their dogs, take a walk through the woods, or just sit and do whatever people can think of to do together in a car in a secluded spot. Play Scrabble or listen to *The Archers*, for example.

Lime Tree Avenue is a public highway, so access is free. The rest of the park is National Trust property, and you non-members have to pay to get in. There are little sentry boxes manned by students and such, where cars are supposed to stop. They don't all do that, of course. A quick burst of speed over the ramp can save you a bit of money, so why not? No student is going to leg it after you to demand a few pennies.

And there they are, all these cars. Practically abandoned in their little secluded corners, parked up on patches of grass, well hidden by trees and clumps of rhododendron bushes. These are cars owned by tourists and families out for the afternoon. This means they're full of cameras, binoculars, radios and other items useful for doing a bit of business with. You will also, I swear, find wallets and handbags, cash and credit cards, and driving licences galore if you take the trouble to carry half a brick in a sock to smash the odd back window with.

Can you believe that people leave themselves and their property so vulnerable in this day and age? I can. All too easily. Because they never learn, remember?

These thoughts were going through my mind as I sat in the Subaru with Nuala. I just can't help it. She was talking, of course, and my ears had kind of turned off. Shortly my body might pay attention, but my brain tends to remove itself from involvement. Even the squirrels that were coming down from their trees to pick up the debris from the nearest picnic looked fascinating to me just then. A squirrel is only a rat with a fluffy tail, after all. Fascinating, though.

Nuala is different from Lisa. It goes without saying, I suppose. It's why I do this - for the change. She's dark and somehow sort of mysterious. I don't know how that can be when she talks so much, but it is. Maybe it's because she talks a lot but says nothing. It leaves you wondering whether there's anything really in there. That's a kind of mystery. She has lots of dark hair, and where Lisa is slim she's, well, what's the word... voluptuous? Plenty of curves, know what I mean? Something to get hold of. When she talks, which is most of the time, her arms fly about and her sweater bobs and quivers violently as if she had a couple of bunny rabbits under there.

Nuala works part-time in that travel agent's Moxon was banging on about. I think she's probably good at selling things, talking like she does. But I don't know. If the customers get awkward or something, she's likely to lose her temper. And that's a nasty experience, I can tell you.

Right now, I think she might have been telling me something about a problem with a holiday to the Seychelles. There was some mention of a cancelled flight and luggage that ended up at the wrong airport, and a mix-up over a visa that she'd sorted out single-handed. She made it sound as though she was Cat Woman cleaning up crime in Gotham City.

I stifled the yawns, looked at the scenery, and waited for Nuala's spring to wind down so the real action could start.

Eventually, she turned towards me and indicated she was inclined to use her mouth for something other than talking. Her sweater bounced and waggled. I swear that all that yakking gets her in the mood. She was certainly gasping for a bit of social intercourse now, and within seconds the windows of the Subaru were steaming up. The scenery disappeared as if a warm mist had fallen. Then, for a while, it was goodbye squirrels, hello bunny rabbits.

*   *   *   *

In the car on the way back to Medensworth, Nuala said something really strange.

"Tomorrow, Stones," she said. "Will you take me out again?"

"Eh? We've just been out. Didn't you notice all that green stuff on the floor and the big sticky-up brown things? That was out."

"No. Somewhere nice, I mean."

It was baffling to me that Nuala didn't think Clumber Park was 'nice'. This place is one of the jewels in the crown of the National Trust. The tourists flock to it. They pay to get in, for heaven's sake.

"You could take me out for lunch again. A drink at least."

"Oh, right."

Twice in two days? This was in danger of becoming a habit.

"So that I know you're not ashamed to be seen with me," she said.

"No worries. I know just the place."

When we got back to the house, I pointed Nuala in the direction of the kitchen while I made a few calls, careful with my words in case the clattering of plates wasn't loud enough to cover me.

Nuala had nearly finished producing a microwaved steak and a beer when the phone rang. I answered it a bit hesitantly, nervous at

76

doing it in front of her but not wanting to miss the call in case it was business. But it wasn't. It was my Uncle Willis.

"Now then, Livingstone. How are you?"

"All right, Uncle."

He's almost the only person alive who can call me Livingstone and get away with it. I hate the name. It makes me sound like a bad music hall joke. The next person to utter the words 'I presume' will get my boot up his Stanley.

"And how's, ah... what's her name?"

"She's fine too, Uncle."

He has no idea, of course, who the current 'what's her name' is, but feels he has to ask anyway. It's one of those conventions, like telling someone you must meet up some time when you've got no intention of setting eyes on the pillock ever again. Uncle Willis lost track of my 'what's her names' a long time ago and doesn't bother trying to keep up now. This is a bit of luck, since it means I can insert any name necessary into the conversation with him, depending on who happens to be in earshot at the time.

"But how are you keeping anyway, Uncle? Is everything all right at Rolling Meadows?"

Willis is in one of those nice modern nursing homes. You know the ones. The old folk in these places are not being looked after, they're 'in a personal care situation'. In the mornings they spend their time practising something called 'living skills', which as far as I can make out means making your own bed and burning a bit of toast for your own breakfast. Then in the afternoon they move on to 'social and recreational skills', which means watching Countdown on the telly and listening to Val Doonican records. I think the Doonicans were probably bought at the car boot sale. Well, somebody has to buy them.

In keeping with this approach, the nursing home is called Rolling Meadows, which obviously means that it's in the middle of a modern Wimpey estate that has never seen a meadow in its life, let alone anything rolling. Still, Uncle Willis likes it, which is all that matters. He says he appreciates the proportion of women to men in there. Maybe I'm just a chip off the old block after all.

"It's as bad as ever, youth," he said. "But they've let me have my annual phone call, you see. It was either my lawyer or my nephew, and the lawyer wasn't in."

This was his joke, and just in case I'd forgotten and was about to take him seriously, he let loose a painful metallic rattling that ought to have me sending for a British Telecom engineer to mend my phone, except that I knew it was just my uncle laughing.

"Right. What have they been doing to you now then, Uncle?"

"Torture it is, bleedin' torture. They've cut down my cigarettes. Can you believe it?"

"Why's that?"

"Oh, they had some pimply youth in here called Darren, who said he was a doctor. He can't have been more than fifteen. Do they let them do house calls while they're on work experience these days? Honestly, Livingstone, I don't know how they think they can fool me. I told him, I've had more varicose veins and gurgling chests than he's had clean socks. When I'm sick I expect to see a doctor who really is a doctor, not a snotty-nosed fifth former doing GCSE Biology."

"But did he say what's wrong with you?"

"Oh just a wheezy chest. Have to cut down for a bit, youth. Still, it's made all these old girls cluck round me like a lot of hens. Nothing like it for getting the women going, you know, thinking that you're ill."

I could imagine it. Uncle Willis's charm isn't lost on the elderly female residents of the Meadows. Or on some of the staff, for that matter. I had a bit of a fling with one of the care assistants myself once, and I had to drop her like a ton of bricks when she started comparing me unfavourably with my aged uncle. Women really know how to hurt.

"Would you like me to come and see you, Uncle?"

It might sound as though I shouldn't have to ask this. I do go regularly to see the old bloke, but if I don't ask I'm liable to turn up and find that he's out somewhere gadding around. They go for day trips to Alton Towers, Mansfield Brewery, stuff like that. And other days he's just off for a stroll in the car park with one of his admirers. That's when he's not practising his compulsory social and recreational skills, anyway.

78

"Yes, that would be nice, Livingstone. Come tomorrow afternoon. There's only *Jurassic Park* on the telly, and I've seen it three times."

"No problem."

"I've something I want to talk to you about anyway."

"Yeah? What's that?"

"I'll tell you tomorrow."

Nuala brought the steak in just at the right time to take my mind off what it might be that the old man wanted to talk about.

"That your uncle?" said Nuala when I put the phone down.

"Yes."

"That's nice."

"What is?"

"Looking after your uncle, of course. You take care of him don't you, Stones?"

"No - he's in a home, Nuala."

"Well, I know. But you look out for him. You're concerned. You're close, like a family should be. That's what I mean. You're a real caring sort of man, aren't you? You'd make such a good father yourself, it's a shame."

I dug my knife into the steak a bit too hard and almost went through the plate. Me, a dad? I've spent the best years of my life trying to avoid it. Not to mention the money I've spent on condoms.

"I don't think so, Nuala."

But she'd gone all dreamy now. You know, the way women do when they get the least sniff of a nappy on someone else's brat. I could see what was going through her mind. This was ridiculous. Nuala was supposed to be the new bird. How come I'd ended up with two of them getting all broody and meaningful? There was something very wrong here. Was it me? Was I pulling the wrong sort of women? Was I getting too old? Maybe I could ask Uncle Willis when I saw him.

"You don't really want to be living in this house on your own, do you, Stones?" said Nuala.

But she might as well have been talking to herself as far as I was concerned.

"Yes."

79

"It's lonely for a man on his own. You can't look after yourself properly, can you?"

"Yes."

"I'm sure the reason you haven't married is because you've just been looking for the right woman all this time, isn't it?"

"No."

You can see I was trying to keep it simple for her, but she still didn't understand. Spell it out, Stones, quick.

"I don't want to get married, Nuala. I'm perfectly happy as I am."

She smiled at me understandingly. Or rather non-understandingly. It was a look that said she was a woman and could therefore see right into the shallow depths of my male soul. Having looked in there, she felt - what? Pity, probably. Her look meant she knew what I wanted better than I did, but was prepared to let me go on believing my pathetic little fantasy that I knew my own mind. Women, eh?

"I could always just move in with you, Stones. We don't have to get married. How would that be?"

"No. And no. And awful."

Well, I'm not made for living with, that's all. But I realised I'd perhaps been too abrupt. She was starting to look hurt now.

"It's not you, love. I just I prefer to be on my own, that's all. It's the way I am."

She smiled, reassured that I wasn't a totally lost cause.

"We'll see."

Okay, we'd see. But what we'd see wasn't what she thought we'd see. Not by a long way, see?

Unfortunately, the steak and the beer seemed to have had more of a softening-up effect on me than Nuala's arguments. After a bit, she started to look very desirable and a visit to the bedroom seemed called for urgently.

She was right, after all - I did need looking after, in a way.

8

Monday morning there was bad news. A 'load lost' message on the answering machine. Not a big job like the French rig, but bad news all the same.

I'm reasonably good in the mornings as a rule, but this particular Monday morning my brain didn't seem to be able to get into proper gear, like there was dirt on my clutch plate. I got Slow Kid on the phone. I thought he might have had something to tell me about Rawlings and Lee by now, but he was about as informative as a Council Tax demand.

"As far anybody can tell, they're working for themselves," he said.

"Yeah? So what have they got against you and me?"

"Pass."

"So what did Sean say?"

"Not much. Just kept telling me to stay clear of Josh Lee. He doesn't know Rawlings at all."

"Great," I said. "What about on the streets? Anybody new dealing round here?"

"Dunno, Stones. There's always rumours, but you know I don't have anything to do with 'em."

"Come on, Slow. What rumours?"

"Well, just someone around the pubs and clubs, chatting to the kids. A few may have scored from him. Just talk, though. Nothing you can pin down."

"Could it be Lee?"

"Can't tell, Stones."

"This is great, this is. Some organisation we are, pissing about in the dark like nuns in a power cut."

"Aw, Stones, you know what it's like."

"Keep trying, Slow."

"Course."

A bit later I was in the Cow's Arse for lunch with Nuala. I'd promised her the best, and I always follow through on a promise. She'd get her lunch, and be seen with me too. She would even get the genuine Cow's Arse ambience.

I was thinking about Rawlings and Lee and that burnt-out van. Nuala may have noticed that I was a bit distracted, but she kept up the conversation on her own, without my help.

Then I spotted Moggie Carr across the bar, and something seemed to click in my mind. Moggie is the sort of bloke who doesn't do anything much himself, but seems to know everyone who does do something. This makes him a top class source of information, and that's what you need these days.

And something else too - Moggie is a member of the other travellers' clan, the Carrs. No love lost between them and the Lees, of course. But he knows what's going on there. It's in his interests. In a moment I was across the room, my hand on Moggie's sleeve. He jumped as if he'd been shot. It doesn't do to sneak up on somebody like Moggie unless you want to give him a heart attack.

"Oh, shit," he said, slopping beer on my boots. "Don't do that."

Moggie's face was brown and creased, like one of those bits of leather on Ernie and Stella's stall at the Sunday market, but more genuine. He always looked as though it was a long time since his last square meal and even longer since his last proper wash.

"Nervous, Moggie? Who were you expecting?"

"Nobody at all. I just don't like surprises."

"Nor me. Particularly the sort somebody nearly gave me a day or two back with a van load of stuff."

"What's that, Stones?"

Moggie looked intrigued. He scented a new bit of information. I told him about the burnt-out van, and how the goods had nearly been in my possession.

"You're joking," he said.

I wish people wouldn't keep going on about me joking. Sometimes I do joke, yeah. I can be a real comic. There are times when I can be so hilarious that I have them rolling on the floor and wetting their pants with my wit. But this wasn't one of those times.

"What do you know about any drugs business around here, Moggie?"

"Me, Stones? I'm not into stuff like that. You've got to be - "

"Don't say it, pillock. I'm not chuffin' joking. You know what's going on, Moggie. Who's into the drugs now? Is there someone new?"

"I wouldn't know anything like that."

"Oh? Would you know what's it's like to have that glass shoved down your throat? Tell me."

Moggie looked worried. But was it me he was bothered about, or something else? Time to try a different tack.

"Do you know someone called Josh Lee?"

"Shit. If you know about him already, why are you hassling me?"

"Moggie. Come over here and whisper in my ear."

"Er, I think your bird's looking for you," he suggested.

I looked round. Sure enough, Nuala was staring my way. She was sitting on her own and she didn't look happy, but at least she hadn't stopped talking. It was just that the words she was using weren't very complimentary, and you could tell that even from a distance. I gave her a quick wave with my free hand and tried to suggest with a few facial expressions that I wouldn't be long. She mouthed something at me that I couldn't make out, but the first word definitely began with an 'f' and the other with a 'b'. She might have been asking for a firkin and a basket, but they don't serve those at the Cow.

"Over here, Moggie." I pulled him into an alcove out of sight. I wasn't really worried about anybody seeing us, but Nuala was putting me off.

"There ain't nothing I can tell you, Stones. Honest."

When people start saying 'honest', I know they're lying. I do it myself. Moggie Carr was only honest when he was really leaned on hard, and I hadn't started leaning yet.

"Josh Lee," I said. "Tell me about him. Everything you know."

"Well, I can tell you he's one of the Lees."

"Yeah, yeah. Even I can figure that one out, pillock."

"He lives at the caravan site out at Highbrook."

"The Lees run that place themselves, don't they?"

"Old man Daniel Lee runs it. He's the gaffer. Josh is his grandson."

"And Josh is into drugs? That's a bit out of the usual for the Lees, isn't it?"

"Yeah, right. If old Daniel found out, Josh would be out on his ear. If he still had any ears by then."

"Not their scene then, the Lees?"

"No way. Anything else, but not drugs. Try the Nottingham Yardies. Or there's Craig, of course. But I don't need to tell you that, Stones."

"Yeah. Craig."

I let Moggie go, but his jacket stayed crumpled.

"What about a bloke called Rawlings then?"

He shook his head firmly. "Never heard of him. Is he new?"

I didn't like the way Moggie was turning the conversation round so that he could get information out of me. That was a knack he had, a bit of a talent. Everybody has to have a talent. Moggie would make a good television interviewer, if they could smarten him up enough not to break the camera.

I was about to turn away and find my back to Nuala when Moggie made his mistake. He'd been thinking about Rawlings, trying to file him away in his mental filing cabinet, and he let something slip.

"Maybe he's working with the other bloke then."

I turned round again so fast that he didn't have time to back off, and we collided hard enough to make his glasses fall off and land in his beer.

"Shit. Now look what you've done."

"What other bloke?"

Moggie fished around in his pint with a finger and dragged the glasses out. "The lenses will be all sticky now."

"What other new bloke, Moggie?"

"I won't be able to see my way to the bar to get myself another drink. You've ruined my beer as well."

"Okay, okay, I'll buy you a drink," I said through gritted teeth. "But first you tell me - what other bloke?"

"Well, I dunno really."

"Moggie, I'm getting seriously pissed off."

"It's just one or two things I've heard around. No names. Just that some of the blokes have been getting work from somewhere.

Not from Craig. They ain't talking about it too much. It's been going on for a bit, but word is that the outfit is expanding now. Starting to exercise a bit of muscle. Maybe that's where Josh Lee fits in. Does that help?"

"I need a name, Moggie."

"I told you, no one's saying."

"Who's not saying?"

"Well, there's Mick Kelk for one. He's had a driving job this week, I think. For God's sake, Stones, don't tell him you found that out from me."

"Course not."

I bought Moggie the drink I'd promised. It always saddens me when greed gets results where threats fail. Then I remembered Nuala. To my surprise, she was still there. I thought by now she would have stamped out in disgust. But she was sitting at the same table where I'd left her. The only trouble was, now she had company. I could see her mouth going nineteen to the dozen, spilling her guts to the nice, polite bloke who'd just bought her a vodka and who had no doubt told her that he knew Stones McClure very well, that he was an old friend in fact. Yes, that's just the sort of trick DI Frank Moxon would pull. It should be in the Police and Criminal Evidence Act - the use of intrusive and unwarranted niceness strictly prohibited.

I was torn now, between a reluctance to encounter Moxon face to face and a tearing anxiety about what Nuala might be telling him. At the rate she talked, she could have given him my entire life history already, if she actually knew it. Rapidly, I reviewed what she did know about me, what she might have noticed during the short course of our relationship. I'm careful, but sometimes there are moments when I stop thinking too clearly, and Nuala has been intimately involved in one or two of these moments, if the truth be known.

* * * *

The drive home was tense. In my mind, all I could see was Frank Moxon's oily smile as he'd slithered away from the table and slimed his way out of the door of the Cow.

"He told me you had a nickname," said Nuala, blissfully unaware of my mood. "Not Stones, I mean. Another one. One that you don't tell people and you don't use any more, because you don't like it. But Frank knows it - he knows a lot of things about you, he said."

I bet he did. My only worry now was whether he knew even more about me since his long chat with Nuala. Also hearing her call the bloke Frank was starting to turn my stomach.

"He's talking through his backside."

But Nuala just smirked.

"Tufty. I thought that was really sweet. Can I call you that?"

She giggled loudly. One vodka too many, by the sound of it. I said nothing, but concentrated on driving. We'd be home soon, and then I thought I might be able to find a way to shut her up.

"Frank said it was because of your hair cut. I can't imagine it now. Tufty. How sweet."

"Stay away from Moxon, Nuala."

I hadn't intended to speak, but it needed saying. Her eyes lit up, loving it. She thought I was jealous, the silly tart.

"Oh, but he's ever so nice. And he knows a lot about you."

"Yeah, you said."

"He says he's met a lot of your friends too. He's going to tell me about them next time we meet."

"Yeah?"

"Tufty."

That giggle again. It was a good job Nuala had compensating qualities, otherwise I would have had her out of the car right there and then, without slowing down. When a woman thinks she has power over you, you're sunk if you don't get out immediately. And here she was thinking I was worried about a deadly rival for her favours in the shape of Detective Inspector Frank Moxon. Me, jealous of the Bill Gates of the Nottinghamshire Constabulary, the supernerd of the CID?

"He's a plonker."

"Now, tut, tut. Why are you calling him names? He was very nice about you. He said you were old friends. He couldn't understand why you didn't come over to talk to him. Did you have to speak to all those people at the bar, Stones? I'm sure you were only pretending. Some of them looked quite surprised. You even bought them drinks. It was almost as if you were trying to avoid Frank. I told him that, and he laughed. He said he couldn't believe it, not of an old friend like you. It was then he told me your nickname. Tufty."

By now, my hands were gripping the steering wheel so hard that my fingers were leaving impressions in the rubber. I realised I'd been imagining the wheel was Frank Moxon's neck.

The fact was, Moxon had hit me where he knew I was vulnerable. I couldn't tell Nuala to stay away from him because he was copper. She had no idea I was the sort of person who needed to avoid coppers, and that was the way I preferred to keep it. Ignorance is bliss, but it's also security.

"Oh, I nearly forgot, I've got to call in at the church," I said.

And Nuala's eyes lit up, just like Lisa's had.

*   *   *   *

Medensworth isn't all one big housing estate, though it might look it at first glance. There is still an Old Medensworth. It's bypassed by the main road now, which moves rapidly on towards the sprawl that is New Medensworth. But the old village has an eighteenth century pub serving eighteenth century meat and potato pie. It has some dinky stone cottages lived in by old ladies who've been there since the Year Dot. And it has a manor house, looking a bit battered and neglected, which is often the subject of speculation that it's about to be turned into a conference centre or nursing home. Probably it'll just fall down before they get round to it.

Best of all, though, it has St Asaph's Parish Church. Bits of this god box are Saxon, and bits of it are Norman, with later congregations adding their fancies to it in a wonderful sort of hotchpotch. It's like a complete record of the last thousand years of what passes for civilisation in this part of the world. Around it there's the churchyard, the quietest spot you'll find for miles, full of crumbling gravestones and ancient yew trees.

Lisa says there's nothing quite like an old churchyard for making you feel in touch with the past. All those dead folk lying under your feet. You can tell which of them were rich gits by the size of their memorial stones. I'm more interested in the plain ordinary folk, as you've probably guessed. They're a bit special to me. Among this lot will be the actual stonemasons and carpenters and labourers who built the church. Just go inside and look at the thing if you still want to know why they're special.

When I walk in that churchyard, I can hear them talking to me. What they say isn't always complimentary, true - but I can take it. They agree with me on one thing, though - the rich gits should be in the lower, hotter bit of eternity.

Down at St Asaph's you'll find the Reverend Gordon Bowring, usually just known as The Rev. He's one of those young vicars - by which I suppose I mean that he's younger than me. Not much above thirty anyway. A child of the Sixties, like. And that means his ideas are more, well... modern than some of the C of E types I've come across before.

He isn't from round these parts, as anybody can tell from his habit of leaving his car unlocked outside his house. In fact, he's a bit of a southern nancy, to be honest. He was in a parish in Berkshire or Buckinghamshire or somewhere soft before he came to Nottinghamshire.

The story goes that he got carried away one day and preached a sermon that said it was basically okay to nick things from supermarkets. He meant that if you were poor and hungry, the big businesses wouldn't miss the odd tin of chicken and mushroom soup or a packet of chocolate Hobnobs.

But the details of the message sort of got ignored, as they do. This scary vicar had said it was okay to steal things. Shock horror, stories in the tabloids and questions asked at the General Synod. And before he could get his cassock off or swing his thurible, the Reverend Gordon Bowring had been banished to the arse-end of the Midlands, where he couldn't do any harm. I suppose they thought that if he told folk in Medensworth it was okay to nick stuff they'd wonder what the hell he was talking about. People here are brought up to nick things - they don't need one of the god squad giving them permission, thank you very much.

The Rev is not what you might expect for such a villain. He's no more than five foot six or seven, and his hair is vanishing rapidly despite his age. Perhaps it's all that worrying about sin. I try not to do any worrying at all on this subject, and it hasn't harmed me. The Rev's eyes always look vaguely troubled too. He dresses in a really trendy style - well, I seem to remember it was trendy back in the Seventies - and he talks like the Oxford bleedin' dictionary. They should have sent an interpreter up from Berkshire with him. His congregation here have trouble understanding him half the time. Me, I sometimes understand what he's saying. But I can't understand what he's thinking, no way. His brain processes defy logic.

Just imagine a small child surrounded by Lego bricks. He has to build a model of a cathedral, and he's been told he can only use the white bricks. But he finds that all the bricks he's been given are red ones, and they're such a funny shape that they'll only fit together in certain ways, and the building they make is starting to look more like a set of sheds on an allotment. Somehow the child has to convince himself that his bricks are white, and that what he's building is a cathedral. How does he do it? Well, he turns colour blind and becomes the world's biggest fan of avant-garde modern architecture, that's how. Meet the Rev.

When I parked the Impreza outside St Asaph's, I hadn't intended bumping into him. I only wanted to take a squint at the rotas in the church porch. I'm down on the churchyard rota, you see - which means, I suppose, that in theory I take my turn at tidying up round the graves and keeping the grass in trim. Well, you'd be surprised how fast the weeds grow in the summer. It's practically a full-time job, and obviously the church can't afford to pay anyone. So a group of us caring local citizens put our names down to look after the task in turn. The Rev thinks we're wonderful. And he never seems to care whether we actually do any work, bless him.

For my reasons of my own, I wanted to get my name down for a turn on the rota this week. It was no problem, as there are always plenty of spare periods.

The one thing I had to do was make sure my spell was clear of the times when our churchwarden, Welsh Border, was working. He isn't actually Welsh - far from it, he's born and bred in Medensworth, and he won't hesitate to let you know it. He's

Councillor Border to his face, chairman of the parish council, retired accountant and a bugger for wanting to do things right. I don't fit into his scheme of things at all, and he has a horrible suspicious mind. I can't do with Welsh Border hanging around when I'm putting in my spell of good work.

Lisa knows about this, but it was a new concept to Nuala when I explained to her about the volunteer rota. She looked awestruck, like she'd just had a vision of the Virgin Mary. I nipped up to the porch as quick as I could, but the Rev was just coming out of the vestry door and he buttonholed me before I could escape.

"Ah, Livingstone. Giving of your time as generously as ever, I see. How wonderful. Giving is the greatest of joys, is it not?"

He's the only person who gets to call me Livingstone, apart from my Uncle Willis. Maybe that says something.

"Yes, Rev."

I've found this is the best way to deal with him - just agree with whatever he says. You can't disillusion somebody who already looks so worried and is almost bald before he's thirty-five. It would be cruel, like telling the child with the Lego that he'd just built a public toilet instead of Westminster Abbey.

"I see you've got your delightful young lady with you. Lisa, isn't it?"

The Rev gave a coy little wave towards the car, and Nuala waved back from the passenger seat, for all the world like the Queen Mother or something. I swear these two are on another planet. For a start, the Rev obviously couldn't tell the difference between one bird and another, which in my book makes any bloke a very sad person indeed.

"Yeah, I was just taking her home, so - "

"I've been wondering when we might have the honour at St Asaph's of reading the banns for the McClure nuptials," simpered the Rev. "Might that be in prospect at some date in the not too distant future?"

For a minute I honestly hadn't a clue what he was on about. I always thought nuptials were what Nuala would be up to half an hour later in my bedroom. But I'd never heard the Rev talk smutty before. Was he really talking about banning it? Then I mentally translated his words into English, and the penny dropped.

"Er, I can't say it is, Rev. I'm not really prepared for the, er..." What was the word I was searching for?

"Commitment?" suggested the Rev.

Ridicule was the word I wanted, actually. But I let him have his own way.

"Perhaps you'd like to come and talk to me about it privately one day," he said. "You and the young lady together, or just the two of us if you prefer. Man to man, so to speak. I may be able to put your fears at rest."

He was doing a pretty good job of increasing my fears by the minute. The last thing I wanted was for him and Lisa to get together when this subject was likely to be on the agenda. If marriage was on the vicar's afternoon tea menu, then Stones McClure was on a diet. Fasting for Lent, in fact.

"I'll let you know, Rev."

"Right-ho."

He actually does say that. Until I met him I thought it was something Leslie Phillips had invented to send up RAF types in all those Carry On films. Right-ho, chaps. Wizard prang. Peppered a few oiks. Tally-ho.

I made to set off back down the path, but the Rev hadn't quite finished.

"Oh, when you're here on your mission of goodwill, Livingstone..."

"Yes?" He meant when I was skiving around the churchyard.

"I wondered if you would do me a favour and take a look at the vestry roof." He gestured up towards the church. "We seem to have suffered a bit of storm damage. I didn't notice the wind being quite so bad, but sometimes I get a bit absorbed in my work, you know. In a world of my own, so to speak. But it must have been damaged. It seems to be deteriorating rather rapidly."

I looked up at the roof. There was a bare patch of a several square feet among the ancient brick tiles, and wooden beams and bits of felt were poking through. I looked at the guttering and down at the ground below the roof. There was no sign of any broken bits of tile. Some storm.

"I'll see to it, Rev."

"Thank you, my friend. We do need to maintain the fabric of the church as something the people of the village can be proud of."

In a world of his own was right. When I got back in the car, the first thing I did was make a quick call on the mobile.

"Slow? You there? Do something for me, mate."

"Yeah, Stones?"

"Find out which pillock has been nicking the Rev's roof."

9

Beef, Yorkshire pudding, roast potatoes and a mountain of vegetables. Apple pie, cream, cheese, biscuits, coffee and beer. Doncaster Dave was having a snack.

Dave appeared in court once. It was about the time I met him, actually, but that's another story. He'd got himself pulled in for nicking stuff off the stalls in Mansfield market. Well, nicking was hardly the word for it. When the stallholders saw him coming, they just kind of backed off and invited him to help himself. He only took food, of course. Pork pies and pasties, the odd half pound of cheese or a loaf or two. Even apples and bananas. It's peckish work walking round a market, and there it was, all set out on display. But then some jerk complained one day, and Dave found himself up before the magistrates. Somehow, assaulting the police got added to the charge sheet on the way there. Must have been a mistake.

I've got to know Dave quite well since then - as far as you can get to know anyone who communicates in grunts. And the thing I remember most about his day in court is the moment when the number one magistrate got right up on her high horse and asked him: "Mr Underwood, don't you know right from wrong?" That was a real laugh. Right from wrong? He doesn't even know right from left.

"I need your services, Donc," I said.

"Yeah?"

He waited for instructions, filling in the few seconds by piling more food into his mouth.

"There's something going on that smells wrong to me. I want to see Mick Kelk and ask him some questions."

"Yeah?"

He was looking down at the remains of the cheese as if he wanted to ask a question of his own, like 'where's it all gone?'

"We may need to lean on him a bit."

"Yeah." He nodded. He understood that bit.

"Trouble is, I don't know where he is at the minute. He might be on a job somewhere."

Dave looked towards the food counter, where a whole range of desserts were on display. I could see his eyes flicking backwards and forwards across the gateaux.

"We have to go and look for him down at the Ferret," I said.

"Yeah?"

"As soon as we've done that I'll take you down the Shah Naz for something to eat."

Dave was on his feet then. "Less' go," he said.

*　　*　　*　　*

If you think the Cow's Arse is a bit rough, then you've never been in the Dog and Ferret. Very wise too, if I may say so. I wouldn't touch the Ferret with anybody's barge pole, let alone mine, if I didn't have to call there sometimes for professional reasons. It's been closed more often than a cashier's window at a Post Office counter. It's usually on the orders of the magistrates after complaints by the police about the amount of trouble there.

And it's not as if it's organised trouble. That I could understand, if it was in the course of business. But it's just general mayhem, people beating each other up as a way of having a bit of a laugh on a Saturday night. Smashing up the bar, turning over a few cars, ripping out the toilets and flooding the car park. You know the sort of thing. It's so primitive and 1950s. Haven't they heard of the late twentieth century, these blokes?

In any case, I wouldn't go in there without Dave at my shoulder and Slow Kid outside with the engine running. Some of the customers don't know me and might give me a kicking by mistake. Some do know me and might give me a kicking on purpose. Sadly, this is where Mick Kelk and some of the other Medensworth blokes hang out.

When we walked through the door it was almost like one of those Western movies. You know the scene, when the strangers

94

mosey in, call for a couple of shots of redeye and start demanding to know where the sheriff is? And all the customers go really quiet and start twitching their trigger fingers? Well, it was a bit like that. Only there ain't no sheriff in Medensworth, and the only redeye in the Ferret tonight was the one the lad was wearing who staggered past us out of the door. In fact, his eye was so red the blood was making a mess on his shirt.

Inside, nobody looked as though anything out of the ordinary had been happening. They were just having a quiet drink, as far as anything was ever quiet in the Ferret. The jukebox was on full blast, the fruit machines and video games were bleeping and farting at one end of the bar and a bunch of pool players were arguing about a shot at the other end. In between, everyone was shouting at everyone else to make themselves heard, and those at the bar were having to shout even louder.

As we pushed our way through the crowd, the noise subsided around us, then came back to its full volume after we'd passed. I reckon it was Dave's shadow falling across them, or maybe they saw him coming and were trying to protect their pork pies and crisps, like starlings with a clutch of eggs when the sparrowhawk appears overhead.

Dave forced his way through to the bar by the simple means of putting a huge meaty hand on a few shoulders, as if he was patting them to say hello. When he arrived, he turned to one side, pushing back the tide to allow me to reach the bar unhindered.

This had the effect of attracting the landlord's attention pretty quick, and we got served straight away. Somebody grumbled behind me, but Dave moved his head and gave them his low-grade glower. They shut up.

"Who're you looking for?" The bloke behind the bar certainly caught on pretty quick.

"Mick Kelk."

"Playing pool."

"Cheers."

I suppose he thought we might be less trouble if we did what we had to do and got out. It's an attitude that's probably let him keep his licence this long.

The lads round the pool table weren't really lads at all. They were wearing jeans and t-shirts cut high at the sleeves to show their muscles, and some of them had hair that was a bit too long. But their beer guts were straining their t-shirts more than their pectorals were, and their faces were lined from years of absorbing ale and smoke in places just like the Ferret. Also their tattoos were out of date. Black Sabbath are definitely not the current thing this year.

One of the lads was Mick Kelk. I had a moment of curiosity about the others. I had no idea who they were, which meant they were from outside Medensworth. But I didn't really want to know just now. There was a general shuffling of position as they all took a pace backwards or sideways, arranging themselves into a defensive group with Kelk in the middle. Some of them took their hands out of their pockets, put down fags, picked up beer bottles.

"Kelky. I want a word with you."

Dave strolled up and stood over the pool table. Mick was about to play a shot. He had the blue ball in a good position, but he wouldn't get the white back to where he could pot the pink. Not the way his hand was shaking.

"I'm busy."

"You look it. It's just a friendly chat, like, but it's got to be now. So drop out of the game for a bit then, Kelky."

"I'm still busy."

"Tell you what - I'll just let you miss this shot, then we'll talk."

"I don't miss shots like this, pal."

"Yeah?"

He looked at me and then glanced sideways at Dave, who was watching Mick's cue as if it was the first time he'd ever seen one. Mick couldn't look soft in front of his mates. If it came to real trouble, he wanted them to back him up, not throw him to the wolves, which they would if he ruined his cred now. Act tough and you get accepted. Show you're scared and the pack disowns you. Mick knew that all right.

He certainly took his time lining up the shot, considering how easy it was. The tip of his cue seemed to be wavering all round the white ball, until eventually he whacked it down the table. It hit the blue all right, bouncing it hard off the cushion and away over the table beyond a clutch of reds. The white hovered uncertainly as if sensing the atmosphere, then nipped into the pocket like a mouse going for its hole when the cat appears.

"Well, if that ain't missing, my tadger's a pot plant."

Mick straightened up, his cue gripped firmly in his right hand, ready to shift it to make use of the heavy end if necessary. The other three lads shuffled their feet, not quite sure what was going on. Everybody seemed to be watching Doncaster Dave, except me. I've seen him before, so he's no novelty. But I knew he'd be getting hungry thinking about the Shah Naz. And when he's hungry he loses patience.

Helpfully, Dave leaned forward to retrieve the ball from the pocket where Mick had potted it. He placed the ball on the table, right on the D. He was moving slow, as if he'd lost interest in what was going and had decided to keep himself amused with a game. He reached out a large hand towards the nearest of the lads, and a cue was automatically placed into it. It looked like a toothpick when he gripped it like that.

"I really need to talk to you, Mick," I said. "I'll be upset if you don't co-operate."

"I told you, I'm busy."

"Well, personally I can wait, but it'll mean Dave here going past his supper time."

Mick's eyes followed Dave, fascinated, as he handled the pool cue. He had a funny grip on it, as if he'd never held one before. For a moment, I thought Mick was going to put him right. It wouldn't have been wise.

He turned back towards me instead. "I've got nothing to say, McClure."

Suddenly, Dave had hold of the narrow end of the cue in both fists. It whistled through the air and the blunt end came down on the cue ball with tremendous force, smacking it with a great thud that sent the ball flying off the table at two thousand miles an hour and accelerating. Its trajectory took it skidding past Mick Kelk's right ear to shatter a beer glass standing behind him on a head-high shelf.

There was a pause in the conversation. I could hear the drip of the beer running down the wall and even the trickle of Mick's

97

blood as it drained from his face. He was working out that if the ball had been an inch or two to the right, he'd have been able to go to the next fancy dress party as Admiral Nelson. One of his mates bravely hefted his own cue, a reflex action only. It accidentally snapped on Dave's hand and the bloke had to sit down on the floor suddenly out of surprise. Dave was being quite restrained. I hoped he wasn't getting too weak from hunger or something.

"Okay, what do you want to know?" said Mick shakily.

Conversation started up again. The landlord came and cleared up the broken glass with a resigned expression. We sat in the corner while Mick's mates pretended to carry on with the game under Dave's critical eye. He grunted with disapproval every time a wavering shot went wide of the pocket.

"I'm interested in any driving jobs you've had recently, Mick, that's all. Nothing to worry about."

"I drive all the time. That's my business. I'm a driver."

"I know that, Mick. That's why I'm talking to you. If I want to know who's been doing driving jobs recently, then that's who I ask - a driver. Right?"

He licked his lips. He looked as though he wanted his beer, but it was soaking into the floor, and I wasn't about to buy him another. Two free drinks in one day was beyond the call of duty. He was nervous, and I thought it might not be entirely because of Doncaster Dave.

"So. What have you been driving recently, Mick?"

"I took a load of pallets down to Derby on Monday."

"Pallets? Are you kidding me?"

"There's a bloke pays cash for 'em."

"And where did these pallets come from?"

"You know, here and there. Surplus stuff."

I shouldn't have asked really. Well, you don't. Of course they were surplus stuff. That means they were nicked from factories, warehouses, transport depots. Pits too, if he'd been able to find one that hadn't been cleared out already. Anything that's left lying about is 'surplus'.

"Pay well?"

"Next to nowt."

"So what did you bring back?"

"A bit of scrap, that's all. For one of the yards in Mansfield."

"And then?"

"Eh?"

"That was Monday, Mick. Today's Friday. What have you been doing since? I can see you haven't been practising your pool all that time."

He sighed. "I can't tell you, Stones. It's not worth it."

I had a sneaky sympathy for him, but I needed to know.

"Is it a new firm? A fresh bit of business?"

"Maybe."

"Who, Mick?"

He said nothing. This was worrying. "If I have to tell Doncaster Dave that his supper will be late because you don't want to talk, he won't be happy."

"Look." He was starting to plead. "They're not people to cross, Stones. I'll be right in the shit as it is."

"Are you working for a bloke called Rawlings? How about Josh Lee? "

"I know 'em. All right?"

"What's their game? Is Rawlings the boss, or is there someone else?"

But then the pub really did go quiet. Silent as the grave. Suddenly I could see right across the room, as if the Red Sea had parted for Moses and the Israelites. But this was no Moses. This was a hefty bloke with a broken nose, a badly fitting suit, and teeth like Stonehenge. I recognised him straightaway. He used to do a lot of boxing round the local amateur circuit until his last brain cell died. His nose is a particularly distinctive shape, like one of those novelty potatoes that people keep because they look like Mickey Mouse or General de Gaulle. Only this one was shaped more like Dumbo the Elephant.

They call this lad Sledgehammer Stan, but I won't bother you with the technical reasons. More importantly, he's one of Eddie Craig's favourite boys. With Stan were three more big lads, looking mean and shouldering people aside. If this was the landlord's way of calling 'time', he had a point.

"What the hell are Craig's boys doing here?"

99

Dave was eyeing up the three apes speculatively as they came our way. I might have put odds on him in a fair fight, but Eddie Craig's lads were usually tooled up some way. It might be time for a strategic withdrawal. Pity - a few more minutes and Kelk might have turned co-operative.

Dave's back passed in front of me, so I couldn't see Sledgehammer Stan any more. Even better, he couldn't see me. There was a fire door behind us, and I began edging backwards, ready to make a run for it, with Dave as my rearguard if necessary.

As we got to the door, I took a quick peek round Donc's shoulder. Stan wasn't even taking any interest in us. He'd zeroed straight in on Mick Kelk, who was now propped up between two of the lads, his feet dangling just short of the floor.

Poor old Mick. The balls really weren't breaking for him tonight. Or then again, perhaps they were.

* * * *

It was a relief to get away from the Ferret. I didn't have much concern for Kelk's welfare. If he'd upset Eddie Craig, then there was nothing to be done for him. Keep out of the way, that's the thing when Craig and his boys are about.

If you ever saw Eddie Craig, you'd think he looks harmless, like some middle-aged businessman or bank manager, someone who has a comfortable house, grown-up kids, a villa in France and membership of the local golf club. No doubt Craig has all of these. But he also has the best organised and toughest little empire in north Nottinghamshire.

Our paths don't normally cross much. Even now that I was trying to move up a bit, I wouldn't expect to run into trouble with Craig. What I'm involved in is small beer to Craig - a bit down market, like. There's big money to be made in his game, if that's what you're into.

Personally, I wouldn't spit on Eddie Craig or his type of business. It seems to me he's only making money out of people destroying themselves. In some circles that's thought to be okay these days. Enough big companies do it, so why not people like Craig? It's only free enterprise, after all. Right. Pass the sick bag.

Wherever there's big money involved, there's always people prepared to do anything to get it, or to protect it when they've got it. Craig doesn't need to dirty his hands with that side of it any more - not while Stan and a hundred others are willing to jump at his command, lump hammers at the ready. And Craig is never reluctant to give that command. There are enough blokes around here with the scars and the permanent limps to testify.

Dave had only one thing to say as Slow Kid drove us towards the Shah Naz.

"That was my trick shot, Stones."

"Brilliant, Donc. Does Steve Davis know about it?"

"I dunno. Do you want me to lean on him a bit and find out?"

"Never mind."

It was the most I'd heard him say in weeks. He must have been bubbling over with it.

Slow Kid was taking us back out on Baulk Lane, which curves north of Medensworth, to get to the end of the village where the Naz could be found.

Maybe it was the lack of conversation that made me notice the car that was following us all the way, refusing to take any of the turnings off towards Edwinstowe or Warsop, staying a constant distance behind us - far enough so that I couldn't make out the occupants or the registration number in the dark.

It just shows my positive outlook on life that I assumed they were the police. I certainly wouldn't have put it past Frank Moxon to put a tail on us, even though we were all perfectly innocent. That's the way the cops operate these days, harassing innocent citizens

I nudged Slow Kid. No point mentioning this to Dave. He wasn't quite asleep, but his brain had gone into a sort of suspended animation while he waited for the food to arrive.

"I think we're being followed, Slow."

He nodded and put his foot down. He soon had the Subaru up to seventy, and then eighty, on the long stretch past the bridge. The car behind stayed with us. I hated the thought of the cops catching up with us out here. Like the sheriff's last words, it was much too quiet.

"Can we lose them?"

"No probs. Just hang on. I'll take the twocker track."

At the back of the old pumping station there's an area of land like rough heath, covered in weeds and scrub, and some trees further in. Across this are tracks much favoured by the Medensworth twockers for a burn-up in their nicked motors, before they literally burn them up in some quiet spot among the woods. There are plenty of scorched trees in there and a few burnt-out hulks still waiting for someone to take them away. In its official guide, the council describes this as an ancient woodland beauty spot. And I'm Lord Byron's mother.

I was glad Slow Kid was driving. Given a suitable bit of tarmac, I knew he could let the car behind get right onto our bumper, then hit a handbrake turn and be away back down the road before they knew what had happened.

No cop car in Nottinghamshire ever caught Slow when he was racing. Unfortunately, after a while, they all knew where he lived, so they didn't have to chase him at all. They just went round to his house and sat and had tea with his mum while they waited for him to come home. Such is fame.

The speed had woken Dave up in the back seat.

"Woss going on?"

"Cops are after us."

"Yeah?"

"Slow's going to lose 'em, so get belted up."

"Hang on, I can't get it fastened," he complained, stretching the fabric over his belly. Right enough, the seat belt was adjusted for someone of normal size, like me.

"For God's sake, breathe in or something. The track's coming up."

It was no more than a fire break in the woods really, but the kids used it a lot, and the corners were nicely chewed off. Slow Kid seemed to reckon he could make it, even at sixty miles an hour. We might mangle the undergrowth, but who cares about a few bits of broken bracken? Would it ruin the ambience of the ancient woodland beauty spot? I think not. Doncaster Dave's weight falling around the car willy nilly was a different matter. It would be like steering a rowing boat with an elephant balanced on the side. There was a lot of grunting, and finally I heard the click of the belt.

"Now - lean this way!"

We both lurched to the right just as Slow Kid jumped on the brakes and spun the wheel to the left. Thank God I went for something with power steering as well as four-wheel drive. Dirt sprayed and the back end swung towards a birch tree, scything down bracken and brambles. But the wheels stayed on the track and we kept going, accelerating up towards the trees. It would be no problem to lose the cops once we got on the hill.

"Can you see them?"

Dave turned round and watched the end of the track.

"Yeah, lights," he said, just before we disappeared from view round the first bend.

Slow Kid was away now. If he took a left turn by the wrecked Nissan that was up there and went round the pond, we'd be on the far side of the hill and into the access road for the pumping station. The cops would never follow us. They're all townies, and it's a different world out here.

"Still see anything?"

"No. Have we lost 'em, Stones?"

"Maybe."

The Nissan had been there a long time, just a blackened lump of metal now. Slow Kid knew exactly where it was on the track and screeched round with inches to spare. Then, up ahead, there was another car. It was a Peugeot hatchback, its lights off and its windows smashed. Three kids stood round it pouring petrol onto the seats. They were laughing and shouting to each other as they got ready for their bit of excitement. They looked up in amazement as our tyres slid round the corner and our headlights caught them.

Slow Kid pulled the wheel to the right and the car tilted at an angle as we skidded half off the track to get past. The white face of one lad was so close to the window as we went by that I could have counted the spots on his chin. The kids didn't have time to react before we were past them and away again. One more minute, though, and we could have been copying those stunt riders who go through burning hoops.

"Close thing, that," said Slow cheerfully as he floored the accelerator and got back onto the track to take the hill.

A minute later we heard a bang and the horrible grinding of crumpled metal. I craned my neck to look down through the trees and saw lights down below and figures milling about. I thought I could hear voices, too - several of them, and they sounded angry.

"Looks like one of them expensive German jobs. Saloon car."

"Nice motor," said Slow Kid.

We drove on for a few minutes, then Slow Kid stopped on the edge of the access road, killed the lights and switched off the engine. I pressed the button to lower the window.

All we could hear were an owl complaining in the woods and the sound of someone having a party down on the estate below us. It sounded like Meatloaf's *Bat out of Hell* turned up to full volume. I kind of wished I was there right now.

"Nothing. We lost 'em."

"We going to the Shah Naz now then, Stones?"

"Right, Donc."

The Naz it was. Maybe I'd find the party later. We'd gone like bats out of hell ourselves for a few minutes there, I thought. But hell was closer than I knew right then.

10

On Tuesday morning I called some of the boys round for an emergency meeting. There were three of them making my sitting room look untidy. Untidier than usual.

"We lost another load last night," I told them.

"Shit, Stones, what's going on?"

Slow was slouched on my second armchair, kicking his trainers over the arm like some street kid. Metal Jacket was flat on his back on the floor, meditating or something. There wasn't much room for him on the settee, because it was occupied by Doncaster Dave.

"I don't know," I said. "I'm getting nowhere and things just keep getting worse."

"It's a pisser all right."

"Is it the police?" asked Metal.

"No, no. Somebody's tipping them off, that's what."

"Only, I hope it isn't my fault, what with that nicked motor, you remember. The Citroen."

"I don't think so, Metal. Forget it."

"Ta."

They all had cans of Mansfield Bitter in their hands, at my expense. It was supposed to make their brains work, ease their ideas out. But it wasn't having any effect so far.

"What you going to do then, Stones?"

"Yeah, what you going to do?" That was Metal, doing his impersonation of an echo.

"Some planning meeting this is, if all you lot can do is sit there and ask me what I'm going to do. Why does it have to me who has the ideas? You've all got a brain, haven't you?"

Slow Kid did an eye roll towards Dave. "Sort of. Well, two out of three ain't bad."

Dave stirred, like a slag heap settling. "Is he taking the piss, Stones?"

"Never mind, Donc. We'll skip the brains bit. What we need is some cunning."

"Right," said Slow.

"Right, right," said Metal.

"Uh?"

"The thing that's worrying me now is Eddie Craig."

"No. You think he's in this somewhere, Stones? That's real bad," said Slow Kid.

"Me and Dave saw his lads last night at the Ferret. And they were looking for Mick Kelk. It's like they were just a few minutes behind us, as if they knew where I was going and what I was doing. I don't like that."

"You could have sorted 'em out, Donc, yeah?"

"Yeah."

"Baffled 'em with your wit, I bet."

"Eh?"

"Only Stones is always saying we've got the brains to take this market."

"What you on about?"

"Give over, Slow."

"Is he taking the piss again, Stones?"

"Here, have these biscuits, Donc."

"Right."

"You think Craig's got it in for us? Is he trying to sink us just when we're getting going?"

"Could be, Slow. Maybe he sees us as a threat."

"But we're not, though. Nowhere near. Hasn't he got the sense?"

"Doubt it."

We all thought about Eddie Craig for a bit. At least I did, and I reckon Slow Kid did. Not Dave, obviously. And Metal Jacket looked to be asleep, dreaming of Morris Travellers.

"What can we do then, Stones?"

"Hell, I dunno. Just keep our eyes and ears open. And be careful."

"Yeah, right."

106

"That includes you too, Metal."

"What? Course."

"We keep our heads down. Keep out of the way of the cops, don't try anything too ambitious. And don't attract attention."

"You going to keep Dave indoors then?"

Doncaster Dave looked pissed off, and I'd run out of chocolate digestives. It was time to bring the meeting to an end.

*　*　*　*

I wanted some time to turn things over in my mind, but Nuala didn't understand. Does she ever? She can't get the idea that sometimes people need to think about what's going on in their lives. Thinking doesn't feature much in Nuala's lifestyle. Basically, it's something unpleasant that happens to her brain when she has to stop talking.

You'll have noticed that she doesn't give up talking very often. Maybe it's like that film a few years ago - you remember, *Speed*, with Keanu Reeves? Where he has to keep driving the bus, because if the speed drops below fifty miles an hour a bomb will go off? Maybe if Nuala stops talking at fifty miles an hour her head will explode. It's just a theory.

The person I really needed to talk to at the moment was Lisa, but she'd swanned off to Sheffield. Heritage Bleedin' Management. When was she back? Thursday? And she hadn't even phoned me, had she?

For some reason, this made me feel really bad. I dwelled on it for a while, until it really rankled. Then I found myself on the phone ringing a list of hotels in the centre of Sheffield. Did they have a Heritage Management course on? They wanted to know who was running it. But how the hell could I tell them that? I hadn't asked.

After a lot of this stuff, I finally got through to the Old Victoria Hotel. It felt like the three hundredth phone call I'd made, and I was losing enthusiasm. So it took me a bit by surprise when they asked for the delegate's name and said they would get a message to her when her seminar broke up for lunch.

I put the phone down regretting what I'd done. What was Lisa going to think when she got the message? 'Here's Stones, phoning up to pester me. He can't do without me even for a couple of days.' Oh, shit. What a mess. That wasn't what I wanted at all.

I still had this feeling inside, as if I was missing something that I really ought to take notice of.

Slow Kid called in. "I got the word out about that roof job, Stones."

"That's good, Slow. Thanks."

"You want me and Dave to lean on the boys that done it when we find 'em?"

"I mainly want them to put the roof back, Slow."

"Yeah? Them roof slates sell really well. There's lots of places being worked on out Retford way, and that. Old barns and things. The council tells the builders they got to use old slates, like. But the builders can't get hold of enough of them."

"I want them put back," I said.

"Right, right." I heard him make a mental note. I knew it would get done.

Next I had to drive down to the cop shop at Ollerton with Dave so that we could make statements about our little French connection. There was no sign of Moxon and Stubbs, which was a small mercy. We just got some DC, with a pimply youth in police uniform to do the writing. There was nothing they could argue with really. It was all down to a communication problem. This is one of the major benefits of the European Union - there are a lot more communication problems to blame when things go wrong.

Dave's statement was pretty brief anyway, and it was all in words of half a syllable. Even the young bobby had no difficulty writing it down. But then they really threw Dave with a tough one when they asked him to sign his name. After a bit, they were panicking about whether to send for a doctor to see if he'd gone into a coma. But I took pity on them and dictated it to him a letter at a time. 'D' for dinner, 'a' for afters... otherwise, we could have been there all day.

I was feeling even more depressed by the time we got back to Sherwood Crescent. It was this depression that made me do the one thing that brought me even worse trouble. I took a walk up through the estate to see if it would give me any ideas.

You might not think the Forest can possibly be the sort of place to bring anybody inspiration but you'd be wrong. Sometimes it tells me what's up with the world.

Take a look down First Avenue, for example. You can see down the hill into Oak Avenue and right round the corner into Birch and Maple Crescents. There are rows and rows of grey council houses with tiny porches over their front doors. Those porches are covered by a sheet of lead to keep the rain out. If you can collect enough of them, you can turn the lead in for scrap. Some of the kids take it as a challenge to see how many they can strip.

If you look a bit closer, you'll see that the latest in style round here is to decorate the top of your porch with one of those garden ornaments made out of resin and moulded into the shape of an animal, like an otter or a toad, really rural. Or an Alsatian dog maybe, if you want to look tough. The trouble is, they don't wear well in the weather up there, and nobody ever takes them down for cleaning. So after a while it's like looking at the grisly trophies that used to be stuck over the huts of Celtic tribesmen to warn strangers away. Maybe it has some deep significance, I don't know.

The estate is in two halves really. The older streets at Top Forest are the old British Coal houses. They were actually built by the company that sank Medensworth pit, long before nationalisation and the NCB. Medensworth was one of that flurry of pits sunk in the 1920s, along with Rufford, Clipstone, Ollerton, Blidworth and Thoresby. Suddenly mineral railways and headstocks appeared everywhere among the farms and woods. Huge splodges of miners' houses were grafted onto traditional farming villages. Planned communities, these were called. They have geometric rows and terraces, and grid pattern streets. They didn't need names for these streets - they were called First Avenue, Second Avenue and Third Avenue.

A lot of pit owners took a paternal interest in their employees. The company had complete control over its tenants, giving it the sort of power that the lord of the manor might have envied. At one time, different grades of employees occupied particular streets -

such as at Edwinstowe, where only colliery officials lived in First Avenue. The company owners themselves tended to move into prestige residences. Montague Wright of Butterley Company lived in Ollerton Hall - now derelict and awaiting conversion into a Sue Ryder Home.

At Bestwood, where the first shaft was sunk by the Bestwood Coal and Iron Company in 1872, an entire village was built. The houses all have the initials of the company, BCIC, over the front door, just in case the serfs forgot who they belonged to. When a new village was built for miners at Shireoaks pit, the place was even named after the boss of the mining company. Unfortunately, his name was Rhodes. That's why we now have a place called Rhodesia in North Nottinghamshire, which is about as far as you can get from Central Africa. If you start to look, there's not much difference between these mine owners and the dukes, is there?

Later on, British Coal came up for privatisation, and it sold off all its pit houses. They went into the hands of private landlords.

Down on Bottom Forest, though, the houses are a bit newer, and they're council houses. You can buy your council house these days, and some folk have done just that. You can tell the ones - where the open front gardens have been fenced in with wavy lines of larchlap panelling, like the stockade of a little Englishman's castle. Owning property does funny things to your mind. It can even make you plant a privet hedge.

Some of these houses are tarted up with leaded windows, or even a mock brass carriage lamp by the front door. It's like folk are saying they aren't on a council estate at all, but really belong up Budby Road, where all the big houses are with their landscaped lawns and wrought iron gates.

These leaded windows and carriage lamps say you think you're too good for your neighbours. It's like you're expecting the chauffeur to bring the Bentley round to the front door at any moment, except he can't get it past the second-hand caravan parked on the concrete apron where the front garden used to be, and he's worried about scraping the paintwork on the old Mini Cooper with its wheels off that's been standing in the driveway for the past eight years. The servants just don't put things away properly, do they?

But the most common decoration on the front of these houses is the satellite dish. Your kids can do without clothes, you can go without proper food for weeks, and you can fail to pay the rent, your Council Tax or your court fines. But you've got to have the satellite dish. It's still number one on the list of essentials items for the nub end of the 1990s.

These things tell me what's wrong with the world. It's like all the money's going to Rupert Murdoch, who already has more than enough, thank you very much. And there are lots more Rupert Murdochs around, only they don't make such a shout about it. I read the figures once. They were printed in The Sun, with a diagram. They said the income of the top tenth of society grew by over fifty per cent in the 1980s and 90s, but the income of the bottom tenth actually fell by eighteen per cent. Well, these are the bottom tenth, right here. You don't have to look any further.

Now, they tell us that one child in three lives in a poor household, the highest rate of any European country. A lot of these kids are suffering ill health and stunted growth because of their lousy diet. Well, the European Union has done one thing for us anyway - it's helped us to compare ourselves to others and see what a pathetic state we're in.

Sometimes it feels like there's a mountain to climb. Usually it's on days like these that the mountain seems highest. Why don't I just forget about all this and concentrate on lining my own pocket like everyone else is doing? Why don't I sell up and move to somewhere with warmer rain, like Devon? Well, it's tempting, now and then. Otherwise, I'm going to end up as another daft old sod in a nursing home.

*　*　*　*

Dave was with me on my stroll, but as usual he wasn't making with the witty conversation too much. Eventually we reached the end of the estate and turned the corner onto Ollerton Road, at the end of the village's main shopping street.

It hadn't dawned on me that we'd come out near McDonald's until Dave suddenly began to veer towards the arched entrance as if drawn by a huge, golden magnet.

"All right, then. Maybe a burger and fries will help me think."

There are no tattooed waitresses in McDonald's, so I thought Dave's attention might be totally occupied by the food. This turned out to be almost true, but not quite.

We'd collected what seemed like a huge stack of containers oozing various appetising smells and we were winding our way to a convenient table. This takes a bit of doing, because Dave doesn't fit too easily between tables in these places. He needs a stretch of clear water, like a cruise liner negotiating its way into harbour. While we were doing this, I half noticed four blokes come through the door. I paid a lot more attention when they gathered round us, as if desperately wanting to share our large fries.

"Are you McClure?" said the one in front.

First off, I had this lot pegged as a dissatisfied customer and his mates. It happens now and then. Ungrateful lot the punters, sometimes. They find out they've been ripped off, and some jerk tips them my name, so they come looking for a bit of compensation. It's a sad old world. But you see why I need Doncaster Dave on the payroll.

Yes, these were definitely amateur talent. Local accents, cheap trainers. It's pitiful, really. A few half-hearted bottle fights down the pub on a Saturday night and they all think they're the Terminator. I could have told them they were wrong. The real Terminator was standing just behind me, waiting for a signal.

"We want a word with you, McClure."

This bloke doing the talking, now. He was trying to look hard, but he was dressed in a leather jacket and chains. He had three days of stubble - and he was even wearing shades, for God's sake, as if Medensworth had been transplanted to California suddenly. If you have to dress up to look hard, then you're not hard at all really, just fashion conscious.

"You want a word? How about 'piss off'," I said, trying out the theory. "No, sorry - that's two words, isn't it?"

"Save the clever shit. Just put the stuff down and come outside where we can talk private, like."

"Sorry, but I can't talk on an empty stomach. So you might as well piss off anyway."

He was starting to get annoyed, but I didn't care. At least, not until I noticed that the bloke standing behind him had a noticeable bulge in his jacket pocket. Bulges make me nervous. Somebody can get hurt when there are bulges about, amateur or not. The other two lads had edged their way round so they were near Dave. They were watching him curiously as he dipped into one of the cartons with his fingers and started poking french fries into his mouth.

"I won't say it again," snarled the bloke with the shades, saying it again. "Outside."

I turned to look at Dave. He looked pretty casual, as if the whole thing had nothing to do with him. He'd keep like that for as long as I stayed relaxed.

Dave picks things up like a dog does. I don't mean sticks and slippers and things, but atmospheres and intentions. Just like a good dog can sense you're upset, Donc knows when I'm worried, or I'm about to do something risky. Like an Alsatian or a Rottweiler, he recognises danger and reacts accordingly. I hoped his instincts were working properly right now. There are times when you need a Rottweiler instead of a dopey Labrador. In other words, I was about to do something risky.

"Oh shit," I said. "Hold these a minute."

I shoved the stack of polystyrene containers at the lad with the shades, and he held his hands out and took them automatically. Then he looked round, puzzled, to see what was happening. That was two mistakes at once, so he was definitely an amateur. I grabbed his jacket, swung him round and hoisted him halfway into the air, straight into his mate with the bulge in his pocket. Fries and burgers went flying everywhere. Shades got a face full of Chicken McNuggets, and a carton of coke exploded and soaked two teenage girls sitting with their mouths open. Meanwhile, Dave had come awake, both hands reaching out deceptively slowly to grab the collars of the other two lads. They stood frozen like rabbits in car headlights as his massive fists closed around their jackets and their heads jerked forward to meet each other with a horrible crack. They both fell face forward on the nearest table, which happened to be empty but for the salt. Trust Dave not to waste any food.

A moment later we'd got out of the door of McDonald's without even being wished a nice day. Remind me to complain to Ronald some time about the standard of service.

"Stones?" said Dave as we legged it through the car park and over the back fence.

"Yeah?"

"Do you think I should have shown them my trick shot again?"

I laughed for second or two, breathlessly, as I ran.

"What do you mean, again? Had you seen them before?"

"A couple."

I was amazed at this. With Dave's memory, it would have to be in the last twenty-four hours for him to remember a face.

"Where did you see them?"

"Last night, yeah?"

"Yeah? What, you mean in the Ferret? Mick Kelk's mates?"

"Nah, not his mates. The other lot."

I thought about this. I recollected my hasty exit, hidden behind Dave's shoulder. I'd seen them coming, but my eye had been fixed on the one in front, Sledgehammer Stan, though there had been at least three others with him. Of course, Dave had seen them all right.

"With the broken-nosed bloke, Stones."

"Shit, Donc. Were those Eddie Craig's lads?"

"That's them," he said. "See, I remembered."

＊　　＊　　＊　　＊

Nuala did her best to take my mind of things later on. As it was her afternoon off, we were able to spend some time on foreplay, which means Nuala talking and me thinking about something else. She'd noticed I was a bit fed up, and she was trying really hard. She gave me a talk on the attractions of the Seychelles as an exclusive holiday destination that was first choice for the discerning travel customer. I guessed it was word for word from the seminar she'd been to that day, but with more body language. Eventually, she got herself into such a heated state that she had to start taking her clothes off. Now she was talking.

And then the mobile phone rang.

Well, you can't ignore a ringing phone. It might be business. But when I put it to my ear there was nothing. I said 'hello' all the same. These digitals are supposed to be safe, so that no one can tap into your line and listen to your calls. If that wasn't true, then I was going to sue somebody. Probably Bob Hoskins or Buzby. Somebody, anyway.

But there was a caller there, something like a heavy breather except the breathing sounded faint. Then a distant voice said 'hello' like it was talking to itself and knew the men in white coats were about to come and cart her away for it. It was a female voice, and that was about all I could tell you.

I mentally ran through the list of females that might have my mobile phone number and discovered that it was a pretty long list. I made myself a note to change my number soon.

I said 'hello' again, louder. I got a surprised 'yes' in reply. Then there was more silence. This didn't seem to be getting us anywhere. I tried a 'who's that?' and the breathing became more rapid, as if the mere sound of my voice had stirred up somebody at the other end. But then I always seem to have that effect on women. It didn't narrow it down at all.

"Is that Stones?"

At least that was clear, but it was like a radio station fading in and out of reception.

"Yes. Who is that?"

"Ah. It's Angie Thompson here."

"Who?"

The voice repeated the name, but seemed to be talking to someone else. I wondered whether she had the phone upside down or something.

"Can you speak towards the phone, Angie? I can't hardly hear you."

The next minute I was deafened by a bellow from the earpiece.

"Is that better? I'm not used to these things. That is Stones, isn't it?"

"Yes, Angie, it's Stones. What's the problem?"

"They've taken Lloyd."

"What? What? Who's taken who?"

"It's Lloyd. They've been and taken him. That is Stones, isn't it? He said to ring Stones."

My brain must have been affected by too much tequila or too much Nuala, but at last it was starting to click into place. It was just that Lloyd was never a name we thought to use for Mrs Thompson's little boy.

"Slow Kid? Are you talking about Slow Kid?"

"Yes, that's what you call him, isn't it? But they didn't - they called him Lloyd, very polite."

"Who did?"

"The police. Didn't I say? The police have been and taken him away."

"Tell me what happened, Angie."

"They came to the house, two of them. Not uniforms, the others, you know. Detectives. And they asked for Lloyd Thompson. Then they took him away."

"Did you get their names? Did they say what they were taking him in for? Was he arrested?"

"I don't know, I don't know. So many questions, Stones. They were asking questions too. But I'm sure Lloyd didn't know the answers." She paused. "I think that's why they took him away."

"Is that what they said - they were taking him for questioning?"

"That's right."

"They didn't arrest him? Did they read him his rights and all that?"

"No, they didn't. That's right. They can't have arrested him, can they, Stones?"

Angie Thompson knew about arrests. Her middle son had only recently spent a spell in Lincoln Prison, after all. And then there was Slow Kid's father. He hadn't been seen around for quite a few years, and it wasn't because he was shy.

"These police. What were they like?"

"Oh, now. The one who did the talking had glasses. Very polite, he was. A nice man. The other was fatter, not so nice."

A poor judge of character, Angie Thompson. But then she'd married Slow's father, so it was too late to expect anything better.

"Was it Inspector Moxon?"

"Maybe." she sounded doubtful. "Can you get him back, Stones?"

"I don't know," I said, honestly. "What were they asking questions about?"

"I can't remember. They took me by surprise, you know, otherwise I would've got him out the back. I don't know what they were saying. But Lloyd didn't do it, whatever it was. I could tell."

At least she didn't claim, like so many mothers, that her little Johnny wouldn't do anything like that and never got into any trouble. A mother's love is blind sometimes. Even Jack the Ripper was probably a poor misunderstood boy as far as his mum was concerned.

"I'll see what I can do, Angie. Is it Lloyd's mobile you're using? Will you hang on to it? If it rings, tell people to phone me?"

"I'll try. Get him back, won't you, Stones?"

I closed the call without promising anything. I don't like to promise things I might not be able to do, and this came into the category. And so, unfortunately, did what Nuala wanted me just now. You can't concentrate when you're worried.

"I have to make a few calls."

"Now?"

"Yeah."

"That's not fair."

"Tough. There's things I've got to do."

"Does that mean I've got to get dressed?"

"Not if you don't want." Well, there's nothing wrong with a decent view while you're working.

The first call was to Ralph Catchlock. Ralph is a defence solicitor, and if Ralph can't get you to walk you haven't got legs. Slow Kid wouldn't be on his own down the station for long. Then I made a few more calls, putting feelers out, calling in a few favours, even where I didn't have any owing. I needed to know what was going on. It made me mad to think of Moxon sneaking round to knock on the Thompsons' door, while me and Dave had actually been down the nick doing our duty voluntarily.

Picturing Frank Moxon completely ruined the effect of Nuala lounging around the house in her knickers. She must have noticed my expression, because she got dressed and started to talk to the picture of my mum and dad over the fireplace while I was still on the phone. One of the lads I'd rung thought it might be worth mentioning a bit of action that was supposed to be going on up the top end of the estate. He didn't know if it was relevant. But, relevant or not, I was clutching at straws just now.

11

An hour or two later, and I was left feeling strangely dissatisfied. The calls I needed to make about Slow Kid had already been made, and now all I could do was wait for results. So far, I didn't even know what the coppers were questioning him about, or whether they might charge him. What did they think they could prove?

But there were other causes for anxiety. Some of them made themselves obvious as soon as I started to take the afternoon's calls on the mobile. There were two abort messages, jobs that had been called off or gone wrong. A trailer load of computer parts parked up near Worksop had already been nicked by somebody else when we got there. A delivery of watches and jewellery from Birmingham had failed to arrive for no apparent reason.

The occasional abort does happen. Sometimes people turn out to be not quite so stupid as they seem. Sometimes the coppers stumble across something by accident and we have to back off. Two aborts in one day seemed like bad luck. An omen, if you like. I rang up one or two of the boys, but they didn't seem too bothered. They mostly wanted to ask about Slow Kid. But their talk didn't make me feel any better. Time to clutch at those straws.

"Nuala, I have to go out for a bit."

"Oh, where are we going?"

"I said I was going out for a bit." Nuala's a bit slow sometimes, and I have to repeat things.

"If you think I'm stopping in this place on my own, you've got another think coming. I've got better things to do."

"Look, you'd only be bored. Anyway, it's business."

"Where are we going?"

"I'm going up Top Forest. Just to see some people."

"Wonderful. I'd like to meet some of your friends."

"Who said anything about friends?"

"Will I need my coat?"

"Only a bullet-proof vest."

"Just let me tidy my make-up."

"Nuala, you're not coming."

"Won't be a sec."

Naturally, I walked straight out of the door, pulling on my leather jacket as I went. You can't let women argue with you like that.

But when I got the door of the Impreza open, somehow Nuala was already sitting in the passenger seat doing her lipstick. Her skirt was up round her bum as usual and she looked like she was ready for a Saturday night disco.

"Out of the car," I said.

"What do you think of this colour?" she said, dabbing at her lips. "It's a bit darker than what I normally use."

"Look, you're not coming."

"You don't like it, do you?"

"It's fine, but - "

"I got it to match my hair."

"Nuala -"

"I suppose you don't like my hair either."

I turned on the engine and pulled away from the kerb. I recognised the horrible whine in a woman's voice that warns you she's about to cry or sulk unless you do exactly what she wants. It was better to take her up Top Forest than tolerate that. There's only so much I can bear in one day.

"I could always dye it blonde," she said.

*   *   *   *

Like a lot of these estates, you can easily get lost on the Forest if you don't know the place. There's no sign of a way out once you're in. It's a bit like a maze - any turning could lead you to a dead end or into a crescent that will just bring you back to where you started from. When you stumble on the little shopping parade in the middle, it's always a surprise. To a stranger, it must look like an oasis in a desert of Transit vans and Sky TV. Some oasis. Peter

120

Malik at Malik's Late Night Superstore, Off Licence and Video Hire Centre is always complaining that he spends half his life directing strangers off the estate. It's best to ask Peter, though, rather than one of the kids on the street - they'll most likely direct you into someone's back garden and nick your spare wheel while they're doing it.

Yes, the kids play on the streets here - at least they do down in Bottom Forest. It's really because the streets weren't made for cars, like I said. Once you get cars and vans parked on both sides of the street, the traffic ain't coming through too fast. If it's anything wider than a Transit, it ain't coming through at all. If you have a chip pan fire at the weekend round here, you don't call the fire brigade, you have to call the next door neighbour to come round with a spare blanket. By the time the fire engine gets through, your whole house could be frying.

On the newer, more open sort of streets up Top Forest, it's a bit different. This is where the joy riders rule. The county council has put speed humps here to stop them. Traffic calming, it's called. It took them months to do it, because they couldn't leave any equipment or materials on site overnight. They had to pack it all up and take it away every night and bring it all back again from the depot next morning. Otherwise it would have been regarded as surplus, and there would have been none of it left within twenty-four hours.

Anyway, they've put these little red hillocks in the roadway and bollards either side to narrow the road down to one car's width. The only people it slows down are folk like me, the ones who are worried about damaging the suspension on their nice new Toyotas. And there's nothing calming about that. Of course, the chuffin' joy riders aren't bothered - it's not their cars they're driving, is it? They're nicked, didn't you know? In fact, these lads soon found out that if you hit the humps fast enough, you could get airborne. Wowee, new game. Traffic calming? What a load of crap.

So the young kids stay off the street up in Top Forest. You never know when some pillock's going to come screaming round the corner on two wheels, dead set on killing himself and anybody else who gets in the way. But there *are* places to play. In two directions, the estate peters out into the edge of heathland to the north of the village. There's also the car park of the old Miners Welfare. The Welfare's not a bad place to go, in fact. The beer's still cheap in there, and the pool tables are free. There just aren't any miners.

Nuala chatted happily as we drove up the estate. She seemed to be commenting on the choice of curtains in the houses that we passed. Then she started cooing over the fact that someone had attached a bit of trellising to the wall next to their front door and had managed to get a clematis to survive long enough to produce a flower. I thought for a minute she was going to tell me to phone Homes and Gardens with the news.

There weren't many people about, except at the shops. There were a few blokes hanging around outside the betting shop and the newsagent's. They weren't speaking to each other. In fact, they had nothing much to do except kick used crisp packets about on the pavement until they were too wet and shredded to move. Anywhere else, it might have been an aluminium drinks can they were kicking. But those cans are like gold round here. If you drop one, a kid will dash up and grab it before it has chance to hit the floor. Crisp packets don't make good substitutes - instead of a satisfactory rattling, there's nothing but a pathetic rustle. That says it all, really.

Malik's Superstore was open as usual, but the chippie was shut and its steel shutter was firmly down. The hairdresser's and the motor spares shop didn't look like they were doing much business. The other two units had been closed and derelict for a long time. A few starlings were perched on the edge of the roof, picking at the weeds growing in the gutters.

This area around the shops is about the only place on the estate where you can find rubbish bins. They're put there by the council for the empty chip papers. But the bins are red and they look ridiculously like post boxes, so people sometimes get them mixed up. I mean, they drop bits of burning paper into the litter bins to set fire to them, when they really meant to drop them into the post boxes. They also get phone boxes mixed up with public toilets. I blame the teachers, you know. Why don't they give classes on this sort of thing? What hope have these kids got of landing a job in some high tech computer factory if they can't figure out whether you speak into a phone or piss on it?

I found two of the blokes I wanted standing with some mates looking into the engine compartment of a Ford Capri. This is a favourite hobby round here, when there's nothing much on the telly. Engine compartments can be really, really interesting when you've been on the dole for a bit.

Jeff and Colin are ex-miners, employed at Medensworth Colliery up to the day it shut. Their dads had worked there as well, and probably their granddads. But their sons never would.

"Hey up, lads."

"Hey up," said Jeff cautiously. It was his driveway, so he was the spokesman. The others just nodded at me. Then I saw them all turn and stare at the Subaru behind me at the kerb. I gathered that Nuala was getting out. And I'd specifically told her to stay in the car, no matter what. I could well imagine the bits of her that were showing as she struggled to make it to the pavement in that skirt. They were bits that some of these lads probably hadn't seen since they retired the pit ponies.

Four pairs of eyes swivelled as Nuala came to stand at my side, hitching up her blouse where it had fallen open a bit more over her lacy bra.

"Hello," she said. "I'm Nuala."

She didn't even get a nod in reply. She might be the most exciting thing they'd seen all month, but she was only a woman.

"I'm a friend of Stones," she tried again.

This made no impression either, except that one or two of them looked from her to me and quickly back again. You could see their minds making the connections in all the right places.

"Are you friends of Stones too?"

Nothing.

Well, this was really good. Compared to them, I was going to seem really courteous and caring to Nuala from now on. I might be a bit rough and ready, but at least I know how to be polite to a woman.

"Piss off back to the car, you silly tart," I said. "You're in the bloody way."

Nuala sniffed and backed off a bit towards the Subaru. I knew she hadn't actually got in. I knew this not only because I didn't hear the car door shut, but also because there were four pairs of eyes angled past me on a course that I reckoned would end at about Nuala's thigh level. I guessed she was doing her Motor Show pose draped over the bonnet. I tried to act as if this was perfectly normal.

"I'm looking for some help," I said.

I had their attention a bit now.

"What sort of help?" asked Jeff.

He was looking hopeful suddenly, as if he thought I might need some help with Nuala. Well, I did, but not that sort of help.

"I know you blokes keep your eyes open. I wondered if you'd noticed anybody new working this part of the estate. Anyone selling, you know what I mean?"

They knew what I meant all right. When I said 'you keep your eyes open' they knew I meant 'you lot are all unemployed and have got nothing better to do.'

"We don't take any notice," said Jeff. "Why should we?"

"You care about what goes on round here, don't you?"

"Maybe. But that's our business."

"No bugger bothers about us, do they?" said Colin. "Forgotten about us, they have. The council, police, government. Nobody gives a toss about us down here. We've got the worst crime rate in the area, but we haven't had a beat bobby walk down this end of the village for years. And do you know they're shutting the old community house now? So why should we help anybody?"

"That's terrible," said Nuala, moving away from the car again, ears flapping. "Somebody ought to do something. There should be a community action group."

They looked at her, then back at me. I was starting to get the impression they felt sorry for me.

"You know I can make it worth your while."

"What's this, charity?" snapped Colin.

"No. Payment. Information is valuable."

"Well..."

"Well?"

"There might have been some bugger," admitted Jeff.

"Who?"

"Don't know his name. Our Ryan said this bloke come up to him and some of his mates outside the Welfare. They'd never seen him before. He was selling."

"Drugs?"

"Well, he weren't the Avon lady," said Jeff.

"What did he look like?"

"You'd have to ask Ryan. He's down at the rec, playing football."

"Okay. Anybody else?"

"There was that car hanging about," said Colin.

"Yeah? Whereabouts?"

"Couple of places I've seen it. Same car. Waiting, like."

"What make of car?"

"Dunno. Blue-coloured thing. German. Not the usual sort of motor that visits round here. You'd think it might be the doctor on a call or something. But it wasn't, not this one."

"Oh yeah, and somebody from the Gazette was round asking questions," said Jeff.

The local press? Blimey, it must have been something earth shattering like a golden wedding to bring them out onto the Forest Estate.

"What were they after?"

"Background."

"Eh?"

"That's what they called it. Two of them, there were. One with a camera. Doing an article on drugs."

"What did you tell them?"

"Nowt. We don't talk to the Gazette."

I bit my lip impatiently, but said nothing. I knew it would be a waste of time. Not good old Nuala, though. She walked straight into it.

"Why not?" she said. "Have they done something to upset you?"

Jeff and Colin turned to look at her as if she was an invader from the planet Mars, or maybe even some soft southerner who didn't know any better. For a moment, it seemed as though they were just going to ignore her question. She was still only a woman. But a faint stirring of defensiveness won the day.

"We don't talk to the Gazette since the strike," said Jeff. "Nobody does."

Nuala had every right to look gobsmacked at this. The miners' strike was in 1984. To her, it was ancient history. It might as well have happened just after the Battle of Hastings and the Spanish Armada. It was something you read about in books that have grainy black and white photographs of men with donkey jackets and long sideburns standing round braziers, facing columns of helmeted police. Maybe, at a pinch, you might accidentally catch a snippet of TV archive footage showing Arthur Scargill in full rant, his words meaning no more to anybody now than King Harold's address to his troops before Hastings - and I'm not forgetting the fact that Harold would have been speaking in Anglo Saxon.

But these men were ex-miners who'd lived through the strike, and they had long memories. Come to think of it, they still had the donkey jackets and the sideburns too.

Although geographically in Nottinghamshire, some of the local pits had been part of British Coal's South Yorkshire area. In the Yorkshire coalfields they were NUM men, the National Union of Mineworkers, some of Scargill's brave, ageing lads. The breakaway union, the UDM, had recruited its members from the Nottinghamshire coalfield, whose pits that stood no more than a mile or two away. It was no wonder this had been the scene of so many bitter confrontations.

But Nuala wasn't to know that. She'd missed the mass pickets and the intimidation, the armies of police, the strike-breakers and the communities ripped apart by violent feuding. She wasn't to know that these men had taken a decision not to talk to their local paper following a front page editorial during the strike urging them to go back to work. As far as they were concerned, the paper had taken sides, and it had been the wrong side - the side of Maggie Thatcher and the bosses. The decision not to speak to the Gazette had probably been taken during a heated meeting of an NUM branch that was now long since defunct.

Their pit itself had closed years ago. The newspaper had been taken over by a big national group, and the owners and editors had

126

all moved on since 1984. But Jeff and Colin were still sticking to the decision not to speak to the Gazette. They would stick to it until they died. They were NUM men.

"It seems a bit short-sighted to me," said Nuala.

For God's sake, didn't she get the vibes? I thought women were supposed to be sensitive to people's feelings? These blokes were suddenly giving off hostility like a barbed wire fence. And if their thoughts weren't enough, they were giving it some body language too - shoulders hunched forward, heads lowered like bulls about to charge, eyes staring unblinking at this irritating thing in their midst. Their sideburns bristled like the spines of hedgehogs about to perforate an inquisitive cat.

"Well, I mean - they could help you, couldn't they? If you asked them, they might give you some support here. A bit of publicity for your problems."

God knows what might have happened if the Fiesta XR2 hadn't screamed round the corner on two wheels just at that moment. I don't suppose Jeff or Colin would actually have hit a woman. They might have taken the preferable course and hit me instead. Once the first fist went in, that would have been it - they would all have been on me. One in, all in. That's solidarity.

But as it was, they turned as a man, their jeans stretching over their spreading hips and their false teeth twitching angrily as they eyeballed the Fiesta and its occupants. The car bounced off one kerb and was in the air for a few seconds as it hit the speed ramp before disappearing round the next corner.

"Bloody joy riders!" said Colin.

"Who is it? We'll have the buggers."

"Them two pillocks from the Villas again."

"They'll kill somebody one day."

"It's their mam and dad's fault, I reckon. They've got no more sense than to let the silly sods do it."

"Let's go round there and sort 'em out."

"Aye, Jeff, you're right. Time somebody did that."

"Bloody police are useless, any road."

"Police? They'll be sitting on their arses at Ollerton."

"Come on, then."

And off they went, chuntering among themselves, suddenly converted from aggressive left-wing trade union radicals to equally aggressive reactionary property-owning citizens. The moment saved us - or me, at least. But it hadn't got us any further.

Before we got to the car, I stopped dead on the pavement and turned to speak to Nuala.

"Nuala - clear off. Go. Quick."

"Don't talk to me like that. I was only trying to help."

"Sod that. Will you just get away? Move!"

I gave her a shove that sent her tottering off down the street. She threw her arms in the air angrily and flounced off, muttering abuse. As she went, she got a couple of appreciative leers from the windows of the big car that had been cruising quietly up behind us. I must have been thinking too hard, or I would have noticed it before. Anyway, I stood quite still as it came alongside me, letting Nuala get clear.

A rear door came open as the Jaguar pulled into the kerb in front of a parked-up Transit van with a smashed wing. There were three lads in the car. The one in the back was Sledgehammer Stan, as ugly as ever. The other two looked like ageing rejects from the Hell's Angels, but without the bikes or the hair styles. I recognised the stubble on one of them. He'd left his shades off today - probably so that he could give me the evil eye better.

"McClure. Eddie wants to talk to you."

"Fine, fine. I'll give him a ring some time, when I'm not so busy."

I kept walking, at a brisk pace. I was gambling that Stan and his mates wouldn't resort to extreme violence here in the street in broad daylight, but it wasn't a certainty. Since there were three of them and only one of me, and one of them was Sledgehammer Stan, I'd already decided to co-operate for once, if they insisted. I know, I know - it's not like me, but it was one of those days. I just couldn't be bothered taking them on.

The car had to pull out to go round a roadside skip and an old Ford Cortina that hadn't moved for years. It wasn't likely to, either, with those bricks under the wheels. Then the Jag got back to the kerb and the door opened again.

"McClure. Get in."

"Nice of you to offer me a lift. But I've got an urgent appointment up the Cow's Arse."

"Eddie wants to talk to you *now*," said Stan.

No sense of humour, Stan. I reckon he's been watching too many films, the sort where the heavies only have one line. I knew better than to try engaging Sledgehammer or his mates in conversation. You can't communicate with pondlife.

Stan and one of the lads started to get out of the Jag. I resigned myself to a ride. Then they stopped and went suddenly into reverse. It was like one of those old silent films when they run the frames backwards for comic effect. Had they decided I was too hard for them after all? Had my wit put them off?

As the Jaguar pulled away and accelerated down the street, another motor came cruising the other way. This one was less flashy, a red Mondeo with mud splattered on its door panels and a pair of glasses glinting behind the windscreen. I kept walking. DI Frank Moxon may be slightly preferable to Sledgehammer Stan, but it doesn't mean I have to say thank you.

12

Then I remembered I'd promised to visit Uncle Willis. Rolling Meadows seemed as safe a place as any to be just now.

As I passed St Asaph's, I could see a local builder, Gary Lockman, and a youth I didn't know up a couple of ladders on the vestry roof. A second youth was helping Gary's mate pass up some roof tiles. It looked like the Rev was getting his hole fixed.

Gary spotted me as soon as I arrived, and his eyes lit up. The lads were doing it for nowt, of course, but Gary had to be paid - he has a legit business to run and a tax man to satisfy, poor sod.

"It's not my normal sort of job this, you know, Stones. I'm a craftsman builder, not a chuffin' social worker."

"Yeah, yeah."

"I mean, I've got to watch these kids all the time. They might nick me tools or something."

"Just let me have the bill, Gary, okay?"

"All right, all right. I'm only saying."

It does that to you, being legit. It makes you treat everybody else as though they're suspicious persons. I know this because I was legit myself once.

"Ah, the roof repair men," said the Rev's voice. "Thank you so much. It's wonderful, what you're doing here. God bless you all."

The Rev favoured Gary and the two sullen kids with his best smile. "Let me know when it's time for your break, gentlemen, and I'll brew up. Or mash the tea, as I'm told I should say in these parts."

The lads looked baffled. Naturally, they expected this poncy vicar bloke to be really pissed off with them for nicking his roof. And here he was thanking them and offering to brew up. But they didn't know the half of it. The Rev is on a totally different planet, permanently. I mean he's a brick short of a privy; a pickle short of a jar. This is the bloke who once found four glue sniffers in the churchyard just getting their snouts into the plastic bags behind one of those big eighteenth century tombs, where they'd pulled some stones down to crash out on. And what did he do? He only invited them into the vestry for a chat and a Bible reading. So they went in, laughing, taking the mickey, thinking they might do the old bloke over for the collection money. Six months later, two of them are still in the church choir and their spots have healed up.

I wanted to sneak away before the Rev started asking me about nuptials again. I sometimes think he has a one-track mind - he's always on about people making commitments. As if we could all commit ourselves to something, like he has. Just how long will he have to live in Medensworth before he discovers that you can't go looking for the good in everybody when there's none to be found? Commitment isn't in our shopping trolleys. They haven't sold it at Cost Cutters for years.

When I turned away from the Rev I almost bumped into a big, red-faced man with a grey moustache and no more than a few wisps of hair on his head. He was dressed in an old boiler suit, trouser legs tucked into a pair of boots as if he was ready for work. He was carrying an electric strimmer and a suspicious expression. Right now he was looking at the ladders propped against the wall of the vestry.

Welsh Border. How could my timing have been so bad?

"What's going on here, then?"

When he says that, he sounds so much like a copper it makes me want to reach for the roll of cash I keep in my back pocket for emergencies. I mean emergencies like a quick bung to keep me out of the nick. But it wouldn't work with Councillor Border anyway. Pillar of the community, he is. Straight as a die. He's making up for a lifetime working as a company accountant, you see. If you want a professional crook, try those guys. There's more money goes missing in the small print of company accounts every year than in a thousand Great Train Robberies. They call it modern business practice. I call it authorised robbery. Anyway, Councillor Border is desperately trying to balance his own personal profit and loss accounts before that Great Auditor in the Sky finally gets a look at his books. All right, you might say - let him get on with it. But the trouble is, he can't bear to let the rest of us get on with a bit of creative accounting of our own. Me, I'm happy to let the bottom line take care of itself. I don't need Welsh Border trying to keep me on the straight and narrow. And he's *so* suspicious. Unhealthy, that is.

"Where have those roof tiles come from? Who's paying for them?"

The last question pained the Rev. He prefers not to think about who's paying for things like this.

"Don't worry about it, Rev," I said quickly.

"Do you know who these people are, Mr Bowring?"

"Well, I'm sure - "

Whatever the Rev was sure of, it wasn't enough for Welsh. He recognised Gary, who was a perfectly reputable tradesman. But he was frowning at the two lads, and I could see him mentally slotting them into a category. No matter how right he might be in this case, I don't like to see that. It makes me go into righteous mode, and that's not a pretty sight. It can take me days to recover, and it feels like going I'm going through cold turkey. No wonder I try to avoid Welsh Border.

"And what's McClure got to do with it? If he's involved, there's something crooked going on. Mark my words, vicar."

"Oh no, that's a terrible thing to say."

The Rev was defending me like a martyr, bless him. He might be naive and ready to believe the best in people, but on the other hand Welsh is too clever for his own good. I know which I prefer. And it wasn't a very nice thing to say, was it? As a Christian, Welsh had definitely got on the wrong bus. I hate to admit that I worked for him at one time, in a way.

Me and the councillor eyeballed each other for a bit. This was the Rev's territory, and I didn't want to antagonise Welsh any more than necessary. It might become necessary at any moment, though.

"Livingstone and his friends have kindly volunteered to repair the damage to the vestry roof," pointed out the Rev in a hurt voice. There was a general shuffling of feet and dropping of jaws behind me as four pairs of ears picked up the word 'volunteered'. Not now, Gary, I thought - don't go on about your invoice right now.

"Very noble, I'm sure."

"The Lord provides a roof over our heads," said the Rev mysteriously. The Lord? I was impressed that he'd granted me a title, but I didn't really want it. Me and the nobility don't mix.

Welsh Border glowered at me again. It must be his party piece, he does it so often.

"Would you like to help us, Councillor Border?" I offered. "I'm sure we could find you some bricks that need chewing." There - you can't say I don't try to make peace.

The Rev hovered uncertainly, aware that the conversation was rising a bit above his level. Then he invited Welsh down to the bottom of the churchyard to look at some rhododendrons that might need tidying up. He gave the impression that only Councillor Border's opinion could decide their fate. It was like the intervention of the United Nations. With one last glower, Welsh went.

Next thing the mobile rang again, and it was Lisa.

"Oh, hi."

"Hello, Stones."

"How are you?"

"I'm okay. You?"

"Yeah, great. How's the course, then?"

"Fascinating. We've been doing Footfall Optimisation today."

"Brilliant."

I hadn't a clue what she was talking about. But she went on a bit before she wound down. Then, in the silence, I remembered it was me that had been trying to get hold of her. Now what was it I wanted to say to her?

"Is everything all right, Stones?"

Oh yeah, that was just it. Everything wasn't all right.

"Yeah, fine. Just fine. I was just, er, wondering when you were coming back."

"I told you. Tomorrow. Can you pick me up at the station? If you're busy, it doesn't matter. I'll understand."

"Sure. What time?"

"If I get away promptly, I should get the five-fifteen train. I'll be in Mansfield about six o'clock."

"Is there any reason why you shouldn't get away on time?"

133

"Not really. It's just that, you know, if we get involved in a discussion..."

I didn't like the sound of that 'we'. There are 'we's and 'we's, and this sounded like the other one. It didn't conjure up a picture of a load of old biddies from evening classes to me.

"Has there been anybody interesting on the course with you?"

"Oh, a few people I've managed to talk to. In the bar at night, you know."

"Yeah, I can imagine."

"Actually," she said, "there is one that you've met."

"Really?" Definitely not an old biddy. I could tell by the tone of her voice. In any case, I don't know any old biddies. The only evening class I ever went to was an educational visit to Lazy Maisie's brothel when I was fifteen.

"Yes, I'm sure you remember." Lisa laughed, but the laugh didn't sound quite right. "You introduced yourself to him just the other day. At Hardwick."

I must have got the heating turned up too high in the house. A hot flush had gone through my neck and there was sweat on my forehead. Also I was gripping the phone too tight, like it was someone's neck that I wanted to do some damage too.

"Cavendish."

"That's right," she said. "What a coincidence him being on the course, isn't it? But of course he's very interested in heritage. It's in his blood, I suppose."

"Michael bleedin' Cavendish."

"It's Michael Holles-Bentinck-Cavendish, can you believe it? All those historic family names still surviving in somebody alive today. Incredible."

"And I suppose Mr Holles-Bentinck bleedin' Cavendish has just happened to be one of the people you bumped into in the bar at night?"

"Well, yes. But there have been a group of us usually."

I didn't like that 'usually' either. It had the same taste as that 'we' earlier. Nasty.

"Actually," said Lisa. "I'll tell you all about it when I see you tomorrow, but he's asked me to do some work for him."

"Who has?"

"Michael. Mr Cavendish."

"Tell him to stuff it."

"Stones, are you all right? You send very irritable."

"Bloody hell, do I?"

"I know you didn't take to him, but this is business."

She'd used the magic word, and she knew it. I could hardly object to her having some business of her own. Just so long as it really *was* business. If I found out otherwise, Mr Four-name Cavendish was going to get his hyphens mangled by a bit of Stones McClure footfall optimisation, right in the crutch.

*   *   *   *

When I got to Rolling Meadows, Uncle Willis was already waiting for me. He was sitting in what they call the sun lounge - a sort of greenhouse with chairs. The chairs were the kind they make old people use when they think the poor souls might have forgotten how to sit up without falling over.

A care assistant flapped away from my uncle as I arrived. She was a bit on the hefty side for me, employed for her brawn, I suppose - handy for lifting old people on and off their beds and other things I'd rather not think about. But Uncle Willis had always liked his women big. My Aunt Mary wasn't exactly a wee lass. I think that's why they called her 'Two Ton'.

"They won't leave me alone, youth," said Willis, without bothering with a greeting. "They give me no peace in here, you know."

"I know, Uncle. But you never really wanted peace, did you?"

"Ah, well. I've had an active life, I suppose."

I perched on one of the high chairs, examining him for signs of deterioration. Like my dad, he'd been a pitman. But he'd been the older of the brothers by seven years, and he'd got himself a trade, working up to a chargehand electrician at Medensworth pit. So far, at seventy-two, he wasn't looking bad. A bit frailer and slower than he used to be, but otherwise fit. His eye was bright, and he certainly had his faculties about him, which was more than could be said for some of the other poor old souls in here. He always had a sharp brain, my uncle. That, and an ability to get directly to the point.

"I've made my will, Livingstone."

"Oh, yes?"

"At last, you mean."

"I didn't say that."

"Ah, but you know that I should have made it a long time ago. I could go at any time, the way they treat me in here. I'm permanently at death's door, I am."

"Sure."

He sighed at me. "No, really. It was something I had to do."

"I don't know what you're trying to tell me, Uncle. But I don't want your money, you know."

"Of course you don't. Business is good, so you keep telling me."

He fixed me with a sharp eye. Some folk think all the residents in a place like this are a pickle short of a jar. They'd be making a big mistake in my uncle's case.

"That's right, it is," I said.

"Good. I'm really pleased."

"So?"

"So I've decided to leave my money - and I do have a little bit put aside, you know, insurance payouts and all that. I've decided to leave the lot to St Asaph's Church. I'm going to set up a fund."

"Really?"

"Really. Do you approve?"

"Of course. Yeah. It's a great idea, Uncle. Well done."

"What do you think they might use the money for?"

"A swimming pool at the vicarage? A holiday in the Bahamas for the choir? I dunno."

"I thought a new youth club. Get some of the kids off the streets, give them something to do. You'd agree with you that, wouldn't you, Livingstone?"

"Sure."

"Good. Because I'm making you chief executive of the Trust."

"Hey, wait a minute, what trust?"

"The one that will run the McClure Memorial Fund. The trust will build and run the youth club."

136

"Hang on, Uncle Willis. I'm much too busy for that sort of thing."

"Business?"

"Yeah, right."

"Well, I think you'll find that it's in your business interests to accept this responsibility."

In the silence that followed, I glanced around idly, looking cool. Inside, my mind was hurtling. What was my uncle getting at? How much did he know about my business interests? He'd been in Rolling Meadows for so long that he'd only ever seen me at work in my previous life. I thought I'd been suitably vague ever since.

It was good enough for Lisa and Nuala, and for the Rev. But Willis McClure was my uncle, and therefore not daft. Was he really threatening me here? Would he interfere in my business interests if I didn't agree to this ridiculous trust fund idea? Well, he was my uncle. I reckoned he damn well would.

"Uncle Willis, if you reckon it's a good idea, I'll think about it, I promise."

"Well, that'll do for now, I suppose. We'll talk about it again soon."

"Right."

"Because I'm not going to do die right now, you understand."

"That's okay."

"Do one more thing for me, Livingstone?"

"Of course, Uncle."

"On your way out, tell that bonny big girl I need her services again."

"No problem."

It's true that there's precious little in Medensworth for the youngsters to do. Everyone lives next door to everyone else here, and we know each others' kids intimately. These are the sort of kids who soon learn to fight, thieve, smash the place up and mug old ladies for their pensions - until eventually they get thrown out of the playgroup. By the time they get to school they're already professionals.

You'd think with all this talk about regeneration of the mining communities after the pits shut, it might occur to somebody that these kids were the future. Maybe somebody would even think to spend a bit of that European money on them. But it seems there are more important things to think about, like what to do with all the derelict bits of pit left over - how to tart them up and make them look cool and stylish.

Near the Miners Welfare and the community centre there's a patch of grass. This is notable enough round here. But in the middle of the grass, sunk into a concrete plinth, is the Medensworth Colliery sign. It's about a mile from where the colliery was, you understand. But the sign is Heritage, and therefore sacred.

Every village round here wants to cling on to a bit of its mining past. It helps to make up for watching the pits go down one by one, like ten green bottles. So a village decides to have an old winding wheel painted up and stuck in a prominent position, or goes for the three wagons and bit of line from an underground coal train like the ones that sit by the road in the middle of Warsop. This is Heritage too.

As you know, I'm all in favour of history. But there's history and history. It's got to be real and alive, not dead and torn up by its roots like a diseased shrub rose, or replaced with a plastic imitation like a corner of an insurance broker's office. But that's the way the heritage business is going.

In the town of Worksop, they must have had a bit of a dilemma. When they built the pedestrianisation scheme in Bridge Street, they had a couple of ideas about how they'd decorate it (they probably said 'give it a focal point' or something). One was a modern sculpture of coal miners, very relevant to most folk around there. The other was a series of crests representing the dukes that the Dukeries are named after, all very heraldic and meaningless. The dukes won, of course. You would have thought the days were long gone when the Duke of Newcastle and the Duke of Portland dominated the whole of Worksop, but apparently not. We still have to walk over their family coats of arms to get to Superdrug and Poundstretcher. Me, I try to see them as boot scrapers.

Uncle Willis was right in a way. Something needed doing for the kids round here. But no matter what good use you found for your money, there would never be enough. It'd be like pissing into the sea at Skegness. You can't put problems right by throwing a bit of dosh at them - not when things have gone on like this for so long. It needs dedication from people - long term. Bear this in mind next time you hear the government or the council or somebody boasting about the latest investment in the area. What sort of investment? A Korean textiles company persuaded to set up a factory by hefty grant hand-outs? A few hundred thousand pounds on a leisure centre? A new school? Like I said - pissing in the sea.

Soon, somewhere around here, they'll be building a new visitor centre. It'll be designed to bring the Japanese and Americans flocking in. They'll be able to sit in the reconstruction of a 1940s concrete council house, with a two-bar electric fire and an uncut moquette sofa that's been chewed by the dog, where you have to pay extra to sit in the wet patches. It'll be a full sensory adventure, smelling of piss and dirty nappies and old tea bags. There'll be four or five half-naked kids sprawled on the floor, with a telly tuned to a re-run of *The Simpsons* and turned up too loud.

Featured prominently in the midst of this setting will be a scruffy bloke with a beer gut and three days' growth of beard slumped in an armchair with half a packet of Senior Service and a can of Mansfield Bitter. If you're lucky with the timing of your visit, you might see him belch and poke at the remote control. Visitors will be able to join the eldest son fiddling about in the electrics of an old Escort as he learns how to hot-wire, or to gaze at a typical mum as she works out how to feed seven people on a tin of stewed steak and a bag of McCain's frozen chips.

This will be called 'The Unemployment Experience'. It'll thrill 'em in their thousands. Hey, we might even be able to get European funding for it.

That's what life always comes down to these days - money. When there isn't much of it about, people think of nothing else. When you come to The Unemployment Experience, that's what the exhibits will be thinking about as they light up the next fag or open the bag of chips. So get your purses out and give generously for the postcards and the souvenirs. Let's make it really authentic.

13

Rufford Abbey hasn't seen sight or sandal of Cistercian monks for over four hundred years. But it does have a hundred and seventy acres of grounds. Enough to get a few villages in, let alone the gardens, lakes and ice houses that the earls fancied. Earls of Shrewsbury they were originally, and they had big ideas. Not surprising, because one of them was married to old Bess of Hardwick. And the Earl decided to turn this place into a vast country house.

There is one building here I particularly like. According to Lisa, it was an outdoor bath house back in the eighteenth century, and at one time it must have made your average heated swimming pool in the commuter villages of Surrey look like my granddad's old tin tub in front of the fire. But a hundred years later some other lord or earl, one of the Saviles, decided to build a glass roof over this thing and convert it into an orangery. You know, like you grow your oranges in. You haven't got one? Well, it was all the thing in Nottinghamshire then. Everybody had to have one.

But then Rufford suffered a disaster. It was sold on by the Savile family and ended up in the gentle hands of the British Army, who used it during the Second World War for storing ammunition and basically let the place fall down. You won't be surprised to hear that Nottinghamshire County Council and English Heritage are planning to finish restoring Rufford Abbey. When they can get the money.

There's also a permanent sculpture collection here, that Lisa showed me once. Really modern stuff. Interesting. There's a big Easter Island sort of stone head and a woman with no head at all. Then there's something called Iron Equinox, which is an inventive creation combining the contrasting tones and textures of cast iron, steel and lead. Well, all right, it's a lump of metal with bits of wire trailing from it. Interesting, though.

One of these sculptures is by some bird called Siobhan Coppinger. Basically, it's a bench on a stone base, and it sits in a corner of the orangery. At one end of the bench is a bloke in wellies and a hat, with his coat collar turned up. At the other end is a curly horned sheep, all four hooves on the bench, like it was sitting up ready for a bit of intelligent conversation. Both the bloke and the sheep are made of chicken wire and ferro-concrete, but there's more life in them than there is in some of my neighbours on the Forest Estate. There's also room in between them on the bench for people to sit, so that's what I did. It's the sort of thing that amuses me.

I sat for a while staring at the sculpture opposite me. It's a bronze thing called the Charioteer, but to me it looks more like a duck falling off a plinth. I haven't figured that one out yet. I'll have to remember to ask Lisa about it.

When the lad I was meeting arrived, he first clocked me from behind a tree in the arboretum. I saw him stop, gape and dodge back behind the trunk like someone playing cowboys and indians. That irritates me. These idiots have always watched too much telly.

Finally, it seemed to dawn on him that the other bloke on the bench with me wasn't real, and he sneaked up gradually, pretending I couldn't see him until he was a few feet away. I humoured him. He already looked nervous enough without me startling him with a display of supernatural powers, like being able to see him creeping up on me in full view. Even if I hadn't been looking, I'd have noticed the smell approaching. It was like a mixture of motor oil and chips. You get a lot of it wafting round the Forest Estate and it makes me feel at home.

The lad still hesitated in the doorway of the orangery, his eyes shifting sideways, taking in the art. Old Siobhan had obviously made an impact. In case he hadn't realised, I pointed out that the bloke in wellies wasn't really with us, not even in spirit.

"Don't worry, he's made of concrete, so he ain't listening. In fact, he's stone deaf." But the bloke was looking past me at the other occupant of the bench. "Oh, got a thing about sheep, have ewe?"

"This is weird, man. What's it all mean?"

"Good question, Trevor. It makes you think, doesn't it?"

"Er, yeah."

"Sit down."

"Is it safe?"

"What do you think's going to happen - the sheep's going to bite you, or what? But of course you're a city boy, aren't you, Trevor? Nobody's ever explained to you that real sheep aren't made of concrete."

He eventually sat down next to me on the bench. I might say he looked a bit sheepish, but I won't. I don't know quite how to describe what he did look like in his tattered jeans and army boots, with a filthy, smelly anorak pulled over his t-shirt. That anorak was so shiny with grease it could have deflected the glare from a nuclear explosion. His lank hair wasn't much better. But at least there was life in there among that oily tangle, which is more than could be said for his eyes. He looked as though he was just coming down from a trip, and it had been a bad one, worse than a works outing to Skeggie. When I said I was clutching at straws, I really meant it.

"They made me pay a quid in the car park," he complained.

"You've got a car, Trevor? I didn't even know you'd got a licence again."

"I haven't. But how the hell do you get here from Nottingham on the bleedin' bus?"

"You telling me you nicked a motor to come here?"

"That's what everybody does round here, ain't it? Why couldn't we have met somewhere else? What's wrong with a pub? This place gives me the creeps."

"There are supposed to be a lot of ghosts here."

"Eh?"

"Don't worry about it, Trevor. Just enjoy the sculptures."

"Is that what they are?"

"Of course."

"So why do they call it the orangery then? That's what it said on the sign. Orangery."

"Bloody hell, did you think they were oranges? You've lived a more sheltered life than I thought. Have all my sheep jokes been wasted then?"

"You're always bleedin' taking the piss, you are, Stones. I don't know why I bother coming when you shout."

"Yes you do, Trevor. It's because you love me as the caring human being I am, and want to express your friendship and admiration for me."

"Piss off."

"Here. Take a look at this."

At first, Trevor shied away from the piece of paper I held out to him. He looked as though he might be about to claim he couldn't read, but I knew better than that. He'd been to Nottingham High School and got nine 'O' levels and four 'A' levels, followed by a degree in Sociology. But everyone has to have a role to act out, don't they?

"What is it?"

"It's a love letter from me to you, Trevor. I've hidden my feelings for too long. It's time we came out. Why don't you read it and see what it is for yourself, you pillock?"

While he read it, I admired the scenery in the orangery. An old couple down the far end were reading an interpretation board about the history of Rufford Abbey. I heard the old biddy commenting on one of the sculptures, complaining about the way it had been treated. It wasn't the Charioteer, but a sort of fractured concrete ball, three feet high, that was split wide open at the top. The old girl was outraged that somebody had left their sweet wrappers in it. I hadn't the heart to tell her it was an avant-garde rubbish bin.

"This is a list of names," said Trevor cautiously.

"Well done. Your education wasn't wasted."

"Who are they?"

"That, old mate, is what I want you to tell me."

"I've never heard of any of them."

"Are you sure?"

"Well, not a hundred per cent," he said. "I'd have to check."

"That's more like it. Do all the checking you like, youth. That's what you're for, isn't it?"

Trevor crumpled the piece of paper into the pocket of his tattered jeans and wiped his nose on his sleeve.

"It'll cost you, Stones."

"And I suppose your services come as expensive as usual?"

"I've got a living to make, haven't I?"

"Right. How much do you want?" I started to reach for my back pocket where the emergency roll lives.

"It doesn't matter just now," he said, getting up from the bench. "I'll get my assistant to send you an invoice."

As he walked out, the old couple gave him a curled-up nose look. The air freshened considerably as the smell of motor oil and chips receded with him. I walked part of the way after Trevor to watch him as far as the car park. He got into the passenger side of a gleaming new Vauxhall Senator with a smart blonde woman in the driving seat. He immediately chucked his smelly jacket onto the back seat and started to change into a suit.

They don't make private detectives like they used to, do they?

The mobile rang just as the old couple came out of the Rufford orangery behind me. When I answered it, they turned to look at me as if I was mad or a philistine or something.

"Business," I mouthed at them. They shrugged at each other, convinced they were right the first time.

"Yeah, Ralph? Brilliant. And he's not been charged? What was it all about then? Yeah, I heard it was drugs, but I didn't believe it - not Slow Kid. Where is he now? Right, thanks, Ralph."

Lawyers can be the biggest crooks out, even worse than accountants. Did you know that? You probably did, if you've ever sold a house or gone through a divorce. This is the only profession where a bloke can get away with having his secretary type a letter, than charge you a couple of hundred quid for his valuable time. If I could do that, I'd be printing my own money by now. Have you heard the story about the solicitor's clerk? This poor bugger had to justify an account to a client that said: "For crossing the road to speak to you, £50. For finding it wasn't you and having to cross back again, £50." This is no joke.

But they do have their uses, lawyers. In this case, Ralph Catchlock does the nudging and levering for me that sorts things out, like when Slow Kid gets himself in a cell at Mansfield nick. I could do it personally, use my own influence, but why bother when you've got the paid? In any case, I know a thing or two about Ralph Catchlock that would give the Law Society a fit. That gets me a discount.

And so Ralph had come up with the goods. Slow Kid was free, and on his way back home.

* * * *

The Thompsons' house is at the far end of Top Forest. Away from the main road, there isn't much traffic noise on the estate at the best of times. Just an occasional White Arrow van delivering something from Reader's Digest, or the council dog warden cruising the streets looking for strays.

They hang around here in packs - the dogs, I mean, not the wardens. Folk get these appealing puppies, you know, for the kids to play with at Christmas. Then, blow me, the puppies grow into bloody great Wolfhounds and Dobermans that need feeding and looking after and taking to the vets, and all that sort of effort. Who'd have thought it? We can't do with that, can we? So the mutts are turned loose on the streets to run wild with all the others.

Come Tuesday morning, when the binmen head round this way, the local dog pack does a tour of the wheelie bins to see if there's anything worth getting to first. If your bin's a bit open, or there's a plastic bag left next to it, the dogs will get at it. Then your rubbish is all over the pavement, and the neighbours can see that you've been eating tins of Lo-Cost own brand baked beans every day this week and that you don't throw your knickers out until they're more hole than polyester. Not that your neighbours are any different, of course - but you don't want people to see that.

And it's not only the dogs. Kids are turned loose on the streets the same way, when they get a bit older and raising a family turns out to be too much effort as well. Sod employment training. It's time somebody trained this lot to be parents.

Round the back of one of the houses, somebody was turning over a starter motor, desperately trying to kick life into an ancient car engine. The starter was whining in protest, and soon the battery would be flat. The dog pack was barking on the other side of the estate, its baying competing with the shouts and screams of the kids. Nearer at hand, a radio was playing Roxy Music, probably some housewife reminiscing while she did the ironing. There was

145

a predominant smell of washing and dog crap. But somewhere down the street a redundant pit electrician was endlessly trying to make the world a better place by creosoting his garden fence.

Down there, behind the houses, is a canal. It always has a few multi-coloured umbrellas brightening the landscape where blokes are fishing. Round here, there's fishing and there's allotments. There aren't many options for hanging about all day without spending any money. Time is the enemy of the unemployed man. It's bad enough for the middle aged ones. But time bites so deep on the young lads who've never had a job that it's no wonder they turn to crime.

Number 23 Beech Street is much like the other houses. The area in front has been concreted over and half a plank jammed against the kerb to make it easier to get a car across the pavement. But weeds are growing through the concrete, and a couple of elder saplings are quite well established. Soon they'll be causing trouble with the drains and undermining the foundations, but it won't be the council's responsibility any more, because they sold the house to the Thompsons, cheap. What an opportunity.

I knew Slow's mum would be in, so I dusted myself down and straightened my belt before I knocked on the door. I wanted her to think I was fit company for her son. Mums are sensitive about this, especially when their little boy has just come back from the cop shop. Has Lloyd been keeping the wrong company? Is it that nasty, working class Stones McClure leading him into bad ways, scrumping apples, then knocking on doors and running away?

"Oh, Stones," she said when she opened the door. "I'm glad you've come. He'll be pleased to see you."

Actually, Angie Thompson isn't so bad. I think she has a soft spot for me, like most women. If I decide to exercise a bit of charm, I can twist them round my finger, no problem. Angie might be a bit old for me, but she's still susceptible to a bit of that McClure appeal.

She was staring at me right now. "You owe him something anyway, for all this time he's spent down the police station. I know it's all your fault, so don't look so smug. He's in the front room."

Slow Kid looked tired more than anything. Shifty, yeah, as if he'd let me down somehow, but not guilty. He was in front of the telly with a bottle of beer when I walked in on him. His feet were up on a coffee table, and he pulled them off quick when the door opened, thinking it was his mum. There was a game show on the telly. *Celebrity Balls*, or some such. Housewives' brain death.

"Have you gone dirty on me or what, Slow?"

"You know I ain't into drugs, Stones," he said, handing me a beer. "Me mum'd kill me."

"Yeah, I know." I sighed. "So what was it all about, then?"

"I honestly dunno. They kept asking whether I'd delivered a big load for someone recently. Shit, I just didn't know what they were on about half the time."

"Was this Moxon?"

"He was there, but there was some other guy as well. Big guy, not in a suit like the others, dressed in jeans. I didn't know him at all."

"Drugs squad probably."

"Yeah, well. If you ask me, they must have known about some delivery and just pulled in a load of drivers. I think I saw Danny Cross in there too."

"Not Mick Kelk?"

"I didn't see him. But there could have been others about somewhere."

"So they don't really know anything. They're just chancing their arm? The usual suspects, they call it."

"I'm not a usual suspect, Stones. Not for drugs, I'm not."

"I know, I know."

On the telly, some comedian I vaguely recognised was mouthing inanities at a middle-aged woman contestant, who rolled about in hysterics. Even with the sound turned down, I could tell that his jokes weren't funny. You only had to look at his eyes. Deep down, he was the most embarrassed bloke I'd ever seen.

"Did you pick anything up about this load, Slow? A where, a when, or a what? Did they let anything slip?"

"It was around this area, that's all I got. They asked me about people I know."

Slow hesitated, looking at me sideways around his bottle. I always tell people not to deny they know me. There's no point in lying when the cops know perfectly well it's a fib.

"They asked about me?"

"Yeah, they did. But they can't think you're dealing, can they? You've never done that, Stones."

"No."

This made me a bit thoughtful, though. It's too easy to fit somebody up for a drugs bust. All it needs is a few grams picked up in one place and then 'found' again in another. There's quite a few of the plods down the local nick that don't like me over much, let alone the top boys at Sherwood Lodge. Moxon, though? I doubted it. It's not his style. In fact, it's probably against his upbringing. But if he wasn't in charge of this business, I'd have to watch my back.

"When they took you in, Slow, did they search the house?"

"No. They didn't have a whatsit, a warrant, and I think my mum scared 'em off."

"Have a quick look round anyway, whatever rooms they went in."

"Do you think it looks bad, Stones?"

"Maybe."

Slow Kid thought about it, staring at a minor soap star giggling and shaking her tits on the screen.

"How was business while I've been away then?"

"Not good, Slow, not good. But I'll tell you about it later. Right now, I've got another job to do."

He looked hopeful. "Anything you need me for?"

"No thanks. This is something I've got to sort out myself."

It was nearly half past five already. The TV game show was finishing, and I'd just made a big decision. Cue hysterical applause.

*   *   *   *

"Metal, you pillock, what do you mean - you've still got it?"

Metal Jacket shrugged and waved his hands in the air.

"I couldn't think what to do with it, Stones. I mean, how do you get rid of a cop car?"

"Metal, you're making me mad."

"Sorry."

148

I had to think. The last thing I needed was a hot pig-mobile sitting round in a workshop that I could be connected to. Not with Slow only just back from a cell. For all I knew, Moxon and his crew could be on their way here now with a search warrant. And today even my own uncle was threatening to shop me. I didn't like the signs. They all pointed downwards, into the brown stuff.

"Get some plates on it," I said.

"What?"

"Plates. Any plates. And is that wreck over there driveable?"

"Yeah, sure. You want it?"

"I don't want it, Metal. We're going to use it to get you and me out of this mess, right?"

"Okay, Stones."

Metal looked relieved. He may be good at nicking motors, but when it comes to using his brain for anything else, he was happier taking orders.

"You're going to drive the Citroen," I said. "Dave and me will be in front of you in the Morris. If you get pulled in, you don't know us, and we don't know nothing. Right?"

"Right."

"You drive normally, you don't break the speed limit. Don't do anything that will give 'em an excuse to stop you."

"Right."

"Get in the car, then."

"Right. Er, Stones - "

"Yeah?"

"Where are we going?"

"You'll see when we get there. And bring some wellies."

In the south and east of the county there are lots of disused gravel pits. They're deep, these things, and after they're abandoned they fill up with water. One of the biggest, Attenborough, has been made into a nature reserve. Really, you'd never know what it was.

I know a couple of flooded quarries that nobody has bothered with for a long time. There are signs to point out how stupid it is to go swimming in freezing cold water thirty feet deep with only gravel to get a grip on, but that's about all. People do need telling these things, but there aren't many of them who go out that way, stupid or not. Except us, occasionally.

149

By now it was getting dark. I drove up the track first in the Morris with Dave, and Metal came up a bit behind us, his headlights bouncing all over the place in my rearview mirror. The Traveller was struggling, but the Citroen didn't do too badly up the track. That's the point of these hydraulic suspensions - you get a better ride.

I parked near a gap in the fence, and we manoeuvred the Citroen through to the concrete apron on the edge of the quarry. When I switched on my torch, Dave gazed down at the green water far below and started to look dizzy. I pulled him back from the edge.

"Careful. We need you to help push."

"It's a long way down."

"Yeah. We could make a really big splash here."

"I don't like it out here, Stones," said Metal, coming out of the Citroen. "It's a bit spooky."

"Spooky? There ain't no spooks here, Metal. Other than the ones haunting that chuffin' car."

Metal eased the Citroen up to the edge, looking a bit nervous, maybe wondering whether we'd tell him to stop in time before his front wheels went over. I was annoyed with him, but not that annoyed.

"Right, take the handbrake off. Have you got your wellies?"

"I dunno what I need these for," he moaned as he swapped them for his trainers. "I'm not going in the water, am I? I feel a real yokel."

"Just get on with it, Metal."

We whipped the plates off and began to push. The concrete apron was pretty level, and the three of us soon got the car moving. Dave could have done it on his own. In a moment or two the front wheels slipped over the edge and the underside of the Citroen hit the concrete with a bang. Now the pushing was harder. The horrendous scraping of the metal against the apron sounded much too loud in the night air. But then the car reached its point of balance and started to tip. We gave one last heave and it lurched suddenly.

So we all backed off quickly and watched as the back end of the Citroen reared into the air and disappeared. It seemed an age before there was a huge splash, and waves of spray flew over the edge, sloshing around our feet. Now Metal knew why he needed the wellies. The algae in that water was sheer poison. It would have ruined his Reeboks.

I shone my torch over the edge. The boot and rear window of the Citroen were just visible above the surface. The car bobbed and settled, sinking a bit lower with each movement. The splash had stirred up all sorts of silt and rubbish that swirled around it like a shoal of piranha fish in a feeding frenzy.

Finally, water filled the passenger compartment and forced out a spurt of bubbles. The bumper of the Citroen was the last thing to sink out of sight, cocking itself in the air like the arse of a Parisian tart.

That's so typical of the French - arrogant to the last.

14

Next morning, Lisa was tapping her foot on the station forecourt when I arrived, her bags at her feet and a scowl on her face. I jumped out and put her luggage in the boot like some bleedin' chauffeur. I didn't even get a peck on the cheek. See how I'm treated?

"Sorry I'm a bit late, sweetheart."

"Oh?"

"It was business."

She said nothing, but turned her head away as I drove out of the station towards the A60.

"I'm glad to see you back."

"Thanks."

This stuff is really hard work. I don't have to do it with Nuala. If I did, she wouldn't listen anyway, so I don't bother.

"Was it a good course?"

"Yes, excellent. We had another very interesting discussion in the bar last night."

"Right. Optimising footfall?"

"Customer interactivity. Mr Cavendish was particularly knowledgeable on the subject."

Now she was trying to make me jealous. But this is Stones McClure she's dealing with. It doesn't work. Why should I be jealous of this hyphenated Cavendish plonker when I was already planning on getting shut of Lisa anyway? He was welcome to her. Let them get interactive together. I didn't care.

Lisa turned towards me then, and smiled at something she seemed to find in my face. Women are supposed to be sensitive and intuitive, aren't they? But she obviously couldn't read what I was thinking at that moment, or she wouldn't have decided to be so nice to me suddenly. She leaned across the car and kissed me on the cheek. It was quite a long kiss to say I was only the chauffeur.

And her hand rested on my leg too. This somehow put a different slant on things, and my thoughts began to turn to how we could fill in the time until I found the right moment to tell her she wasn't wanted any more.

"Are we going back to your place?" she said.

I nodded and put my foot down. The Subaru surged forward and we hurtled through Warsop at seventy miles an hour, which is always the best way to see it.

"We also had a session on the one-to-one feel good experience," she said.

"Now you're interesting me. I can manage that one."

*   *   *   *

Barely more than three hours, Lisa later brought me a cup of coffee. I was still in bed trying to get my energy back from all the effort. My eyes were just about open, and as I drank the coffee I watched Lisa wandering about the bedroom. She seemed to be taking clothes out of her bags and putting them away in my wardrobe and drawers. She was moving my own stuff aside to do it, and tutting over the untidiness.

This was such a bizarre thing for her to be doing that I thought I must still be asleep and dreaming. She'd left odd things lying about occasionally when she stayed overnight, but there's a line you don't cross when you aren't actually living with someone. You know what I mean, don't you? Chucking the other person's odd socks on the floor to make room for your knickers and tights is definitely over the line. Okay, the sex had been good, but it looked as though the crunch was coming. Lisa was pushing me too far here. It was time to have it out.

"Where are you going?" she wanted to know when I started to get dressed. What was this, had I suddenly gained a nanny?

"I've got some business to do downstairs. Phone calls to make."

"Oh no, you don't. You're taking me out."

"But - ."

"No buts. Get your jacket on."

Well, that's women. Give them an inch and they'll take a mile. Give them six inches and they think they own you. I reckoned Lisa had a big shock coming. She was really on her way out. I'd have to tell her soon, and let her know about Nuala. When the time was right.

I put my jacket on. "Where do you want to go, then?"

"A craft centre. It's time you bought me something nice."

"Oh."

So I had to take her to Rufford. Twice in two days? I was starting to look like a regular. I might apply for a season ticket.

And of course I bought her something nice in the craft centre. Well, if that had been all that happened at Rufford, I could have put up with it. A bit of misshapen pottery, or a sweater with lumps of fluff sticking it out of it, followed by a small hole in my wallet. That would have been okay. Even when we had to go for coffee and cake in the Buttery restaurant, that wasn't too bad. It isn't the sort of place we have in Medensworth. We had to sit and behave ourselves, and talk quietly, without swearing too much, so as not to upset the old biddies and make them choke on their Darjeeling. I can put up with that, see? I'm not a complete yob.

But accidentally bumping into Michael Holles-Bentinck-Cavendish while we were there? That was taking things too bleedin' far.

First we'd taken a glance at the Abbey, to see how far the restoration had got. I was happy to see the plastic sheeting and scaffolding had gone off the Jacobean south wing, which is almost all that's left of the sixteenth century house. The north and east wings had to be demolished after the army had finished with them.

"Thank goodness it was the south wing they managed to keep," I said, showing off. "It's the bit with Savile's cupola on it."

"Salvin," said Lisa.

"Eh?"

"The architect who designed the cupola and the west front was called Salvin. He designed Thoresby Hall too."

"Yeah. I knew that."

So we did the craft shop bit, and I bought Lisa a set of hand-made bowls and jugs. They had no colour to me, just being a sort of patchy brown, like the stains left on your plate after a hot beef curry. But Lisa seemed to like them - and at that price, she damn well ought to think they were hand-painted by Picasso.

This artistic reflection made me think about my visit to the sculpture park the day before. I broached the subject while we were in the Buttery. We were eating Battenburg and fairy cakes and drinking coffee strong enough to melt your false teeth into a plasticine model of the Peak District.

"Lisa, love."

"Yes, Stones?"

"You know that Charioteer thing in there. What's that all about then?"

"I don't know," she said. "It looks like a duck falling off a plinth to me."

And then I saw him. He drifted in through the doors of the Buttery while we were only halfway through the cake. He was ponced up to his eyeballs and had a look on his face as if he expected all the old biddies to rush round him begging for his autograph and a sniff at his socks. Lisa had her back to the door, so I spotted him first. She saw my expression, followed my gaze, and did her double take. She was very good, an Oscar candidate if ever I saw one. Better than that soap actress shaking her tits on the telly, anyway.

"Oh, it's Michael Cavendish, look."

"Don't forget the hyphens," I said. "Don't make him sound as though he's just some ordinary bloke."

She waved. Cavendish clocked us and began to walk towards our table. I shoved in the rest of the cake and stood up with my mouth so full that I couldn't say what I was thinking. But Lisa had her hand on my arm, hanging on to my sleeve. She'd grabbed my punching arm too. Sneaky.

"Why, hello there, Lisa. What a wonderful surprise to bump into you here."

"Amazing, Michael. But it's lovely to see you again so soon."

They beamed at each other for a minute, while I reflected how they'd gone from Mr Cavendish and Miss Prior to Michael and Lisa since I last saw them together. That's what comes of getting interactive. Then Cavendish pretended to notice me for the first time. It was as if he'd just trodden in something unpleasant that the Golden Retriever had left behind on the terrace.

"And your brother too. How nice."

I've never heard anybody put so many different meanings into the word 'nice' without having to write their own dictionary. It made me choke so hard I spat crumbs of Battenburg onto his trousers. Judging from his expression, Cavendish took this gesture exactly the way it was meant.

"I don't suppose you've given any more thought to my proposal, Lisa?" he said, dismissing me from existence.

"As a matter of fact, I have," she said.

"Wonderful. Do you mind if I sit down?"

"Have my seat," I said. "I was just leaving."

"Leaving to bring us some more coffees, of course. Michael takes one sugar, Stones."

"Thanks a lot, old chap."

Well, you can't spin out the act of buying three cups of coffee for long when there isn't even a queue at the counter. You can count your change a few times, but that gets boring after a bit. The sums aren't big enough to be really interesting. I was sort of hoping Cavendish's coffee would be cold by the time he got it, or that he'd have to rush off to an urgent appointment with his tailor.

It's not that I was jealous, you understand. But people like him have this strange effect on me. Basically, Cavendish was the walking symbol of a disease that society will never cure. Genetically, me and him are at opposite ends of a seesaw, and it seems to me like he's the bigger boy who always has all the weight at his end.

With people like this, I get the impulse to lighten their load a bit in any way I can. Childish, I know. But if you've ever sat in the air on the end of a seesaw opposite a great, grinning fat lad, you'll know what I mean.

When I turned back to our table, I could see Lisa and Cavendish smirking at each other, and nodding. A warm bile rose into the back of my throat. I could taste the sourness of that damn coffee coming back again.

I picked a few condiments from the counter, then stopped off to smile at a couple of middle-aged biddies, all slacks and cashmere sweaters. They looked at me like a Yorkshire terrier bitch looks at a Great Dane. I like you, big boy, but you might hurt me. That was okay. I was only after their savouries.

"Do you mind if I borrow this?" I said, all charm, using my bold stare.

"That's quite all right," said one of the biddies. Another conquest, then.

I put the little jug of tartare sauce on my tray, then moved away to the next table where a family with two kids had been eating chips - or french fries as they're called on Sundays.

"Have you finished with this?"

"Yes, mate."

The tomato sauce went on the tray with the rest. A few steps further on, a bearded bloke in walking gear was tucking into a nice healthy salad.

"All right if I take that?"

"Be my guest."

I've always liked proper mayonnaise. One that's really runny and doesn't need to be scraped out of the neck of a bottle with a knife. I put it on the tray and, as an afterthought, loosened the top of the vinegar bottle next to it. Ease of access - that's the buzz phrase, isn't it?

Now all I needed was some cream. Ah yes. I made a small detour to the old couple's table, who saw me coming and were just leaving anyway. Now all the ingredients were at hand.

Lisa and Cavendish hadn't even noticed I'd been away so long. They were grinning at each other like idiots, and I had the feeling something had been agreed while I was out of the way. That suited me. I hoped the proposal Cavendish had mentioned was marriage. I was even prepared to go to the wedding and cheer from the back, as long as I didn't have to be best man and pretend I was his friend.

"Michael has offered me some part-time work," said Lisa, barely looking at me as I hovered with the tray.

"Oh?"

"He wants me to trace any living relatives he has. Other descendants of Bess of Hardwick. He wants to organise a family gathering, perhaps a Cavendish society of some kind. Don't you think that's a terrific idea?"

"Utterly bleedin' marvellous."

A family gathering? It was the last thing I'd want with any of my relatives. Most of them wouldn't be allowed out to attend it anyway. But people like Cavendish take a different attitude to family. It seems to matter. Well, of course it does - because that's the way they've kept their wealth and property and privileges over all these centuries. That's how they stay better than the rest of us, with their titles and public schools, and their poncy accents. They're all passed down from father to son, like syphilis.

Presumably Cavendish wasn't interested in finding relatives who happened to be poor, or were born on the wrong side of the blanket. He didn't want to find himself meeting Alf and Mavis Cavendish of 16B Grime Street and their kids Darren and Tracey. My guess was that he hoped to find some rich ones who could do him a good turn, for the sake of the old bloodlines, don't you know. And having Lisa involved would be a bonus. Well, good luck to him. I couldn't give a toss what they got up to. Not a toss.

It was at this point that my hand slipped and the whole trayload of coffee, milk, sugar, tartare sauce, tomato ketchup, vinegar, mayonnaise and double cream went flying. If they'd all landed together on a plate in a nice pattern, I could have got an Egon Ronay commendation for it.

But you can never tell with liquids how far they're going to travel when they spill. Sometimes they fly across the room in a huge splurge without you even trying. There were three cups of coffee on the tray that hadn't been touched, so there was plenty to hit Cavendish's shirt when they landed. The milk and vinegar followed pretty closely, and the other stuff made dramatic streaks and splashes of colour on top. Very modernist. Never mind Egon Ronay, give me the Turner Prize.

Cavendish sat there stunned for a minute. He was figuring out the correct etiquette for the situation. It probably doesn't happen too often when the vicar comes for afternoon tea at a gentleman's country residence. Then Lisa picked up a couple of paper napkins and began dabbing at his chest as if she was trying to stop the bleeding from a shotgun wound. I wish.

I suppose some folk would have said 'sorry' at this point. But I couldn't remember how to pronounce it properly. That's the result of a second-rate education, you see. Terrible. I can't play croquet either.

Trust Lisa, though - she had to do it for me. "I'm sorry about my brother," she said, dabbing away. "He's a bit uncouth."

"It's all right, really," said Cavendish, though you could see it wasn't. The look he gave me said that if Lisa hadn't been there he would have called up the grooms and footmen and had me horsewhipped.

"That's the trouble with family," I said. "It isn't always quite what you'd like it to be, is it?"

I walked out of the Buttery and through the courtyard into the Abbey gardens. Maybe I'd go and stare at the ducks on the lake for a bit. Maybe I'd climb up the tower and spit on the stone paving below to see how far it splashed. There are plenty of other ways to enjoy life, if you know how.

Naturally, we didn't speak on the way home. I put some U2 on the cassette player to drown out the silence. It was *The Joshua Tree*, starting off with *Where the streets have no name*. It seemed quite appropriate as we reached Medensworth and turned into First Avenue.

Then I saw another figure I recognised. He was lurking at the corner of the street, like a bungling spy from a John le Carré novel, the one who gets horribly done in by the Russians. This bloke has a particularly crawly line in lurking. You can see him do it any Sunday at St Asaph's, creeping round the people he wants to get in with, giving the evil eye to those he doesn't.

It was bad enough having to get used to the cops watching me, and Craig's boys as well - not to mention someone trying to wreck my business. And Cavendish had left a really sour taste in my mouth, worse even than the coffee. But this was the limit. Bleedin' Welsh Border with his nose stuck out, sniffing the air, clocking my every move. One of these days I was going to do something that he'd find really interesting. Just watch me.

*   *   *   *

It was a big Mercedes van, fifty-five hundredweight - that's five thousand five hundred kilos in foreign money. It was white, with a blue flash down the side that said 'Inter Euro Transport'. The company claimed to have offices in London, Paris and Brussels.

When I pulled up, Metal Jacket and two other boys, the Harman brothers, were standing around looking shifty. They didn't say much, just opened the back doors for me to have a look inside for myself.

The van was full of numbered boxes labelled 'Aero engine components'. Some of the boxes had been ripped open, and I took a peek. They contained lumps of metal moulded into shapes whose purpose I couldn't even guess at. I was quite prepared to believe they really and truly were aero engine components.

This was a pisser. These boxes were supposed to contain toasters, hair driers and portable CD players. Maybe a few steam irons and electric can openers. There wasn't much call for aircraft parts on the Sunday market.

"What is this shit? No, don't tell me, Metal, I can see. Spares for a Jumbo jet maybe. Have we got a Jumbo jet stashed away somewhere that needs spares, Metal?"

"No, Stones."

"Were you planning on nicking one from Woolley Services?"

"No, Stones."

"Then what the bloody hell use is all this lot?"

I slammed the door shut, a bit harder than I'd intended. The boys flinched as the noise echoed around the workshop. The van stood where the Citroen BX had been not too long ago, and it was just as unwelcome.

"But Stones, it was supposed to be - "

"I know what it was supposed to be. I know what you told me it was supposed to be. But where did the information come from?"

"The driver, Stones."

"The driver?"

Metal shuffled his feet. "He told us what he'd be carrying, and where he always stopped. It was a gift."

"You're joking."

He wasn't joking. He thought he'd pulled off a real coup, and this was how it had turned out. He thought he was making up for the cop car, and this is what he'd brought me. I suddenly felt sorry for him.

"Who was this bloke, this driver?"

"He's name is Sid Jones."

"Jones? Oh yeah."

"That's what he said. You don't ask too much, you know... "

"Yeah, all right, I know."

"Chocky met him some place."

Metal indicated one of the Harman brothers. The other tried to look as though he suddenly wasn't there.

"It was in the truck stop at Markham Moor," said Chocky. "I just got talking to him, like we do."

"See?" said Metal. "So Chocky told me, and I went with him to check the bloke out. He seemed straight up, Stones. And there were no cops about when we lifted the van."

"You sure? Are you certain they're not sitting out there now getting ready to walk in with the cuffs?"

"Positive. We gave the car park a good going over. I'm dead sure there was no tail. We did the job proper, Stones."

"Right."

Okay, these things do happen sometimes. And it wasn't unusual to find a driver keen to earn a bit of extra cash by co-operating with lads who wanted to lift his vehicle. But this was the third screw-up in twenty-four hours. Not to mention the Citroen. That was three loads lost.

Like Oscar Wilde said, to lose one is bad luck, to lose two looks like carelessness. But the third piss-up starts to smell like some bastard's got it in for me. And that's not on, Lady Bracknell.

*   *   *   *

The Rev was out and about in front of the church, shepherding his cassocks or something.

"Ah, come to put in a few hours on the churchyard, Livingstone?"

"That's right, Rev. We thought it was looking in need of a bit of a tidy-up round the graves, like."

"It is, it is. You know where the tools are, don't you? Would you like to log your hours in the book. For income tax purposes, of course."

The Rev will have his little joke. But I put my name and Dave's in his workbook and signed us in as having arrived at 8am.

"Eight o'clock? Well, dear me, you've been at it two hours already. You must be getting thirsty. I'll put the kettle on in the vestry, shall I?"

"That'd be just lovely, Rev."

Dave came back clutching a spade, a fork and a hoe in one hand, and an electric strimmer in the other. He held them effortlessly at arm's length, as if they were mere illusions. You could tell from his face that gardening wasn't his favourite occupation. His expression suggested he'd just sat in something cold and squashy and knew it was about to start leaking through the seat of his trousers.

"It's just for a bit, Donc. Got to get your hands dirty. Gardeners always have dirty hands, don't they?"

Dave dropped the tools and looked at his hands, vaguely puzzled. I could see why - his hands were hardly a model of cleanliness at the best of times. But he said nothing. I think there was a shallow level of understanding there, even if he didn't show it.

I set to work with the strimmer along the edge of the grass, while Dave brandished the fork viciously at some flower beds that had done nothing to deserve it except burst into a splurge of tasteless yellow and pink.

The graveyard was pretty tidy, actually. It looked as though the Rev or one of his parishioners had been working on it recently. But we cracked on at such a pace that we soon had an impressive pile of debris in the wheelbarrow and several feet of earth glistening and freshly turned. Personally, I was sweating a bit already, and I was glad of the strong tea the vicar brought.

"Have you had a successful week?" asked the Rev, twinkling at me over his glasses. Sometimes he gives the uncomfortable impression that he thinks I'm a sort of boy scout who goes round helping pensioners and blind people cross roads all day long. The only time I've ever done that was when I was a teenager, and then it was a rich old biddy whose mock crocodile skin handbag was a good bit lighter by the time she got to the other side.

"You could say that, Rev."

"Good, good." He beamed at me and then at Dave. "What are we put on this earth for, if not to help others, eh?"

Dave sensibly kept quiet. Or maybe he just didn't understand the question. He was still on *Janet and John Learn to Use the Potty*, and wasn't quite up to high level theological discussions yet. Besides, Dave thought he'd been put on the earth for only two things, and neither of them involved helping others.

"I'm considering that for my theme on Sunday," said the Rev, taking our silence for respectful interest. "St Luke Chapter 10. The story of the Good Samaritan, you know - but updated, naturally. One must make certain one's sermons are in tune with the modern congregation. A propos, but de nos jours. Germane to the 90s."

Congregation? From what I'd seen of the pew jockeys at St Asaph's, the only 90s they could relate to would be the 1890s, which is when most of them were born. They loved the Rev's sermons, mainly because there was no danger of being kept awake. I could see Dave staring at the Rev as if this bloke with a bit of margarine tub round his neck had just descended from the Tower of Babel talking in foreign tongues. The trouble with Dave is that he will listen. Understand, no. But listen, yes.

"Perhaps you'd like to come along yourselves, gentlemen," suggested the Rev, encouraged by the rapt attention. "I think I can promise you an uplifting experience."

"Er, we'll think about it," I said, and frowned at Dave. He didn't need much frowning at. He was back at work on the flower beds before you could blink, and I passed the empty mugs to the Rev.

I set to again, waving my strimmer at a ragged-looking border, thinking what a real plonker that Good Samaritan bloke must have been. What idiot would stop to pick up somebody lying in the street, without knowing who they were or where they'd come from? Try doing that these days. You'd have a gang of yobs screeching off in your car in no time, while you lay bleeding at the roadside, doing an imitation of a hedgehog that hadn't quite made it through the traffic. You wouldn't catch me doing that, no fear.

Nowadays the equivalent of the Good Samaritan would be the bloke who's willing to ring for an ambulance on his mobile as he swerves round your body. No use telling the Rev that, though. He'd only look pained and drive about looking for a chance to try it out and prove me wrong.

I was occupied by holy thoughts like this when an unmarked police car pulled up at the kerb. From the passenger window DI Moxon stared at me without expression. He didn't even bother getting out of the car, but made Wally Stubbs squeeze out of the driver's seat to stumble up the steps into the churchyard.

"Detective Sergeant Stubbs," he said, flashing his warrant card at the Rev. "Can you tell me how long these two have been here, please, vicar?"

"Mr McClure and his friend? Since about eight o'clock. They're early risers. Very admirable, don't you think? And they heard the voice of the Lord God walking in the garden in the cool of the day."

"Really?"

Wally looked dubious. Admirable wasn't the word he usually heard applied to me down at the station.

"It's in the book. Would you like to see it, sergeant?"

"No, thanks."

Wally looked at us and the results of our work, no doubt comparing it to what he could achieve in a couple of hours in his own garden back home. Looking at the blubber round his waist, I reckon we hadn't done too badly.

"We've just been spending a little of our time in discussion of a biblical text," said the Rev happily.

He was gilding the lily now, I thought. Definitely stretching credulity a bit too far.

"The parable of the man who fell among thieves," he added helpfully.

"Oh yes?" said Wally, his ears pricking up. There was a tense silence for a moment. "What thieves would these be, then?

The silence went on and on, like even the Rev might have realised he'd said the wrong thing.

"S'Luke," said Dave, surprising us all. "The Good S'maritan."

164

"Oh. Right," said Wally. His hand twitched as though to reach for his notebook. His instinct was to get the words down at every opportunity. It could be evidence. He looked at Dave, hoping for more. The big dork could have let it rest there, but it wasn't in his nature. Not Dave.

"The nose ewer," he said.

"Eh?" Wally gaped at him, baffled.

"German to the nighties."

Dave was giving it his intellectual look. Or maybe he just had indigestion. But that was definitely a little twitch of the eyebrows, just like the Rev does when he's talking at you.

"What are you trying to tell me, Underwood?"

"Acro prop the nose ewer."

"I see."

Wally Stubbs was backing away now, looking up at Dave with dismay, like a man who's just got on a long-distance bus and finds Billy Graham sitting down next to him.

"You can come if you like! On Sunday. It's my sermon," called the Rev as Wally scuttled back down the steps. "All welcome!"

Wally got back in the Mondeo and spoke a few words to Moxon, who turned towards us again, his glasses glinting in the sunlight, unbelieving. They drove off with a screech of tyres.

I looked at Dave with new respect. But he only looked down modestly at his hands, as if it was the fork that had done it.

15

Nuala was off work that afternoon, which was handy, because Lisa was due at Hardwick. Trouble was, the new bird was getting suspicious. For a start, she claimed the way I was treating her meant I didn't care about her. Rubbish, of course. But there was worse. Nuala isn't too bright, but she does have that highly developed sense of smell that seems to come with women and dogs. As soon as she got in the car she started sniffing. Well, I could smell the cigarette smoke myself, but that didn't mean anything. What else could she smell, though?

"Do you like my scent?" she said. "It's Givenchy. It's expensive usually, but I got it at the Sunday market. You wouldn't believe the price."

I would, probably.

"You smell lovely, as usual."

This was the wrong thing to say, but it slipped out. She'd just told me she was wearing a new scent, and those words 'as usual' suggested that it didn't smell any different from the old scent. It was as bad as not noticing a new hair style. You see how tuned in I've got to those subtle meanings that women read into what you say? The only problem is, I don't remember how to do it until after I've already said the wrong thing. The charm usually gets me by. And it's all lost on Nuala anyway. If she's not speaking herself, then no one is.

"Have you had a woman in the car?" she said.

"Only in the course of business, love."

She sniffed. "Well, it's a funny business you run if you have women in your car smelling like that, that's all I can say. My mum always said you couldn't trust a man if you found knickers in his glove compartment."

With this baffling comment, she opened my glove compartment and began rooting about. There's nothing incriminating in there, honest. I just don't like people poking about. It gets me annoyed.

"Give over, you silly tart."

"What did you call me?"

"You're getting right up my nose now. Business is business, and it's got nothing to do with you. So just keep your nose out of my affairs, and your fingers out of my glove compartment."

"Oh, something to hide then, have you? My mum always said - "

"I couldn't give a shit what your mum always said. Will you just shut up for a bit? You're making my ears bleed."

Magically, she shut up. For thirty seconds.

"You can drop me off here," she said.

"Don't be stupid. We're in the middle of nowhere."

We were, in fact, just passing through a little tea shop village called Norton, where they might not like to be called 'in the middle of nowhere'. But it wasn't somewhere for a silly tart with her skirt up her bum to be walking along the roadside on her own. Nowhere is, these days.

"I'll hitch a lift," she said. "I can always get somebody to pick me up."

"I bet."

"Anyway, you smell of oil. You've been playing about with cars again, haven't you?"

"Business, duck, business."

"If you think we're going to have sex in them bushes again, you've got another think coming," she said. "After you speaking to me like that? It's not on."

I didn't say anything. I'd just noticed how much her skirt had ridden up as she wriggled about angrily in her seat. It was revealing such an expanse of thigh that I couldn't resist just resting my left hand on it for a while to see how it fit. Her leg was smooth and warm, and it moved instinctively under my hand as I stroked it gently.

After a few more minutes, she sighed. "All right then," she said. "You've talked me into it."

Making love to Nuala is like walking into a busy nightclub. It's noisy and full of energy, and you have to fight your way through a lot of writhing, sweaty limbs to get to the bar. I hoped there weren't any rare birds nesting in the bushes we'd chosen, because they'd just been disturbed from their habitat, no doubt moving out in disgust at the behaviour of the neighbours.

They say that part of Clumber Park is where they re-introduced some Red Kite a few years ago. These are huge birds that died out in England once, but a few kept going in Wales. Now they're back in these parts. I remember a court case once where a farmer got charged with wounding a couple who were having it off his cornfield. He said he mistook the bloke's bum going up and down in the corn for the backside of a rabbit, and that's why he blasted it with his shotgun. I don't think there are folk wandering around with shotguns in Clumber. But sometimes, when I'm with girls like Nuala, I do think of those Red Kite. They've got sharp talons, those buggers. And they hunt rabbits.

All the way through the proceedings, Nuala kept up a constant running commentary, telling me what do and where, commenting on my performance, cheering and shouting at the exciting bits. It was sort of like John Motson commentating on an England v Germany game. At any moment I expected her to criticise my ball control or my poor finishing. But somehow we always seemed to go into extra time and end up with a nail-biting penalty shoot-out.

When it was over, there were a few seconds of silence. I started to doze a bit, turning my face up to the sun and listening to the sounds of the birds complaining and the mums and dads screaming and shouting at their kids as they enjoyed a family afternoon out.

Then Nuala started to talk again. She was recalling a particularly successful sale she'd negotiated recently - a holiday for a retired couple in the Canadian Rockies. Apparently, the trees pictured on the brochure had looked not unlike those around us now in Clumber Park, in that they had leaves and things. The old couple had flown to Toronto from Heathrow and then caught an internal flight to Ottawa before getting on a train to some place in the foothills of the Rockies, and then they hired a car to drive a few hundred miles... Then I fell asleep. I used to think that nodding off after sex was something to do with your body's metabolism slowing down after the release of energy. Not always, though. Sometimes it's just sheer boredom.

I came round again a few minutes later, blearily thinking that Nuala's drone had became particularly monotonous, as if she was repeating the same phrase over and over again in a sort of peevish, high-pitched tone. This was perfectly likely, so it was a bit longer before I realised that the noise I was listening to was, in fact, my phone ringing.

I sat up, trying to look as if I'd just been thinking, and saw Nuala was talking to two ducks that had wandered over from the lake on the off-chance we might have some food about us. She looked as though she was getting more response from the ducks than she had from me. They were particularly riveted by a detailed inventory of facilities at the log cabin in the Rockies. A sauna and a jacuzzi? Flap of wings, gaping of beaks. The old couple had been delighted, had they? Flap, flap. gape. But the manager hadn't even bothered to say 'well done, Nuala'? That was enough to drive you quackers.

"Hello?" I said.

"Stones, it's Teri."

"Now then. How are you?"

"Okay, cut the crap. I had some sort of message. What is it you want?"

I'd almost forgotten she was one of my calls. I ought to be ashamed of myself. My contacts in the constabulary are down to one, and DC Teri Brooker is it.

"Aren't you going to ask me how I am, for old time's sake?"

"No. As far as I'm concerned, you're bad news, Stones. I'm only ringing so I can get you off my back. I don't want you pestering me at work."

"Now, I wouldn't do that. I don't want to prejudice your career, love. I know you're after a corner of the office to call your own and all that."

"Yes, and I'm not going to bollocks it all up by being caught talking to the likes of you. You're Reggie Kray and the Yorkshire Ripper rolled into one for some folk round here, you know. I wouldn't give much for your future if they ever got the chance to invite you in for a visit on a long-term basis."

"I'll bear it in mind. But I need to meet you, Teri."

"No."

"Somewhere discreet. No problem."

"It's too risky."

"You know I'd run any risk for your sake, Teri."

"I didn't mean - ." She sighed. "Is it important?"

"Of course it is. I wouldn't ask otherwise. I can feel the shit rising round me, and if I don't do something about it, your mates might just get that chance you were talking about."

"Where were you thinking of?"

"The Dukeries Garden Centre. You know the one, at Welbeck?"

"You're kidding."

"It's safe as houses. It's out of your patch, for a start."

It also wasn't Rufford, where my face might be starting to look a bit too familiar. But I didn't mention that to Teri.

"None of your lot are going to be sniffing about among all those respectable citizens," I said. "Not unless they're looking for stolen gladioli. We can park over by the far end of the walled garden and nobody will get close. We can visit the art gallery as well, if you're feeling intellectual."

The phone went quiet for a minute, as if she'd covered it with her hand.

"It'll have to be right now," she said. "It's the only chance I've got. Take it or leave it."

"I'll be there in half an hour, love."

Well, of course, Clumber Park is right next door to Welbeck. But somehow I had to dispose of Nuala before I met Teri.

She'd abandoned the ducks and was hovering nearby, listening to the last part of the phone call. I could see her brain connecting that 'love' with the scent in my car. She opened her mouth to make five, but I got in first.

"Do you fancy doing some shopping, Nuala?"

"Eh? Yeah."

"Come on then. If you've finished with the birds, that is."

She was in the car in a flash, and just as quickly she was rattling on about clothes and what she was thinking of buying. She seemed to imagine there'd be department stores and boutiques,

170

River Island and Next. I hadn't the heart to break it to her that I was dropping her in Worksop, which is more Oxfam and Help the Aged.

Even Nuala cottoned on quick when we pulled into the car park at the Priory Centre. When she got out of the car, there was only a canal and the back of Kwik Save, where she'd expected to see the atriums and fancy brickwork of a shopping mecca like Meadowhall or Crystal Peaks.

"Is this it? Have they got a C&A? Or only a Marks and Sparks?"

"Neither. But there's a good choice of charity shops. Save the Children have got a sale on."

She peered down at me through the driver's window. She'd left some of the buttons of her blouse open after I'd adjusted it for her in Clumber. It was a spectacular view from I was sitting. What a pity.

"So what exactly were you thinking of buying me?" she said.

I slid a note out of the roll in my back pocket and stuffed it carefully into her cleavage. It was a fifty, so you can't say I'm not generous.

"There's a place where you can buy almost the entire shop with that," I said. "It's called 'Owt for Next to Nowt' or something like that. They've got a lovely range of plastic kitchenware."

While she was fishing out the note to throw in my face, I eased the handbrake off and reversed towards the car park exit. When I did my three-point turn I could see her in my mirror, mouth still flapping. I was getting good at lip reading. But they certainly didn't sell that in Worksop.

On the way to Welbeck, I couldn't help casting a professional eye at a truck parked by the A60 near the Worksop bypass. It was another with French plates on, and I've learned enough of the lingo to translate the Frog croakings on the side to mean it belonged to an international haulage company based near Caen that specialises in electrical gear. I thumbed a number on the phone and mentioned the location of it to one of the lads, just in case. Business has to go on.

Did you know that over three thousand trucks are stolen in this country every year? Add an incredible twenty-five thousand

171

trailers, with goods inside them worth about the same as the national debt. This is straight up, too. I read about it in *Trucking International*. We're not talking peanuts here.

Someone once unloaded ninety-two thousand pounds' worth of Caterpillar boots after cropping open a container parked in a lay-by on the A45 in Northamptonshire. Three weeks before, seventy-five thousand quid in kids' clothes disappeared from a slashed curtain-sider on the same road. In the course of fifty days, no less than £280,000 in goods went from trucks in that area alone. I wasn't involved in any of that, of course. But I know a man who was.

Me, I prefer to target the continentals. It's a personal prejudice, but it gives me pleasure. You see all these Scanias and DAFs and Mercs, huge beasts some of them, trundling through our English counties bringing in stuff from all across Europe. There are no barriers now, they say, since they created the EU. So they come in their hordes, complaining that our roads aren't good enough and griping about the food in the transport caffs. Some of these French drivers bring their own frog's legs and picnic together by their wagons like they were too good to eat a plate of pie and chips like the locals do. As far as I'm concerned, if they make the mistake of stopping in Nottinghamshire, they're fair game.

Employers prefer drivers to park in official truck stops, but they don't always do it. This means they're a bit reluctant sometimes to admit where a load has been nicked from. Hampers the police no end, that does. So can a driver carrying on to his destination before discovering and reporting a theft. Hell, if you can't say where and when it happened, what can you expect the plods do but make an entry on their computer and write another one off to insurance? Victimless crime, see.

Let me tell you, this is nothing to what happens to British drivers over there. You've heard of the truckers hijacked and their loads of lamb burned at the roadside while the police looked on? You've heard of the haulage firms put out of business because of strikes and blockades by French drivers that their government doesn't do anything about? You've read about the Frog police wading in to open the borders to Germany and Spain, but not bothering about the blockades on Channel ports, because it only affects the English? European unity, this is.

A couple of years ago a lad from Staffordshire spent months in some arsehole of a French jail before a campaign by his family and public pressure got him out. What had he done? Crossed the Channel and picked up a container unit to bring back. Unknown to him, it contained drugs somebody had stashed in there. He'd been in France twenty minutes and had never even seen inside the trailer, which was locked and sealed when he collected it. How could he have hidden the drugs? But they banged him up straight away, left him shackled in chains without contact with his family and wouldn't let him have a lawyer when he appeared in court. He doesn't fancy going back to France now. You and me both, mate.

And you know what? We put billions of pounds every year into EU funds, and what do we get out of it? About ten million pounds in subsidies for rich git farmers to grow nothing, and a load of regulations that would stop you having a crap if it wasn't coming out the right shape. There needs to be a bit of equalisation, I reckon. If the French and German governments can subsidise their manufacturing industries, then maybe we ought to be having some of the benefits trickling down to us on the Forest Estate. Those Adidas tracksuits will do, for a start.

*   *   *   *

Teri Brooker is a nice girl really, and she doesn't deserve to be a copper. Putting on a hard front is just part of the job description. Really, she's another one with a soft spot for me. We go back quite a long way, actually, and our relationship has been fruitful in more ways than one. Now all we exchange is information, but not for want of trying on my part.

We were in the car park by the Dukeries Garden Centre. There is nothing else here, on the edge of the Welbeck Abbey grounds, apart from the Harley Gallery. Beyond the high walls at the back of the garden centre there's the Abbey itself, with its vast underground ballroom and the miles of tunnels built by the 5th Duke of Portland. You don't get the chance to get in there to see the place very often, being as how it's leased to the Ministry of Defence as a training college, while the last descendant of the dukes lives in a cottage in the grounds. The MoD don't make much fuss about their presence here - especially since someone strolled in one night and nicked half the Duke's paintings off the walls. Not me, honest.

I like to come to places like this, where the cops aren't likely to call. They're not generally known for their love of modern art or garden plants. Teri knew this, of course, but she was still edgy. She's been like this around me for a while now. You'd almost think I was the wrong sort of company for an ambitious detective constable.

I had to wind down the windows of the Subaru because she was smoking, a habit she must have picked up in the CID room to be one of the boys. She didn't smoke when I knew her better, but things have changed since then. She's after a sergeant's job these days. Meanwhile, I've gone right down the nick, of course. Teri was a few relationships before Lisa, probably three or four, maybe five. I lose count. But once they've had a fling with me they don't forget me. The charm works wonders. It always gets me what I want.

As we sat in the car, we were both watching the traffic coming in and out. Occasionally old couples would totter to their Fiestas and Nissan hatchbacks with armloads of geraniums and bags of compost, and families would emerge from their Peugeot estates, with the kids making a bee-line for the ice cream freezer. The art gallery was as quiet as the grave.

"I supposed you're going to ask me about Lloyd Thompson," she said.

"Well, yeah. A bit strange that, wasn't it? They can't have anything on him, not really."

"Why? Because he works for you? You're always so careful, aren't you, Stones?"

"It's what my mum always told me to be."

"No, they had nothing on him. It was Gleeson's idea. Moxon wouldn't have done it."

"Gleeson? Is he drugs squad?"

"Drugs squad? What ever gave you that idea?"

"Er... just a rumour."

"Detective Inspector Gleeson is Serious Crime."

"What sort of serious crime?"

"Can't tell you that, Stones."

"Shame."

We jumped as a couple of kids ran round the car, screaming and laughing. Their parents called them away, and Teri relaxed again. Me, I was still on tenterhooks.

"It was because Thompson's known as a driver," she said. "Gleeson wanted to pick some drivers up and lean on them, to see what it might produce. He was just chancing his arm."

"Teri - is this all about the new outfit that's supposed to be moving in?"

"You're not involved in that, are you, Stones? I don't suppose you'd tell me if you were. But I didn't believe the theory. It was just talk on the streets."

"No, I'm not. You know me better, Teri."

"Yes, I suppose so."

"So how come your lot are shooting in the dark looking for drivers? Why haven't they picked up the dealers?"

"Dealers? You're on about drugs still. What's the matter with you?"

"Sorry. Not drugs then, something else. Some major consignments of... something you can't tell me about. But you've never picked up the main men?"

Teri sighed. "We got close. Gleeson's lot had observation on them, but the operation went wrong."

"Wrong? You mean they spotted your people?"

"Not exactly."

"What, then?"

She sat mum and gazed towards the gallery. There's a nice fountain and some landscaped water gardens. Restful to look at, particularly when you want to avoid answering somebody's question.

"Teri, I need to know if they've got inside information. Is someone leaking to them from your side?"

"No, it wasn't that. To tell the truth, someone took our car."

"What?"

"Our lot had followed them to a motorway services. For some reason, both officers went into the building and left their vehicle in the car park. It had gone when they got back."

"Really?"

"The chief hit the roof. It wasn't the usual type of car either. It was something no one would expect."

"Oh? What?"

"A Citroen BX. You know, the one with hydraulic suspension? It's a good car. And nobody ever suspects it's one of ours."

"Is that right, Teri?"

Now it was my turn to look away, so I stared at the displays of flowers in the garden centre. The carnations were a lovely blushing pink. Just over the wall were the tunnels built by an eccentric duke to avoid having to see anybody. He must really have had something to be embarrassed about, mustn't he? But I think I knew how he felt.

"And I suppose the two blokes are in deep trouble for losing it?"

"Very deep." She sighed at the badness of the world, bless her. "I don't know, Stones. Some folk will nick anything, won't they?"

"Too true."

A bloke came past the car carrying an enormous rose bush that hid his face. Just the trick an undercover cop might use. But he wasn't looking at us, and anyway his feet were too small. I came back to a comment that Teri had made a few minutes earlier.

"This talk on the streets, Teri?"

"There's a new operation. Well, not new maybe, but expanding fast."

"Getting serious?"

"Yes. A few small-scale thefts might go by without attracting too much interest. But once things move up a notch, it's a different matter. That gets attention."

"And somebody's been saying that I'm involved in this operation, is that what you mean?"

"So Gleeson says. His lot have informants all over the place. They listen to everything that's being said."

"Somebody's spreading this deliberately. I'm on somebody's shit list."

"You mean hit list."

"Not really."

"Well, the talk is catching. You'd better watch yourself."

I thought about the German car that had chased us over the heath at Medensworth.

"Teri - have your lot been tailing me?"

"Not that I know of. Why?"

"Just thinking."

"Don't get paranoid. You're not that important."

Teri got out of the car, taking her tobacco smoke with her, as well as a certain sense of security.

"Can't I even buy you a pot plant?" I said.

"I can't grow pot in the office - not with the drugs squad about."

"Thanks then, Teri."

"I can't do any more to help you, Stones. I'm sorry."

"It's okay, love."

She drove out of the car park at a sedate pace. Nobody followed her. Yet it was only a matter of seconds before the passenger door of the Subaru opened and somebody slipped into the seat next to me. The smell of tobacco was replaced by motor oil and chips.

"Copper, ain't she? Nice looking piece, though."

"Where were you hiding, Trevor?"

"That'd be telling. I bought this, look, while I was waiting."

He was clutching a cactus in his grimy hand. It was one of those plants with obscene-looking fleshy fingers. You know the ones - they stand at attention, rigid and spiky, and don't change for what seems like for ever. They burst into flower about once every ten years, then go all limp and drooping. I remember they made quite an impression on my fertile imagination when I was pubescent teenager.

Trevor's clothes were just as filthy as they'd been at Rufford the day before. I winced at the threat to my seat covers and opened the windows a bit further.

"It's very nice, Trevor. I suppose you'll put it on expenses?"

"It's necessary camouflage. Justifiable expenditure."

"Right." Funny how he slipped into accountant-speak whenever you mentioned money. It was the one weakness in his performance. "Did you get me some stuff on those names?"

"The names? Of course." He pulled my crumpled bit of paper from his pocket. "One in particular. This name." He pointed at the list. "He's got a bit of a background all right, this bloke. Been away for a bit, but he's back in action. And the word is that he's got his eye on bigger things now."

"Operating in this area?"

"Likely."

"Only likely, Trevor?"

He shrugged. "You add two and two together, and you've got a likelihood, not a certainty."

"Really? When I was at school they told me it actually was a certainty. Four, in fact. Every time."

"You obviously didn't do Differential Calculus, mate."

"You're bloody right, I didn't."

"Well, then."

Trevor was fingering his cactus, rubbing his thumbs over the spines as if he was counting them. Presumably he got a different number each time.

"So. This is the bloke I'm really looking for, is it?"

"No, I wouldn't say so."

"What? Is there someone else on the list you know about?"

"Well, the rest are low level. I mean there's one who isn't on your list at all. These others are working for him now. They're aiming to be on the up, and he's the one with the right contacts, see."

"Tell me about him, then."

"A bloke called Perella. That's all I know."

"All? All? Not even a first name?"

He shrugged.

"Is he Italian or something, with a name like that?"

He shrugged again.

"What's up, Trevor? Aren't I paying you enough?"

"You haven't paid me anything yet."

"So what's wrong? What's happened to your famous methods?"

178

"Well, this Perella - he might be a bloke with contacts, but he also seems to have no past. Not one that I can dig out anyway, so far. Give me time, then maybe. But he hasn't got a record, and he's not been involved in any previous jobs I know of. Basically, no one knows nothing about him. He works through second division blokes like these on your list, and he only contacts them by phone. He's careful. A bit like you, Stones."

"Yeah, thanks. That was the sort of conclusion Eddie Craig was coming to as well."

"So you're not Perella, then?"

"Bloody hell, Trevor."

"I only asked. Your name has been mentioned, see. In passing."

"It's about time people stopped mentioning it. All this talk makes me nervous. It could do me damage."

"I reckon it has already, hasn't it? That's what they're saying. Someone's trying to close you down, Stones. Is it Craig?"

I could see Trevor working out whether his invoice was going to get paid, or if he'd have to go through the hassle of claiming off my estate after my premature death.

"Funnily enough, I think Craig's on my side."

"Lucky you. Because he's not a happy man at the minute."

"Tell me about it."

"That's what I'm doing."

"You could have fooled me. Not unless you're talking in code. So far you've told me sod all. I could have found out more reading the growing instructions on that cactus."

"There aren't any instructions on it," he said, turning the pot round and nearly skewering my eye with the spikes.

"That's exactly the point, nerk."

Trevor looked at me disapprovingly. "As I was saying, Eddie Craig isn't happy. In fact, he's got his blokes running round like idiots. They're liable to flatten anybody who gets in their way, and I don't intend it to be me, Stones."

"Why the hell should it be?"

"If you ask questions in the wrong place, it can have consequences. We might have to discuss risk payments."

179

He squirmed in agitation, shifting his plant from one hand to the other.

"Trevor, keep that bloody thing out my face."

We both struggled with the cactus pot for a minute until we got it firmly wedged through the steering wheel. I started trying to pick the spines out of my hand.

"So what's up with Eddie Craig exactly?"

"Craig's hopping mad since one of his clubs was turned over," said Trevor. "They nicked the takings and trashed the place. Right mess, it was."

"Shit. You mean the Blue Bird? That's one of Craig's places?"

"That's it. Of course, he's scared that word will get round he did nothing about it, and then his reputation as the top hard man would be completely shot. That would be the end for Craig - all sorts of people would start moving in on him, and his lads would go off to find better jobs with other firms. He has to come down heavy on somebody, but he doesn't know who. Soon he's just going to pick on someone and make a scapegoat of them, I reckon."

"Right."

"Might be you, Stones. So they say."

"That's why I have to prove to him it was someone else, Trevor."

"I get you."

"So you have to find more on this Perella for me, mate."

"Well, I'll do my best. But it gets costly in these circumstances."

"Do you want to take your cactus and go home and write out your invoice, then?"

"I've got people to do that for me."

Trevor tugged the plant free of the steering wheel, leaving a bit of it behind to catch me out later on when I wasn't looking. He got out of the Subaru, carefully manoeuvring his cactus so that it didn't catch on the door frame. The garden centre was closing for the evening, and he hated to look conspicuous.

"Is that it for now?" he said. "Have you done with me?"

I looked at him. Was he laughing? "Do you know something else, Trevor?"

"Well, I know about the job that Perella's lot are planning for tomorrow night," he said. "If you were interested, that is."

16

The Jewellery Box had been ram raided before. Watches, rings and necklaces are valuable stuff, easily scooped up in armfuls through a smashed shop window. The council is thinking about extending the anti ram raid bollards down as far as the Jewellery Box, but it hasn't got round to it yet. So it looked as though the shop's insurance premiums were about to go up again.

The day had been spent making a few preparations, and now it was the early hours, still dark. Even the nightclubbers had long since gone home to their sweaty beds.

"Hey, they've nicked one of those Mitsubishi Shoguns," said Slow Kid admiringly over the phone next morning. "Nice set of wheels. Brilliant for this job."

"Yeah, Slow. But what's the getaway car?"

"Looks like an old Sierra. White." He gave me the registration number. "There's two in the Jap wagon, one in the Sierra. They're about to go for it any minute."

"Are they pointed the right way?"

"Sure. Nose towards the roundabout. They won't be wasting any time doing u-turns. This stuff is strictly wham-bam, thank you mam."

There was no one about on the roads at all, except for those up to no good at all, like the police and milkmen. These lads in the Shogun were relying on having no witnesses when they hit the Jewellery Box, and no cops nearer than Ollerton. They would have been right too, if it hadn't been for Slow Kid, who had an old Astra parked up by the wall of the Dog and Ferret across the road, making it look like the motor of some drunk who had the sense to leave it there and walk home.

"Wow! Hear that?"

Even on the mobile I could hear the bang and shattering of glass, followed a second later by the shriek of a burglar alarm.

Watches and jewellery would be disappearing about now into a couple of sports bags as the lads grabbed the contents of the window display like supermarket dash contestants on a TV game show.

They wouldn't be long about it. In a few seconds, they'd be back across the pavement to the Sierra and away, with no lights until they got round the corner and into the back streets. By the time the cops had woken up, had a scratch and cranked the handle on one of their clapped-out Rovers, these lads would be long gone. They hadn't reckoned with me, though.

Then Slow Kid was back on. "Here they go, legging it for the Sierra. Third bloke's revving the engine, he can't wait. Yeah, in they go. And off."

"Don't let them see you. Let them think they're clean away. Then make sure you disappear before the cops arrive."

"No problem, Stones. The Sierra's half way down the road. No lights. He'll hit the roundabout in one minute. I'm off now."

"Cheers, mate."

I dialled a new number. I could hear the Sierra's engine now, getting nearer, and very distantly the first wail of a police siren. The ram raiders would aim to clear the roundabout and be into the middle of the estate before the cops came over the hill and got a sight of them. They were going to make the roundabout, but I didn't intend them to reach the estate.

Just in time, I heard the sound of another, larger engine. From my vantage point, I could see a pair of powerful headlights spring to life as a car transporter began to back out of the garage by the roundabout. It immediately blocked the near side of the road and rapidly narrowed the gap on the far side, where the wall of the chip shop stuck out towards the corner.

The brakes of the Sierra screamed as it came into the roundabout and found no way onto the estate. As the driver swung the wheel to the right he saw, dead ahead, the back gates of the old pit site. They stood invitingly open, some vandal having sheared off the lock earlier that night. Beyond the gates was a vast, dark expanse of steep slopes and dusty roadways where they could surely abandon the car and make a run for it. It was either that or go back round the roundabout and meet the cops coming the other way. No contest.

With only a second to make his decision, the driver went for it. The Sierra skidded through the gates and vanished into darkness. The driver of the transporter braked, revved his vehicle back up into the garage and thoughtfully locked the pit gates behind the Sierra. Then he, too, disappeared into the night.

I watched the car plough its way over the rise and down the other side, moving cautiously now as it lost the street lights and the driver had to search for a roadway. They got to a nice flat stretch where the road curved behind a heap of rubble. Down in the village, a police vehicle went by, lights blazing, and vanished into the estate. Its siren masked the funny popping noise made by the Sierra's tyres as they burst on the sharpened nails buried in the roadway. Those vandals again.

The car bounced on for a few more yards before it stopped, with its wheel rims starting to dig into the dust. The driver got out, cursing like anything, and didn't see me as I stepped out of the shadows. I grabbed him as he bent down to look at the tyres and flattened him across his own bonnet. A moment later, Doncaster Dave had hold of the other two blokes.

"Do you need some help, sir?" I said. "To our members, we're the fourth emergency service. We're the AA, you know. 'Ard Arseholes."

* * * *

The winding engine house is still standing there on the remains of Medensworth pit. Do I need to tell you that they plan to restore it one day? The money will come from the government, the European Union, or the National Lottery, or wherever. One day. But at the moment it's occupied only be the pigeons that roost on the spattered window ledges.

The only people who come to look at the winding house and the headstocks are the miners who used to work here. The cage that lies jammed just underground is the one that took them down into the earth every day to work. It isn't heritage for them. Not yet.

184

They've put up a steel security fence around the site to deter intruders. Otherwise the kids would be in here, smoking and shooting up and having sex. Inside the fence sit the concrete and brick walls of the winding house, with its arched windows. There are huge vents, two feet across, and skips full of rubbish waiting to be taken away. A boiler about twelve feet high lies abandoned, leaning at a drunken angle. When you look at the winding gear itself, it's amazing to think that men's lives hung from those wheels on two steel cables no more than an inch thick.

These wheels are the most distinctive markers on the landscape. They tell us we're in coal mining country. Like two big blue bicycle wheels, they sit at the top of the headstocks and can be seen for miles. The modern superpits hid them inside concrete towers, but they're still there. As pits have closed, a use has been found for some of these wheels. A couple even decorate the front of the Wonderland Pleasure Park. I kid you not.

But maybe this is better than the sad fate of the old headstocks at Brinsley, which are abandoned in the middle of a field, like some unexplained megalith, a twentieth century Stonehenge. In the future, people will wonder about them. What did anyone do here? What strange rituals did they go through under this mysterious structure?

At the top of the engine house are two narrow slits, where you can step out onto the diagonal girders supporting the wheels. There are handrails to help you walk up the girders - because that's what they had to do to keep the winding gear maintained. A ladder takes you from the girders to the platform around the wheels. Below you then are four concrete pillars, with two cables hanging between them, and the cage just visible in the hole in the ground.

A few new industrial units have been built by the road, and some of the old pit offices and store rooms are still standing, their yards full of bits of old cars and junk so useless that no one can be bothered to nick it. The rest of the site is grassed over, awaiting development. But the grass has that peculiar brown look that tells you it's growing on something other than soil. Here and there a birch or a clump of bracken is trying to re-colonise the area. At the entrance, a sign says the pit site has been designated under the

New Deal for Nottinghamshire programme. The sign is starting to look old.

The site of this old pit is probably one of the most barren places in the country now. It has been levelled into a plateau, but great grey mounds of rubble have been left, mountains of dust and shattered lumps of concrete, broken drainage pipes and bricks. Around them still lie the piles of black spoil and dusty roadways carved out by heavy-wheeled vehicles. The ruts they've left fill up with evil black mud in the winter. Here and there rusty metal rods protrude from the flattened earth. Lumps of iron with no apparent purpose lie abandoned among the slag and stone and the scrubby plants.

A sign says 'Warning to children and parents - building sites BITE'. But there's no building going on here, no work of any kind. The bulldozers have done their job and left. The rails and sleepers have been pulled up from the old mineral lines, though the signals are still there, and even a little signal box up the line. The shaft itself is well filled in, and sealed over tight with concrete. No memories here. The whole thing has been obliterated.

In the middle of the devastation, some joker has planted a red flag. Its fluttering is the only movement, apart from the pigeons and the occasional rabbit scuttling towards the scrubby undergrowth.

Well, that's during the day. At night, it's nowhere near so pretty.

It's quiet up here on the plateau, only the sound of birds and the traffic going by on the back road under the old rail bridges. The gates are well blocked with heaps of spoil to stop vehicles getting on, but to those in the know the new roads give easy access to the pit site across the bridge. Then you drive between the mountains of debris and you find yourself in a dip, a little hollow hidden by great clumps of bramble and bracken. No one can see you here. No one can even see a thirty-foot truck down here.

I had the Subaru parked up behind the winding gear house. To the east, a faint glimmer of light was coming up over the hills near the M1. If I strained my eyes hard, I thought I might see the outline of Hardwick Hall.

Slow Kid and Metal pulled up in the Astra, and Metal wound down the window.

"We could have got that Jap car away while the cops weren't looking, Stones. There was hardly any damage."

"You're kidding."

"There's a bloke in Holland just can't get enough of them four wheel drives."

"Not now, Metal."

In the back of the Sierra were two figures slumped low on the seat, and between them a great hulk of something that looked a bit like Doncaster Dave. Come to think of it, it *was* Doncaster Dave, but he looked a lot more handsome than usual, because he was wearing a stocking stretched over his head. Lovely. Look no further for the Face of the New Millennium.

I opened the gate in the steel fence and the two cars pulled in behind the winding gear house. Slow parked the Astra in the shadow of the derelict boiler, and they all got out. The two lads in the Sierra needed a bit of help, as their legs seemed to have gone wobbly. But Dave was quite willing to give them a hand. It must have been a bit like being helped across the road by Godzilla. When the four of us had gathered round them, they were looking definitely nervous.

The lads weren't much to look at, typical weedy scruffs from the council estates in Mansfield or Ashfield. Neither of them would make the meat in a sandwich for Doncaster Dave. They were scared already, not know what was going on. It's like that when things go wrong unexpectedly. It's the unknown that does it. Of course, this makes it easier for us.

Metal and Slow tied the lads' hands behind their backs with some blackened rope and fastened it to one of the steel cables that held the cage suspended from the winding wheel. We all looked down, and the lads looked too. There was a big black hole down there below the cage that looked as though it went down into the earth for miles. Well, it did once. But now it's only a few feet down to the concrete cap they used to seal the shaft. I was betting these lads didn't know that, though.

"Right, lads. Sorry to leave you hanging around like this. But if you don't tell me everything you know, you're going to feel really let down. Know what I mean?"

"We're working for a bloke called Rawlings," said one lad straightaway.

"That's a good start, youth."

It didn't take long to find out what we needed to know. They were only amateurs, well out of their depth. They opened up beautifully.

Afterwards, we dropped the kids off on the edge of Mansfield and left the Sierra in a lay-by on the A60, minus its most valuable contents. Maybe the car's owner would get it back after all, if somebody else didn't nick it first.

On the way back to Medensworth, Dave had a question. For once, it wasn't about where we were going to eat.

"Stones," he said, trying out the sound of his voice.

"Yeah, Donc?"

"These ram raids, like."

"What about 'em?"

"I was just wonderin'. What do they need all these rams for anyway?"

"I dunno, Donc. Maybe they use them to baa-ter for drugs."

"Maybe," he said, not convinced.

I didn't think it was funny either. But right now I was fresh out of sheep jokes.

17

"Parish registers, electoral rolls, estate records, court proceedings." Lisa had chosen Saturday morning to give me a bit of an insight into researching someone's family tree.

"Court proceedings? Not relatives of Mr bleedin' Cavendish, surely?"

"They would have been sitting on the bench perhaps, in his case."

"Right."

"It's fascinating what you can dig up once you start trying," said Lisa dreamily. "All it needs is a bit of time and someone who knows where to look."

"That's you, of course."

"Well, I think so."

"I'm glad you've got so much time."

"Well, the Hardwick Hall job is only part-time, you know."

"Yeah. And there's nothing else for you to do with yourself, so obviously you need Cavendish and his little job to occupy you. I understand."

"Come on. Get those numbers filled in."

"I can't think of any."

"You don't have to think of any, they're printed on the cards for you. You just have to cross a few off."

"It's hard. It's too much like maths."

"The numbers only run from one to forty-nine. Surely you can add up that far?"

"Not necessarily," I said. "I can see you never did Differential Calculus."

"If you don't stop messing about and fill those numbers in, we'll miss the draw."

I can't really see the point of the National Lottery. Let's face it, all we're doing is rushing like lemmings to pour our money into the pockets of a load of fat cats. Okay, so someone has to win a few million now and then. But it won't be you or me, I guarantee it. I've never been one for gambling. I prefer a safe bet. Life itself is too much of a gamble as it is. Sometimes it seems like we spend our entire lives queuing up with all the other mugs in Peter Vardi's 24-hour superstore and video hire, clutching our lottery tickets and hoping that one day some big glittery finger will come down out of the sky and make the whole bleedin' thing worth while. But then one day our number really does come up, and it's bingo! Sorry, is that the wrong game?

No use saying this to Lisa, though. She's the sort who reads the horoscopes in six newspapers and ten magazines every week - and believes them all without blinking. She has a lucky teddy bear and a lucky pixie on her key ring and won't open the door to a tall dark stranger if there's a 'p' in the month. When it comes to the lottery, she naturally picks her numbers using the birthdays of her mum, dad, sister, boyfriend and dog. Then she sticks with them every week, for God's sake. This is a disaster. It's exactly what they want you to do. Because you can't miss a week then, can you? You're obsessed with the fear that your numbers will come up the week you don't bother. It's a prospect too terrible to contemplate. Awful. What would become of you? Well, actually, you'd be in exactly the same position you were before - except a few pounds better off from the money you didn't spend on lottery tickets.

"Have you done it yet?"

"Oh, er... can I have 12 six times?"

"You're in an awkward mood today, aren't you?"

"Is that 'no'?"

"Are you jealous of Michael Cavendish?"

"Don't forget his hyphens. His name might fall apart without them."

"You are, aren't you? That's what all that business was about at Rufford yesterday. I thought at first you were just being obnoxious as usual."

"Thanks."

"I'm only working for him, you know. Nothing more."

"Sure. Helping him to make a family."

"Helping him to *find* a family. Silly pillock."

190

"He is, duck, I agree. I'm glad you've seen through him."

"I meant you."

"It's no use trying to talk me round. Let me get on with my lottery numbers. What's two and two?"

"In your case, whatever you decide to make it."

"That'll do, then. Two hundred and thirty seven million, nine hundred and twelve thousand, four hundred and sixty."

"What?"

"Two. Three. Seven. Nine. Twelve. And Forty-six."

"Oh."

"Are we off now?"

"Did you hear what I was telling you, Stones?"

"Yeah, yeah."

"I'll be upset if you keep this up."

Lisa thought she really had my number, but she was wrong. She was just acting out her part. Have you noticed how women are like that? I don't want to sound sexist or anything, but it's true. Some women seem to accept whatever role is forced on them, as if they're in some kind of play and have no choice. That's okay if you get a good part. But sometimes the Great Director in the Sky says to you: "All right - here's your part, kid. You're going to be a bloody martyr for the rest of your life. Everyone's going to shit on you from a great height, and you'll just have to lump it." A bloke, now, would be likely to say: "Stuff that, mate. I'd rather have a part where I can knock about with the lads a bit, watch some football on Saturday, go to the pub, you know? I'm not bothered if it's a small part, as long as I can have a bit of fun." But women? They go along with it, play the role to the hilt as if they're going for a bleedin' Oscar. Year's Best Portrayal of a Martyr or something. 'And I'd like to thank my dear old mother, for whom nothing I ever did was good enough, and my dad who really wanted a boy, and of course my husband who put himself about all over the county for years, got drunk every night and beat me black and blue. Not forgetting my kids, who walked all over me without a word of thanks. I couldn't have done it without them.'

But to me they always seem to ham it up too much, overdo the melodrama. If I was a critic, I'd give most of 'em a two-star rating.

You'd only go and see it if the tickets are free and there's nothing on the telly except *Blind Date*.

Personally, if I wanted a bit of dodgy method acting I'd go and watch some old Marlon Brando films. At least you can get back out into the real world after a couple of hours. And you don't get those long-suffering looks when you eat your popcorn either.

*　*　*　*

We walked down to Vardi's to get our lottery tickets. I don't know what my stars said I had in store, but I knew my luck wasn't in, not this week.

I hung about outside the shop while Lisa went in to queue for the tickets. Idly, I read the postcards in the window. Most of them were offering second hand Sega Megadrives and unused baby buggies. There were several adverts for homeworkers, promising earnings of up to three hundred pounds a week. For some reason, all the companies seemed to be based in Birmingham.

From here, I could see the health centre down Yew Tree Avenue and the roof of the junior school. Just past the shops was the alleyway that led to the old people's bungalows with their concrete fencing and postage stamp gardens. The path was decorated with Walkers crisp packets and small heaps of dog muck.

A couple of blokes carrying snooker cues in leather cases walked past on their way to the Welfare. A dog was barking somewhere as usual, and behind me I could hear stirrings in the Bombay Duck takeaway as they got ready for the lunchtime trade. This week, their window posters were promoting a special offer on doner kebabs and naan bread. The Duck was the only shop in the parade not to have steel shutters on its windows. Who'd want to nick some chicken curry?

I was thinking about this when I noticed a car parked past the Bombay Duck, outside the little motor spares shop. It was pulled into the kerb, with its boot towards me, but I noticed it because its brake lights were on. If somebody sits with their brake lights on while they're stationary, it tends to make you think they're ready for a quick getaway.

The car was a dark blue saloon, a German job with alloy wheels. And it made me think. It made me remember the car that had followed us the other night from the Dog and Ferret, the one that Slow Kid had managed to lose on the heath. There was a figure in the driving seat, and I decided it would be interesting to see who he was. I started to walk up the pavement and almost bumped into another bloke who came out of the spares shop. He had a carrier bag in his hand and looked to be in a hurry.

He was already at the door of the car before he looked up, and we recognised each other.

"Rawlings."

He didn't have time to talk, his expression seemed to say. He opened the door and shouted something to the bloke at the wheel. As I came up, the driver turned quick and looked at me with those dead eyes. I was too slow to dodge the door that flew open and cracked me hard across the knees. Hell, that hurt.

That was how I came to be lying sideways on the pavement as they drove away. And that was why I could only remember part of the registration number, on account of my head being at the wrong angle. Oh, and my eyes being shut with the pain.

"Stones, what the hell do you think you're doing?"

"Hello, love. Just resting."

Lisa stood over me, looking less than sympathetic. "You're making a fool of yourself. Get up."

"I think I might have broken my leg."

"Rubbish. Get up, you pillock."

I struggled to my feet, wincing at the agony in my shins, and worrying that the fancy pattern on my boots might have got scratched. Dan Posts these, you know. Three hundred dollars, at least.

Lisa did nothing to help me, just stood there with her hands on her hips, looking just like my mum when I hadn't washed behind my ears properly.

"If I didn't know better, I'd say you were drunk."

"At this time of the morning? In any case, you've only had your eye off me for two minutes."

"Mmm. You're up to something."

"Me? Never. Can't you see I'm injured here, woman?"

"You're always pissing about, Stones. Always."

*   *   *   *

Then we called in at the Cow for an early lunchtime drink - me hobbling and Lisa wearing that tight smile she uses when she disapproves of me. I couldn't have got any further than the Cow just then, with my injuries. Fortunately, Lisa's not proud about where she drinks. Good job too. I've been banned from all the places that have ash trays.

It was only two days since I'd been in this same bar with Nuala, of course. But it didn't worry me. People in the Cow don't talk more than they have to, not about each other. It's likely to shorten your life span a bit, which is why I had to lean on Moggie Carr so much. No daft bugger's going to come wandering up and ask who the other bird was that I was with the other day.

In a way, it would have been a relief if they'd done that. I hadn't come up with any good ideas yet on how to ease Lisa out. I was hoping Michael bleedin' Cavendish would do the job for me, but I might have to give her a bit of a push. Sounds cruel, I know, but that's me. Love 'em and leave 'em and move on to the next thing. You take root if you stand still.

"Hey, Stones."

I looked around me. In the corridor to the gents, Slow Kid Thompson was lurking behind a doorway, out of sight of the bar.

"What you doing there, Slow? You owe somebody money again?"

He shook his head. "I've got something to tell you."

"Spit it out, then. Let's go in here."

He followed me into the gents. I wouldn't normally have felt uneasy about this with Slow, if it wasn't for the way he kept looking around like a guilty old pervert.

"What is it?" I said as I let a golden stream hit the stainless steel. It made a nice hollow drumming noise that you could almost play tunes with. I fancied something with a bit of a heavy beat today.

"Eddie Craig," he said.

The stream faltered and the tune became a harpsichord sonata. Sir Thomas Beecham described the noise of the harpsichord as 'two skeletons copulating on a corrugated tin roof'. How appropriate.

"What about him?"

"He's looking for you, Stones. He thinks you had something to do with the ram raid that went wrong."

"What gives him that idea?"

"Talk."

I was dry now, mainly around the mouth.

"I don't particularly want to see him just at the moment, Slow."

"What you going to do then?"

"Go back and talk nicely to Lisa."

"Right? So - "

"You wouldn't understand that, Slow. Sometimes that's what you have to do with women. Talk nicely to them."

"To keep 'em sweet, you mean?"

"No. I mean when you want something."

*　　*　　*　　*

We went in Lisa's Fiat. It wasn't fast, it wasn't posh, it wasn't even clean. But with a bit of luck it wouldn't be recognised by Craig and his boys, or anyone who felt like blabbing to them.

"I'm not sure how long I can put you up for, Stones," she said. "I'm a bit busy right now."

"I know, love. But I won't be any trouble. It'll just be until they get the problem sorted out."

"It was a bit sudden, wasn't it?"

"These old gas pipes, you know. The council should have replaced them ages ago. I suppose it's been building up for years, then suddenly the gas leaks into the house. If I stayed in there another night it could have been 'poof' - no more Stones McClure."

I just had one overnight bag with me, containing a few clothes and stuff. But I also had a rather important sports bag, which I have to admit did not contain my tennis gear. It had arrived by special courier one night, sent by a business contact who'd recently taken delivery from me of a French-registered lorry full of leather jackets, jeans and denim shirts.

"It's terrible," said Lisa. "I hope you get compensation from the council."

"Well, you know - I don't like to insist on anything like that. It's all our money, isn't it? Us taxpayers. The Council Tax, I mean."

"Still. They'd better do a proper job."

"I'll complain to Councillor Border if they don't."

That made her laugh. "I didn't think you liked him. I once heard you call him a grade one plonker."

"Just because I'd rather vote for a rabid dog doesn't mean he's not there to represent my interests."

"I'm sure he'd love to give you some advice."

"Yeah, I can imagine."

It was going to be hell shacking up in Lisa's house. The frilly curtains and the pot pourri were really depressing. After a day or two, I'd go away smelling of patchouli oil and rosewater. I'd probably get banned from the Cow's Arse for offensive behaviour. And then there was the teddy bear. I've had a problem about sharing a bed with furry creatures ever since my older brother slipped a mouse under my sheets when I was eight. So I could foresee a bit of bedtime conflict there.

We stopped at the little shop in Lisa's village to stock up with a few bottles of wine. Lisa came out with pasta, red peppers, sun-dried tomatoes and a bottle of olive oil. It looked like we weren't on fish fingers and chips tonight then.

Once in the house, Lisa headed for the kitchen while I found a discreet place to tuck the sports bag away. It would have to stay there until I got chance to take it to the bank. I wasn't worried - if Lisa noticed it, she'd just assume it was my dirty laundry or something. Then I grabbed the TV remote control and got my feet up on the settee, remembering to take my boots off first. It was getting close to news time, and you've got to keep up to date.

After a while, Lisa stuck her head round the kitchen door a couple of times to look at me. I caught her expression one of these times, and expected it to be a bit of irritation about this obnoxious bloke idling about on his backside while she did the cooking, getting inside her house and straightaway taking her for granted as the skivvy. But that wasn't what I saw on her face at all. It was something much more worrying. I missed half of what Anna Ford was telling me about the latest Middle East crisis while I turned the subtleties of that expression over in my mind. Impatiently, I thumbed the remote and got a load of adverts about cars and clothes and electrical gadgets that we really had to own. Then it came to me. That was the expression on Lisa's face - possessiveness.

I nearly walked out of the house right then. Any self-respecting bloke who values his independence would feel the same. But, to be honest, I was getting a bit peckish and the aroma from the kitchen was starting to smell pretty good. It even overpowered the pot pourri.

I hit the remote again and went back to Anna. In Scotland, a gang had raided the Microsoft factory and nicked half a million quids' worth of software CDs. That's something I've never got into. None of the lads round here would recognise Windows from a wildebeest.

Later, we sank a bottle of wine with our meal and chatted about this and that. The fate of Lord Byron's Newstead Abbey, where old mining activity was likely to send the building crumbling into a big hole, tourists and all. A scheme to plant millions of trees on the slag heaps to restore some of the old Sherwood Forest. I can talk quite intelligently on subjects like this with Lisa. Especially when she doesn't mention Michael Cavendish once.

I looked out of the little front window into the street. The terrace opposite was starting to disappear as dusk fell, and lights were coming on in the houses. I could hear Lisa washing up in the kitchen, singing quietly to herself. The pot pourri was starting to beat back the scent of pasta and Liebfraumilch. Porcelain nicknacks and dried flower arrangements stared at me from every corner of the room. The rug looked so comfortable in front of the

197

gas fire that it ought to have a sleeping cat on it. Upstairs, a teddy bear waited.

"Lisa?"

"Yes, Stones?"

She pulled her hands out of the sink. She was wearing yellow plastic gloves covered in green suds, and the kitchen smelled of artificial lemons. A tea towel with greetings from Edinburgh hung invitingly over a chair, waiting for someone to pick it up and start drying.

"Can I borrow your car for a bit?"

"Well... yes, I suppose so."

She waited for me to tell her where I was going.

"The keys are on the sideboard, aren't they? I noticed you put them there."

"That's right."

I pulled my leather jacket on and collected the keys. There was an old dog lead lying next to them on the sideboard, and it seemed to be attached to the key ring. I recalled that Lisa had once owned a dog, a cocker spaniel, but it had got the push for disturbing the scatter cushions or something. I couldn't get the lead free from the keys, so I took it with me.

"Will you be long?" Lisa had picked up the tea towel and followed me to the front door with it, as if offering an irresistible temptation.

"Just a bit of business I have to see to."

We kissed on the doorstep, and she watched me as I drove away, back towards Medensworth. On the way, I finally managed to get the dog lead untangled from the keys and shoved it in my pocket. I immediately felt better.

*　　*　　*　　*

I got hold of Dave straightaway on the mobile. I don't know what he does with his spare time, but if it doesn't involve food, then it's probably an activity unknown to anthropologists. When he answered the phone he sounded as though somebody had just switched him on and his valves were still warming up.

198

"Donc, it's Stones."

"Lo."

"Are you doing anything?"

"Nope."

"Can you meet me in about ten minutes?"

"Yeah."

"Not at my place or at the Cow. Outside the churchyard at St Asaph's."

"Right."

"You know where I mean, don't you?"

"Yeah."

"And Donc?"

"Yeah?"

"Don't go shooting your mouth off to anyone about me, right?"

I was at the churchyard first. I parked Lisa's Fiat on the little lane that runs up the side of the church and killed the lights. Dave was pretty recognisable, and I wanted to be able to see him coming, in case he had unwanted company. It was a dark spot here, with no street lights past the last cottage across the road. In the churchyard, there were plenty of shadows to lurk in.

I got out to stretch my legs for a few minutes while I waited. The church is built on a mound above the level of the street, and I could easily see in the direction that Dave would come from as I walked past the porch towards the graveyard. Dark graveyards don't hold any terrors for me. There's only one ghost that I'm ever likely to meet here, and it doesn't frighten me.

But where was Dave? I looked down into the street. No sign of him. Then I looked the other way, and forgot about Dave for a second. There was a car outside the vicarage. Not the Rev's puke-coloured Metro, but something bigger, flashier, with tinted windows. When I got closer I saw that it was a Jaguar, lovingly polished and with a pony-tailed thug sitting tapping his fingers on the steering wheel.

I thought of Eddie Craig, and it wasn't a nice thought. If Craig was in the vicarage talking to the Reverend Bowring, it was a fair bet he wasn't there to ask for the Rev's advice on filling a yawning spiritual vacuum in his life. Craig had so many sins to confess that

199

hearing them would take a regiment of Revs working twelve-hour shifts until the next Millennium.

I suddenly had a cold feeling in my stomach. Whether Craig was in there himself or not, there would be at least two of his louts. I didn't think he'd want the Rev hurt too badly. It was information he was after - information about me. He wanted to know where to find me. And if the Rev had any sense, he'd tell what he knew rightaway, before the knuckle dusters came out and 'love thy neighbour' degenerated into a bit of Old Testament brutality.

But hang on, this was the Reverend Gordon Bowring we were talking about. Sense didn't come into it. This was the bloke who was stupid enough to give me an alibi whenever I asked for one, because he thought I was 'good at heart'. This was the same brainless jerk who went round to visit Badger Watts in his sick bed when he got both his legs busted by three blokes with baseball bats - even though the Rev knew perfectly well it was Badger who'd smashed in the vestry door two weeks before and nicked all the collection plates.

Well, you don't talk sense to this man - he works by some mysterious rules of his own. Chances are he'd refuse to tell Craig anything on principle. Principle? That's a word I've heard him use sometimes. I'm not sure what it means.

When the Rev eventually came round in hospital, he'd probably be pleased that he'd done his Christian duty. Just how stupid can you get? But if that was what he wanted, then where was the point in me trying to stop him? Let the fool get his head kicked in if he liked. He ought to know better after all this time living on the Forest. There was no sense in me walking in and getting my head kicked in as well.

No, the only thing to do was to slip quietly away, pack a bag and spend a few nights at the Travel Lodge in Blyth. You can't get more anonymous than that. When things had quietened down a bit, I might drop by one night after dark and offer to push the Rev's wheelchair round the churchyard for a while, as a way of saying thanks.

While I was planning this sensible course of action, I found to my amazement that my feet were moving of their own accord. They were edging me round the back of the Jaguar, as if they were set on getting me nearer to the lad at the wheel, putting me in his blind spot. At the same time, my hand reached into my jacket pocket and found the old dog lead I'd picked up at Lisa's.

Before I could puzzle this out, my brain had joined in. The sound of acid house music thumping into the street told me that the driver's window of the car was partly open. That was a mistake, of course, even on a warm night. In two more steps I was at the door. The driver saw me coming in his wing mirror, but it was too late by then.

"Come on now, Rusty, come on. Leave the gentleman's car alone. We'll find you a nice tree in a minute. Just hang on, lad. No, no, not the tyre. Oh dear, oh dear. Sorry about that, mate."

I grinned at the thug inanely, clutching my dogless lead at arm's length as if struggling to control an extremely small but stubborn canine.

"He has a bit of a thing about car wheels. I don't know what it is, but he can't pass one without watering it, if you know what I mean."

The bloke curled his lip as he stared at me, no doubt classifying me as a local halfwit. Then he made his second big mistake. He stuck his head out of the window to peer down at the imaginary mutt that was supposedly cocking its leg against his Michelin radials.

"Hey, there's no bloody - ."

But he didn't get any further. My right hand whipped in through the open window and grabbed his pony tail hard. I've always been keen on pony tails - they're dead handy in an emergency. While he thrashed around trying to turn his head towards me, my left hand got the car door open. I pulled hard and the bloke flew out of his seat and hit the tarmac head first, with a loud crack.

He twitched a bit, then lay still, his legs still trailing across the door sill. That was good. It saved me the trouble of hitting him. I felt guilty enough about the dog trick already. I'd only been taking the piss.

There was a sound of running feet on the road behind me. I didn't look round, because from the way the whole street vibrated at Richter scale eight I knew it was Doncaster Dave coming up fast, scowling no doubt, because I'd got into a fight without him.

"No problems, Dave," I said.

"Yeah?"

Rather than go straight up to the vicarage I climbed the steps into the churchyard and went through a little wooden gate at the side, which led to the Rev's back door. It isn't one of those old vicarages with fifteen bedrooms and drafts from hell. The old one had been demolished years ago and replaced by this red brick bungalow. Fortunately, it has a set of French windows onto the back garden. So by the time I got to the end of the path I could see people standing about in the sitting room admiring the furniture. Well, two of them were standing around. The Rev was sitting in an armchair. His back was to me, and I could just make out the top of his head. He wasn't moving much, but his visitors were smiling. Bad sign.

Only two, though. And neither of them was Eddie Craig, and neither of them was Lump Hammer Stan. Good sign.

Dave arrived behind me, following like the faithful dog that the lead belonged to. Time to make a move, before the bloke by the car came round. I gave Dave his instructions, then sent him round to the front to ring the doorbell. What? Did you think we were going to bust straight in like the SAS? That sort of stuff is for kids. Why bother with all that energy and aggro, when you can use brains and make it easy?

I lurked near the French windows, out of sight behind an overgrown shrub that the churchyard rota party really ought to get round to one day. I knew about these particular French windows - they're dead easy to get through. A quick tap in the right place and the catch falls open on the inside. I knew this because I'd done it before - only so that I could point out to the Rev how vulnerable he was to thieves, of course. I'd told him his second hand Victorian sideboard and his old Remington typewriter could be nicked at any moment, but he didn't take any notice. But at least that meant the catch would still drop open when I wanted it to.

I heard the doorbell ring. A good long ring. The two lads in the sitting room stopped what they were doing and looked at each other for instructions. That's the drawback to sending out this sort of low-class heavy out on a job. They're programmed for one thing only, and if something goes wrong with the script they don't know who to start kicking first.

Finally one of them walked through a door into the next room, which looked out onto the front of the house. He couldn't see who was at the door because of the nifty little brick porch that had been built round it. But he could see the Jag parked at the kerb, and he could see his mate was no longer sitting in the driver's seat. Therefore it must be his mate at the door. Two and two, you see? Boy, those maths can really get you into trouble.

I watched number one come back into the sitting room and mouth something at number two, who smirked. Then he went out again, this time through the far door, into the hallway. He was going to answer the door to the driver, or so he thought. And maybe he was going to take the piss out of him for leaving his post to go to the loo or something.

It went very quiet for a while. Nobody came back into the room. I could see number two fidgeting, doing everything but stick his head round the door into the hallway to see what was happening. He didn't seem to want to take his eyes off the Rev. This was obviously what he'd been programmed for, and he was sticking to it.

I waited until he was good and edgy, then I stepped out from behind the shrub and gave the French window a smart rap with my fist. Spot on. It sprang open and I stepped into the room as the lad whirled round to face me, his hand going straight for his pocket. The trouble was, he had his back to the hallway now, and it wasn't me he had to worry about. The door swung open and a huge fist came round in a snappy arc. The lad may just have felt the breeze from it a split second before the fist connected with the side of his head. He crumpled like derelict pit buildings do when the demolition blokes set off their explosives. Thump, crumple and a cloud of dust. Gone.

"You all right, Rev?"

The Reverend Bowring looked a bit battered. His dog collar had slipped, and there was blood on his lip and trickling from his nose. He'd have a nice black eye tomorrow. On Sunday he'd be able to address his congregation on Gordon and His Face of Many

Colours. But, ridiculously, he looked completely calm. Serene even. What's up with this bloke?

"Livingstone? Hello. And David, isn't it? Thank you for dropping by."

"It looked as though you needed help."

"Very strange. I don't know what they wanted. I offered them the sideboard and the Remington, like you said, Livingstone, but they just laughed. Are they colleagues of yours?"

"Hardly."

"Oh. It's just that I got the impression from what they said that they might be in the same line of business. Rivals then, perhaps? Your name was certainly mentioned."

"What a surprise."

"I don't really know what to do now," he admitted, eyeing the body on the carpet. "Does one offer tea and an aspirin from the first aid tin? Or will they just go away? I'm not used to this sort of thing."

"If anything like this happens again, you phone the police straight off, no messing."

"One hardly likes to bother them."

"Well, don't let the buggers through the door in the first place. Get proper locks fitted. You need security, Rev, I've told you before."

I was getting a bit cross with him, probably because he was making me feel guilty. I don't know how he does this trick - I had my conscience taken out with my appendix years ago.

"I have my own form of security, Livingstone," he said. "The security of my faith."

"Oh yeah, right."

"Worldly goods mean nothing in comparison to the riches that await us in the kingdom of heaven."

"I'd best hire a van then, when I go."

He looked again at the lad Dave had dropped. "Perhaps if I gave them some of my little brasses from the fireplace in the dining room it would make up for their unhappy experience."

"Shit, Rev, you don't understand."

But he smiled. "Nor do you, Livingstone, I fear."

Dave was standing over the body, waiting for advice. Whatever we did, I knew Eddie Craig was going to be really pissed off with me now. Even Blyth wouldn't be far enough away. It might have to be Yorkshire.

"Let's dump them in their car, Donc."

Dave grunted and heaved the body over his shoulder. In the hallway I stepped over another crumpled heap so I could peer out of one of the little side windows into the street. Outside stood the empty Jag. But in front of it was now parked another one, same colour, also empty. My brain started digesting this fact for future reference. I decided it was definitely a bad sign. Then a lump hammer came smashing through the door.

18

When I opened my eyes there were two Eddie Craigs in front of me, swimming nauseatingly together. My head ached and, come to think of it, so did several other parts of my body. I was firmly fastened to a chair with my own belt. I could feel the VW buckle digging into my wrists.

I couldn't place where I was just yet, but the room smelled mainly of piss. I took a guess that it probably wasn't Craig's nice house in Ravenshead. Maybe it was Lump Hammer Stan's place I'd been invited to today. He's a pisser all right, if ever there was one.

I had a vague memory of a few minutes of violent chaos after Stan had smashed in the door of the vicarage. That's the difference, isn't it? Me, I got Dave to knock politely when we went in. But you don't get the civilities in some firms. Stan had two or three lads with him, and they'd barged me aside so that they could wade into Dave, who was already handicapped with a body just starting to come awake over his shoulder and another under his feet. I remember turning round to help him out, but I didn't get very far. There'd been a movement that I only caught out of the corner of my eye, and then something hit me hard on the side of the head. I'd gone down, seeing the floor through a sort of red haze, and waited for the boots to go in.

When nothing happened for a second, I looked up. I could see Dave giving a couple of leather jackets a good thumping. He was enjoying himself far too much to notice what was happening to me. I'd tried to call his name, but my voice came out as a croak. And I didn't get a second chance as the first boot arrived, and my face hit the floor. They'd dragged me out head first after that.

Now here was Craig himself, gradually starting to come into focus, looking fat and complacent. He's a short-arsed little bloke with a pot belly and a bald head, too many jowls and a lot of flashy rings on his fingers. He was sitting on a white plastic garden chair, with a glass of beer in front of him on a white plastic table. He looked like Willie the Gnome on his holidays.

Like I said, I try to keep out of Craig's way. But he knows me, of course. My reputation precedes me.

"Ah, McClure. Glad you could drop in. I hope you're comfortable."

Comfortable I was not. As the room came more into focus, I saw that I was facing a big window behind Craig's head. The view out there wasn't encouraging. There was a great tangle of undergrowth, the top of a high fence, and an even higher screen of dark conifers. I guessed the nearest house was some distance away.

Craig took a drink of his beer, shifting his pot belly, and looking at me with a little smile on his face that didn't make me feel any better. It was the sort of smile the rabbit sees on the face of the ferret.

"Nice garden," I said. "Did you design it yourself?"

"It's a mess," he said. "It needs work. But, of course, I have people to do the heavy stuff."

"Yeah?"

"Cutting and burning, that sort of thing," he said. "Chopping. Digging."

Lump Hammer Stan laughed. It was the worst noise I'd heard since the last Bjork single. Then I noticed the racks on the wall to my right. They were full of tools, beautifully polished and sharpened. There were spades, forks, a rake and a hoe, secateurs, shears, Stanley knives, pincers, a soldering iron, a baseball bat and a couple of electrodes attached to a car battery. Some funny gardening went on around here.

"Was there something you wanted to talk about, Eddie?"

Craig stopped smiling and looked a bit miffed. Since he got to be top man he prefers to be called Mr Craig. I knew that, and he knew I knew that. He also seemed to think I was lacking in the social niceties by getting straight to the point. He leaned forward, spraying some of the froth from his beer as the smile turned into a snarl.

"I've sent some of my assistants to chat to you twice this week, but you wouldn't co-operate. I don't like that, McClure. I don't like that at all."

Twice? Up Top Forest the other day, yes, when Moxon had miraculously appeared. But when else? Well, there was the day before, when we wasted all those large fries.

"Hell, I didn't know those plonkers at McDonald's were your lads, Eddie. I hadn't realised that you employed amateurs these days."

There were stirrings behind me, and heavy breathing, like I'd accidentally wandered into a cave where grisly bears were hibernating and they'd taken offence. I was feeling a bit hurt that Craig had only sent the second string out for me that first time, when even Mick Kelk had earned the attention of Lump Hammer straight off. This sort of thing is important to your prestige.

"Sorry about that, Eddie. But now we've met up, what was this chat about?"

Craig poured himself another drink, slowly, as if giving himself time to calm down. He still didn't offer me one. No manners, this lot.

"How's business at the moment, McClure? Going well? Any problems?"

I hesitated at that. Craig probably knew all about my business. He'd never interfered so far, but there was no point in lying to him.

"Things have gone a bit quiet at the moment," I said. "The plods are a bit keen too."

"A bit of a downturn, eh? A rough patch? And of course you lost the services of young Thompson for a while, didn't you?"

"Do you know something about that?"

He waved his glass. "Only what I hear. It seems somebody's causing a bit of trouble. A few spanners in the works here and there. Being a nuisance, you might say."

I knew he couldn't really be worried about my problems. So did this mean Craig's business was being affected too? If so, it put a whole different slant on things. Apart from anything else, if whoever had been responsible was prepared to upset Craig as well as me, they maybe weren't safe to mess with.

"I wondered whether you might have any suspicions about the source of your problems," said Craig.

"None at all," I said.

"Are you sure?"

"Certain."

Craig put his glass down, almost sadly. "You see, McClure," he said, "when I observe you apparently doing nothing at all about the downturn in your business, and when I see that one of your boys has been taken in by the police, I start to wonder."

"Wonder what?"

"Whether I need to look any further for the spanner in the works. Whether your so-called problems aren't just a smokescreen. I'm thinking Stones McClure is getting a bit greedy. Moving in on my territory."

He was snarling again now, and his hand was shaking so much the beer was slopping over the edge of his glass onto the plastic table. I reckon he must have a blood pressure problem.

"I'd be very disappointed if that was the case. Very disappointed."

Craig made disappointment sound fatal. Maybe it was time to try a bit of appeasement.

"I'm not interested in that sort of game, Eddie. I'll stick to my own business, thanks very much. It smells better."

He didn't like that either. Maybe I need a bit more practice on my appeasement skills. Craig ended up with his finger poked almost in my face, grimacing at me like a frustrated gargoyle.

"So why was your Thompson boy taken in by the Serious Crime Squad? What's their interest in him?"

"I don't know."

Eddie was well informed in these areas. No doubt half the squad were on his payroll anyway. He must have read the expression on my face correctly, because he leaned back and took another drink. Lump Hammer Stan and the other two lads relaxed a fraction. I was glad about that - I didn't like to see them so tense, it might give them indigestion.

"A driver, isn't he? Thompson?" said Craig.

"Yeah, among other things."

"Has he been moonlighting? Working for someone else?"

"I don't think so."

"You see, McClure, I know you were asking questions of poor old Mick Kelk the other night. He was quite eager to tell us about

209

it." Craig paused deliberately, smiled that ferret smile again. "Poor old Mick."

"Yeah, poor old Mick."

I felt a bit sick in my stomach. As soon as I got away from here I'd have to find out what happened to Kelk. Poor old Mick.

"Kelk's been driving for somebody," I told him.

"I know. That was something else he told me. Now I want to hear how you're involved."

"Look, I told you - I'm not involved at all."

The dried blood on my head was itching, and I instinctively tried to raise my hand to scratch it, forgetting the belt. Stan grabbed me and thumped me back upright. He did it a bit harder than necessary, I thought.

"It's got to stop, McClure," said Craig in his Mister Nasty voice.

Did he mean all this senseless violence? If so, I was right with him.

"You're right. So let me go and we'll forget all about it, eh? I'll shake hands with Stan, and you can pay for a new door for the vicarage. Then we'll all sleep happily in our beds."

"Don't be clever. I did try to warn you, in a friendly way. But it doesn't work, does it? We might have had a peaceful arrangement of interests once, but that's over now. A shame you've gone and spoiled it."

"I don't know what you're talking about, Eddie. All I want to do is get on with my business. Why do people keep interfering?"

Craig didn't take much notice. He shook his head, as if he didn't believe me. Did he know me that well?

"Did you think your friends in the police would help you?"

"Friends?"

"Maybe they decided to use you to try and close me down. You and the police would like that, wouldn't you?"

"You've got it all wrong, Eddie."

Even to me my voice sounded weary. I saw Craig hesitate for the first time. He isn't stupid. He's got to have good judgement or he wouldn't have survived in this business so long.

"There's been an awful lot of talk about you, McClure."

"Don't I know it. And I suppose you think there's no smoke without fire? I suppose you've added two and two together somewhere along the way?"

A saw that movement out of the corner of my eye again. It was Lump Hammer Stan taking a step towards me. He thought the big words were swearing. I flinched a bit, trying to hide all the bits that already hurt. But Craig just lifted a hand to hold him back, and Stan went back to lurking just outside my field of vision.

"You've been making a nuisance of yourself. Asking a lot of questions. Dealing in information. That's a long way from your car boot stalls."

"The information I wanted was about who's been fouling up my business. I've been suffering here, Eddie. Like, you, I guess."

"Not like me, I don't think."

Craig lit a cigarette. I was glad he didn't offer me one. I gave up smoking a long time ago. Besides, my mouth hurt.

"There's always been a lot of this sort of thing going on. Petty crime - your sort of crime, McClure. It never really occurred to me before that it was organised on any scale. Now it seems as though it is."

"Not by me. I've hardly got started."

"I think you've stirred somebody up. They've been bringing in a lot of cash, on the quiet. But now they're upset, and they're lashing out. At you. And even at me. It won't do."

"I don't know anything about them."

Craig nodded. I instantly tensed, thinking maybe it was a signal for Stan to start doing a bit of gardening with the baseball bat. But nothing happened. Craig nodded again. I realised he was trying to tell me that he actually believed me.

"But you'd like to know this person is, wouldn't you, McClure?"

Craig looked at the end of his cigarette for a while. I just hoped he was planning on smoking it and not using it for anything else.

"This person - he's the one who's been fouling up my deliveries?" I said.

"They call him Perella," said Craig, with a smug look. He was relaxed now. He thought he was completely in charge, that he

211

knew everything and I knew nothing. He thought he had control over me. His calmness was more worrying than his high blood pressure.

"You knew who it was all along? But why - "

"It was him or you. Maybe both of you together, who knows? But you were the most convenient to get hold of."

"That'll teach me to be accessible to my public."

"Well, relatively convenient," said Craig, with a glance towards Stan. For the first time, it occurred to me that I wasn't the only one in Craig's bad books at the moment. You can't over-rate fellow feeling too highly, even when you have to call somebody like Lump Hammer Stan a chum.

"Perella, now, I can't find him at all," said Craig. "No one knows where he lives or where he comes from, or where he hangs out. So obviously I had to start with you. We do have some interests in common, don't we?"

I didn't like the way he said this. I don't like to think I have too much in common with the likes of Eddie Craig. So I kept mum and admired the garden. I'd just noticed that it wasn't all wild undergrowth out there after all. Somebody had recently been doing quite a lot of deep digging in a bed just under the window.

"So you do believe me, Eddie? We're on the same side in this, you and me."

"Well, I thought you might say that, McClure. In fact, I'm delighted that you're so willing to take up my proposition."

There was a small silence. I got the feeling there was something I was supposed to say. A little voice at the back of my mind suggested I didn't say it, just to see what happened. But the silence, and Eddie Craig's way of staring at the end of his cigarette, were just too convincing.

"What proposition?"

"You see, I'm a stranger outside Mansfield, I don't know your area too well. But you're a man with a lot of contacts round here. You know how to ask questions in the right places. With your friends in the police, for example."

"I don't have any - "

"Yes, yes. But also you're not so high profile as myself. I think that you're the ideal man to find this Perella. Then we both benefit, don't we? It's quite obvious to me that you have a personal interest, and you've already put yourself out to make inquiries. So we make use of your enthusiasm."

"And if I find him, what? You'll deal with him?"

"No, no. This is too risky for me, in my position. I'm sure you understand. You, McClure, will find this person. And then you'll take him out."

"I won't do it."

Craig made an odd noise. I thought he was choking on his beer at first, and wondered why Stan or one of the lads didn't rush over to help him. Then I realised the noise was a genial chuckle.

"A pity," he said. And he looked past me and a few feet above my right ear. Though I couldn't see what he was looking at, a picture of Stan's face drifted into my mind, frightened me enough to give me nightmares, and drifted out again.

"I'll try to find him, Eddie. I can probably do that. But after that, it's up to you."

"I don't think you fully understand the situation. There's another aspect you haven't considered yet."

I took in his continued eye contact with Stan.

"I suppose you mean what you'll do to me if I don't agree. Is that it?"

"Oh, not you," he said. "I don't think that would achieve very much. I think you're too stupid for that. It wouldn't be what I'd do to you, but to your girlfriend."

A little cold shudder went through me. For the first time, I felt real fear.

"Miss Lisa Prior, isn't it? A nice looking young lady. Very intelligent, and well-educated. Too good for you, McClure."

"You bastard, Craig."

He shrugged. "Stan here has always wanted to visit Hardwick Hall. He's a bit of a culture fan on the quiet. You wouldn't think it to look at him, would you? But, being shy, he's likely to spend a lot of his time lurking in the car park or among the trees, outside the gate in the dark perhaps, just to catch one of the staff to speak to privately as they go off duty."

Craig's quiet words were worse than anything he'd said or done so far.

213

"I'm telling you this," he said, "so that if Miss Prior doesn't come home one night, you'll know to make inquiries at the hospital. Casualties go to King's Mill at Mansfield, I believe. Unless there are serious head injuries, in which case there's a special unit at Sheffield. You see how I'm trying to help you, McClure?"

"Piss off."

He sighed again, like a man who really hates what he does. Well, I can be a hypocrite too.

"Your choice," he said. "I can't put it more plainly. Give him his belt back, Stan."

Stan untied me, not gently.

"Is that it then?"

"I hope we understand each other now."

I said nothing. But I was horribly afraid that I really did understand.

Eddie Craig had me by the short and curlies, and the bastard knew it. No way could I let Lisa be involved. Well, not until I'd given her the push, and then it wouldn't matter to me anyway. Meanwhile, she was my bird and I couldn't let Craig get his hands on her. On the other hand, I couldn't think of a way of getting her away from the area, not without telling her about the danger she was in. A cleft stick, with the shitty end pointing my way.

Basically, I was going to have to do what Craig said. When I say basically, I mean Craig was going to have to think that I'd done what he said. This isn't quite the same thing. Not quite.

*   *   *   *

Craig's boys dumped me on the edge of Ollerton and made me walk the rest of the way home, with no cash in my pockets and no mobile phone to ring for a taxi. They even went out of their way to make sure I had to walk past the police station, the bastards.

I don't object to exercise - in fact, I've even been known to jog in my time. But there are times when you want exercise - like when you've got a bellyful of tequila from the night before to work off or something. And there are times when your body protests at the very idea of putting one foot in front of another. Especially when your bruised shins are starting to ache, and it's dark and cold and you're wearing boots with snip toes and cowboy heels, and you've still got five miles left to go until you reach home and you can finally curl up in bed and feel *really* sorry for yourself.

There are also times when a car is good protection, so you're not exposed like you are when you're out walking on your own. Exposed to the attention of any pillock who happens to be driving past and sees you slogging along. Today was obviously my day for being offered lifts. I'd got half way down the road between Ollerton and Medensworth and my legs were starting to complain when the car pulled up. I thought about running, but my feet said 'no'. What the hell, it was only Moxon and Stubbs anyway. Out cruising for some fun, and they found me, lucky buggers.

Wally Stubbs opened the back door of the Mondeo for me, and I got in. I was at such a low ebb that I could barely stop myself saying 'thanks' as I collapsed into the seat. I was so relieved not to be walking the rest of the way home that even these two looked like my best mates just then. Stubbs didn't pull away straightaway. They both turned to look at me, like they were gawping at a chimpanzee in the monkey house at the zoo.

"Yeah, you've recognised me. You win a tenner if you happen to have a copy of the Daily Mirror and you can answer a simple question."

"What are you on about, McClure?" said Stubbs.

"No, I'm supposed to ask the question. You just lost the tenner."

Moxon had a gleeful little grin that I didn't like. "Rather a funny time to choose for a walk, isn't it? And you're not really dressed for it. You should be wearing an orange cagoule and a woolly hat."

"That's right, inspector. Perhaps I got mugged and had them pinched."

"I suggest you walk back to the station at Ollerton and report it."

"I can bear the loss."

"I do hope they didn't hurt you too much, these muggers. That looks remarkably like blood on your face."

"I cut myself smiling too much."

Moxon took a bag of sweets out of the Mondeo's glove compartment and passed one to Stubbs. They smelled like pear drops from where I was sitting, but that was as near as I got to them.

"Things aren't going too well for you at the moment, McClure, are they?"

"I've known better, thanks. I take it you're going my way, are you?"

The car still hadn't moved. Moxon was in the mood for a bit of a roadside chat.

"You know, McClure," he said. "You're going to slip up very soon. Slip up badly. I know you are."

"I can't think what you mean."

"In fact, you may already have slipped up. That's something for you to think about."

"I'm really tired. I'd just like to go home."

"A hard day, was it? Sergeant Stubbs and I have had a hard day as well. So much information to sort out and put on record, you wouldn't believe it. You're not keen on all the paperwork, are you, sergeant?"

"No sir," said Stubbs. "But it has to be done. When you've got so much information to file."

"Computers can help," said Moxon. "We have computers at the police station, you know."

"Congratulations. Have you tried Sonic the Hedgehog? You'll never beat my high score."

"We don't play games on them. But we find them very useful for information gathering."

"Oh well." I yawned. "If you drive on for a mile or two, you can turn left into Medensworth. Just in case you'd forgotten the way, like."

Wally Stubbs tapped the wheel irritably. His boss hadn't finished yet.

"Computers get everywhere. That young lady of yours uses computers at the travel agent's, she tells me."

Shit. He'd been talking to Nuala again. No wonder he had all that information for Wally Stubbs to file. Just pray that most of it was about special deals on Eastern European holiday destinations and fluctuating exchange rates for the South African rand.

"Very helpful, your young lady. Wasn't she, sergeant?"

"I'll say," agreed Stubbs. I didn't like the grin on his face either. It wasn't a smirk, like Moxon's, more of a leer.

"It's Sherwood Crescent. Down the bottom of First Avenue. And don't spare the horses."

"Funny thing is, though," said Moxon, "some people we talk to seem to be under the impression you have a different young lady. Someone by the name of Lisa Prior. How can that be?"

"Can't imagine. Just drop me off at the end of the street if you like."

"It seems to us like something that needs checking out. I don't like inconsistencies. We haven't asked the friendly Irish girl yet, but I dare say she'd be able to put us straight on this one. Just for verification. We like our records to be accurate."

"I've had enough of this."

"You're quite free to go on your way, of course. Open the door for the gentleman, sergeant."

Stubbs leaned back and opened the door. I got out. My feet woke up and began screaming.

"You'll miss that cagoule, I'm afraid," called Moxon. "I believe it's starting to rain."

*   *   *   *

I set off to walk the rest of the way to Medensworth. It was another hour before the Forest Estate came in sight, and my mind was wandering with tiredness by then.

Whenever I look at these houses, I remember what it was like round here during that 1984-85 miners' strike. You can't imagine it if you didn't live through it. From the day a young Yorkshire picket called David Lee was killed in the streets of Ollerton, the death of the coal industry was sure to follow. A Greek tragedy, that's what folk have called it who wrote books on the subject. I think they mean it was inevitable. They're right.

217

There's been a lot of stuff about the mining industry since then. Some of it is true enough, but it only tells half the story. Some pretend the closure of a colliery brings out the best in people, things like unity and comradeship. Community spirit, and all that. Oh yeah? Here in Nottinghamshire, they remember that it was those same Yorkshire pit men who tried to bully them into striking against their union's instructions, who hurled abuse and bricks at them day after day, who smashed up their cars and their homes, terrorised their families and brought chaos to their communities. And these were men who'd belonged to the same bleedin' union. Try telling the Notts miners all about unity and comradeship.

Even in 1997, when they closed Asfordby pit in Leicestershire, some of the men there turned down transfers to the Yorkshire area. They preferred to go on the dole, rather than work than work in an NUM pit. And that was twelve years after the strike had finished.

Or tell it to those NUM men, who stood shoulder to shoulder behind Scargill, loyal to the core, believing wholeheartedly that they were fighting to save the coal industry. Those were the blokes who watched their own mates break ranks and turn scab, working right through their strike to keep coal production going. They were the men who resisted when Margaret Thatcher turned the might of the British police against them, massed ranks of southern bobbies waving their bulging pay packets at picket lines while striking miners and their families queued at soup kitchens right through the winter. They were the same men who finally had to give in, drifting back to work, angry and defeated, until the inevitable outcome - their pits closed after all. Those lads know a thing or two about bitterness.

Almost the whole of Nottinghamshire sits on what they call the coal measures. This is a huge slab of the earth's crust, tilted at an angle so that it comes right up to the surface near the Notts-Derbyshire border. But to get the best coal you have to deep mine. This means sinking shafts a mile down into the ground to reach the good black stuff.

There are lots of different seams of coal below Nottinghamshire. There's High Hazles, Wingfield Flags and Brinsley Thin. Dunsil, Abdy and Sutton Marine. Combs,

Mainbright and Manton Estheria. Their names are like a poem when you hear them said by a miner. But the really good stuff is called Top Hard. Its seam is thicker than the others, and the coal is better quality too. It's the hard, dull stuff that burns for a long time, as distinct from the soft, bright coals like the Combs and Gees and High Hazles, which are flashier looking but burn quicker.

Most of the collieries round here were originally sunk to work Top Hard. You could sell the coal for more money, the pit became more viable, and the blokes' jobs were safer. Any pit with a workable seam of it was onto a good thing. Yes, Top Hard. It would be a miner's dream if the stuff wasn't such a bugger to dig out. It's killed as many men as it's saved. But that's life around here. You only survive if you work yourself to death. We live as if we were always in Top Hard.

From the plateau at the back of the Forest Estate you can see over the whole of North Nottinghamshire, as far as the power station cooling towers on the banks of the Trent. On good days the real forest lies below you, a dark blanket of trees across the county. It's as if a large cloud has cast its shadow there, while the hills beyond still sit in sunlight.

From here, too, you can see more of those strangely shaped hills. Man-made, of course. Landscaped spoil heaps where coal mines used to be. During the strike, the Yorkshire pickets used to swarm over these spoil heaps to get to the pit entrances when the police blocked off the roads. They don't need to bother now.

You can tell by the state of the spoil heap how long the pit has been shut. Some, like Shirebrook, are grim black cliffs, with deep rivulets down their sides where rain has carved out channels in the slag. But others are green, unnaturally smooth and suspiciously contoured, with sheep turned out on them to graze the stunted grass. This is where pits have been closed and landscaped over.

My mum always said that's what they did to my dad. Closed him down and landscaped over him. He didn't last long once they'd chucked him on the dole. He just withered away, like a bit of old root dug up from the earth and left to rot on the surface. Now he's in the graveyard at St Asaph's. They put him back into the same ground that he'd spent his life working in.

Of course, pitmen get redundancy money when they're laid off. This buys them a newer car maybe, a holiday in Majorca, a few new carpets and curtains. It doesn't buy a man what he had before - self respect. That was what my dad lost the day he walked out of the pit gates for the last time. When he washed off the coal dust that afternoon, it was like he'd washed off all the outer coating that made him a man and left some sad white, squirming thing exposed to the air. He said goodbye to his mates, and he hardly ever left the house again until the day he died. In the end, maybe the grave is the only escape from a life in Top Hard.

The old miners will tell you this sometimes. But only sometimes, and then probably at another pitman's funeral. When you've been through this shit a few times, it tends to leave a scar on you that never heals and never goes away. My scar itches a lot. Sometimes, it burns.

19

"What you going to do then, Stones?"

I'd called another planning meeting, which just showed how desperate I was. After hearing about the night before, it was Slow Kid who asked the usual question. What was I going to do?

"Yeah, what you going to do?" said Metal.

"Don't ask me," I said.

"Who else is there to ask, Stones?"

Slow Kid looked around the room meaningfully, first at Metal, then at Doncaster Dave, who was well out of it with a bag of Cheesy Wotsits.

"You expecting Dave to come up with a master plan, or what?"

Slow was right, of course. When I'd got back to Medensworth the previous night, I'd met Dave walking out of the village towards me. The joy of seeing him was undermined when I realised that it hadn't occurred to him to get any transport. Now my feet were like raw steaks. And I still had to drive Lisa's car back to her house and go through all the performance of lying to her about where I'd been for so long. She'd kept sniffing my breath, as if she couldn't believe anyone could stagger in so late looking such a mess and not have been drinking. Well, I must admit my story about going for a walk in the woods and getting lost sounded a bit weak. I was too tired to approach the question of whether or I'd be allowed into Lisa's bed, so I slept on the settee. At least it meant I didn't have to face the teddy.

Now I was pacing up and down in my own sitting room. No need to hide from Craig any more.

"Let's face it, Slow, if we go looking for this Perella bloke, we ain't going to find him, not for bleedin' months. So..."

"Yeah?"

"We've got to get him to come to us, right?"

"Right," said Slow. "But why would he want to do that?"

"Because we've got something he wants?"

"Have we?"

"We could have."

"Like what?" asked Metal.

"Well, what does he want, do you reckon?"

"Money," said Slow.

"Yeah, and the goods," said Metal.

"And customers for it."

"And what doesn't he want?"

"Hassle from the cops."

"Yeah, or trouble from other firms."

"Bigger firms, Metal?"

"Well, he'll be worried about what Eddie Craig's up to, dead sure."

"But is he worried about me?"

"He might be."

"Yeah."

"He might be worried about what you know, Stones."

"Or I could be a threat, a challenge?"

"How's that?"

"All this stuff... it started to happen when we tried to expand the business, right? Nobody bothered with us when we were just handling the small stuff. But as soon as we moved up, somebody went out of their way to shaft us. The cops got tipped off about a load, a van's set up for us with the wrong merchandise. And that fire bomb - somebody meant that for us, Slow."

"Tell you what, Stones - he doesn't give a toss, this Perella bloke, does he?"

"What do you mean?"

"Well, those lads that did the ram raid. They could easily have gone down, couldn't they? And there's Rawlings and Lee too."

My brain was running now. They did work these meetings, after all.

"Slow, do you reckon he's worried enough about what I know to follow me?"

"Well, maybe."

"I'm thinking about the other night, when we left the Ferret."

"Wasn't that the cops?"

"How do we know?

"You're right, we don't. But, shit, they were amateurs all the same."

There was a pause.

"So you're trusting him, then," said Slow Kid.

"What? Me? Who?"

"Eddie Craig."

"Never in this world. What makes you say that, Slow?"

"I mean, we don't really know that all this isn't just Craig trying to close us down."

"Craig all along? Yeah?"

"And he's fed you this stuff to send you looking for someone else. Could be, right?"

I sighed. "We do have interests in common."

"Like shit."

I rubbed my bruises as I stood up from the computer desk. I still had my memories of Craig and his mates. But you have to let bygones be bygones sometimes. When you're on the same side.

Suddenly, I was struck by an unpleasant mental picture of Lump Hammer Stan. In my vision, he was lurking in some bushes near a car park at Hardwick Hall.

"Off you go then, lads. I'll catch up with you later."

I took a quick glance at the paper for the results of the National Lottery draw. My numbers hadn't come up. Well, I was gobsmacked. Just when things were going so well, too.

*　　*　　*　　*

I made it to Hardwick in record time, irrationally worried about whether Lisa would be there. In fact, I saw her coming out of the staff exit as soon as I arrived. She was surprised to see me, and I thought she looked around a bit uneasily, as if expecting someone else. The thought went through my mind that maybe she'd already seen Lump Hammer Stan or some other charmer stalking about the grounds. We stood for a few minutes under the big lime tree.

"Hi, love."

"Hello, Stones. What are you doing here?"

"I thought you might like to go for lunch, so I came to pick you up. Or, if you've got your car here, we could meet up somewhere. Where do you fancy?"

"I'm really sorry, Stones, I've got other plans today."

"Oh yeah? Funny, you seem to be the only person round here who's got plans that don't involve me."

"What do you mean?"

I really wanted to tell Lisa what was happening, but I couldn't. How could I warn her she might be in danger without explaining why? And she wouldn't be in danger anyway, if I did what Craig wanted.

"I'd like to know what you're going, Lisa. It's important."

"What's the matter with you, Stones? You seem edgy today."

"I'm all right."

"Still sore from last night?"

"I'll be fine."

"I still don't understand why you went for a walk in the woods in the first place. Not on your own."

"I was just thinking."

"You *were* on your own, weren't you, Stones?"

"Honest, love."

"Mmm."

"Look, don't worry. I've got everything sorted out."

We walked together across the gravel towards the car park. There were visitors arriving constantly, being directed by car park attendants onto the grassy area. I wondered for a second why Lisa had parked her car out here with the public, instead of in the staff section.

"Stones," she said suddenly. "You've been in some sort of trouble recently, haven't you? I can tell."

"Yeah, but it's nearly over now."

She smiled. "I get the feeling someone's going to regret it if they've been causing trouble for Stones McClure."

"You bet. There's a bloke out there got it coming very soon."

Careful. That was close enough.

"Just take care, won't you?" she said. And she sounded really concerned.

"Anyway, how's the detective work going? The Cavendish job."

"Very well, thank you."

"Found lots of clues to his relatives?"

"They're adding up."

"Are they? Two and two?"

She frowned. "There's definitely something wrong with you."

"Why?"

"You haven't made any crude remarks about Michael Cavendish yet."

"Why should I?"

"Because you're an inverted snob, that's why. And you're jealous of him."

We were standing on the grass now. I couldn't see Lisa's Fiat, and she was looking from left to right among the cars as if she couldn't spot it either. It still didn't click with me.

"You've got me all wrong. I've got nothing against the bloke. It's just his hyphens I don't like. They're bad taste, like having furry dice in your car window."

"That's more like it."

"I suppose you've got to keep seeing him. To report on progress or something?"

"Actually, it's him I'm meeting."

"Ah."

"In fact, he's taking me for lunch."

"I see. Somewhere nice, I suppose."

"Goff's at Langwith."

Very nice too. No pub lunch, then. Something a bit better than I'd be tackling later on, anyway. I watched a gold-coloured Range Rover nose its way onto the grass a few yards down. Michael Cavendish got out and began to stroll casually towards us, brushing his suit as if he'd got bits of real life on it from having to use the same car park as the plebs.

"So I'm a spare part?"

"Don't be like that, Stones. I'll make it up to you some time."

225

She put her hand on my arm. She thought I was being jealous again, when I was only concerned about her safety. I couldn't have cared less if she'd zoomed off with Cavendish in his Range Rover to live in his mansion and never come back. But would he be able to protect her from Lump Hammer Stan and his mates?

Cavendish hesitated a few yards away, as if he didn't want to speak to me for some reason. But now Lisa saw him and gave a wave, and he kept coming.

"Hello, Lisa. Hello, er... old chap."

"Stones they call me. As in rolling, standing and you can't get blood from."

"Ah yes. And what are you doing at the moment, rolling or standing?"

"Well, just standing, I suppose. As you do."

"A change from last time we met here, then."

I stared at him. The bugger was being cleverer than me. In another minute I might have to call on all my intellectual reserves and punch his lights out.

Cavendish smirked. "Are you ready, Lisa? There's nothing keeping you, is there? Our table is booked."

"I'm ready," she said. She looked at me a bit nervously. "I hope you really do get your problem sorted out, Stones."

"Oh? What's that?" asked Cavendish, his ears pricking up for further signs of my inferiority.

"Nothing to do with you," I said. "It's not something that can be sorted out with a cheque book."

"You never know, old chap. I might be able to help. I could suggest an alcohol addiction clinic, for example. A good psychiatrist. I've had some experience in welfare work. I doubt if I can do anything for your dress sense though, I'm afraid."

"Piss off."

"Or your lack of vocabulary. Shall we go, Lisa?"

They walked off and got in the Range Rover. Cavendish revved the engine and gave me a little toot of the horn as they went past towards the gates. Lisa stared at me, almost expressionless. Somehow Cavendish had got the better of me, and I'd let him do it. What was wrong with me?

Well, Lisa was the only person I could have asked a question like that. But she wasn't there any more.

* * * *

I met up with Slow Kid and Dave and we went to the Cow's Arse. The usual crowd were in, some of them looking at me a bit sideways and keeping clear. Word soon gets around when you're in trouble. But word getting around was just what I had to rely on.

I went to the bar myself to get the drinks. Baggy Prentiss has known me a long time, and he's not about to snub a good customer.

"Hey up, youth. Everything all right?"

"Between you and me, I've been having a few problems recently, Baggy."

"Aye, I heard."

"But I've got it all sorted now. I've worked out the situation, like. Spotted where the problem is."

"That's good, Stones."

"Me and some good mates, know what I mean?"

Baggy slid the glasses onto the bar. "I know what you mean."

"So things are going to be picking up again very soon."

"Bloody marvellous. That'll be five quid twenty-eight then."

I took the drinks back to the table, where we chatted loudly about how good things were going to be again and laughed about someone being sorted. On the way to the loo I passed Moggie Carr and gave him a friendly pat on the shoulder. He almost spilled his beer on my feet again, but I dodged in time.

"I just want to say thanks, Moggie, old mate."

"Eh? What for?"

"The bit of information you gave me the other day. It really helped."

"Yeah?"

"I know who I'm dealing with now."

"Who's that?"

"Oh, can't say." I gave him a big wink, right there in the middle of the pub. "But you'll probably hear."

"Right."

227

Across the room, Slow Kid had got into conversation with a couple of drivers he knew. They were all nodding knowledgeably, tipping bottles back and looking cool. Metal was leaning over to the next table, where a thin bloke in overalls was sitting with a Guinness. I had a suspicion they were probably talking about car engines. Nobody was talking to Dave, of course. He was just there for decoration.

Next I sent Slow Kid and Metal down the Q Tip snooker club for a game while I went with Dave to the Ferret. Mick Kelk wasn't playing pool today, just watching. This was probably to do with the plaster cast that he wore on his arm and the swelling over his eye that limited his vision.

"I don't know nothing," he said straightaway. "I didn't know nothing then, and I don't know nothing now. I told those blokes of Craig's, I haven't got any names."

"That's all right, Mick. I just came to say thanks for your trouble. We managed to get what we wanted in the end."

"It was nothing to do with me."

"Here - this is to pay for the cue that Dave broke, and a bit extra to buy a few drinks for you and your mates."

Kelk looked at the fifty quid note. I thought he was going to refuse it. But he couldn't have been doing much driving recently, not with one arm. He pocketed the note with his left hand. I stood back to make sure his mates saw him do it.

We didn't hang around at the Ferret, but got in the car and drove back through the village. As we passed St Asaph's I saw activity in the churchyard and pulled in.

"Morning, Councillor."

Welsh Border straightened up from the grave he'd been tidying. Dad's plot is near the east side. Not the newest graves, but still well tended. The older memorials are crumbling with the effects of weather and general neglect. Some of the dead are long forgotten by their descendants. Now and then vandals visit and smash up someone's stone for a bit of fun. If they ever do that to my dad's grave, I'll stick their baseball caps so far up their arses the elastic will get stuck on their teeth.

"What do you want, McClure?"

"I'd just like to shake your hand, Councillor."

"What?"

"I know we haven't seen eye to eye sometimes, but we can't bear grudges, can we? Not on church premises."

Border glowered at me. He made no move to put down his garden shears, let alone take off his work gloves to shake hands.

"Mr Bowring said there was some trouble here yesterday," he said. "Was that caused by you, McClure?"

"Did the Rev say it was?"

He pulled his face. "He was vague about it. But I have my suspicions."

"Actually, the Rev has been helping me work through some personal problems. I won't bother you with the details."

"I don't want to know."

He took a step towards me, not to shake my hand, but to peer more closely at my face. He was clutching the shears like a bayonet and he smelled of soil and freshly cut weeds.

"Have you been fighting, McClure?"

"Like I said, I've had some personal problems. But I'm on the way towards getting them sorted out. That's why I wanted to make peace with yourself, Councillor. What about it?"

"I can't ever tell what you're on about," said Border. "You're just taking the micky again, aren't you? You're always taking the micky out of the vicar."

"Not at all. We're practically best mates."

He snapped his shears together irritably. We stared at each other for a bit.

"Oh well," I said. "If that's the way you feel. It's just that I thought we might be able to make a fresh start."

"All this means nothing to me."

"Maybe. Maybe."

"I'm in regular touch with the police, you know, McClure."

"Yeah? That's nice." I made a mental note to ask Teri Brooker about him. Somebody had been talking about me, isn't that what everybody said? Just at the moment, I couldn't think of anybody more likely to go around bad-mouthing me than the Born Again Accountant. "I suppose you have a lot to talk with them about, Councillor? People you've seen dropping cigarette packets in the street? Old ladies whose wheelie bins are obstructing the

229

pavement? Or have you hit the big time and nailed somebody with their telly on too loud?"

Welsh began to work the blades of his shears violently, as if decapitating flowers that had dared to bloom in the wrong place. The clack of the blades punctuated his words.

"I know..." Clack. "Things..." Clack. "About you..." Clack. "McClure." He lunged past me with the shears and slashed off the head of an inoffensive hydrangea. The shears looked pretty sharp, all right. "And I'm not afraid..." Clack. "To stand up and be counted..." Clack. "In the cause of justice." Clack, clack, clack.

I backed away towards the car, fearing some accidental pruning of my personal twigs and branches.

"He's not on the right bus, that bloke," said Slow Kid, eyeing Welsh Border as he stood snapping his shears in the graveyard.

I don't know why I equated Welsh Border with the likes of Moggie Carr and Mick Kelk. But I knew he could talk, and I was covering all the options. I wanted word to get around that Stones McClure had his eye fixed on a target. I was hoping somebody would get worried. I wanted them to feel they needed to know what I was up to.

We went back to the Cow and had lunch. Dave would have fainted otherwise. While we ate, I tried to detect any changes in the atmosphere around us. I listened for whispering, any sudden silences. I watched for curious glances, a knowing tilt of the head. But there was nothing that I couldn't honestly put down to pure paranoia.

*   *   *   *

Eventually I took Slow Kid with me and we drove the Subaru under the viaduct, heading out of Medensworth. It was Sunday after all, and I made it a rule to visit the Sunday market every week, just in case.

We'd crossed the A60 at Cuckney and were winding our way towards the Derbyshire border before I realised we were at Langwith. Here, Goff's Restaurant is set back off the road in a converted mill overlooking a pond.

230

"Pull in a second, Slow."

We parked across the road and I examined the car park. I couldn't make out Cavendish's Range Rover among the BMWs. In any case, it was after two o'clock. Surely they'd be long gone from their business lunch. Unless it involved more than business, of course. I dialled Lisa's home number, but the phone rang and rang. Maybe she wasn't quite home yet. Maybe she had some shopping to do. Or possibly she was just avoiding answering the phone, in case it was me.

But if she was with Cavendish, at least she should be safe. In a way.

At the Sunday market, the same bloke in the blue suit and short haircut had the usual admiring housewives gathered round his demonstration.

Ernie and Stella were still busy. "What can I sell you?" said Ernie. "Nice leather waistcoat?"

The brothers, Carl and Vince, weren't so busy. Watches and jewellery weren't the choice today. "It'll build up for Christmas, I reckon," said Carl, hopefully.

Marlene had three or four kids with her today. They were okay too. But it was Marky Benn's stall I wanted to see.

Marky watched me sideways out of his blotchy eyes as I poked about among the radios and hair driers, electric alarm clocks and toasters. And CD players. Although he was dealing with a customer, I could feel his eyes flicking towards me as I picked up boxes and turned them over to look at the serial numbers and names of manufacturers.

"All right, Stones?" he asked. He had other customers browsing further down the stall, but he wanted to know what I was doing. Was it my imagination, or did he look worried? Who could tell with eyes like that?

"Where did these CD players come from, Marky?"

"What?"

"These CD players. French make, aren't they? Where did they come from?"

"Can't remember, Stones. They'd be in a batch I got off your lot, wouldn't they?"

"I don't think so, Marky."

He shrugged. "I get most of my stuff from you, Stones. You give the best deal."

"Yeah, I know. That's what keeps you in business, Marky. If you had to pay full whack, you'd never make a profit."

He glanced nervously at the women fingering some heated hair curlers.

"You sure the CD players didn't come from you, Stones?"

"I'm so sure I can smell it."

"I'd have to look it up in the books, then."

"Do that, will you, Marky? And let me know. Give me a ring, or have a word with one of the boys. Don't make me have to come round and ask you again."

I picked up Slow Kid down the end of the aisle, where he'd been lurking near a display of conservatories.

"Just Jean to check on, then we're off, Slow.

"Brill."

The smell from Jean's stall was overpowering. Her perfumes and cosmetics were getting sampled big time. But Jean had something she wanted to tell me.

"There were two blokes, Stones."

"What? Only two? You must have had more customers than that."

"No, I mean... you know. Blokes. They were hanging around, asking questions like."

"When was this, love?"

"Earlier on. They went over towards Marky's stall."

"Yeah?"

I looked towards Marky Benn's pitch, but he was busy re-arranging his stock.

"What did these two look like, Jean?"

"One was big, balding. The other was younger. I didn't like the look of the young one at all, Stones. A nasty bit of work, if you ask me. I've seen 'em around before too. Last week they were hanging around. I thought you ought to know."

"Ta, love. You've done the right thing."

"Rawlings and Lee?" asked Slow Kid as we walked away.

"Sounds like it."

"You want to go looking for 'em?"

"Not now. Not here."

Halfway across the parking area, I stopped suddenly.

"What's up now?" said Slow.

"There, look. The dark blue saloon with the alloy wheels."

"A German job, I reckon."

"Not *a* German job. *The* German job. It's the same registration, I'm sure of it."

"It's a good trick that, Stones, remembering registration numbers."

"It comes naturally," I said, as I stepped closer to the car. Actually, I'd only remembered part of the number. But I was almost sure it was the same one - the blue car that I'd seen Rawlings and Lee in outside Peter Malik's, maybe the one that had followed us from the Dog and Ferret, and the one that had been hanging around Top Forest. I walked round the front and saw the dent in the nearside wing that had been hastily knocked out and touched up to stop it rusting. Somebody didn't have time to get it repaired properly after clattering it into the joy riders' Peugeot on the heath.

"There's no alarm in it," I said, squinting through the window at the dashboard. "Can you lift it, Slow?"

"How? I've got no tackle on me. We can't go putting the window in here. It's too public."

"Isn't this an old model? You know, with the vacuum thingy in the lock?"

"Actuator. Yeah, you're right."

"Hold on, then."

I'd spotted a group of young kids kicking a ball about on the grass near the toilets. They looked as though they'd been left to amuse themselves while their parents stocked up on dog chews and cushion covers.

When I got closer to them, the ball rolled conveniently towards me. I picked it up, as if to throw it back to the kids. It was a nice intact rubber ball, about the size of a tennis ball, with plenty of spring in it.

"Here, kids. I want to buy this off you."

The lads stared at me like I was Ian Brady and Myra Hindley combined. This was Suspicion Corner - and no wonder. I'd have to make this a quick transaction, or I'd be lynched by a posse of angry mums and dads in a minute. A strange bloke chatting to someone else's kids? I felt as though I was taking the biggest risk of my life, bar none.

"Whose ball is it?"

"Mine."

One kid put his hand out tentatively for the ball. I pulled a fiver from the back pocket roll and shoved it in his hand instead. That act alone was probably enough to get me permanently on the paedophile register and hounded out of town.

"Buy yourselves a proper football. There's a stall over there."

"Yeah!" said one of his mates, and the kid grabbed the note. They all ran off, leaving me safe with my rubber ball.

"Here, Slow. You don't know what I put myself through for you."

Slow Kid took out his knife. It was nice and sharp, and it sliced easily into the ball, opening a small hole. He shoved the knife in his pocket and approached the driver's door of the blue saloon. I leaned against the windscreen as if admiring the view, shielding him as best I could with my body. It didn't take more than a few seconds. Slow placed the ball over the lock and smacked down on it hard, so that it squashed flat. The hole pushed air into the lock, and the button inside clicked up. Slow Kid got in the car.

"I don't suppose you've any pliers either," I said. "Do you want me to go and get some from that hardware stall?"

"Nah. I can manage this bit."

He'd hardly got the words out before the wires connected and the car's engine burst into life. Slow gave me a grin.

"Okay, off you go. I'll see you at the workshop."

The blue saloon pulled away across the grass towards the exit. I walked to my Impreza and followed him. I looked round, but could see no sign of Rawlings and Lee. Pity. I would have liked to see their faces when they found out their nice car had just been nicked.

20

"Come on, love, you can do this for me."

"No."

"Just one little favour."

"No again. You've already had your one little favour for this century."

My car smelled nice when Teri was in it. Eddie Craig was right about one thing - I do have a friend in the police, sort of. Sometimes I thought I could forget Teri was a cop and start chatting her up seriously again. But then I'd hear some faint noise, like the rattling of her handcuffs, or maybe some echo from the past, and I'd think better of it.

"Teri, love -"

"No."

"This is mutual interest. It's a number you might be interested in as well."

"Oh?"

Notice that when women say 'no', they still carry on listening, just in case you say something more persuasive? Teri has that down to a fine art.

"You remember a little surveillance operation that went wrong? A certain delivery? Wouldn't you like to trace the top bloke involved?"

"Straight up, Stones?"

"Would I lie?"

"Yes."

"Trust me, I've seen a doctor."

Teri took another look round the garden centre car park. It looked innocent enough to reassure her. I could have told her about Trevor watching us at our last meeting, but that would have destroyed her illusions.

"This is *his* car, the number you've got?"

"His, or close."

"Not good enough."

"It's the best I can manage, love."

"If I do this, will you pass on any other information you get hold of?"

"Do you take me for a nark?"

"Mutual interest, remember?"

"I'll help you all I can in this case. But there's something I have to do for myself first."

"Give me the number."

"You're a darling. We must meet up again some time when you're out of uniform, so to speak."

"You've got to be joking, McClure. I wouldn't touch you with my baton. Not any more."

*   *   *   *

"There's not much in it," said Slow Kid. "But it's a nice motor. I can find a buyer for this, no problem."

"Hold on, hold on. Let's have a look."

The blue saloon was in Metal's workshop, and the two of them had already been through it by the time I got there. They're used to working fast.

"Some crappy tapes, look. A couple of coats and hats - large ones."

"No car phone," said Metal. "That's a pity."

"They probably had a mobile with them."

"Radio's all right, though. It's a Blaupunkt. CD deck too. You want me to whip that out, Stones?"

"Later, later."

"Handbook and service book in the door compartment," said Slow. "It's been serviced properly. A main dealer in Mansfield."

"Yeah?"

"Tax is up to date too."

"These tyres are worth a fortune, Stones."

"Leave them on, Metal."

"Some road maps on the floor, and a few bottles of Budweiser on the back seat. And somebody left their shades on the dash."

"Look at this engine," said Metal, yanking up the bonnet. "Clean as a whistle. Two-litre job, and only twenty thousand miles on the clock. We could turn that back a bit if you want, and it'll pass for practically new."

"Is it a nicked motor, do you think?"

"I reckon not," said Slow Kid. "No signs of it. Wires in the ignition are tidy. Plates haven't been changed, so far as I can see."

"Let's hope so. What's in the glove compartment?"

"It's locked, Stones."

"Yeah? So?"

"They're tough locks on these jobs. We didn't know if you wanted us to force it. It might bring down the value a bit, like."

"Never mind that - get it open."

Metal produced a slim jemmy and within a few seconds the glove compartment was hanging open. There was a dull glint of steel.

"Well, look at that."

"Bleedin' hell, this lot are serious, ain't they?"

"Get rid of it, Slow," I said.

"You mean...?"

"No, I don't mean find a customer for it. Get rid of it. I don't want guns hanging around."

Slow Kid handed the gun to Metal, who dropped it into a plastic carrier bag. "It's done, Stones."

I poked about at the back of the glove compartment and pulled out a few bits of paper. Bassetlaw District Council car park tickets. A petrol receipt from an Elf station in Tuxford. It didn't add up to much.

"Wipe it and dump it."

"We not going to do business with it?" appealed Slow.

"We could flog it to that bloke who sends 'em to the States," said Metal.

"No. Leave it somewhere obvious. I'm going to tell the police where to find it."

"Like shit!"

"The cops?"

237

"I'm using it to bargain, lads."

"Oh, right."

"Right, right."

"Have you ever heard about using a sprat to catch a mackerel?"

"Er, no."

"No."

"It's a fishing expression."

"I know about floats and wagglers," said Slow Kid helpfully. "Our Derron's in the Meden Vale Angling Society. He took me down to the canal a couple of times to catch some roach."

"Oh, for heaven's sake. Do you know about ground bait then?"

"Yeah."

"Well, think of this car as a pound of nice juicy maggots."

"Oh, right."

"Hey, you can sell them buggers," said Metal.

*　*　*　*

Teri came through with the stuff I needed later that day. The name meant nothing to me, but then people use so many names these days it's hard to keep track. The address tied in, though. It was one in one of those rich gits' villages out east towards the River Trent.

This is the affluent part of Nottinghamshire. There's a whole money belt there, stretching from Newark, right round Tuxford and up towards Gainsborough. It's a big area, but it's also the most sparsely populated bit of the county.

Few of these villages have council estates. There are farms and old manor houses, converted barns and vicarages, farmworkers' cottages that have been done up, and a few new ranch-style bungalows built for people who drive off to work in Sheffield or Nottingham in their Range Rovers and Fourtraks. They think they're the real country people now. They wear wellies at weekends and carry a walking stick when they take the labradors out for walkies. They support the hunt and maybe bag a few birds now and then. Otherwise nature stops at the double glazing. The real dirt and noise of the countryside is sent round to the tradesman's entrance.

The sad thing is that these people live in an area where history practically bursts out of the ground. Take the Pilgrim Fathers, for instance. This is where they came from, the villages of North Nottinghamshire. It was here that the Separatist movement started that ended up with Ronald Reagan, where folk were so stubborn about refusing to grovel to the established church that they had to leave the country in the end.

The Pilgrim Fathers are one of the biggest draws for American tourists and all those lovely dollars. But you'd never know it. You see Robin Hood everywhere in Nottinghamshire - the World of Robin Hood, the Tales of Robin Hood, Robin Hood's Larder, the Robin Hood Statue, the Oak Where Robin Hood Hid from the Nasty Sheriff's Men, and the Dead Patch of Grass Where Robin Hood Got Caught Short and Had a to Have a Quick Piss. Welcome to Robin Hood Country, God help us.

But the Pilgrim Fathers? Somewhere in a dull museum room in Worksop you might find a wax dummy that looks a bit like William Brewster. And, er... well, that's about it, really. And Worksop's at least eight miles from where the real action was - Scrooby, Babworth, Austerfield. You know about those places, of course? No? What a surprise.

Okay, so it's true the pub at Scrooby is called the Pilgrim Fathers. It was opened in 1771 for travellers on the Great North Road, and its name was the Saracen's Head until some enterprising landlord in the 1960s decided to cash in and change the name.

Apart from that, your hordes of Brewster and Bradford descendants can steam through North Nottinghamshire without seeing a sign of their courageous forebears. The cameras stay unclicked and the dollars stay in their pockets as they disappear northwards into Doncaster looking vaguely puzzled. It's as if we're shy about our history, and we have to keep it hidden.

We drove out through Ollerton and Tuxford, circled the Markham Moor roundabout and turned eastwards on the A57 towards Lincoln. Half way towards the River Trent at Dunham Bridge we found a little 'B' road and wound our way through corn fields and dense patches of woodland, with some low hills appearing to the north and west. These were real hills, too, not landscaped slag heaps. These were the Wheatley Hills, the rolling slopes where an army of Parliamentarian soldiers once camped to watch for attack from the direction of Yorkshire.

To our right, we could see the monsters that local people call the 'cloud factories'. Power stations - three of them, the giants of Megawatt Valley. They dominate the landscape for miles on the western bank of the Trent here. They may not be picturesque, but they're the biggest customers for coal produced at Nottinghamshire's pits. For now anyway. All it would need would be for these power stations to switch from coal to gas, and the last pits would be gone. So the western parts of Nottinghamshire, the villages between Worksop and Mansfield, rely on the eastern side for their living, just like the peasants always relied on the gentry at the big house.

Many of these rich gits' villages shelter behind hills and woodlands, so they can't actually see the power stations. West Laneton is definitely one of those rich gits' villages. And Old Manor Farm is a typical rich git's house.

We came to wrought iron gates across the end of a drive, with two brick pillars and little stone creatures sitting on them - just like the garden ornaments over the porches on the Forest, except these were griffins rather than toads. The drive was beautifully swept gravel, without an oil stain or a kid's toy in sight, and the hedges were yew instead of privet, and neatly trimmed instead of straggling over the pavement.

Come to think of it, there weren't any pavements anyway. The spaces between the road and the hedges were grassed over and planted with flower beds. Obviously nobody ever walked in this part of the world, except to get from the garage to the Range Rover. If you were a pedestrian, you must be some poor plebby oik from Worksop or somewhere, so it didn't matter if you got run over by the mobile library because you had to walk in the road.

The front garden of this particular house looked like something out of *Practical Gardening*. Geoffrey Smith had been round and shown them how to create the perfect rockery and an interesting water feature that would be totally maintenance-free. It probably would be, too, since most of it was likely to be plastic.

240

The house was older than the garden, if that doesn't sound ridiculous. According to the plaques on the brick pillars, the house was called Old Manor Farm. But this place hadn't seen a real farmer since Bernard Matthews was last on the telly. There was a double garage, so it must be a pretty low-class house for these parts - most of them have triple garages. There's one for hubby's four-wheel drive, one for the little lady's Volvo estate and probably one for the bleedin' nanny to park her second-hand Mini. When they get going, this lot can chuck out more air pollution than any one of those power stations.

"Stay here and watch my back, Slow."

"What you going to do?"

"Just a bit of a recce."

I left Slow in the Subaru and dodged across the road, wary of traffic coming round the bend from behind those big hedges. The gate opened easily - no electronic devices here, anyway. It seemed to take half an hour to walk up the drive, and by the time I reached the top I was breathing hard.

I rang the bell, hoping that no one would answer. No one did. Perhaps it was my lucky day. While I waited, I weighed up the front door. Georgian style, but good wood, not those that they sell for tuppence at the DIY stores. The frame and lintels looked pretty solid. This property had gone up in the days when blokes knew how to build a house, before they started using papier maché bricks held together with chewing gum because it's cheaper.

Getting no answer again after a second attempt, I walked round the side of the house, taking a quick peek through the front windows as I went.

There was oak furniture, a bit dark for my taste. A grand piano and a big open fire that looked as though it was never used except for roasting chestnuts at Christmas. The paintings on the wall certainly hadn't come from Woolworth's and didn't show Spanish ladies or kids with runny eyes. In fact, one didn't show much at all - just a few splashes of colour. This was someone with more money than sense, then. Unfortunately, art isn't my field, so I didn't know whether one of those paintings was worth nicking while I was there.

I found a side door that seemed to lead to a passage and into a kitchen. A fitted oak kitchen, of course. It must have had a cooker and a fridge and all that sort of thing, I suppose, but they weren't in any form that I recognised.

Was this the home of some mate of Welsh Border's, I wondered. It could easily be some business contact of his, a well-heeled property developer or other low-life he'd got in deep with through the council. There's always the stink of corruption hanging around those town halls, if you ask me. And this place certainly smelled of something not right.

A window in the garage was low enough for me to peer through. It was empty, but there was plenty of space for a couple of cars, and dark patches on the floor indicated that something normally stood there - presumably the German motor that was still in Metal Jacket's workshop. I ought to decide what to do with that very soon.

At the back of the house were manicured lawns, mature trees - and an actual tennis court. It was all properly maintained and marked out, with the net still up and everything. It looked like something Tim Henman might have got disqualified from after bouncing a shot off the ball girl's head. So who called round here to play tennis? The neighbours, a few business chums, the teenage daughter's boyfriend in his flannels and straw boater? I found I was picturing the cast from a Noel Coward play, which always makes me feel nauseous.

But near the trees was another building that made me stop and stare. It looked at first like any old barn, built of ancient, crumbling stone. Then I looked again, and it registered on me that it was circular. It was about twenty feet high, and near the top were a whole series of holes built into the stonework. I wanted to wander over and peer closer to be sure. But I felt pretty confident that this was a medieval dovecote, sitting right here in the grounds of a house in this rich gits' village.

Of course, this had been a farmhouse at some time, belonging no doubt to the manor down the road. Somehow this dovecote had got left behind and neglected over the years. I had a dim recollection of Lisa telling me that there were just three circular medieval dovecotes in Nottinghamshire, and they were all further south in the county. Well, never mind - it looked genuine to me, and that was enough.

Now I could imagine the farmworkers toiling across the fields to harvest their crops and tend their animals. Old buildings do this to me. I go all sort of dreamy, just like after I've had sex. Must be an illness or something. Lisa says I'm sensitive, but what does she know?

There was a movement beyond the yew hedge. A hat appeared - one of those white canvass hats, squashed and floppy like the hat on a Sunday cricketer who's been to the bar during the tea break. I thought I knew the face that would be under a hat like that, and I wasn't wrong. It was that Neighbourhood Watch face you get in these places, red and suspicious and constantly teetering on the edge of a heart attack. A rich gits' version of Welsh Border, no less.

The bloke stared over the hedge at me. Somewhere behind him would be a wife, hovering near the phone, ready to ring the cops. 'Hello, hello, come quick, it's an emergency. Working class oiks are walking up our neighbours' path. The estate agents told us there was a by-law against the working classes. We wouldn't have retired here otherwise.'

I only needed to put one foot wrong and I'd be a statistic at the next meeting of the Police Liaison Sub-committee. Another number logged in the book by the eagle-eyed busybodies of West Laneton. I'd be long gone by the time the police arrived in a place like this, of course. They'd have our registration number, but that wasn't what worried me. I didn't want them alerting Perella and his friends at this stage.

Luckily, I had a handy pen in my top pocket and a notebook in my hand.

"Good morning, sir. We're doing some work in the area, and we've had a job cancelled this morning, so we have some materials available. My boss has authorised me to offer householders in the area the chance to have their drives re-surfaced at a very reasonable price. It'll just be a few pounds for the lads. I wonder if you'd be interested, sir?"

243

Mr Neighbourhood Watch had me weighed up now. He looked smug and satisfied. He knew how to deal with people like me, all right.

"We don't do business with cowboys like you round here," he said. "We know all about your shoddy tricks. You might as well clear off. Nobody will have anything to do with you."

"The cost is very reasonable, and I couldn't help noticing that one or two of the drives here need a bit of patching up."

"Did you hear what I said?"

"Fair enough, sir. But I wonder if you could suggest anybody else in this road who might be interested?"

"If you're not out of here in thirty seconds, I'll call the police!"

That was exactly what I wanted, of course - to be out of there. Neighbourhood Watch Man makes me uncomfortable. It's like coming face to face with some lumbering prehistoric creature, which will die out soon, but might just step on you in the meantime.

I hurried back to the car, conscious as always of being an alien in a foreign land. I had the wrong clothes and the wrong accent. My hands were probably the wrong shape, made for carrying a useful tool instead of a tennis racquet. If there were border controls, I'd never have got through.

There are different degrees of foreign, of course. These folk are low-grade foreign, just your basic bundle of incomprehension and resentment. I reserve the real aversion for nuclear-grade foreigners, like the French.

You've heard of twinning, haven't you? Medensworth is twinned with some poncy village in Brittany, where they nick our fish and burn our lamb and blockade our lorries. Every year a bunch of our school kids go over there to be insulted and shrugged at. Then the Froggies send their kids on a return visit to sneer at our houses and turn their noses up at our food and our M & S sweaters. This is all done for the sake of understanding, of course. Entente bleedin' cordiale isn't in it. If what they've got is European culture, give me *Coronation Street* and egg and chips any time.

And then there's the Germans. Did you know they subsidise their coal mining industry by four billion pounds a year? That's forty thousand pounds per miner. No wonder they can dump shit-cheap anthracite on us. It's anthracite now, but what next? Meanwhile, our own pits are closing. Nottinghamshire had twelve coal mines left in 1992, when Heseltine got in on the act and seven of them went. That's nine thousand jobs, nine thousand men on the dole. Later, when the electricity generators discovered gas and cheap German imports, the rest began to shut.

When it comes to twinning, I've got a better idea. Why not twin Medensworth with one of these rich gits' villages, like West Laneton? No need to trek across the Channel to be insulted - you could get the experience right here. And they're two different cultures all right. Shit, these rich kids would get a shock if they had to walk home down First Avenue to a grey council house with a resin toad over the door.

*   *   *   *

When I got back to the car, Slow hadn't moved. He was staring at the village churchyard, trying to figure out how the sundial worked when there wasn't any sun.

We drove by the church and looked at some more big houses. Each was in its own grounds, set back from the road, with carriage lamps and magnolia trees. The only magnolia you ever see on the Forest Estate is the colour of the paintwork that goes with woodchip. Here, even the 'For Sale' signs had to be different. Every one claimed to be advertising a 'Home of Distinction'.

The whole lot reeked of new money. I'd been to places like this before, in my past life. Some of the times I'd been welcome, sometimes not. I had a feeling this was going to be one of the nots.

"We need Hooper for this, Slow," I said.

"He's tagged, Stones. He's got another year to go for that last job they done him for."

"Are you telling me those tags don't go wrong sometimes?"

"Oh, yeah. Right."

"Get me Hooper, then. And tell him it's got to be tonight."

245

21

Yes, I was definitely getting paranoid. When I saw there was a car parked opposite Lisa's house that I didn't recognise, my first thought was of Craig's crew watching me, making sure I carried out my part of the deal. Deal? More like blackmail.

There was no one in the car just now, but they'd be around somewhere. Mentally, I gave them a wave. Look, I'm doing my bit, like the deal says. But if you hurt Lisa, you're dead, pal.

Lisa wasn't home, though, no matter how much I knocked. Again I found myself peering through windows. I could practically smell the pot pourri, as if her spirit was lurking there. I rang my home number to get the messages from my answer phone. There were no messages from Lisa.

Finally I gave up and drove home. When I went through the e-mails on my computer it was obvious business still wasn't good. But then I'd been neglecting it these past few days.

So I got to work again. Things to do, arrangements to make. A vital operation to plan. I needed gloves, a balaclava. What else? A torch. Were the batteries working? No. Shit, this isn't my sort of thing at all.

I jumped when there was a hammering on my door, but it was only Doncaster Dave reporting for duty. He stood on the doorstep chewing a bar of chocolate, like a huge kid wanting me to come out and play. I had to find a way of telling him he wasn't coming with us tonight. He would only be a liability.

We drove along Sherwood Crescent, down First Avenue and out onto Ollerton Road by the shops. There was a faint grey drizzle falling, and women walking towards the bus stops were swinging and dipping their umbrellas with disregard for the safety of other pedestrians. It's dangerous on the pavements sometimes. Maybe it's time they got everybody off the pavement and onto the roads.

We pulled into the car park at Cost Cutters and I let Dave push the trolley. I stocked up with some stuff from the freezers and plenty of beer, plus milk and coffee and loo paper. And batteries for the torch.

"I'll have a job for you tonight, Donc."

Dave was concentrating on steering the trolley. It looked like a toy in his hands, and it was showing a tendency to shoot madly off in the wrong direction.

"Yeah? We're going out to this village?"

"Not you, Donc. I want you to go somewhere else."

"Right."

It was impossible to tell whether he was disappointed, relieved or just couldn't care less. The expression on his face didn't change. Of course, he could just have been trying to thaw out the frozen steak through sheer will power so that he could eat it before we got to the checkout.

"Donc, I want you to go to Lisa's place and wait for her to come home."

He nodded. He knew who Lisa was, I think. Even though she hadn't got tattoos, he'd noticed her around occasionally.

"When you see her, you stay with her. I don't want anyone getting near her, right?"

"Right."

A harassed housewife with two kids in tow barged our trolley with hers as she reached across us to grab at the soap powder. Dave gave her a hurt look as she pushed past without a word. It was a cut-throat world in here.

"You can take the Impreza. I won't be using it tonight. Slow and Metal are getting us something inconspicuous."

Dave nodded cautiously. He is able to drive, but only at ten miles an hour, because his accelerator foot gets jammed against the floor and his elbows stick out of the windows.

"If necessary, get Lisa in the car and bring her back to Medensworth. For her own safety."

We got into the queue at the checkout. Dave had gone very quiet. I picked up a handful of chocolate bars from the display by the till and dropped them into the trolley, in case he needed a quick fix of energy. But when it came our turn at the checkout, I saw

247

where his attention had turned to. We'd picked the queue for the heftiest, most muscular checkout girl in the place. Underneath the uniform, she was bound to have tattoos.

I saw Dave admiring the way she shot the barcode reader at each item and how her thick fingers thumped the keys of the till. He seemed charmed by the high pitched screech that came out of her mouth when she announced the total. When I handed over the cash, the bird smiled at him, not me. Amazing.

On the way back from the supermarket, Dave got talkative. It was like that cement toad suddenly flexing its legs and hopping off the porch.

"Stones?"

"Yeah, Donc?"

"Can I ask you something?"

"'Course."

"Do you think I'm well muscled, or just a fat bastard?"

I thought about this for a minute. If a bloke asks you a serious question like that, it deserves a bit of thought.

"Does it matter?"

"Well, yeah."

"Why?"

"It's, you know... what people think of you. It's important sometimes, ain't it?"

"Donc, have you got off with one of those waitresses you're always drooling over?"

"Don't be daft."

"Because if that's it, then I'm the wrong person to be giving advice. I don't give a toss what women think of me. They have to take me or leave me. That's the way to do it, Donc. Don't let them get their claws into you, because they'll try and change you, and it doesn't do you any good. Are you listening to me, Donc?"

"Yeah."

"Good."

"So.

"So what?"

"Do you think I'm well muscled, or just a fat bastard?"

I sighed, and tried to ignore him for the rest of the walk back to Sherwood Crescent. But the brain's a funny thing, isn't it? It was right then that my mind started to put two and two together, the way it does sometimes when there's no bird or booze to occupy me. It hadn't seemed important while I was actually at Eddie Craig's place, but now I started to wonder how his lads had known to visit the Rev to find out where I was holed up. Craig isn't strictly a local villain - his home manor is Mansfield and Ashfield, where the market for his stuff is. So for information, he must have to rely on local snouts.

I wondered who had tipped him off to tap the Rev for my whereabouts. Who knew that I'd visited St Asaph's the day before I skipped off? Only my own crew, and one other person.

Yeah, and another thing. Who had been gossiping to Moxon and Stubbs about my private activities, my personal liaisons? I could think of someone who had. And those two someones were one and the same person.

"Dave?"

"Yeah?"

"Food later. Let's go visit St Asaph's for a few minutes."

The Reverend Bowring came out of the vicarage when he saw us in the churchyard. He was dressed like a chat show host in a bright woolly cardigan. Perfect evening wear for Medensworth.

"Where is your young lady, Livingstone? I haven't had the pleasure of seeing her for some days. No trouble, I hope?"

"Trouble? You don't know the half of it, Rev."

"Oh. Would you like to tell me about it?"

"Not really."

"Has there been a disagreement between you? Not a permanent estrangement, I trust?"

"To be honest, I think some other bloke's got her, Rev."

"Ah? A rival? Dear me, how sad."

"Don't worry, I'm going to do something about it."

"Remember that God giveth, and He taketh away," said the Rev. "That's what the Bible says. Sometimes we must accept His will, Livingstone."

"The Bible doesn't say God taketh it away from one bloke and giveth it to another who doesn't deserve it."

The Rev smiled understandingly, damn him. "Ah, but it may say that. In a way."

"What do you mean, it may do? It's written down there in words, isn't it, Rev? Either it says it or it doesn't."

"Hardly. The Bible means different things, according to our interpretation."

"Well, holy shit. Nobody ever told me. So can it mean whatever you want it to? That must make your job a lot easier, Rev."

"Mmm. On the other hand, there are a number of basic truths that we must live by, Livingstone."

"Yeah, yeah."

There wasn't much fun in baiting the Rev. He was likely to take it seriously and decide I needed to join Bible classes, like the glue sniffers. So far I've managed to get away with not coming to services because of my voluntary work in the churchyard. But if the Rev got the idea that I was some poor soul facing eternal damnation instead of being the original Good Samaritan, he'd have me with a Good News Bible in one hand and a hymn sheet in the other before you could say Moses.

The sound of a petrol mower drifted across the graveyard, along with the smell of cut grass. There was a horribly familiar boiler suit moving backwards and forwards by the graves at the end of the churchyard. It was Welsh Border, still toiling away in the gathering dusk like the Gadarene Swine.

But no one keeps me away from my dad's grave. The Rev went over to speak to Councillor Border while I walked down the row to the lump of stone that's the only thing commemorating the day that Granville McClure gave up the fight. My mum is here, too, but she lasted longer and died of pneumonia in the end. Somehow that doesn't seem as bad - at least it's something that God did to her, not someone else.

Border had switched off the lawnmower to empty the grass box when the Rev wandered up, and I was vaguely aware of him kicking his boots against the side of the mower as they talked. His voice was rising in agitation, and it occurred to me for a second or two that maybe he was still smarting from our previous encounter. He'd got it into his head that I was a hooligan or an unsavoury character. People come to all sorts of wrong conclusions about me.

Then I looked up and met his eye. The Rev was getting anxious and flapping his hands about, as if to ward off a swarm of midges. A large figure loomed in the background by the church wall, unwrapping a Mars bar.

"All I'm saying, vicar," said Border, raising his voice so that I could hear, "is that we ought to be a bit more careful who we allow to be buried in this churchyard. Some families that quite undesirable and always will be, in my opinion - no matter what jobs they manage to weasel their way into. People expect a churchyard to be a respectable place, not a hangout for criminals. They're entitled to think they're going to be buried with decent Christians, not alongside the relatives of thugs and crooks."

Well, that was it. Patience finally runs out for everyone. I had my limits, and Welsh Border had just crossed them.

"Donc," I said. "Help Councillor Border with his grass cuttings."

Dave ambled forward, his chocolate bar still sticking out from between his teeth. He reached down and pulled the full grass box off the lawnmower, like he was pulling the leg off a fly. It was one of those plastic boxes with net sides, and it was full to the brim. Bits of chewed grass spilt over the lip onto Border's beautifully mown patch.

"Just a minute. I don't want your help. I can manage perfectly well myself."

"I don't think so, Councillor. You look tired. In fact, you look so tired you might fall over at any moment."

The grass smelt green and dark and juicy, the sort that stains your hands and clothes as soon as you look at it.

"The compost heap is over there," said the Rev helpfully, pointing away towards the back of the churchyard, trying to ignore the atmosphere. Poor bloke, he doesn't know what to do when it comes to taking sides between the sheep and the goats. The thing about goats is that they're stubborn where sheep are meek, wayward where sheep are regimented, independent where sheep are submissive. You can count me in with the goats if you like. No kidding.

"No, Rev, I think the compost heap is right here in front of me."

Welsh Border took a step towards me. His hand came out, a finger pointing aggressively at my face. His mouth opened to say something offensive, but he didn't quite get round to saying it. His face suddenly went bright red and tears came to his eyes. It would have been nice to think it was his guilty conscience troubling him. But it could have been my boot trampling on his big toe.

"Get off my foot, McClure. I'll have you charged with assault."

"Oh sorry, Councillor. I thought I was treading on a worm."

"I'll - !"

Just then Dave swung the grass box and slipped it neatly over Border's head, smothering his latest gem. Grass poured over the councillor's shoulders, slithering into the collar of his shirt and down inside his boiler suit. A high-pitched screeching, choking sound came from somewhere inside the box.

"Oh my goodness," said the Rev. "Are we having a contretemps?"

With Councillor Border incapacitated, Dave and I decided to make our escape from the churchyard.

"Grass," I said to Dave as we walked back up the road.

"What?"

"Grass. Do you think he got it?"

"'Course he got it, Stones. I tipped it right over his nut."

"No, I mean the message, the meaningful pun. Grass. He grassed me up. So we grassed him up. Right?"

"Some of it were dandelions," said Dave.

We walked on a few yards more.

"Yeah, that might have confused him a bit," I said.

* * * *

After I'd sent Dave off in the Subaru, there was nothing else much to do except wait for dark. I ate a pizza from the freezer and downed just one can of Mansfield Bitter while I watched TV.

I was anxious for news that Lisa was safe, but no call came. There was nothing from Nuala either. Had I upset her? Was it something I said?

The call that did come was from Uncle Willis. I had the answerphone on, but when I heard his voice, irritated at having to talk to a machine, I picked up the phone.

"Hello, Uncle."

"Livingstone? In person?"

"Yeah, in person."

"Why do you give me a message saying you're not in, when you are?"

"It depends who's phoning."

"Well, it seems a bit funny to me. When I phone, I want to speak to the person, not a robot."

"What is it you're calling about, Uncle?"

"I wondered whether you've had a think. You know, about that little thing we were talking about the other day."

"Well, to be honest, I've been a bit busy."

"Working hard at your business, no doubt."

"Yes, Uncle."

"That's good. I want your business to do well, you know."

"Do you?"

"Yes. I was wondering, you see, after you'd been to see me, whether you properly realised what I was saying."

"Well, I think so, Uncle. You're leaving your money to set up a trust to help kids."

"That's right. But my money won't be enough on its own."

"Well, there's never enough, is there?"

"What a trust like that would need is a regular income."

"Yeah? We'd all like that, I suppose."

"It would require, let's say, a successful local businessman willing to put in a percentage of his profits each month. Do you understand what I'm saying now, Livingstone?"

There was a nasty silence. Uncle Willis was waiting for me to respond. Me, I was trying to convince myself that a member of my own family hadn't just made such a suggestion. We both listened to the silence for a bit. It said a lot.

"It would be a really good move, I think," said Willis. "For public relations. And, er, your standing in the community."

It was incredible, but true. The old bugger had just threatened me.

"Tell you what, Uncle. I'll ask around, see if anyone's interested, shall I?"

He carried on as if I hadn't spoken. "I really hope you'll do it, Livingstone. I know how good you are with young people."

"You must be mixing me up with some other nephew."

"You were always like that. I remember you with your cousins, young Charlie and Frank. They always thought the world of you. And of course, you had a lot to do with young people in your job. I mean your proper job."

"I don't have that job any more, Uncle."

"No, I know. But you were good at it, Livingstone. You always cared about the young lads you dealt with. Not like the others. Some of them are right bastards."

"For goodness sake, that's all in the past. It's nothing to do with me now."

"Maybe. But *you* don't change, Livingstone. Not in yourself, you don't."

"Don't you believe it, Uncle."

I don't like being reminded of my previous life. Like I said to Uncle Willis, it's well and truly in the past. If I was going to let these things get to me, there are reminders all around me, all the time. DI Frank Moxon and DS Wally Stubbs, for a start, who seemed to be very much around me just now.

"You were good at that job. It was criminal what they did to you."

Criminal? That was a laugh. *It's supposed to me that's the criminal, Uncle, didn't you know?* But I didn't say that. Well, you don't.

"What's this got to do with what we were talking about? I'm in a different business altogether now. I'm not in a position to help these kids that you're on about, Uncle."

"Yes you are," he said. "That's what I mean. You're still you, the same Livingstone McClure. You still care about the youngsters. But now they'd trust you even more, wouldn't they?"

This was ironic, but probably true. I just wished Uncle Willis would stop going on about my previous life. In a moment he was going to say it outright, and it would all come flooding back again, the years of hassle and frustration, and that final humiliation and betrayal. I wanted to forget it. Forget it, right?

"Are you still there, Livingstone? You haven't put me back to the machine?"

"No, I'm still here, Uncle."

"So this is what I was thinking, you see. That you've got the right background, the experience. But now you're more in a position where the kids would take notice of you. Now that you're not a policeman any more."

There, he'd said it. A policeman. Stones McClure? Surely not. That was someone else entirely. It was some naive bastard who thought he was doing a worthwhile job for the community, until reality hit him like a baseball bat. That was some gullible pillock who reckoned he knew what justice was and tried to put it into practice until they squashed him with the rule book. That McClure was a bloke who turned a blind eye once too often to some poor, desperate sod nicking a bit of stuff to feed his kids, and who got shafted by his own side as a result, stitched up and stabbed in the back by a bunch of treacherous creeps in and out of uniform.

No, that was a previous life. I've been reincarnated since then. Born again, like one of those fundamentalist Christians. Yet I'm still dragging all the bad karma along with me, which is not the way it's supposed to happen. Thanks for the memory, Uncle.

"Of course, you were a very good policeman," said Uncle Willis, misunderstanding my silence. "You were the best detective inspector that Nottinghamshire has ever had."

22

When we called back at West Laneton later that night, Slow Kid was in the driver's seat of an ex-BT Combo van, and Lenny Hooper was in the back. Hooper was treating it like a works outing - his electronic tag didn't allow him out of Bilsthorpe, as a rule, so a drive to West Laneton in the dark was like a coach tour to Skegness for him. He'd got fatter and balder and pastier than when I saw him last. I suppose that's the result of sitting round the house all day getting under the feet of the wife and watching the Columbo repeats on the telly. If they ever try to tag me, I might opt for prison. There's a nice one near here, at Ranby, where they provide you with all the facilities you could want, and you seem to be able to pop out any time you like.

Tonight, I'd made Hooper wear a woolly hat so that his bald head didn't reflect the light. What's the use of wearing dark clothes if your head stands out like a bleedin' Millennium beacon?

"I wouldn't be doing this if I didn't need the money," he said.

"Join the club."

"If they find out you fixed my tag, my probation officer's going to be right narked."

"What's up, Hooper? Are you married to him? It's just a tag, not a wedding ring, you know."

"I'm just saying."

"Right. Well, you've said it. How easy will it be for us to get in there?"

"Dead easy."

"What about the burglar alarm?" asked Slow Kid.

"No problem."

Hooper sounded more confident than I felt, but I knew he had his little tool bag with him. This was a workman's van, so why shouldn't it have tools in the back, officer?

It was just after one o'clock in the morning. The residents of West Laneton were tucked up in bed. There are no street lamps in these little places, but the big houses like Old Manor Farm all have their security lights. Some are on sensors and come on when you walk into their range. But there's a trend to have lights that stay on permanently, covering the drives in a nasty glare all night. These don't make any difference if you're going in the back way, where no one can see you anyway. Naturally, we were planning on going in the back way.

Ideally, you'd watch a place like this for a bit to see who comes and goes, and to get an idea how many people there are in the house. But you couldn't do that in West Laneton. We could only see the entrance to the driveway of Manor Farm from one spot on the bend, and there are no pavements, no shops, no pub, not even a bus shelter to provide cover. You'd be blocking half the road and making yourself so obvious that you'd have every horse rider and Range Rover driver in the area ringing up to report your licence number for obstructing the highway. Right now, I didn't even know if there were any cars in the garage at Old Manor Farm. But I had to assume there were, and that the owners were somewhere in the house, counting piles of money in their sleep.

"Drive round the corner then, Slow. Watch for a gate into those woods about half a mile on."

We drove past the house of Mr Neighbourhood Watch. He'd left a couple of lights on in strategic places to convince blokes like us that he was sitting up all night with a shotgun on his knee. But I wasn't worried about him. His type are only aggressive in defence of their own property. All hell could break loose next door, and he'd dial 999 with his head under the pillow.

Slow Kid pulled into the gateway and I cut through the chain of the ancient padlock that held the gate together. With our lights out, we crawled back through the woods towards the village. We left the Combo on the edge of the trees, and the three of us skirted a hedge and hopped over a narrow drainage ditch to get to the back of the garden at Old Manor Farm. There was patchy cloud and no moon tonight, but I was still nervous. This sort of thing just isn't my scene.

Sure enough, there was a security light at the back, but no one to see us as we nipped through the glare and hugged the side of the house. It was a low-built farmhouse, and they hadn't bothered to get the control box for the burglar alarm too high up. Hooper grinned when he saw it and opened his tool bag. All the bits and pieces inside were carefully wrapped in cloth to stop them clattering against each other. He took out a mastic gun with a long thin nozzle and snipped the end off the tube with a pair of long-nose pliers. Then he got me to give him a leg up against the wall. It would have been easier if Dave had been with us, but who'd want Doncaster Dave lumbering about on a job like this?

Slow Kid helped me to support Hooper, both of us leaning against the wall while he did his bit with the alarm. Faintly disgusting squelchy noises came from overhead, like someone with a bad case of the balti belly dance.

"It's dead quiet, Stones," whispered Slow.

"Well, they don't have all-night acid house parties round here."

"Yeah?"

"Not on a Wednesday night anyway."

"Why not?"

"Why not? The excitement of *Panorama* wears them out and they have to go to bed early."

"You're full of shit, Stones."

Hooper was starting to wobble a bit on our shoulders, and I heard him give a little squeak of panic. A small blob of black mastic landed with a splat on Slow Kid's shoulder. He squirmed his face to the side to look at it.

"Do they have seagulls round here, Stones?"

"Nah. They hang around the rubbish tips and gravel pits, don't they? They'll have posher birds round here, like peacocks."

"I think a bleedin' peacock just shat on me then."

More wobbling and grunting suggested that Hooper was ready to come down. We grabbed him and hoisted him back to ground level.

"That'll fix that bugger," he said. "It's stuck solider than a constipated cow."

"Okay, now the door."

258

Hooper dug into his bag again and bent down to the back door. It was a stable-type affair in two halves, and Hooper had the bottom half open so fast that it might as well have been a giant cat flap left open specially for us cat burglars. That's the trouble with rich gits - they think anyone who hasn't got as much money as they have is stupid as well. This lot were about to learn a lesson in crude peasant cunning.

We left Slow Kid at the back door while Hooper and I moved about the house. Hooper had no idea what I was looking for, but I needed his experience to keep me from stumbling into an infra-red sensor or something. The only other thing I worried about was a dog. But if there had been one, it ought to be telling us about it by now, and I for one would have been back in those woods like Linford Christie, clutching my lunch box.

Just inside the back door was a hallway with coats and stuff. Then there was the kind of room that doesn't exist in houses on the Forest Estate. I did see a picture of one once in a Sunday magazine, and the caption on the picture said it was a utility room. I suppose it's where you'd keep your croquet equipment or send your butler to polish the silver. This one looked like you could have kept a couple of horses in it. But it was nothing compared to the next room, where you could have kept the carriage as well.

Hooper was nodding his approval as he eyed the place up, taking stock of the china and the more movable bits of furniture. I know of one job that Hooper and a couple of his mates did not far from here, where they took everything out of the house, including half a dozen solid oak doors. They just drove up in a furniture van and took it all away. That time there was nobody at home to complain about the draught.

We walked down a long, dark passageway and passed a door into a dining room with a kitchen beyond it. Doncaster Dave would have been sticking his head in the fridge by now to get at the chicken legs and left-over caviar. But I moved on, trying the next door and hitting lucky. This looked like a study, with bookshelves and a big desk over near the window. Even this was bigger than my entire house. We'd come past five rooms, and we hadn't even seen the stairs yet.

Hooper gave the study a quick once-over and dropped me the nod. I went straight to the desk and shone my torch on the surface, looking for letters, bank statements, address books - anything to give me a handle on who we were dealing with.

A couple of letters had been left lying about. Nothing exciting - offers of investment opportunities, credit cards that supported charities, insurance deals, mobile phone offers. It was the usual stuff - the bloke had got himself on a mailing list at some time and his letter box would be jammed up for ever more. But they did confirm the name - Mr N. Perella. What would the first name be, I wondered. Nigel, Nathaniel? Not a Norman, surely? Perella sounded vaguely Italian, but I couldn't think of any Italian first names starting with 'N', apart from Nero.

There were four drawers, all locked, but Hooper soon whipped them open for me with a little sliver of stiff plastic. The first contained bills and a wallet full of bank statements. Just as I thought - a rich git. My eyes widened as I looked at some of the figures, and my brain started to tick over with schemes for relieving Mr Perella of some of that excess wealth. But then I remembered why I was there and started on the second drawer. This was even more boring - share certificates, tax vouchers, letters from the Inland Revenue, copies of invoices from solicitors, accountants, estate agents. It looked like Perella hadn't owned Old Manor Farm for more than a few months. Such a pity that he hadn't got round to replacing the out of date burglar alarm yet.

Hooper got the first of the left hand drawers open and I heard him draw in his breath sharply.

"Bloody 'ell, I don't like guns."

It was an automatic similar to the one we'd taken out of the German car. If Perella had his own private arsenal, then I was with Hooper on that one. I suddenly felt even more uneasy and itched to get out of the house.

"You never told me there were guns involved, Stones."

"Shh."

There was just one more drawer to go, and now I hit lucky - if you can call it lucky. At least it solidified something I'd been feeling recently. I took a leaflet off the top of the pile and barely needed to glance at the papers underneath, neatly filed away in a blue folder. Yes, I'd found what I was looking for after all. I read the front sheet again, and then a third time. Boy, I was going to like this.

Hooper was looking at me strangely.

"Out?" he mouthed.

"Yeah."

We crept back down the corridor, hearing nothing from inside the house except the usual little creaking noises from an old building at night. Hooper pulled the back door shut. They might never know they'd been broken into, until the next time they had the burglar alarm tested.

Slow Kid met us in the garden and the three of us set off back towards the trees. Then I had a thought, or a sudden impulse, and veered off towards the old dovecote that loomed out of the dark across the grass. Slow and Hooper came after me, baffled now, but not able to make a fuss.

The door on the dovecote was fairly new and solid, and it fit well. It wasn't the sagging, loose-hinged mess that you usually see on old farm buildings. There was a smooth run up the grass to the doors, and it looked to me, even in the dark, as though cars regularly pulled up here. The dovecote was plenty big enough to use for storage. There'd be no interior walls, just tiers of nesting places reaching up to the tiled roof.

Hooper shrugged and snapped open the lock. We pulled the door back, and it moved quietly and easily. A strange smell hit us, a mixture of old timber, dry earth and ancient stones. It was the sort of smell that takes me straight back through the centuries to imagine the blokes who'd built the thing. Real craftsmen, who achieved the most amazing things with primitive techniques. Show me a building that's been put up recently and tell me whether you think it'll still be there in five hundred years' time. No? We may have learned a lot of things since the Middle Ages, but we haven't learned much about craftsmanship.

The space inside also held the ghosts of all the folk who'd used it in those five hundred years - farmhands, labourers, shepherds and general peasants. But there was another smell. It was the sweet, sickly stink of something more recent that didn't belong here.

A flicked my torch around the floor of the dovecote, keeping its beam pointing downwards. We didn't want any stray chinks of light creeping out through these old walls. At the far side was the inevitable collection of rusty farm equipment - a baler, a chain harrow, bits of less identifiable rubbish. There were piles of blue fertiliser sacks tied up with baling twine and an old water trough standing on its end against the wall. To one side was a stack of roof tiles not unlike the ones that the Rev lost off the vestry roof. Old bits of horse tack were hanging from six inch nails knocked into a beam.

Nearer to hand, my torch picked out some cardboard boxes. Quite a lot of them, actually. They came from France, and they looked as though they might contain portable CD players.

Then I noticed the wire leading from a sensor by the door. A burglar alarm on a dovecote?

"Hooper, what's this?"

Hooper frowned at the sensor and began to follow the wire round the wall. It disappeared behind some of the boxes. Slow came over and went with him to move a box or two. Then they both froze.

"Shit, Stones."

"What?"

"It's a timer."

Oh. A vision of that burning Renault van shot through my mind. Fertiliser and sugar, and a timer set to go off half an hour after a box had been opened? Or maybe after a door had been forced with a jemmy?

"Out! Everyone, out! Now!"

I shoved Slow Kid and Hooper out of the door. Then everything was lit up by an almighty flash and we hit the deck, cursing. The explosion blew out the front of the building and sent lumps of stone flying across the garden. As soon as the debris started to settle we were up again and running. Hooper was swearing and clutching his arm, and his hat had come off. The flames from the dovecote were starting to reflect off the sweat on his bald head.

In the trees, I stopped and turned to look back. Although lights were starting to come on and faces were no doubt appearing at windows, I had to watch the dovecote burn. There is nothing more tragic than a piece of history going up in smoke, and this one could have been avoided.

Slow Kid looked at me, puzzled.

"Come on, Stones. We need to be out of here."

"I won't be a minute. You two clear out."

Something about the figures now emerging from Old Manor Farm had caught my attention. Against my better judgement, I slipped back towards the dovecote. The smoke was black and acrid, but billowing away from me and towards the house. No doubt everybody in West Laneton had phoned the fire brigade by now. But for a couple of minutes I had the chance of getting closer to see who we'd flushed out.

When I peered round the corner, I could see only one bloke now, running about like mad in front of the house. He was struggling desperately to untangle a length of garden hose, but the hose was winning. There was something familiar about the figure, but I couldn't make him out too clearly. I felt sure that if I waited a bit longer he'd turn his face to the fire and I'd be able to recognise him.

But I waited too long. Suddenly there was a movement close to me - a dark shape forming out of the smoke at the corner of the dovecote. I caught a brief glimpse of a pair of stuffed-cat eyes, then a glint of steel flashing towards me through the grey swirl. I pulled my shoulder away sharply from the wall and heard the scrape of the knife as it skidded off the stone.

Panicking, I lashed out with my foot towards where I thought the bloke's legs might be and felt contact with something solid. If I'd been wearing my boots, he would have been down, but instead I was wearing sodding trainers and all the kick did was throw him off balance. He lurched into me, his shoulder crashing into my chest and his left hand scrabbling for a grip on my belt. I tried to stop him getting the leverage on me to push himself upright, and we stumbled about for a minute in an ungainly dance in the dark.

Every second I was expecting the knife to strike upwards, and my guts contracted with the anticipation of the pain. His head was right under my nose, and I could smell his sweat and the grease from his hair. Finally, I managed to twist his arm and push him away from me. He cursed as he collided with the wall, but he was still up.

It was enough for me to get a head start as I slipped and slithered across the grass, legging it as fast as I could towards the trees. I could hear the bloke grunting behind me as he followed. He didn't seem to have a torch, but he didn't need one with the amount of noise I was making. Even in the panic, my mind was working, and I knew where I'd seen those dead blue eyes and the flat-top that had just been shoved in my face.

I saw the hedge coming up ahead of me and remembered the ditch just in time. I jumped and landed in a scramble on the other side. A crash and a squelch, followed by a barrage of curses, told me that my pursuer hadn't seen the ditch. I was grinning to myself with self-satisfaction when I heard a strange whistling in the air near my ear. Something that glittered in the patchy light from the flames spun past me and buried itself in the ground with an awful thud. It might have been a wild throw, but if he'd been just a bit more accurate with that knife, I'd be dead meat.

My legs were wobbly by the time I reached the trees. But Slow Kid was waiting for me with the van door open and the engine running, anxious to be off.

"You all right, Stones?"

"Shut up and drive."

Even as we headed out of West Laneton, I could still see the dead eyes of Josh Lee as they appeared through the smoke. And the bloke wrestling with the hose had been his mate Rawlings, for sure.

Yeah, Rawlings and Lee. Fire bombers to the gentry.

23

On Monday morning, I went in the newsagent's on Ollerton Road. As well as papers and magazines it sells stationery - the stuff that more literate folk up Budby Road use. It doesn't quite stretch to books, of course, except for stamp albums and the 'make your own will' type of thing. Perhaps I ought to have got one of those while I was at it.

The old woman behind the counter is called Betty. As far as I can remember, she's always been there.

"What can I do for you, duck?"

This 'duck' business takes folk by surprise when they're from out of the area. Some don't like it, but those are usually soft southerners. They don't have a greeting down there that they can use for men or women equally without sounding patronising. But 'duck' does it. Well, you know you're at home when they call you 'duck'. It's like seeing the first headstocks from the M1 coming north. Or that's what it used to be like. Now instead you have to watch out for the first tourist signs. Robin Hood Country seems to be the new name for the area that I used know as Nottinghamshire. I suppose it's all run by UK Heritage plc these days, since our history was privatised.

"I want a street map."

"Where of, duck? We've got Mansfield, Newark, Worksop, Nottingham. We've even got one with the whole of the county. That has places on it I didn't even know had streets."

"No, I just want Medensworth."

"Medensworth? Oh." She looked doubtful. "I think there was one they brought out a few years ago. Let me have a look in the back."

Yes, the street map of Medensworth was produced by the Chamber of Trade. It carries adverts promoting the delights of Bernard's Quality Pork Butcher's and the Curl Up and Dye hair salon. I don't know how the tourists can bear to stay away. It doesn't have the Forest Estate on it, though. You won't find it on this, or any other map. This is because it's not really called the Forest Estate. Not officially. Not by the council or the Royal Mail, or anybody like that. But with streets like Birch Avenue, Oak Crescent and Chestnut Close, what else would it be?

The map is also a bit out of date now. It still shows the pit for a start, though it closed in 1992. Remember the fuss at the time? No? That old Tory Heseltine wielded the axe on the pits, just like Dr Beeching did on the railways thirty years earlier.

But the writing had been on the wall since the 1984-85 strike that left the miners' union exhausted, defeated, and split in two. They hadn't the strength left to fight the closures when they came. And everyone knew that privatisation was planned. Now British Coal itself is long gone, and the pits left over belong to a private company. This doesn't stop them closing, of course - if they're not making enough profit.

There are plans to turn our derelict pit site into an alternative technology park, all solar panels and water power and battery-driven cars. Anything but coal, in fact. That's old technology, ancient history.

One thing that made me laugh on this map was the claim that its publication has been supported by Neighbourhood Liaison. This is some sort of token organisation run part-time by a copper and an office boy from the county council, which is supposed to sort out problems in the most deprived areas of the county.

In some places, like Newstead, they have the Corner House, a mini community centre where a corner shop used to be. When the pit closed, so did the shop. But at least they've got some advice on the doorstep. And what have we got here in Medensworth? Neighbourhood Liaison. What neighbourhood's that, then? You might well ask. It's not in the neighbourhood of the Forest Estate, that's for sure. The office is conveniently located somewhere in the depths of Sherwood Lodge Police headquarters. This nestles in its wonderful leafy isolation in Burntstump Country Park, where coppers can escape from all the stress of big city crime fighting. As far as Medensworth folk are concerned, it might as well be on a satellite orbiting Jupiter.

When I'd got my map from Betty, I marked a spot on it with a red felt tip pen and dreamed a bit. Either this was going to work, or I was totally up shit creek. Lisa's safety was in my hands, not to mention my own future if they should drive me into doing something really stupid.

But for this part I needed Lisa's co-operation. Everyone knows how well my charm works with women, but I was going to have put myself out a bit to soften her up for this one. I might even have to pay a bit of attention to all those things that women think are important, like having a shave every day and not leaving the toilet seat up. That's the desperate situation I'd been driven to.

* * * *

There are moments when we're all amenable to a bit of gentle persuasion. When you're lying naked and fully satisfied in bed is usually one of them. So that afternoon I waited until I reckoned Lisa was looking sufficiently flushed and softened up before I explained the idea to her. And, blow me, she didn't like it.

"You only need to make one phone call, love."

"Only one phone call? But I'd have to tell a lie, Stones."

"It's in a good cause, honest."

"But you say you can't tell me what that cause is."

"It's important to my business."

"And you won't tell me what that is either."

"Don't you trust me?"

Lisa propped herself up on one elbow and looked at me hard. Her breasts swung round and aimed themselves towards me like a pair of ouija board pointers picking out the person the spirits want to communicate with. A message was about to come through, in duplicate.

"Well?" I asked.

She was taking an uncomfortably long time to answer such a simple question. I could practically see the whole of our relationship passing through her mind, incident by incident, promise by broken promise. My face was starting to ache with the effort of trying to look sincere, but still she said nothing. Was she thinking about those little incidents with Cavendish? I might have embarrassed her a bit. But, come on, it was all justified. Was she thinking about the little fib I'd told her about the gas leak in my house? I'd explained about that, though, hadn't I? Or was she thinking about all the evasions she'd got when she asked me questions about what, exactly, I did for a living? That was for her benefit, though. The less she knew, the better. So what was so difficult about the question? I'm about the most trustworthy person anyone could hope to meet in Medensworth. Well, unless you happen to be a rich git. Or a Frog or a Kraut. Or a member of Nottinghamshire Constabulary. Or one of Eddie Craig's boys. Or Welsh Border. Or... well, for God's sake, you can't be trustworthy all the time.

"I suppose so," said Lisa.

"Of course you do." That was better. She's a good girl, is Lisa.

She sighed. "I'm a fool though, really."

"By the way, you have, er... you have nearly finished that little job that you've been doing, haven't you?"

"For Michael Cavendish? Yes, nearly finished."

"Do you want to tell me about it?"

"Well, it's..."

"Because, if you like, we can talk about it later. After I've explained exactly what I want you to do."

"Stones...?"

"Yes, love?"

"Did I ever tell you you're a pillock?"

*   *   *   *

"I knew you'd find a use for it," said Metal. "It's a great motor, ain't it?"

Ironically, since Metal Jacket had actually bought the Morris Traveller, it was the only legal set of wheels we had access to at the moment, apart from the Impreza - and I had a reluctance to risk the bodywork on that.

"Have you heard that noise it makes when you throttle down?" said Metal. "It's just like someone's farted. No kidding. You've got to hear it."

"I can't wait."

"Some daft buggers pay good money just so they can hear that, you know. This thing'll be worth a fortune when I've done it up. A real collector's item."

"Metal, are you thinking about going straight or something?"

"Eh?"

"All this car restoration and collector's stuff. It sounds almost legit to me."

"Nah. It's just... cars, you know, Stones? A get a right buzz out of 'em. This one - well, somehow I wanted it, but I didn't want to nick it. Do you know what I mean?" he appealed.

"Yeah, it's called ownership, Metal. The desire for property. It's an old story."

He looked a bit crestfallen. And I hadn't told him yet that he wasn't going to be driving the Morris himself.

"Anyway, have you heard the saying 'Property is theft'?"

"Sounds all right to me," he said.

"All right? It's what the world is based on, mate."

Slow Kid had found us a couple of ancient sports jackets and flat caps.

"They were my granddad's," he said. "Mum never chucks things out."

"Brilliant. They're just the job. Metal, I want you to drive the van."

"What, the Telecom van? But it's hot. Somebody might have seen it last night."

"That's exactly what I'm banking on, Metal."

"On my own? Can I have Dave with me?"

"Yes, but he'll be in the back. I don't want anyone to see him. You're the only one of us they won't recognise, Metal."

"Right."

"Are you up for it?"

"All right. Just one thing, Stones."

"Yeah?"

"Look after the Morris, will you?"

269

"Oh yeah, I'll even rub its tummy when it farts."

The blue German saloon was gone from the workshop now. In fact, we'd returned the motor to its rightful owner, just like any decent law-abiding citizen would. It was almost undamaged too, thanks to the way Slow Kid had lifted it from the Sunday market. I'd even added a few hidden extras. I'm so generous sometimes that I get all soppy and sentimental just thinking about myself.

So if Lisa had done her bit and made the call, this plan might actually work. I had complete faith in her, of course. She was the only person I knew who could sound genuinely respectable and convincing. Besides, I was well aware why she'd agreed to do what I asked. She hoped it would give her a bit of leverage over me. Dream on, sweetheart.

We split up and set off in opposite directions. Slow Kid was driving the Traveller, with his flat cap pulled down so far over his forehead that it made his ears stick out just right. I was slumped in the passenger seat in my own cap and sports jacket. From behind, we should look like a couple of old fogeys out for a Sunday drive on a Monday. We'd be comparing our false teeth and arthritis, and talking about the next reunion of the Decrepit Order of Water Voles.

For a while, though, we old fogeys were parked up by the Parliament Oak, a tree even more ancient than we were. King Edward I is supposed to have held a parliament of his barons under this tree. They'd been hunting in the royal forest near Clipstone when they got the news that the Welsh were revolting. It wouldn't be news to me, but they were a bit innocent in those days.

The oak itself is just a rotten, blackened stump. Not surprising, when it's getting on for a thousand years old. But there's a new tree too - a sapling oak, sprouting from the same spot. It's thriving, and even helps to prop up the old one that the visitors come to see. Some folk could make a meaningful symbol out of this. You know, like regeneration and all that. Bringing in new life, but keeping the old traditions alive at the same time. Preserving the best of our heritage while adapting to the young and vibrant modern world. Yeah, you could see all that in this little oak tree, if you want. Me, I think someone nicked all the acorns off the old tree, but dropped one and a squirrel shat on it. That's the way real life works, believe me.

My mobile phone rang, ruining my image as an old fart.

"They've picked us up, Stones," said Metal's voice. "A blue kraut saloon, right?"

"How many in it?"

"Three."

"Stay well ahead for a bit."

"No problem. They're hanging back anyway."

"Good. They want to see where you go."

"Dave's asleep in the back, by the way."

"He'd better wake up when we need him."

"Hey, Stones, you know this van we've got?"

"Yeah?"

"What happens to it afterwards?"

"It vanishes along with you, Metal."

"Dump it and burn it?"

"That's right. You know the drill."

"Right. I was just wondering. Because there's a stereo in here, and some real good steel racking built into the back. I can find a good home for them."

"Look, once you've disappeared, Metal, I don't care. I just don't want to see it still sitting round in the workshop in a few days' time like that Citroen, get me?"

"Right, right. Can I tell Dave not to bend the racking then? Only he's lying on it, like."

"Tell him whatever you want, Metal. Have you still got that car in sight?"

"Oh yeah. Gotta go anyway now, Stones. The Budby junction's coming up. See you in a minute or two, eh?"

I nodded at Slow Kid and he started the Morris. We crept out from under the Parliament Oak and edged towards the road. I was watching for a white van coming over the brow of the hill.

"Okay, here they come. Let's go."

He let out the handbrake and we pulled across the road. He flattened the accelerator to get a bit of speed up and we were approaching the first bend by the time the van closed in behind us. Metal just managed to overtake us before we were into the bend, and we saw him turn sharp left. We followed him, and the blue saloon came up in the rear. They would have liked to get past us, but the lane was too narrow and there were hedges and ditches on either side. Slow Kid managed to deter them from overtaking by carelessly wavering across the road a couple of times just at the right moment, like a doddery old fool who was falling asleep at the wheel after a lunchtime steak and kidney pie and half a Mackeson. The blue car skimmed the right hand ditch a couple of times before pulling back over. In the wing mirror, I could see a lot of mouthing and gesturing going on back there. Some folk have no respect for their elders, do they? But in the end, the driver gave up and settled for third place when he realised that the van wasn't getting too far ahead.

This was the back road into Medensworth. There was a view across an enormous ploughed field towards the old pit site. The spoil heaps stood out, a range of low black hills against the grey sky. The houses that clustered beyond them were as grey as the sky. Away to our left were the eastern fringes of the heath.

A minute or two later, we emerged suddenly into the top end of the Forest, the hedges giving way to rickety fences and fancy breeze block walls. In a rush, the houses gathered round us as we entered their territory, the white van slowing to lead the way into Lime Avenue and right onto Birch Road. Sure enough, the Morris Traveller farted as Slow Kid throttled down to take the corner.

If the driver of the blue saloon thought he could get past the Morris now, he hadn't reckoned with our famous traffic calming measures. Even these can come in useful, sometimes. Every few yards on Birch Road there are bollards narrowing the carriageway to a car's width, and a fearsome hump to get over. Slow Kid braked to a crawl to take the humps, just like a careful driver would. Even between the humps he drove slowly, sticking to the middle of the road as if afraid the parked cars might reach out and grab him.

As we approached First Avenue, the van started to pull away from us. The blokes behind saw this and panicked. The driver began to sound his horn at us, but all he could see was the back of two heads and a pair of flat caps. We took no notice. There were cars parked on both sides, and a lot of kids in the street, with it being school out time. We were almost where we wanted to be, the exact spot on the map I'd chosen.

As we went over the last hump, the driver of the German car was so distracted by the sight of the van disappearing that he didn't notice we'd stopped. Just to help the moment along, Slow Kid slipped the Morris into reverse and the two cars met with a satisfying crunch. I had to wince as the bonnet of the German motor smashed into the rear end of the old car and bits of broken headlight tinkled onto the road.

Instantly, both cars were surrounded by kids. They were mostly young sprogs, but there were some teenagers among them, crowding round as if we were a scene from a TV cop show. They were staring at the drivers to see what they would do, perhaps hoping there'd be a fight.

We got out of the Traveller and shut the doors. The other car was trying to pull itself away from our boot, and a bit of bumper came away with a ripping sound. But there were too many kids in the way, and behind them were some mums too, shouting at the driver to watch what the hell he was doing, banging on the roof and calling him rude names. The driver looked around desperately for a way out, but he'd lost his chance. The crowd was getting thicker.

An argument seemed to be going on in the blue car. Finally, the driver got out and walked forward towards Slow Kid, his voice unnaturally ingratiating.

"I don't suppose there's any harm done. These things happen, don't they? Bloody road humps, that's what it is."

As he came up the bloke saw Slow Kid more closely, and started to look puzzled. I took off my flat cap. Then he turned and recognised me.

"Shit," he said.

"Hello, Rawlings."

"Shit," he said again, failing the conversational challenge. Rawlings began to back off, bumping into the kids milling about behind him.

"Don't you want to exchange names and addresses?"

One of the kids laughed at this. "He don't live around here, that's for sure."

273

"Maniac driver," said another.

"A bit old to be a joyrider, aren't you, mister?"

"Come back tonight and we'll give you a race on the rec."

"Piss off out of it, you lot."

Rawlings was taking the wrong attitude. He was likely to start a riot going on like that. Some of the mums didn't take kindly to their kids being spoken to that way, and they were a fearsome lot, these mothers. A lot of coppers would tell you they were the worst thing they had to deal with during the miners' strike by far.

"Two hundred thousand miles this thing's done, with a careful owner," I said. "Now you come along and rip the bumper off. That's not nice, Rawlings. You'll have to pay for it."

The passenger door had opened now. Josh Lee stood leaning against the door, apparently unaware of the crowd milling about him. He was staring at me, and his hand was creeping slowly up towards the pocket of his jacket, like a snake slithering towards a toad. I started to wonder where Doncaster Dave was. Metal should have dropped him off just round the corner. Okay, so he was probably still asleep in the back of the van at that point, and he had to walk a few yards. But it was about time he was here, wasn't it?

"Well, what do you say, guys? Are we going to exchange details, or do we have to phone the police?"

The word 'police' seemed to rouse the figure in the back of the blue saloon. He leaned forward to rap on the window, and gestured angrily to Rawlings. I don't think he wanted to exchange details or call the police. What an irresponsible citizen.

"Later, McClure," said Rawlings. Lee didn't speak, but his face said it all. He stopped leaning on the door and got back in the car.

One of the older lads had a German hub cap in his hand, but Rawlings just pushed him out of the way and climbed back into the car. There was another argument inside, and some foul language from Rawlings that seemed to include my name. Then he leaned on the horn and the car began to inch backwards. Some of the kids banged on the panels or sat on the bonnet, grinning through the windscreen. But Rawlings gritted his teeth and kept going, so gradually the kids dropped off until the road was clear. Then the engine roared, Rawlings swung the steering wheel to the right and the German car accelerated away, narrowly missing Slow Kid as it went round the Morris.

A youth of about sixteen on the far side of the car gave me a thumbs-up sign and waved a wheel brace at me. We all stood and watched as the blue saloon got up into second gear and accelerated to take the bend into First Avenue, trying to catch the van. It had almost made it round the corner when one of its back wheels fell off.

There was an interesting spray of sparks as the axle slid across the road and the car slewed to an undignified halt. There were more curses, louder this time. Rawlings got out again, looked at the wheel, then back at me, as if somehow it might have been my fault. Then the first police car came round the corner.

Rawlings bolted up the street, while Lee jumped out of the car and backed away, knife in hand. A shape loomed up behind him, and in the next second Lee was on the floor with Doncaster Dave standing over him. The knife was in the gutter.

But it wasn't Rawlings or Lee I wanted. I was interested in the bloke in the overcoat who came out of the rear passenger door and legged it towards the garden of the nearest house. He was quicker on his feet than Rawlings, and if he got among the back gardens and into the Crescents he might just get away.

There was nothing else for it. I set off after the bloke from the blue saloon, thanking God for the jogging, because without it I wouldn't have made fifty yards.

We ran through one set of gardens and over a fence at the back into Lime Avenue. There was a ginnel here that led between houses to lock-up garages in a back lane. But the bloke ran past the garages, came out onto the corner and went through the gardens on the opposite side. I could hear sirens and wheels screeching somewhere as the police picked up Rawlings, him being the easiest target, of course. But to get to my man the cops would have to go round the end of First Avenue and back down Oak Lane. Long before that, he'd be over the next fence and up the black slope of the slag heap rearing ahead of him beyond the gardens.

He wasn't dressed for mountaineering, but he went up the slope well, only slipping a bit when he got near the top, sending some of the slag sliding back down towards the bottom. I had my boots on, so I was better equipped. But I was starting to get breathless, despite the exercise, and I was wishing the coppers would get out of their cars and come and give me a bit of a hand here.

Over the top of the heap the landscape changed completely. We were on the pit site now, looking at the plateau of rubble and coal dust. The runner was legging it as fast as he could across the site. He probably didn't realise it was only me behind him yet, but in a minute he would, when I got into the open.

At this end, the demolition teams had left a couple of bulldozers and a JCB to give the impression that work was still going on. The bloke ran straight past them, kicking up the dust like a company of cavalry. This just went to show that he didn't recognise an asset when he saw it, and he probably wouldn't know how to nick a bit of machinery anyway. Me, though, I had a pretty good idea about both these things. I also knew that if we kept up this Linford Christie bit much longer I'd be chucking my ring, and the overcoat would get away. I'm not Slow Kid Thompson or Metal Jacket when it comes to nicking a motor, but I'm not Mary Poppins either.

I chose the JCB, being as how it's a bit nippier and has better torque to make cornering easier. There was no stereo and the upholstery was kind of basic, but I wasn't intending to be in it all day. It took me a few seconds to get at the right wires before the engine rumbled into life. I looked through the windscreen and saw the overcoat making ground through a valley between the hills of rubble and debris. I needed to cut him off before he vanished past the engine house and was lost. If I could delay him for a few minutes, I reckoned the cops would eventually catch on and come over the hill.

The JCB bucked and bounced over the rough ground. I jammed the accelerator down as hard as it would go, which wasn't far. Just now, I'd even have been glad of the Morris Traveller. It could have farted as much as it liked, as long as it got me across the next few hundred yards.

Even as I careered across the pit site in my own personal cloud of dust, I thought I could see figures appearing over the slope to my left. This looked like being a fair cop, as they say.

But in the next minute the whole thing fell apart. The figure in the overcoat stopped and turned to face the JCB. As I got nearer, he could see who I was. And Michael Cavendish and I stared at each other with mutual loathing. It was inherent, that hatred. A product of hundreds of years of playing at lords and peasants, and the peasants always losing. Until now, Mr Cavendish.

Or so I thought. But the other side always has extra resources to bring against you. And this time it just wasn't tennis. Cavendish drew aside his overcoat and pulled a handgun from the pocket of his suit. He gripped it in both hands as he aimed it straight at the JCB.

Before I could react, a bullet crashed through the windscreen, showering me with bits of broken glass and setting my ears ringing with the bang as it embedded itself in the roof. I ducked, swerved and ploughed the machine through a mouldering heap of concrete and twisted metal into the steel fence around the engine house. The steel ripped with a painful screech and collapsed as the JCB ground to a juddering halt. A second shot ricocheted off the bucket, and a burning pain seared through my arm as a bullet tore a gash in my leather jacket.

So it was game, set and match. I clung to the torn plastic seat of the JCB, and waited for Cavendish to finish me off.

24

The rain was dripping down my collar from the roof of the shed. I'd already been feeling cold and tired and on edge, and right now I was really irritated.

Ahead of me, in the dark, was a house, and somewhere inside were the blokes we'd been chasing for weeks. My partner was round the corner, covering the back door. The suspects were armed and dangerous, like they say on the telly. But no worries - all we had to do was wait for the back-up to arrive.

And then I was distracted by a noise to the left, coming from a brick lean-to extension near the garden shed. Something like an outside toilet or a coal house. Yes, that noise could have been pieces of coal rattling. A cat or a rat maybe. Or maybe not.

I opened the coal house door carefully and felt along the wall. There was a light switch, but it didn't seem to work. Somewhere in there, I thought I could hear breathing, but I couldn't be sure. With my foot I felt a rough stone step down into darkness as I pulled my torch from my pocket. It was the blackest place I'd ever seen, without a chink of light penetrating from the outside or even from the open door.

I flicked on my torch and did a quick sweep. I registered a few roles of mouldy carpet, a pair of staring eyes, and about half a ton of coal heaped against the far wall. The coal hadn't been used for a long time and was growing mould like the carpets. The eyes were as bright as an animal's, glittering with fear.

The figure back there in the darkness made a dash for it, slithering across the coal towards the door. He was never going to make it, and I had him up against the wall by the arm in a second. I dragged him out into the light, and he dropped a sports bag with a clatter of steel.

We knew who we might expect to find in the house, but the individual I was looking at now wasn't any of them. This was a nobody, a lad off one of the estates, just like a thousand others.

I actually knew this one, too. I'd nicked young Dean before, several times. But he was nineteen now - and that meant he'd go down for this one.

It was tough. Dean had two kids already, one of them two years old and the other no more than a couple of months. Unlike a lot of lads his age, he was sticking by the mother and trying to support the family. That wouldn't stop him going down.

Dean had nothing to do with the job we were there for, surely? He was a petty thief, not a heroin dealer. He wasn't exactly the Archbishop of Canterbury, but he knew where to draw the line. Dean never carried a weapon either. Once, when he'd been disturbed by a householder, he'd almost fainted with fright.

We looked at each other for a minute. Dean's shoulders slumped as soon as he recognised me. With one hand on his arm, I opened the zipper of the bag. Inside were a few tools, an old radio, a roll of copper wire, even a plastic bottle of motor oil - pathetic bits and pieces nicked from the garden shed. Was this all Dean's life was worth - half a litre of Duckham's multigrade?

"You've picked the wrong house this time, son," I said.

He didn't answer. I wondered how much he'd hoped to get for the stuff he'd nicked, and how it could possibly justify risking a spell inside. The whole lot couldn't have been worth a tenner.

I didn't have much time to make my mind up. My partner was round the corner, covering the back door. Any second now, our back-up would arrive - a senior officer to take charge, a Special Operations team issued with firearms and trained to use them. And that would be curtains for Dean.

"Go on, clear off out of it."

"What?"

Dean stared at me, amazed. Then slowly he began to walk away.

"Take the bleedin' bag with you. I don't want it."

He grabbed the bag and began to run. But his footsteps and the clanking of the tools in the bag reached the ears of my partner, *who came thundering round the side of the house and spotted the figure legging it for the road.*

"Stop! Armed police!"

"Frank, you daft bastard, leave it!"

Sergeant Frank Moxon skidded to a halt and glared from me to the vanishing Dean.

"What the hell's going on?"

"Stop shouting, for God's sake, Frank. You'll wake the whole bloody street."

"Stones, you've just let that bloke get away, haven't you?"

An upstairs window in the house banged open and there was a movement between the curtains as an arm poked through it.

"Shit. Get down!"

I dragged Moxon with me and we rolled behind the wall of the shed as the first bullet from a handgun dug a hole in the lawn.

"Jesus. Now you've done it, Frank. The lad was nothing to do with it."

"Oh yeah? How do you know? Have you been conducting a full interrogation out here? Got the tapes of the interview for the record, have you?"

I pushed Moxon off me and used my radio to call the control room and tell them we'd bollocksed the operation. A bullet bounced off the garden wall to emphasise the point.

"Believe me, he wasn't worth it, Frank."

"Worth it? Was he worth your job? Because you've gone too bloody far this time, Stones."

I could hear shouts in the house, and a car engine revving up in the garage. We were helpless while the bloke at the window had us pinned down. It looked as though our targets were about to make a getaway. Frank Moxon was spitting with rage.

"You've turned a blind eye once too often, and this time you nearly got me killed. That's way out of order."

"Frank - "

"Why do you always think you can do things by your own rules? Just because some kid comes from the same estate as you, you think he deserves special treatment. You'd be a good cop if you weren't so bloody soft-hearted about these low-life wasters. Deep down, you're still just one of them yourself, aren't you? You're just

a thieving dosser's kid off the Forest Estate who's had a bit too much education for his own good."

"Let's talk about it later, Frank."

"Later? When we get out of this, McClure, I'm going to see you shafted."

"Thanks, partner."

Moxon knew more than enough about me to do it, too. I wondered whether to walk out into the open and let the bloke at the window kill me there and then. In view of what happened later, I might as well have.

*   *   *   *

Probably Cavendish, too, could have finished me off as I lay in the cab of the JCB. But he must have seen the police appearing over the slope, because when I dared to look over the dashboard he'd turned his attention away from me and was pointing his gun at something off to the left.

It looked remarkably like the gun I'd left in the drawer in the house at West Laneton. It was fully loaded, too, unless he'd used it since then. I'd checked it myself.

Through a crack in the side window I could see the cops had stopped where they were and got busy looking for cover. I knew exactly what would happen now. They'd be straight on the radio shouting for armed support, and they'd be holding off until the lads in the fancy body armour arrived - which might not be for the next half hour.

Meanwhile, there was just me out here, with no standard operational procedures and no Police Manual regulations to hold me back. It looked as though it was up to me again, and there would only be Stones McClure to blame when it all went wrong. Story of my life.

I dropped out of the driver's door of the cab and nearly made it round the back of the abandoned boiler before Cavendish noticed me and decided to come after me. Suddenly I was the hunted instead of the hunter, and it didn't feel too comfortable.

I pushed the debris aside and shinned up onto a skip full of rubbish. From there I reached for one of the open arches into the engine house. I could hear Cavendish coming after me, but he was being cautious.

Maybe he thought I was armed too, in some way. If so, he'd badly overestimated my resourcefulness. I didn't even have a spare sock to throw at him. Maybe I could frighten him to death by pulling faces, but my gut feeling told me I was at a slight disadvantage, like a ladybird on a stalk of grass that's about to be eaten by a cow.

I jumped down from the arch onto the floor of the building and made for the wooden stairs to the top floor. I wasn't halfway there when I heard Cavendish walk through the door. I hadn't even bothered to check whether it was unlocked. People are so lax with their security.

"Just stop there, McClure."

Even without looking round, I could feel the gun pointing at me. I stopped at the bottom of the stairs and turned. Cavendish looked nervous. His coat was covered in coal dust and his brogues were unrecognisable. He was breathing hard, and his eyes flickered round the building as if he expected company at any moment. With a bit of luck, we might get it too. But would they be too late?

"The police are outside," I pointed out. "You haven't a hope."

"Yes, I have," he said. "I've got you."

"Well, I'm delighted to bring hope into someone's life. What exactly did you have in mind?"

"You're going to be my hostage."

"Wow. My dream. Do we get the TV cameras and all that? Global coverage by CNN, and the SAS coming in with smoke grenades? This could be my moment of fame."

"Damn well shut up, McClure."

"By the way, is your name really Cavendish? Or is it Perella? I need to know for the interviews afterwards. I don't want to get my facts wrong."

"It doesn't matter to you."

"Oh, yes it does. I like to know who's been trying to wreck my business, and why."

The hand holding the gun was shaking, and it wasn't just from the exertion. Cavendish was scared stiff. That was risky - he might be trigger happy in an agitated state. But it also gave me my best chance. I didn't want to be still standing there when the cops came clumping up and made him even more nervous.

There wasn't much near me that I could use as a weapon. The interior of the engine house was practically bare - just a bit of rubbish lying about on the floor, and a few lumps of coal. Above me, pigeons were shuffling on the ledges of the windows, dropping their sarcastic comments down the wall and wishing we'd all go away.

"You were just incidental, McClure. I wouldn't have bothered with the likes of you, but you went out of your way to annoy me. I don't forget things like that."

"Oh, I can be such an embarrassment, can't I? 'Course, I haven't had your upbringing. No couth, that's me."

"Was it you that broke into my house?"

"Of course. Shame about the dovecote."

"The jewellery was in there. I lost the lot."

"Not all of it. Some of it is in your car, under the seat. No doubt the police have found it by now. It came from the job you did on the Jewellery Box in Medensworth."

"I thought so. I knew you'd set me up. You've been a big nuisance to me, McClure."

"That's what everybody says."

"First you started muscling in on my territory."

"Your territory? I was here first, mate."

"You're just a council estate yob. My ancestors owned this area."

"Oh, still on that line? I bet your most famous ancestor was just some younger son's bastard by a servant girl, if the truth were known."

His face went red and the tendons stood out on his neck as he snarled at me. Damn, I seemed to have hit a nerve there.

"You're going to pay for that, McClure."

"No!"

I shouted the word as loud as I could, kicking up a great echo against the high walls of the engine house. Above us, the flock of pigeons took off, startled. The immense clattering of wings was like a thunderflash going off.

Cavendish reacted instantly, whipping round and firing up towards the unexpected noise. I bent and hefted a lump of rusty metal from the floor and heaved it towards him. It caught his arm and sent the gun spinning across the floor. He was too surprised to move, and I got to the gun first to kick it away into the furthest corner.

Cavendish read my intention. Since I was between him and the door, he had only one place to go. He ran up the stairs, with me at his heels, and leaped for the arched entrance on the first floor of the building.

He'd gone several steps out into the open air before he realised he was running up the metal walkway towards the winding gear headstocks. He looked down at the ground and began to wobble. I stood in the opening and smiled at him.

"That's what I like to see. Somebody going out on a limb. Like to feel you're up there above the rest of us, do you, Cavendish? Well, tough, because I'm coming after you."

"Stay away, McClure."

"No chance."

Cavendish backed further up the walkway, slipping and stumbling until he reached the maintenance platform running round the twin wheels of the headgear. Somehow the sight of him up there in his Hugo Boss suit made me grit me teeth with anger. At that moment I probably hated him more than ever. What right had he even to go near the last reminder of the pit where my dad and all those thousands of other men had worked and sweated and died?

At last the police were coming, cars and an armoured van throwing up the dust as they raced towards the engine house. Cavendish saw them coming too.

But he must also have recognised the look in my eye as I began to move up the walkway towards him. In a panic, he turned to go round the platform. His muddy brogues slipped and he toppled forward, grabbing at the nearest spoke of a wheel for support.

284

But the wheel wasn't as rusted up as it looked. As Cavendish hit it with all his weight, it began to move, throwing him off balance and carrying him over the edge of the platform. He screamed as he bounced off the blue spokes and cartwheeled in the air. Then he hit the ground below with a horrible, meaty thud.

A moment of silence. I hung on tightly to the rail as I looked down at the spreadeagled body. I'd never seen anyone look quite so dead. His shape was imprinted deep into the coal dust, which hung around him like a fog until it began to settle again, slowly covering his face. I tried to summon a respectful thought into my head, but couldn't manage it.

So instead I rattled back down the walkway and into the engine house. When I emerged into the light I'd hardly turned round when there were more guns aimed on me.

"Stop! Armed police!"

I put my hands up, innocent as the day, and waited nervously while a couple of cops came over in their body armour and frisked me, none too gently. Then they cuffed me, and I had the pleasure of seeing my best mate walk over to stare at me. DI Frank Moxon. Well, I was almost pleased to see him.

"That's the bloke you want, Frank. The one doing the pancake impression over there."

A small group of officers had gathered round Cavendish. An ambulance with its lights flashing was already bouncing across the rubbish-strewn plateau.

"What are you doing here, McClure?" demanded Moxon. "What's your connection?"

"Hey, guv, I was just passing. I thought you blokes might need some help."

"Ah, an honest citizen. A have a go hero, in fact. Is that the idea? Expect your picture to be in the paper, do you? Want a certificate from the Chief Constable?"

"Oh no, you know me. Modest."

"I know you all right, McClure. I've got your job now, remember? You're nothing any more, just shit like all the rest. So keep your nose out of my business."

I held up my wrists with the cuffs on. "Am I under arrest then? I hope you've got some evidence, because you're letting your personal prejudices show, inspector."

"Get in the car."

We got in, leaving the heavy mob and the ambulance to look after Cavendish. Back in the village the crowd in Birch Road had grown much bigger. Uniformed police were trying to keep them back from the damaged cars, but there was a sort of carnival atmosphere. People hadn't seen this much fun in Medensworth since the war.

Blokes in overalls were pulling the blue German car apart, and had even taken the seats out of the Morris Traveller. Metal Jacket was going to be pissed off with me about that.

There was no sign of Slow Kid, but there was a large figure sitting on a garden wall eating a bag of chips. I hoped Rawlings and Lee had already been taken away in one of those nice black vans.

And here was Lisa too, practically pushing Moxon aside to get at me.

"What happened, Stones? Where's Michael Cavendish?"

I explained as best I could, playing down my heroic role, of course.

"That's terrible," she said. "And do you know those youngsters have stolen almost everything out of the car that had the accident."

"You mean the blue car? The one with a wheel missing?"

"Yes, they'd even taken the wheel as well before the police got here."

"It's a disgrace."

"The awful thing is, I heard a policeman say they were expecting to find some stolen jewellery in the car. But that's gone too."

"Shit. That's terrible."

And this time I meant it. That was supposed to be evidence. For heaven's sake, some people will nick anything.

"Why do the police think you've got something to do with the stolen jewellery, Stones?"

"It's a mistake," I said. "I was just helping out."

"This is why you got me to tell Michael Cavendish you'd given me some jewellery, isn't it? You knew about this?"

"I've got contacts, you know."

"There's more going on than you're saying. I'm sure there is."

"Just things I hear. Through business, you know."

"You wouldn't know anything about stealing things, would you? Because I really hate stealing."

"It can't be me who nicked anything, love, can it? Not with these on." I held up the handcuffs, hoping for sympathy.

"Quite honestly, they suit you."

"Oh, come on, love."

"And then there's all that money you've got stashed at my cottage. Is that the right word - stashed? Yes, I've seen it. I was going to do your dirty washing for you, and I found it. There seems to be an awful lot of it, Stones. What is it all for? Where is that going? To finance some other shady venture?"

"Bleedin' hell, Lisa."

"Let him go! He's innocent!"

Even while I was struggling to defend myself, the distant shout caught my notice. I looked round to see a familiar redhead with big tits coming across the road. The police fell back in front of her, the way a lot of blokes do.

"Anyway, about that money, Lisa," I said hastily, desperate to distract her attention. "No need to worry about that - it's going to my Uncle Willis's Trust Fund."

"Really?" Lisa looked surprised, as if she'd actually thought I was a crook. Women can be very hurtful.

"Yeah, I promised him. It'll go to a new youth centre."

"Well, that's wonderful. I'm very proud of you." She paused. "If it's true."

"Well, of course it's true. I - "

"Stones! Are you all right?" Nuala was right in front of me now, her breasts practically poking my eyes out as she threw her arms round my shoulders. She looked really concerned for me. It made a refreshing change.

"Fine, love. Fine."

Oh yeah, just fine. What, with the real shit about to hit the fan? Unable to push Nuala away because of the handcuffs, I looked about me for inspiration. But all I saw was Frank Moxon's satisfied smirk.

"Stones," said Lisa.

Her voice was flat and hard, like the sound of a judge just before he sentences you to be removed from this place and hanged by the neck until dead.

"Stones," she said again, "who exactly is this woman?"

It seemed things were about to turn runny again. So I smiled, scraped some dust off my boots, and reminded myself of the Top Hard Rule. *You can't trust anyone these days.* Not even me.

* * * * THE END * * * *

Author's note:

All the titles in my Cooper & Fry series are set in Derbyshire, and I'm often asked by readers why I've never written a novel set in my home county of Nottinghamshire. The answer is - I have! About a year before I created my two young Derbyshire police detectives, Ben Cooper and Diane Fry, I wrote TOP HARD. This book reflects the situation existing in Nottinghamshire coalfield villages in the 1990s, and the characters give voice to some of the views being expressed at the time. In 1998, TOP HARD was shortlisted for the first ever New Writing Award, presented by the UK Crime Writers' Association (now known as the Debut Dagger). A short story adapted from the first chapter appeared in the 'Criminal Tendencies' anthology, a fund raiser for breast cancer research, and was later chosen for publication in 'The Mammoth Book of British British Crime 8', released in 2011. TOP HARD has never been published in its full-length novel form, until now. I hope you enjoy it.

Stephen Booth

If you enjoyed TOP HARD, why not try a novel in the Cooper & Fry series by the same author? The titles in the series so far:

BLACK DOG
DANCING WITH THE VIRGINS
BLOOD ON THE TONGUE
BLIND TO THE BONES
ONE LAST BREATH
THE DEAD PLACE
SCARED TO LIVE
DYING TO SIN
THE KILL CALL
LOST RIVER
THE DEVIL'S EDGE
DEAD AND BURIED (2012)

And a Ben Cooper novella:
CLAWS

The most recent title in the series is THE DEVIL'S EDGE:

In his most gripping case yet, newly promoted Detective Sergeant Ben Cooper investigates a series of lethal home invasions in the Peak District. During the latest attack, a woman has died in an affluent village nestling close under the long gritstone escarpment known as the Devil's Edge. Despite seething enmities between neighbours in the village of Riddings, the major lines of enquiry seem to lead to the nearby city of Sheffield. But before Cooper and his team can crack the case, the panic spreading throughout the area results in an incident that devastates the Cooper family. And the only person available to step into the breach is Ben's old rival, Detective Sergeant Diane Fry...

Here's a sample to give you a taste:

THE DEVIL'S EDGE

Stephen Booth

CHAPTER ONE

Tuesday

A shadow moved across the hall. It was only a flicker of movement, a blur in the light, a motion as tiny and quick as an insect's.

Zoe Barron stopped and turned, her heart already thumping. She wasn't sure whether she'd seen anything at all. It had happened in a second, that flick from dark to light, and back again. Just one blink of an eye. She might have imagined the effect from a glint of moonlight off the terracotta tiles. Or perhaps there was only a moth, trapped inside the house and fluttering its wings as it tried to escape.

In the summer, the house was often full of small, flying things that crept in through the windows and hung from the walls. The children said their delicate, translucent wings made them look like tiny angels. But for Zoe, they were more like miniature demons with their bug eyes and waving antennae. It made her shudder to think of them flitting silently around her bedroom at night, waiting their chance to land on her face.

It was one of the drawbacks of living in the countryside. Too much of the outside world intruding. Too many things it was impossible to keep out.

Still uncertain, Zoe looked along the hallway towards the kitchen, and noticed a thin slice of darkness where the utility room door stood open an inch. The house was so quiet that she could hear the hum of a freezer, the tick of the boiler, a murmur from the TV in one of the children's bedrooms. She listened for a moment, holding her breath. She wondered if a stray cat or a fox had crept in through the back door and was crouching now in the kitchen, knowing she was there in the darkness, its hearing far better than hers. Green eyes glowing, claws unsheathed, an animal waiting to pounce.

But now she was letting her imagine run away with her. She shouldn't allow irrational fears to fill her mind, when there were so many real ones to be concerned about. With a shake of her head at her own foolishness, Zoe stepped through the kitchen door, and saw what had caused the movement of the shadows. A breath of wind was swaying the ceiling light on its cord.

So a window must have been left open somewhere - probably by one of the workmen, trying to reduce the smell of paint. They'd already been in the house too long, three days past the scheduled completion of this part of the job, and they were trying their best not to cause any more complaints. They'd left so much building material outside that it was always in the way. She dreaded one of the huge timbers falling over in the night. Sometimes, when the wind was strong, she lay awake listening for the crash.

But leaving a window open all night - that would earn them an earful tomorrow anyway. It wasn't something you did, even in a village like Riddings. It was a lesson she and Jake learned when they lived in Sheffield, and one she would never forget. Rural Derbyshire hadn't proved to be the safe, crime-free place she hoped.

Zoe tutted quietly, reassuring herself with the sound. A window left open? It didn't seem much, really. But that peculiar man who lived in the old cottage on Chapel Close would stop her car in the village and lecture her about it endlessly if he ever found out. He was always hanging around the lanes watching what other people did.

Gamble, that was his name. Barry Gamble. She'd warned the girls to stay away from him if they saw him. You never knew with people like that. You could never be sure where the danger might come from. Greed, envy and malice - they were all around her, like a plague. As if she and Jake could be held responsible for other people's mistakes, the wrong decisions they had made in their lives.

Zoe realised she was clutching the wine bottle so hard that her knuckles were white. An idea ran through her head of using the bottle as a weapon. It was full, and so heavy she could do some damage, if necessary. Except now her finger prints would be all over it.

She laughed at her own nervousness. She was feeling much too tense. She'd been in this state for days, maybe weeks. If Jake saw her right now, he would tease her and tell her she was just imagining things. He would say there was nothing to worry about. Nothing at all. *Relax, chill out, don't upset the children. Everything's fine.*

But, of course, it wasn't true. Everyone knew there was plenty to worry about. Everyone here in Riddings, and in all the other villages scattered along this eastern fringe of the Peak District. It was in the papers, and on TV. No one was safe.

Still Zoe hesitated, feeling a sudden urge to turn round and run back to the sitting room to find Jake and hold on to him for safety. But instead she switched on the light and took a step further into the kitchen.

She saw the body of a moth now. It lay dead on the floor, its wings torn, its fragile body crushed to powder. It was a big one, too - faint black markings still discernible on its flattened wings. Was it big enough to have blundered into the light and set it swinging? A moth was so insubstantial. But desperate creatures thrashed around in panic when they were dying. It was always frightening to watch.

But there was something strange about the moth. Zoe crouched to look more closely. Her stomach lurched as she made it out. Another pattern was visible in the smear of powder - a section of ridge, like the sole of a boot, as if someone had trodden on the dead insect, squashing it onto the tiles.

Zoe straightened up again quickly, looking around, shifting her grip on the bottle, trying to fight the rising panic.

"Jake?" she said.

A faint crunch on the gravel outside. Was that what she'd heard that, or not? A footstep too heavy for a fox. The wrong sound for a falling timber.

This was definitely wrong. The only person who might legitimately be outside the house at this time of night was Jake, and she'd left him in the sitting room, sprawled on the couch and clutching a beer. If he'd gone out to the garage for some reason, he would have told her. If he'd gone to the front door, he would have passed her in the hall.

So it wasn't Jake outside. It wasn't her husband moving about now on the decking, slowly opening the back door. But still she clung on to the belief, the wild hope, that there was nothing to worry about. *I'm perfectly safe. Everything's fine.*

"Jake?" she called.

And she called again, louder. Much louder, and louder still, until it became a scream.

"Jake? Jake? *Jake!*"

* * * *

Six miles from Riddings, Detective Sergeant Ben Cooper turned the corner of Edendale High Street into Hollowgate and stopped to let a bus pull into the terminus.

The town hall lay just ahead of him, closed at this time of night but illuminated by spotlights which picked out the the pattern in its stonework which had earned its nickname of the Wavy House. Across the road, the Starlight Cafe was doing good business as usual, with a steady stream of customers. Taxis were lining up for their busiest time of the day. It was almost ten o'clock on an ordinary August evening.

The pubs were even busier than the Starlight, of course. Cooper could hear the music pounding from the Wheatsheaf and the Red Lion, the two pubs on either side of the market square. A crowd of youngsters screamed and laughed by the war memorial, watched by a uniformed PC and a community support officer in bright yellow high-vis jackets, the pair of them standing in the entrance to an alley near the Raj Mahal.

Even in Edendale, there were often fights at closing time, and drug dealers operating wherever they could find a suitable spot. On Friday and Saturday nights, there would be a personnel carrier with a prisoner cage in the back, and multiple foot patrols of officers on the late shift. A change came over the town then, a place that had looked so quaint during the day, with its cobbled alleys and tall stone buildings, revealed its Jekyll and Hyde nature.

"Hey, mate, shouldn't you be out arresting some criminals?"

"Ooh, duck, show us your baton."

Looking round at the shouts, Cooper saw that the bus was a Hulley's number 19 from the Devonshire Estate. Oh, great. He took a sharp step back from the kerb, turning his body away towards the shop window behind him. There were too many eyes gazing from the windows of the bus, and the likelihood of too many familiar faces, people he didn't want to meet when he was off duty. Half of the names on his arrest record had addresses on the Devonshire Estate. He didn't recognise the voices, but there was no doubt their owners knew him.

Well, it was his own choice. Many police officers chose to live outside the area they worked in, for exactly this reason. When you went for a quiet drink in your local pub, you didn't want to find yourself sitting next to the person you'd nicked the day before, or sharing a table with a man whose brother you'd just send to prison.

But Cooper had resisted moving to a neighbouring division. He could easily have travelled into Edendale every morning from Chesterfield or Buxton, but that wouldn't be the same. He belonged here, in the Eden Valley, and he wasn't going to let anything push him out. He intended to stay here, settle down, raise a family, and eventually turn into a cantankerous pensioner who rambled on about the good old days.

That meant he had to put up with these awkward moments - the looks of horrified recognition on faces, the shying away as he passed in the street, the aggressive stare at the bar. It was all part of life. *All part of life's rich pageant.* That was what his grandmother would have said. He had no idea where the expression came from. But he knew the phrase would stick inside his head now, until he found out. He supposed he'd have to Google it when he got home.

He seemed to be turning into one of those people whose minds collected odd bits of information like a sheep picking up ticks.

As he walked, Cooper checked his phone in case he'd missed a text message, but there was nothing. He carried on towards the end of Hollowgate, ignoring the loud group of youngsters. Not his business tonight. He'd only just come off shift, at the end of a long drawn-out series of arrests and the execution of search warrants. With six prisoners processed through the custody suite at West Street, there wasn't much of the evening left by the time he finally clocked off.

At the corner of Bargate he stopped again and listened for the sound of the river, just discernible here above the sound of the traffic. The council had been talking about making Hollowgate a pedestrianised zone, like neighbouring Clappergate. But of course the money had run out for projects like that. So a stream of cars still flowed down from Hulley Road towards the High Street, forming Edendale's version of a one-way system. 'Flow' wasn't exactly the right word for it. Half of the cars stopped in front of the shops to unload passengers, or crawled to a halt as drivers looked for parking spaces, the little car park behind the town hall already being full at this hour.

Cooper studied the pedestrians ahead. There was no sign of her yet. He glanced at his watch. For once, he wasn't the one who was late. That was good.

He decided to wait in front of the estate agent's, looking back towards the clock on the Wavy House to make sure his watch wasn't fast. There was always a smell of freshly baked bread just on this corner, thanks to the baker's behind the shops in Bargate. The scent lingered all day, as if it was absorbed into the stone and released slowly to add to the atmosphere.

It was good to have somewhere in town that still baked its own bread. For Cooper, it was these sounds and smells that gave Edendale its unique personality, and distinguished it from every other town in the country, with their identikit high streets full of chain stores.

He turned to look in the estate agent's window, automatically drawn to the pictures of the houses for sale. This was one of the more upmarket agents, handling a lot of high-end properties, catering for equestrian interests and buyers with plenty of spare cash who were looking for a country residence.

He spotted a nice property available not far away, in Lowtown. An old farm house by the look of it, full of character, with a few outbuildings and a pony paddock. But six hundred and fifty thousand pounds? How could he ever afford that? Even on his new salary scale as a detective sergeant, the mortgage repayments would be horrendous. He had a bit of money put away in the bank now, but savings didn't grow very fast these days, with interest rates still on the floor. It was a hopeless prospect.

"So which house do you fancy?" said a voice in his ear.

It was totally different voice from those that had shouted to him from the bus. This was a warm voice, soft and caressing. A familiar voice, with an intimate touch on his arm.

Liz appeared at his side, laid her head against his shoulder, and slipped her hand into his. He hadn't seen her approach, and now he felt strangely at a disadvantage.

"What, one of these?" he said. "Chance would be a fine thing."

She sighed. "True, I suppose."

Cooper looked beyond the the pictures of houses and caught their reflections in the glass. The pair of them were slightly distorted and smoky, as if the glass was tinted. Edendale's traffic moved slowly, jerkily behind them, like a street in an old silent film. And, not for the first time, it struck him how well matched they looked. Comfortable together, like an old married couple already.

Liz looked small at his side, her dark hair shining in the street lights, her face lit up with a simple, uncomplicated pleasure. It delighted him that she could respond this way every time they met, or even spoke on the phone. Who wouldn't love to have that effect on someone? It was a wonderful thing to bring a bit of happiness into the world, to be able to create these moments of joy. A rare and precious gift in a world where he met so much darkness and unhappiness, so many lonely and bitter people.

"Kiss, then?

He bent to kiss her. She smelled great, as always. Her presence made him smile, and forget about the gaping faces. Who cared what other people thought?

They crossed the road, squeezed close together, as if they'd been parted for months. He always felt like that with Liz. At these moments, he would agree to anything, and often did.

"So, any progress on the big case?" she said.

"The home invasions, you mean?"

"Yes. The Savages. That's what the newspapers are calling them."

Cooper grimaced at the expression, sorry to have the mood momentarily spoiled. It was typical of the media to come up with such a sensational and ludicrous nickname. He knew they were aiming to grab the public's attention. But it seemed to him to trivialise the reality of the brutal violence inflicted on the victims of these particular offenders.

"No, not much progress," he said.

"It must be awful. I mean, to have something like that happen to you in your own home."

"The victims have been pretty traumatised."

The gang of burglars the papers called the Savages had struck several times this summer, targeting large private houses in well heeled villages on the eastern edges. E Division was Derbyshire Constabulary's largest geographical division by far, and the edges marked the furthest fringes, the border with South Yorkshire.

Cooper wondered how he'd feel if he owned that nice home in Lowtown, and someone broke into his house. He'd been told that owning property changed your attitude completely, made you much more territorial, more aggressively prepared to defend your domain.

Well, he'd seen that at first hand. Because it had certainly happened to his brother. He'd watched Matt turn into a paranoid wreck since he became responsible for the family farm at Bridge End. He patrolled his boundaries every day, like a one-man army, ever vigilant for the appearance of invaders. He was the Home Guard, ready to repel Hitler's Nazi hordes with a pitchfork. That level of anxiety must be exhausting. Was owning property really worth it?

"Do you think the Savages are local?" asked Liz, voicing the question that many people were asking. "Or are they coming out from Sheffield?"

There were few people he could have discussed details of the case with. But Liz was in the job herself, a scenes of crime officer in E Division. She'd even attended one of the scenes, the most recent incident in Baslow.

"They know the area pretty well, either way," said Cooper. "They've chosen their targets like professionals so far. And they've got their approaches and exits figured out to the last detail. At least, it seems so - since we haven't got much of a lead on them yet."

They had a table booked at the Columbine. It was in the cellar, but that was okay. In Edendale, there wasn't much of a choice of restaurants where last orders were taken at ten. And even at the Columbine that was only from May to October, for the visitors. Edendale people didn't eat so late.

Cooper was looking forward to getting in front of a High Peak rib-eye steak pan fried in Cajun spices. Add a bottle of Czech beer, and he'd be happy. And he'd be able to forget about the Savages for a while.

They opened the door of the restaurant, and Cooper paused for a moment to look back at the street, watching the people beginning to head out of town, back to the safety of their homes. If anyone's home was safe, with individuals like the Savages on the loose.

"Well," he said, "at least they haven't killed anybody yet."

*   *   *   *

In Riddings, a figure was moving in the Barrons' garden. Barry Gamble was approaching their house cautiously. The last time he'd been on the drive at Valley View, it hadn't been a happy experience. Some people just didn't appreciate neighbourly concern.

He hoped there was no one hanging around outside, no chance of seeing any of the Barrons. He would just have a quick check, make sure everything was okay, then get back to his own house a few hundred yards away in Chapel Close.

Gamble shook his head at the roof trusses and window frames stacked untidily against the wall. That was asking for trouble, in his opinion. It gave the impression the house was empty and vulnerable while construction work was going on.

The Barrons' improvements seemed to have stalled, though. The area that had been cleared behind the garage was supposed to be an extension for a gym and family room, so he'd heard. But the foundations were still visible, the breeze block walls hardly a foot high where they'd been abandoned. Perhaps the Barrons had run out of money, like everyone else. The thought gave Gamble a little twinge of satisfaction.

He wondered if some item of builder's materials had made the noise he'd heard. A dull thump and a crash, loud on the night air. And then there had been some kind of scrabbling in the undergrowth. But he was used to that sound. There was plenty of wildlife in Riddings at night - foxes, badgers, rabbits. Even the occasional deer down off Stoke Flat. The noises animals made in the dark were alarming, for anyone who wasn't used to them the way he was.

Gamble skirted the garage and headed towards the back of the house, conscious of the sound of his footsteps on the gravel drive. He tried to tread lightly, but gravel was always a nuisance. He'd learned to avoid it whenever he could. A nice bit of paving or a patch of grass was so much easier.

He began to rehearse his excuses in case someone came out and challenged him. *I was just passing, and I thought I heard... Can't be too careful, eh? Well, as long as everything's all right, I'll be getting along.*

He couldn't remember whether the Barrons had installed motion sensors at Valley View that would activate the security lights. He thought not, though.

The house was very quiet as he came near it. The younger Barron children would be in bed by now. He knew their bedrooms were on the other side of the house, overlooking the garden. Their parents tended to sit up late watching TV. He'd seen the light flickering on the curtains until one o'clock in the morning sometimes.

Gamble peered through the kitchen window. A bit of light came through the open doorway from the hall. But there wasn't much to see inside. No intruders, no damage, no signs of a break-in or disturbance. No one visible inside the house, no soul moving at all.

In fact, there was only one thing for Barry Gamble to see. One thing that made him catch his breath with fear and excitement. It was nothing but a trickle. A narrow worm, red and glistening in a patch of light. It was a thin trickle of blood, creeping slowly across the terracotta tiles.

*   *   *   *

THE DEVIL'S EDGE is published by Little, Brown under their Sphere imprint.

About the author:

Stephen Booth is an award winning UK crime writer. He is best known as the creator of two young Derbyshire police detectives, DC Ben Cooper and DS Diane Fry, who appear in twelve novels, all set in England's beautiful and atmospheric Peak District. Stephen has been a Gold Dagger finalist, an Anthony Award nominee, twice winner of a Barry Award for Best British Crime Novel, and twice shortlisted for the Theakston's Crime Novel of the Year. DC Cooper was a finalist for the Sherlock Award for the best detective created by a British author, and in 2003 the Crime Writers' Association presented Stephen with the Dagger in the Library Award for "the author whose books have given readers the most pleasure". The Cooper & Fry series is published all around the world, and has been translated into 15 languages. The latest titles are THE DEVIL'S EDGE and DEAD AND BURIED, published by Little, Brown.

For the latest news, visit the author's website:
www.stephen-booth.com

or stay in touch on Twitter:
www.twitter.com/stephenbooth

on Facebook:
www.facebook.com/stephenboothbooks

or the Stephen Booth Blog:
www.stephen-booth.blogspot.com

or visit Stephen Booth's channel on YouTube
www.youtube.com/watch?v=1ssD8g65LK8